The son of a British diplomat, Daniel
Carney was born in Beirut in 1944.
He grew up in the Far East and was
educated in England. He travelled
extensively throughout the world
before settling in Rhodesia in 1963,
where he joined the British South
Africa Police. After $3\frac{1}{2}$ years service,
he resigned to take up a business
career in Real Estate Property
Development. Now he divides his
time between full-time writing and
defending his country's frontiers
against guerrilla attacks. Both his two
published novels, THE
WHISPERING DEATH and THE
WILD GEESE, have been turned
into major films.

Daniel Carney

The Wild Geese

CORGI BOOKS
A DIVISION OF TRANSWORLD PUBLISHERS LTD

THE WILD GEESE

A CORGI BOOK 0 552 10869 3

Originally published in Great Britain by
William Heinemann Ltd

PRINTING HISTORY
William Heinemann edition published 1977
Reprinted 1977
Corgi edition published 1978
Corgi edition re-issued 1978
Corgi edition reprinted 1978 (twice)
Corgi edition reprinted 1979

This book is set in Intertype Baskerville

Corgi Books are published by Transworld Publishers Ltd,
Century House, 61-63 Uxbridge Road,
Ealing, London, W5 5SA
Made and printed in Great Britain by
William Collins Sons & Co Ltd, Glasgow

*Dedicated with love
to Sally*

CHAPTER ONE

LIMBANI

May, 1968

THE Swissair DC8 whispered through the night sky, two hours out of Zurich, en route to Tel Aviv, its crowded cabin darkened, save for the dim glow of the overhead passenger lights.

A stewardess entered the cabin from the flight deck, a tray of empty coffee cups in one hand, shutting the door softly with the other. She moved slowly along the aisle checking on her passengers sprawled in sleep across their seats.

Here and there she passed the brighter light of a reading lamp, silhouetting a businessman poring over company papers, or a mother reading a novel, her sleeping children gathered protectively about her, faintly conscious of the aircraft's vibrations and the distant murmur of its engines.

Towards the middle of the aircraft the hostess stopped beside a sleeping man. His seat was tilted back as far as it would go, and his hands lay relaxed upon the arm rests. He was large with the well-proportioned build of a fighter, aged about thirty-five with a dark, sunburned face and white blond hair. She watched him for a moment. Even in sleep his body had an almost cat-like grace. His face was hard and finely chiselled with creases around the edges of his eyes and his lips. He was, the stewardess decided for the third time that night, one of the sexiest men that she had ever seen. She reached down and touched him lightly on the shoulder. His eyes flashed open, then his mouth relaxed into a mocking smile. The hostess found herself blushing.

'It's time. You asked me to wake you,' she whispered angrily.

The man nodded. She spun on her heel and walked quickly down the aisle. The blond man glaced at his watch, then turned and nudged awake the man sleeping beside him. He was an African of middle age and height, several stone overweight with unusually dark skin tinged a sickly grey. He had a moon-shaped face with large brown clouded eyes which, in the days when journalists had cared about him, had been said to reflect all the misery, the pain and the fear of emergent black Africa.

The African fumbled in his waistcoat pocket and brought out a small case. He opened it and took out two pills. Around his wrist hung a silver chain with a medical alert plate fastened to it. The stewardess returned with a tray bearing cups of coffee and a glass of water. She ignored the blond man as she reached across and handed the African the glass. The blond man smiled contentedly, his eyes arrogantly stripping the clothing from her body. The African swallowed the pills and returned the glass with a murmur of thanks. The stewardess continued up the gangway to the flight deck.

'Sleep any?' the blond man asked. He spoke in English with a Swedish-American accent.

'Not too much,' the African replied.

'You sure you're okay?' the blond man asked again gently. He was a cold, selfish man, but the African had the ability to command devotion in the men who worked for him.

'I'm all right,' the African said softly. 'How much longer?'

The blond man leaned back in his chair and closed his

eyes. ' 'Bout two hours forty minutes,' he said sleepily. The African nodded and turned to the window. He was a very sick man and time was important to him.

With her free hand the stewardess knocked on the flight deck door. As she opened it, a man with a gun in his hand rose silently behind her and followed her through. A second man, towards the rear of the plane, rose and walked along the aisle. He also held a gun in his hand. Suddenly the overhead cabin lights were switched full on and there came the hollow sound of the tannoy starting to life.

The blond man lay deep in his seat, his eyes still closed, yet his body collected and tense, as though he was testing each muscle. Then, in one fluid movement, he threw himself forward, rising to his feet and into the aisle, his right hand reaching up into the left underarm of his jacket. But before he reached the aisle, his legs began to buckle as though he had lost his balance. His eyes were filled with shock and pain and his mouth was shaped into a wordless scream.

The African's eyes were drawn to the empty seat beside him. Three-quarter way up its back, five inches of a long, incredibly thin stiletto pierced through and shone in the now bright light. Sweat appeared on his upper lip and forehead. He was dimly aware of the strong reassuring voice of the captain informing the passengers of a hijack and assuring them that they would come to no harm.

The blond man's gun fell to the floor. He began to move along the narrow aisle. From deep inside him came a sound, a rising tortured scream, his arm twisted grotesquely behind him as he tried to reach for the wound high up in his back over his heart. The sound grew louder. He began to jerk, clawing at the wound in his back. He moved a few feet crabwise down the aisle. Then his knees began to buckle again. He clutched at the back of the seats for support. Slowly, very

9

slowly, he sank to his knees. Tiredly, he lifted his head and his eyes focused on the passenger beside him. It was the woman with the children, her novel lying discarded on the floor.

The blond man coughed. Blood began to form in the corners of his mouth. He reached out to her, frightened of his pain, of dying alone.

'Help me,' he pleaded, 'I'm hurt bad.' The woman did not move. 'Oh, God,' he whispered again. 'Please help me. Help me.' He tried to touch her. The woman galvanized into life. She caught up the child nearest to her then flung herself back towards the window, her lungs sucking in air. Then she let out a piercing scream and kept on screaming until the blond man died in the aisle by her feet a minute later.

The knife was withdrawn. A well-dressed man of about forty-five slid into the seat next to the African.

'Julius Limbani?' he asked pleasantly in a French accent.

The African nodded slowly. He was trembling, mechanically wiping the beads of sweat from his forehead with a cream silk handkerchief. The Frenchman moved his hands expressively, as though erasing all the horror of the previous few minutes.

'We regret the inconvenience, of course, but there is an old friend of yours who wishes very much to meet with you again.'

A haunting suspicion formed in the African's mind. Had Faulkner double-crossed him? His mouth was dry, his throat tight. 'Who?' he rasped.

The Frenchman smiled deprecatingly. 'General Ndofa, my friend. You remember him. Who else would want you so badly?'

The African paused. He needed to think clearly, but he couldn't. All he could hear was the fear screaming out to him in the darkness of his mind. 'How much?' he breathed at last. 'How much to set me free? I can pay you.'

'I am already well paid,' the Frenchman said softly. 'It is useless for you to try. Forgive me, but I must search you.'

They were dragging the blond man away, his limp body bumping along the aisle. None of the passengers moved. In the distance a child cried and his mother covered his mouth. The African turned to the window. He felt the Frenchman's hand running expertly over his body. 'I nearly made it,' he whispered silently to himself. 'Oh God, I so nearly made it. Faulkner! Where's Faulkner? How could he let this happen to me? If he's free, there's a chance, or have they got to him too?'

Ridges of pain knotted the African's chest as his over-strained heart responded to the adrenalin surging through his system. 'My pills,' he breathed. 'My pills. I have a cardiac condition. I need them.'

The Frenchman studied the contents of the case anxiously. Then he glanced at the medical alert plate on the African's wrist. 'Of course,' he smiled relaxing. 'But I shall keep the case for you. Come, Monsieur Limbani. Compose yourself. Perhaps even try to sleep a little. The journey is rather long.'

'Where?' the African asked.

'Algeria,' the Frenchman shrugged resignedly, forestalling the next question. After that it is not my business. But there is no chance for Faulkner. You understand?'

The African turned away. So they'd got to Faulkner. There was no hope now. The utter despair of it all deadened his mind. He should never have come this far. The odds were too great and he was too weak. And yet, in spite of all that, he had so nearly won his country back. Involuntarily, tears filled his eyes. He peered out of the window to hide them. It was dark outside for there was no moon that night and the stars hung cold in the cloudless sky.

CHAPTER TWO

FAULKNER

Heathrow Airport, London. Late November, 1970

FOG was closing in over the runways. Icy drizzle, carried
on the wind, washed against the glass walls of the transit
lounge. Inside, scattered through the large floor area, a few
bored, cold passengers waited in the gathering darkness of a
winter's afternoon.

A man in his late twenties pushed open a door marked
Immigration and walked into the lounge. He had a serious,
efficient face that would fit a hundred other men and his
dress and manner were just as unassuming. He paused for a
moment, scanning the passengers, then walked quickly
towards a small figure hunched in an uncomfortable futuris-
tic chair.

The man in the chair was almost lost in an enormous
overcoat. It reached from his ankles to where a high-winged
fur collar touched his hat, shielding his face until only his
chin showed. On the table before him rested a half-empty
bottle of whisky and an empty glass.

'Colonel Faulkner?' the anonymous man inquired quietly.

A gloved hand pushed back the hat. Faulkner rose slowly
to his feet, seeming to grow in stature as he did so. The
overcoat was typical of him, for Faulkner hated the cold. In

his early fifties, his hair greying at the temples, he had a lean, strongly-made face with high cheek bones and a broken nose. A battered, likeable face that looked well lived in. But it was his eyes that held your attention for they were wide, dark and cold. And they seemed to see straight through you and way beyond.

'You're late,' Faulkner said finally. His voice was whisky-flavoured, the words soft and somehow menacing.

'I know. I'm sorry,' the anonymous man said hurriedly. He felt the dark eyes burning into him and a chill crept up his spine.

'We thought it wiser if your visit to this country was not recorded. That's why we moved you in here. Immigration are kicking up a fuss though. This is their little kingdom and they don't like trespassers. I had to get the Centre to apply some pressure to get you through. You are clean?' he asked anxiously. 'I mean, you're not carrying a gun or anything like that, are you?'

Faulkner shook his head, contemptuously pushing his hands forward in his overcoat pockets, as if inviting a search. Embarrassed, the courier ignored the unspoken invitation.

'If you'll follow me,' he said, 'I don't think there'll be any difficulty now.' He turned and walked quickly towards the door marked Immigration. Faulkner followed more leisurely. The fluorescent lights on the ceiling flickered on. A weary voice on the tannoy began to apologize for delays in flight arrivals and departures.

Faulkner sauntered past the Immigration barrier, oblivious to the hostile eyes that followed him, and on into the main hall of the terminal. The courier nodded to a uniformed chauffeur who stood by one of the exits.

'Be a few minutes yet,' he said cheerfully. 'Gone to get the car.' He looked around at the milling people. Actually, I like airports, always a lot happening.' He was a grey little man and he was making an effort to be pleasant. 'Got a friend who's an airline pilot. He tells a good story. It's about a foggy day like this when the planes can't get in to land and they're stacking them up as far out as the coast.'

'Who's Balfour?' Faulkner interrupted him.

'I don't know,' the courier replied coldly, giving up. 'My job's just to deliver you.'

Faulkner buried his chin in his collar and strode up and down, stamping his feet. He wished now that he had brought the whisky with him. After the warm sunlight of South Africa, even in his enormous overcoat, he was cold. And more than that, he was tired; tired deep down to his soul. Balfour, who in the hell was Balfour? A name he could not place at the bottom of a telegram that curtly bade him come. With the telegram there had been delivered a large, unsigned cheque and an airline ticket.

All through the long night journey around the bulge of Africa, his mind had worried the problem, tried to place the name of Balfour. Faulkner was a man with many enemies. He needed to know who he was meeting. Normally, he would not have come, but for the faint hope of a contract. No one would use him after Limbani's death. They must have known his situation, how desperate he was for work. Not just for the money, but to command men in action once again. The courier, the waiving of Immigration formalities, someone with a pull in Government? Faulkner shook his head to clear it. Who in the hell was Balfour?

A black Rover 3-litre pulled up outside. 'That's it. Your luggage is already in.'

Faulkner braced himself, walked through the terminal doors and hurried down the steps. The courier joined him in the car.

'What's the Centre?' Faulkner demanded as the car pulled away. 'Military Intelligence?' He had crossed them in the past and still had a faint but lurking fear that a British gaol awaited him.

The courier shrugged. 'I'd like to go to South Africa one day,' he said avoiding the subject. 'What's it like, I mean apart from the politics?'

Faulkner grunted angrily. He had already summed the courier up as a lightweight – of no real use to him. 'Cold,' he muttered softly to himself, settling into a corner and tilting his hat over his eyes. 'Bloody cold.' A few seconds later he was asleep.

The courier flushed, then turned to stare out of the window. Visibility had closed to twenty yards. The lights from the oncoming traffic became yellow blurs in the now driving rain.

By six-thirty they had cleared London and were travelling fast along the Brighton freeway. The car decelerated smoothly, then turned left into an almost hidden road. The road narrowed to a lane. Suddenly they were winding through a small village, the stunted houses dark and curtained against the winter evening.

It was as though the village, two centuries ago, had withdrawn from the race for civilization and now lay quietly, fearful of the day when the local pub would boast a juke box and bulldozers would rip away at the outskirts to make room for housing estates. Around it lay the beautiful wooded acres of the banking and publishing house families.

Three miles past the village, the car drew up before a pair of enormous wrought iron gates. On either side a seven-foot high red brick wall stretched into the distance. The driver leaned forward and pressed a button under the dashboard. The gates swung open. The car moved forward and the gates closed behind them.

They followed a gravelled, tree-lined drive for several hundred yards, then drew up before the steps of a rambling manor house. Faulkner hurried up the wide stone stairway. The door opened as he reached it. A butler, immaculate in tails and pin stripes, helped him off with his coat.

The butler quietly asked Faulkner to follow him. Though he was an elderly man, he held himself erect with the proud, authoritative manner of an old family retainer. Their footsteps echoed, following them across the stone-flagged floor. A staircase of polished oak swept up to the first floor landing. Around them there were five doors leading to different parts of the house. The butler chose the first door on the left and knocked softly. A voice answered and he opened it.

'Colonel Faulkner, sir,' he announced.

Faulkner entered the room. It was a beautifully panelled study, fairly large and warmly lit, with rows of finely bound books lining each wall, their polished covers glinting in the firelight. The room smelled of leather and good cigars. Two men were seated in high-backed chairs before a log fire. They rose as Faulkner entered. Both were in evening dress. One of them, in his early forties, slightly built with sandy hair thinning on the crown and a permanently worried expression, moved forward, hand outstretched, to greet him.

'Thank you for coming so quickly. My name's Balfour. Thomas Balfour. You'll remember, it was on the telegram,' he added, anxious that there be no misunderstanding. His voice held a trace of a Scottish lilt. Faulkner nodded. Balfour turned. 'Let me introduce you to Sir Edward Matherson.'

Matherson was in his seventies. He stood six-foot four in a lean straight line with grey, close-cropped hair and a small military moustache, half hidden by a long hook nose. His face had wrinkled into parchment from many years in the sun. His clear pale blue eyes had been watching Faulkner intently while Balfour spoke, his head thrust out from between his shoulders like a hawk. And Faulkner noticed that, like a hawk, his eyelids rarely blinked.

Matherson shook Faulkner's hand briefly. His clasp was hard. His hand appeared to be all bone. Then he retrieved his brandy from the table and settled himself comfortably in his chair. Faulkner stood in front of the fire, his hands outstretched before it. 'Matherson as in Merchant Banking?' he asked. Matherson nodded. He swirled the brandy in the glass, staring through it into the fire. He looked up suddenly. 'Draw up a chair, Faulkner,' he ordered softly.

'I believe that you drink whisky?' Balfour said from behind. 'Do you take soda or water?' Faulkner did not turn his head. 'Large and neat,' he said, then he turned to warm his back. Balfour handed Faulkner the whisky. He pulled up a third chair before the fire. 'It was good of you to come at such short notice. If you accept our contract, we are going to be rather short of time.'

Faulkner smiled suddenly. It seemed to light up his face and his eyes warmed, showing the two sides of the man. One warm, wild, magnetic. The other cold, calculating and ruthless. 'An air ticket and a large unsigned cheque are great persuaders,' he said. 'Besides, you must know I was down to my last bottle.' He settled himself down in the chair, swallowed half the whisky, leaned back and breathed out slowly. He stretched his legs before the fire and sighed contentedly. 'This is the first time I've been warm since I arrived in this bloody country.'

Matherson looked at the now empty glass in Faulkner's hand. 'Please make yourself free with my whisky,' he said drily. 'It would appear,' he continued, half lost in thought, 'that, as the civilized world grows more respectable, it tends to use mercenaries for its more distasteful chores.'

Faulkner nodded. 'It's the new age. The big powers are shit scared of the atom bomb,' he grinned. 'We're even becoming respectable.'

'Most of your colleagues, I believe, are fairly busy at the moment?'

Faulkner leaned back in his chair. 'Yes,' he agreed, mentally ticking them off. 'Peter d'Enis got the oil sheikdoms contract on the Gulf a few months ago. He's to supply and equip a small army for National Defence. Jean Pierre got the Yemen. He's doing well, I hear. Claus the German got the Sudan, but he's having a rough time. Not enough money behind him. And of course Tiny Martin's landed the Angolan contract for when the Portuguese pull out. Mind you, he's on such a bloody great retainer that he'll probably drink himself to death before they leave.'

'It would seem that these contracts, as you refer to them, are only awarded by Government.'

'They're the only people who can afford us,' Faulkner said simply.

'I represent a syndicate that can well afford to use you, if I decide that you are suitable,' Sir Edward said softly.

'I'm the best there is.'

'Yet you have not worked for some time, I believe.'

'No.'

'Your last contract ended disastrously.'

'It never started,' Faulkner said angrily. 'You know that. Someone hijacked my principal.'

'It was felt in some circles that a man who could not protect his principal could hardly be expected to complete a contract satisfactorily. In fact, it is said that you're getting too old. Too much whisky.'

'I'm dry when I'm in action. And compared with you I'm still a boy.'

'My profession requires brain rather than brawn.'

Faulkner started to reply. Then he stopped and took control of himself. He needed this contract badly. 'Limbani was on his way to sign the contract when the C.I.A. took him. I was not in his service at the time.'

'You worked for him before. It was reported that you

were a friend of his, yet you did not try to get him back.'

Faulkner put down his whisky. 'There was no profit in it. I've learned only to work for profit.' He was silent for a moment. 'Besides, within hours of hijacking him, they called at my hotel in Tel Aviv. Warned me that if I moved he'd die before I got there. They watched every move I made until he died. He was a good man,' Faulkner said softly, by way of an epitaph. 'A bloody good man.'

Matherson handed his glass to Balfour and motioned Faulkner to do the same. Faulkner refused. 'I believe that the contract was to depose General Ndofa and reinstate Limbani as head of the Government?'

Faulkner stared into the fire. 'The Congolese people were with us. The army didn't account for much. We would have had to silence the Presidential guard and the paramilitary police units that he had built up. We could have done it too.' Faulkner looked up. 'Anyway, what's the use? He's dead.'

'No,' Matherson said softly. 'He is alive. Very sick and they intend to finish him off soon. But he's not dead, yet.' Matherson raised his hand to stop Faulkner from interrupting him. 'I'll start from the beginning,' he said, 'so that you may know what our interest in the matter is.

'The merchant banks started almost from the time that man first began to trade with money. They grew into a common brotherhood that knew no frontiers or boundaries. We have survived unchanged all known disasters. From wars to plagues and famines. We have learned to ride the changes of Government. In fact, in the old days we financed Governments and, to a lesser extent, we still do today.

'One of the first things that the banks did when they started was to form some of the first true intelligence services. As the banks grew and whilst they pooled much of their information, they found that they also required specific knowledge of what was occurring in other world capitals.

Thus, they began an efficient courier service. For a long time, the more enlightened Governments relied on these services.

'I tell you this merely to illustrate that our intelligence services are still amongst the best in the world. Thus we know that Limbani is alive. And we know where he is.

'Our bank normally operates independently. However, when a project is offered that requires really large financing, we syndicate among our brother banks. We also syndicate when faced with a large mutual problem. At the moment our investments are at risk. I therefore speak to you on behalf of a syndicate.

'You're sure you won't have another drink?'

'I'm waiting dry until I know what you're offering.'

Matherson had been watching Faulkner as he spoke, gauging the strengths and weaknesses of the man. Now he leaned back in his chair. 'Very well,' he said, forming a temple with his hands over his brandy glass.

'You may not be aware,' he continued, 'that Britain had extensive interests within the Congo. The second largest consortium after the Union Miniere du Haut Katanga was British owned, together with a monopoly on the marketing of Congolese diamonds. And, most important, the Benguela railway. The only access by which the copper and cobalt from Katanga could be transported to the sea was British owned.

'Some years ago, while the country was still under colonial rule, our syndicate committed itself heavily to financing the exploitation of the copper mines. On balance it was a good investment. The mines proved some of the richest in the world. They survived the transitional stages to black rule and the civil wars that followed. We were, therefore, not unduly perturbed when General Ndofa led the coup against his old friend Limbani.

'We of course knew of the impending coup and, though unable to stop it, we were able to arrange for Limbani's safe exit from his country. We bought certain of his shareholdings in the copper mines, made the funds available to him in Switzerland and installed him there with the intention of saving him for a rainy day.

'Naturally, we then made Limbani's shareholding available to General Ndofa at a very reasonable price, in order that he might have a personal interest in the mines and would therefore continue to protect our interests. We try not to concern ourselves with politics,' Matherson said reflectively. 'All we require is the element of personal greed – and a stable Government.

'All went well for a while, but unfortunately General Ndofa succumbed to the Nkrumah complex. He distrusted the intelligentsia of the country and had liquidated most of them. Their places in Government had been taken by largely uneducated men who are simply riding the bandwagon.

'After the bloodshed of the sixties, the people left the land and flocked into the cities. The cost of living has spiralled. Foreign aid has poured into the country to the tune of four hundred and eighty million dollars in the last ten years. But dictatorships require the expenditure of vast sums to ensure loyalty. General Ndofa's personal cheque book drawn on the Banque Nationale makes nonsense of budget estimates. Graft and corruption have risen to intolerable limits. The country's financially bled dry.

'Ndofa has played the aid game for several years now. First leaning towards the Russians and then the Americans. Both sides are fed up with him. England can't afford to play and the Chinese are fully committed to Tanzania and Zambia. His last resort to induce some form of solvency into his country's economy is the copper mines. Three years ago, he nationalized fifty-one per cent. Compensation of a sort

21

was paid in fixed assets within the country, which we were not able to dispose of. Since then, profitability on the mines has dropped by half.

'Our information is that now Ndofa intends to nationalize the whole shareholding in the mines without compensation. He further intends to confiscate all our fixed assets. After the first wave of nationalizations he has been unable to persuade any other bankers to trust him, so that he has been denied access to the international money market.

'We believe that he intends to re-offer our holdings to us in exchange for very liberal financing. Thus, we are to be blackmailed into investing more and more money in his country. Part of this money I believe is to be used for building a special village for the Organization of African Unity Summit meetings.'

Matherson rose and took a few quick paces up and down the room. No one spoke. He stared into the fire for a moment, picking up his train of thought.

'Our problem,' he continued, 'is that we have nothing to bargain with at the moment. At least . . .' he paused and glanced at Faulkner. 'That's where you come in.

'Limbani was the people's hope for uniting the country, but the Americans did not think that he was strong enough. So they backed Ndofa against him. Limbani could not hold them both and tried to get the British in to help him. The British Government at that time had enough problems in Africa, so they dropped him. Against our advice, I might add.

'The one person that Ndofa has always been frightened of is Limbani. He knows the power that man has over the people, especially as his own tribe occupy a third of the country. In recent years, it has almost become a mania with him. He tried to eliminate Limbani twice when he was in Switzerland. However, a new Government was in power here at the time and we were able to persuade D.I.6. to protect him. Then Ndofa got wind of your impending coup and was able to persuade the C.I.A. to arrange his abduction.

'You know the rest, of course. Limbani was taken to Algeria which specializes in these manoeuvres, to be held until the fuss died down and then returned to his own country for public execution. What few people know is that the Algerians found that, in holding Limbani, they achieved a large measure of control over Ndofa. So they continued to hold Limbani in spite of Ndofa's protests. Ndofa found it easier to accede to Algeria's demands than risk them setting Limbani free and starting a civil war that he might well lose and couldn't afford anyway.

'World opinion rose against Limbani's incarceration and began to prove embarrassing, even to the Algerians. It was known that Limbani suffered from a heart ailment, so the Algerians moved him into the interior and gave out that he had died. His family, of course, kept silent to ensure his survival. Ndofa having told his people of Limbani's death, was then faced with the terrifying prospect of a reincarnated Limbani walking amongst his people. A man who could well claim to have been sent again by the tribal spirits of the land to free them from Ndofa's oppressive rule.

'The situation has worn thin now. The Algerians have no further use for Limbani, so they are returning him secretly to Ndofa in exchange for certain treaties and considerations, part of which is a substantial share of our copper mines.'

Matherson leaned forward. 'It is now 20th November. Our information is that, on or before 5th January, Limbani will be transported across the lake from the Tanzanian border and will be incarcerated in the Army barracks at Albertville. Ndofa will leave Leopoldville the same day, as he wishes to see Limbani personally before he is executed and his remains are scattered.

'We wish to offer you the contract to get Limbani out of Albertville and return him to England. Alive, of course. We will make available any information that you may require. We can also provide you with personal files on any man of note that you may come up against in the Congo.'

Matherson stopped, his head craned towards Faulkner. 'Do you have any questions at this stage?' he asked. Faulkner thought for a moment, then shook his head. 'They can wait,' he said.

'Monies to meet your expenses will be made available through a numbered account in the Central Bank of Zurich. The account has remained in Limbani's name. However, withdrawals will be met on documents bearing your and Balfour's joint signature. Neither the account nor the bank, which is controlled through nominees, is traceable to us. Apart from this one meeting, we will not in any way be associated with you, nor render you any further assistance. Balfour, who is again not traceable to us, will act in liaison with you in matters concerning information and finance. Balfour also has contacts within D.I.6 who will be prepared to render limited assistance.'

Matherson sat back in his chair and handed his empty glass to Balfour. Firelight warmed his face and glinted in his half-closed eyes. 'Now,' he said softly. 'Your questions.'

Faulkner remained still for a while, marshalling his racing thoughts, striving to control the elation that was rising within him.

'One,' he said shortly. 'It'll take a few days to see if the project is feasible. Two, if it is, I shall require a properly drawn contract.'

Matherson nodded. 'We can arrange for the other signatory to be a member of Limbani's family.'

'Three, how soon can you confirm the actual date of Limbani's arrival in Albertville?'

'We can let you know that within seven days from due date,' Balfour broke in.

'Four, can you detain Ndofa in Leopoldville while the snatch is being made? I believe that he never travels without his Presidential guard and the fewer men that we have to contend with the better.'

'We can arrange that,' Matherson said.

'Right, that's all for now.'

'I would have thought that you might wish to discuss your fee and expenses.'

Faulkner grinned. 'I'll send you an account when I know what it costs.'

'I know that in your particular profession, you get paid for risking your life, Faulkner,' Matherson said drily, 'but I trust that you don't consider your skin too valuable.'

There came a soft knock on the door behind them. Matherson turned as the butler entered. 'Your supper, sir,' he said reprovingly.

'Thank you, Wilson. Tell cook that I'll be along directly.'

Matherson rose and led Faulkner to the door. 'Well, that's all.' He shook Faulkner's hand. 'If you take the contract, I wish you luck and a safe journey. Balfour will return with you to London. Goodnight.' He turned abruptly and crossed the hall. The butler opened the door for him. Before it closed, Faulkner saw a polished table, lit by candles and set in silver for two.

They were halfway to London before Faulkner spoke. 'The bastard,' he said angrily out of the darkness.

'Why?' Balfour asked anxiously.

'I'm half starved. Does he think he's too special to offer us dinner? Or am I a dirty word in his vocabulary? 'Fraid that

25

his wife might disapprove? We colonials have learned how to use knives and forks, you know.'

'His wife's dead.'

'I saw two places set.' Faulkner suddenly smiled. 'So he's go a woman on the side, he's half human after all.'

'Oh, that,' Balfour said. 'No, his wife died six years ago. But they had a rule. No matter what he was doing, he always had dinner with her. Used to talk over his problems with her then, get them sorted out. He still does now, even though she's dead.'

'Do you mean that he just sits there and talks to an empty plate?'

Balfour shrugged his shoulders. 'It's hard to explain – they don't serve her food or anything. But the old boy loved her so much that, if you stay in the house for a while, you get the feeling she's still living there. You can't put your finger on anything. You just get the feeling, if you know what I mean.'

'She must have been some kind of woman to get through to that cold bastard.'

'She was half White Russian, half Chinese. He met her in Shanghai just before the war. She was working out of the Long Bar. And after being so long a bachelor, he suddenly just upped and married her.'

Faulkner whistled in the darkness. 'You mean to tell me that Matherson married a call girl.'

'That, Colonel Faulkner,' Balfour answered shortly, 'I don't know. But I do know that there was more fire, generosity and compassion, more woman packed into her five feet than in any three women I've ever known.'

'What did the children look like?'

'Now I know why I don't like South Africans,' Balfour said angrily. 'There was only one. A son. He got some bone disease and died. Slowly. The old man nearly died with him.'

'Don't judge all South Africans by me. I'm a special kind of bastard. Mind you, it must have taken courage,' Faulkner reflected. 'Especially in that kind of elevated society. It was even more rigid than Singapore. And I knew Singapore before the war.'

'Let me tell you about Sir Edward,' Balfour said. 'He came from the poor side of a great merchant banking family. That meant he was further away from the money than a tart from the altar in a Mormon Chapel. Oh, he went to the right schools and then, because he was a wild one, hell bent on disgracing the family name, straight into the army.

'They gave him a small allowance to stay there. And cut it every time his name appeared in a scandal. As it was, he was a damned good soldier. My father served with him as his R.S.M. When he died in the war, Matherson looked after our family. In fact, he looked after every man who ever served with him. He's the only man I know, apart from you, who could raise a private army overnight. They'd all be old crocks, but they'd fight to the death for him. Anyway, marrying a Eurasian ruined his chances in the army until the war broke out. Then he received some of the fastest promotions in history.

'He was made Major-General in charge of the British Garrison in the Lebanon. When he thought the French were going to turn and while they were still our allies, he disarmed them and put them in prisoner-of-war camps. He then placed mines under the major commercial institutions and the homes of the principal sheikhs. He promised them all faithfully that he'd blow the lot up if they went over to the Germans. They gave him their unswerving loyalty.

'The French never forgave him and, after the war, they demanded his resignation. The British Government at that time was all out for the *entente cordiale* and they forced him to resign. The family took him in, for he was covered in

27

medals and they hadn't done much during the war. They gave him a few minor directorships, but mostly they used him as a nominee, working no doubt on the principle that a soldier has no brain for business.

'He lived up to their expectations for about five years. Then one day they woke up to find that he knew the business better than they did and he had taken them over. None of them were strong enough to stand up to him, so now they work for him.'

'What's your part in all this?' Faulkner asked.

Balfour laughed softly. 'I handled his more private affairs, such as this.'

The car was nosing its way through the heavy traffic around Marble Arch. 'Stop here,' Faulkner ordered the driver. 'I'll stay at the Cumberland.'

The driver looked back at Balfour for confirmation. Balfour shook his head. 'Not this time. You're too well known,' he said. 'This is a private visit.'

The car dropped Faulker outside a shabby hotel in the Gloucester Road. Faulkner got out, turning up his collar against the cold. He looked at the hotel with distaste. Then he turned back to the car. 'When do you sign the cheque?' he asked.

'When you sign the contract,' Balfour replied from the warmth of the car. 'You've got my number?' Faulkner tapped his pocket. 'Anything else you want?'

'Yes. Can you find a man for me in a hurry?'

'Possibly. Who?'

'Janders. Rafer Janders. He used to work with me. I've lost track of him, but he should be here – somewhere in London.'

'Is he an American of sorts? Grey hair? Hemingway beard?' Balfour interrupted.

'That's him. Where do you know him from?'

'Got a file on him as well. Had it out the other day. Don't worry, I'll find him. Goodnight.'

The car nosed into the traffic. Faulkner watched the blue exhaust smoke curl in the freezing night wind. Then he walked up the hotel steps.

CHAPTER THREE

RAFER JANDERS parked his battered old Morris in the courtyard of an ageing but gracious block of flats overlooking the Thames, near the Hurlingham Club. He switched off the lights and leaned back against the seat listening to the rain beat softly on the canvas roof.

He was a big man, in his early fifties, but still hard. His strong, bearded face was strangely attractive for the character it showed. His smokey grey eyes were sad, as though they had seen too much and the pain had seared into his soul. No drugs, he had told them when they made contact. Mister, I'm down. I need the money. I'll carry anything but no drugs. They hadn't listened to him and they were going to pay for it now.

Janders slowly got out of the car and looked up towards the top storey where a row of lights and the noise indicated that a party was well in progress. From his raincoat pocket he brought out a small paper-covered package and he tossed it in his hands. The cold thin rain matted his hair, streaming down the creases of his haunted face into his beard.

He entered the building, following a long carpeted passage to an ancient lift by the stairway, his footsteps padding noiselessly on the floor. He closed the wrought iron grille, pushed a button and the lift whirred and creaked as it rose to the fifth floor. In the dim overhead light, he drew a Russian-made Tokarev 7.62 millimetre automatic from his pocket, worked the action, inserted the eight-round ammunition clip and then replaced it. The gun was a memento from the Congo of the sixties, kept for such a time as this.

The lift shuddered to a halt. Janders walked to the end of another short passage and knocked on the door. He knocked twice more before the sound was heard above the noise of the party. At last a slot covering the peep hole flew open and an eye glared through. Then the door partly opened, still held by a chain.

'What're you doing here?' There was a harsh Southern drawl in the voice of the man who challenged him. 'I warned you never to come to this place.'

From behind him, above the music, came the wild whoop of a younger man. 'Baby,' he was shouting, 'my daddy was the devil and my mama was his mistress. And I was born wild. Oh, baby, wild – just wild.'

Janders posed no threat, for he looked a lonely, broken old man, his shoulders stooped in a grubby, rain-sodden mac. He drew the package half out of his pocket. 'Trouble,' he muttered apologetically.

'Anybody after you?' the big man asked. Janders shook his head. The man unlatched the door. 'All right,' he decided. 'You'd better see the boss. Come in. Hurry.'

Janders was led through a small hallway into a large empty living-room. It was dark, save for the glow of tiny spot lights which shone upon etchings set into niches on the black draped walls. The floor was covered with thick white rugs. A bar stood in one corner littered with half empty bottles and used glasses.

A young man appeared from the bedroom. He was naked, supported on either arm by two equally naked girls. All three were drunk or high. 'What I need now,' he shouted as he came through the doorway, 'is a crate full of whisky, an arm full of woman and I'll just destroy myself.'

He stopped, staring blankly at Janders. 'What're you doing here?' he demanded when his eyes focused.

'Trouble, he says,' the man beside Janders spoke. 'You'd better get rid of the girls.'

'Sure.' The young man turned and pushed them into the bedroom. He came out a moment later, wearing a towel and closing the door behind him. 'What's the problem?' he asked nervously.

'You should have told me that I was carrying heroin,' Janders said gently, looking round, making certain they were the only people there. 'I warned you, no drugs.'

'So what?' the young man shrugged. He was tall, lean, good-looking, apart from a debauched face. 'People like you I buy and sell. I don't have to tell you anything, old man. And now, you know what?' he giggled, a sadistic excitement rising at the prospect of a new diversion. He tossed his long fair hair out of his eyes and crossed the room towards Janders. 'You should have done what I told you first time. 'Cause now Randy here's going to kick your balls in. Aren't you, Randy boy, hey?'

'You should have told me,' Janders said again softly, turning to Randy and pulling his gun from his pocket.

'Go on, Randy boy,' the young man called excitedly from behind. 'Kick the old bugger's balls in. Hurt him real bad.'

Randy did nothing. He was a big, hard man. Dark with a sallow skin and he was beginning to sweat.

'Little punk, why don't you come over here and stand beside Randy boy?' Janders asked politely. His voice was calm but his grey eyes were cold. 'And, little punk,' he said mimicking the youth's accent and indicating with his gun, 'don't you give me no trouble now. 'Cause if you do, first I'll take away your towel, then I'll hang you out of the window for a while, so that all the world can admire your truly glorious manhood. Then I'll drop you.'

The young man stood for a moment, open-mouthed. Then he scampered around to join Randy, clutching his towel.

'Now, Randy boy,' Janders said and he smiled. 'I don't have to threaten you. I mean, you must know that if you cross me, I'll shoot pieces off you. So undo your belt and let your trousers drop. And if you're carrying a gun, do yourself a favour, friend, let it drop too, because I'll surely check.'

'Take him, Randy,' the young man urged. 'Go on, you can do it. He's only an old man.'

Randy looked into Janders' eyes. An expression of exasperation crossed his face. His hands dropped to his belt.

'Go on, take him, you baboon,' the young man urged angrily. 'That's what you're hired for.'

'Shut up, will you?' Randy said tiredly. 'We're in more trouble than you know.' His trousers fell about his ankles, revealing a pair of blue striped jockey shorts below his shirt.

'Kick your trousers well away from you,' Janders said. 'Then your shirt.' The man did as he was told. Janders indicated a bare part of the rug. 'Sit over there by the wall.' He watched them carefully as they moved.

'I . . .' the young man began. His voice was pitched too high with fear and it cracked, so he tried again. 'We'll get you for this.' He indicated to Randy. 'Won't we, hey?'

'Shaddup, will you?' Randy said again. 'Look, Mister,' he addressed Janders. 'I know he's a punk. But he's still just a kid. His old man's something special in the Mafia back in the States. So why don't you clear out, eh? And you won't get hurt. We'll leave it at that, no hard feelings. I mean, so you don't like pushing dope. Well, you've made your point. We'll leave it at that. Okay. Okay?'

Janders took the package from his pocket. He tossed it to the young man. 'Open it,' he said. The young man did as he was told. Before him lay a little white mound of heroin.

'This was my first job for you,' Janders said quietly. 'And

you might have been lucky. Except that when I made contact the girl I met was dying. You're selling bum stuff, my friends. But more than that. As I watched the girl die, it reminded me of my first wife. She died like that a long time ago. I really loved that woman,' he said softly. 'So eat it.'

'What?' the young man yelled, his voice breaking again.

'Eat it,' Janders said coldly. 'Both of you. Half each.'

'No,' Randy shouted and started to move. Janders shot him in the forehead at close range. Randy remained upright for a moment. Then he heeled over leaving the back of his head a bloody mess against the wall. Janders moved quickly across the room and locked the bedroom door.

'Eat,' he said pointing the gun. 'I won't tell you again.'

The young man ate the lot.

'I'll let myself out,' Janders said softly. 'No use praying for a stomach pump, friend. There's strychnine with it. I thought I'd let you know a little pain before you go. You'll feel it in your muscles soon. Then your back will begin to arch, until maybe it breaks.

'You'll be dead in about ten minutes. The girl took a whole lot longer. I'll say goodbye now.' He closed the door as the young man began to scream.

Janders walked unhurriedly out of the building. He stopped in the courtyard and turned up his collar against the rain. He had known about the young man's family, knew they would hunt him now until there was no place deep enough for him to hide. But when a once proud man like Janders was having to carry heroin to earn money, it was the end of the line. There was no point in living – no point in tomorrow.

He looked up to the top floor one last time. And then, abandoning his car, he turned and walked into the night.

CHAPTER FOUR

THE night passed slowly for Faulkner. He lay on his back under the covers of a narrow, uncomfortable bed. Orange light from the street lamp outside filtered through faded net curtains and, together with the glow from the gas fire, cast the room in a weird half light.

The room was small, bare with a wash-stand in the corner, a peeling mirror above. In the drawer by the bedside was a half finished bottle of whisky. Faulkner was determined to leave it there. He had tried to drink himself to sleep many times before, but it never worked. On those occasions, as now, his body rested, but his mind refused to blank out. In the half light of consciousness it wandered back uncontrolled to memories that were better left forgotten and a sadness settled over him.

He remembered the hotel room in Tel Aviv where he had been waiting feverishly for Limbani to arrive and finalize the contract. The men were standing by, everything ready to go in. It was to have been his comeback: his last big contract when everyone said that he was past it, too old, too deep in the bottle. And now men like Tiny Martin who had once served under him had broken away and were leading their own mercenary units.

When word reached him that Limbani was captured, he came apart. He abandoned his men, left them stranded and went on a drunk. A blind, savage, fighting drunk. One morning he awoke from an alcoholic stupor in an Israeli gaol, all alone and there was nothing left. He was finished, washed up as a mercenary leader. Dear God, he had never been so down.

The telephone rang. Faulkner's mind cleared as he lifted the receiver.

'Do you know it's three in the morning?' the porter asked indignantly.

Faulkner glanced at his watch. 'Yes.'

'Switchboard's supposed to close at midnight. Don't you read the rules? Anyway, there's a call for you,' the porter said grudgingly and put it through.

'Hello, hello, Faulkner,' Balfour's voice came on the line. Faulkner swung himself onto the side of the bed, pulling the bedclothes around his shoulders. 'Yes,' he answered.

'Listen,' Balfour sounded worried, his Scots accent coming through clearly. 'That man you asked me to find, that American, Janders. I thought I'd make a few calls before I went to bed last night, to save time. Well, the answer's just come through. The man's in bad trouble. In fact, he's probably dead by now.'

Faulkner pulled the blankets closer about his shoulders. 'What happened?'

'He removed a couple of the Family's men last night,' Balfour said guardedly. 'One of them was a close relative. He's on the run now.'

'Is he still in town?'

'Must be. They've got the whole city sealed off. He's hurt them badly. They've put the biggest contract out on him that's ever been made in this country.'

Faulkner was silent for a moment. In his mind's eye, he could see Janders moving alone in the night through the great sprawling streets of London while the net closed in around him. 'You at home now?' he demanded.

'Yes.'

'I'll be there in thirty minutes. Keep trying to find him. Use all the contacts you have.'

'I've tried,' Balfour started, but Faulkner had replaced the receiver.

'Where's the nearest all night taxi rank?' Faulkner shouted to the dozing porter as he passed the reception area. The porter half started to his feet in surprise. 'Down the Cromwell Road,' he pointed.

It was raining gently, a fine cold drizzle. Faulkner sat back morosely in the taxi. It was now three-twenty on Sunday morning. The streets were deserted, the wet pavements stained orange in the reflected light from the street lamps overhead. A man needed crowds to lose himself in. As the parties broke up, the clubs in the West End emptied, he would grow more and more conspicuous on the streets. No, Faulkner reassured himself, Janders wouldn't be on the streets now. The old fox was far too cunning for that. He'd be holed up somewhere. Somewhere good and deep.

The taxi turned into a mews behind Kensington High Street and drew up before an attractive, white-painted cottage. The lights were already on. The door opened electronically soon after Faulkner pushed the buzzer. He climbed a narrow flight of stairs. Balfour still wore his anxious expression. 'At the moment, the Mafia can't find him and neither can we.' He led the way into a pleasant, warmly decorated living-room. 'My wife's gone to visit her family for the weekend, so make yourself at home.' Faulkner glanced at a photograph of a pleasant, fair-haired woman with twin, freckled, laughing boys.

'They're away at boarding school,' Balfour said proudly. He resumed his anxious expression. 'What happens to Janders now is no concern of ours. The less we interfere the better. Anyway, since you are here, let me get you a drink.' He walked over to the cocktail cabinet.

'Balfour,' Faulkner said softly from the centre of the room. Balfour turned. 'I don't go without Janders.'

'Colonel Faulkner, we know your circumstances. You're hardly in a position to call the tune.'

'You need Limbani badly, Balfour. I know the Congo. I know Limbani. And I can get him out for you. Besides, I'm the only man you've got in the time that's left to you, so get that contract lifted off Janders.'

Balfour thought for a moment. He handed Faulkner a whisky. 'Do I understand then, that if we were to get the contract lifted, you would accept our contract, regardless of risk, as of that date?'

'Provided the money's fair.'

'You'll find us generous. Tell me, why do you concern yourself with Janders? I thought that you only worked for profit.'

'I need Janders. He's the best planner I ever knew. I can lead the men, but someone has to get us in and out of there. Besides,' Faulkner added gruffly, 'I haven't got that many friends left that I can afford to lose one now.'

Balfour had been writing while Faulkner spoke. He rose from a table and handed Faulkner a piece of paper. 'I am, by nature, a cautious man,' he explained. 'I have set out here a brief draft of our agreement tonight. If it is satisfactory, please sign it and keep a copy. It may help to avoid any misunderstandings at a later date.'

Faulkner read it through and signed both copies of the document. When he looked up, there was renewed respect in his eyes for the anxious little man before him. 'I didn't know that the Mafia had moved into England in such a big way.'

Balfour twisted his glass in his hands and sat down. 'I know little more than the next man about them,' he admitted. 'But it seems that, over the last five years, they have been moving more and more men in. Mostly through their respectable fronts. When the police broke the main London gangs a few years ago, it left them an opening – and they took it. They've taken over the organized drug rings and now they're moving into prostitution. The police have been hammering on the Home Secretary's door for years, but it will take martial law and the death penalty to break them now. And none of the politicans will wear that, especially because, on the surface, the mob remain respectable and pay taxes like everybody else.'

'What happened with Janders?'

'It seems that one of the wild young sons of a Mafiosa was sent over here to cool off and learn the business. He thought that the place was wide open, so he set up his own organization on the side. I believe that it was nothing to do with the Family, just making pocket money. Anyway, they used this chap Janders as a courier. It took him one trip to discover what he was carrying. When he found out, he went berserk, shot the bodyguard and made the young chappie eat the lot. There was strychnine with it. Of course, his intestines lit up like a torch. He died pretty horribly.'

'So?' Faulkner said coldly.

'So, Colonel Faulkner,' Balfour replied, 'it will be no easy matter to get this contract lifted. However, we have a great need of Limbani at the moment. We'll do our best.'

'Are the police looking for him yet?'

Balfour shook his head. 'Not officially anyway. The Mafia avoid this kind of publicity.' He rose. 'There is nothing more that we can do now. I suggest that you return to your hotel and get some sleep. Sir Edward has already been informed. I am breakfasting with him in the morning. I'll inform you of developments.

'Oh, and Colonel Faulkner,' Balfour called after him as he was going down the stairs, 'please don't look for Janders.

This is not your territory. If you were hurt, our contract would be void immediately.'

Faulkner returned to his hotel and began work on two lists. The first contained every friend or acquaintance of Rafer Janders that he could remember. It was a short list, but it took him a long time to compile, for Rafer was by nature a lonely man. The second list was longer and contained the places he knew that Rafer used to haunt.

By seven a.m. Faulkner had finished and he realized how little he knew about an old friend. He stopped at a café for a light breakfast, studied the lists, trying to pair people with places. Then he began to walk the streets of London.

It was a cold, cheerless Sunday. Sometimes his footsteps followed him. Sometimes they were joined in the rush of others. As the day wore on, he grew more and more despondent. People had moved, though the places remained the same. He was following the shadow of a lonely, rambling man who stayed in each place long enough for a drink, to watch the people, and then moved on, leaving no friends to remember him.

In the good days after the Congo, Janders had taken a large flat in Mount Street. There he had been content to live amongst his paintings, his books and his music. He once told Faulkner that he welcomed old age: a chance to think without the passions of living, to reach into his mind and seek his God and find a peace within himself.

Faulkner visited the flat. Janders had moved on some time ago. He secured an address off the King's Road, found that Janders had moved on again. He visited three more addresses, each one more shabby than the last, until he reached a grubby rooming house in Bayswater which had been Janders' last known address.

The Mafia had reached there first. Two men waited in a car parked by the kerb. Faulkner was sure that two more waited inside. He walked slowly past. At least Janders was still in front, but for how much longer? The evening was drawing in, bringing with it a light cold drizzle. He stopped by a street lamp and consulted his lists again.

CHAPTER FIVE

11.30 a.m. Sunday, 29th November

THE weather had cleared sufficiently for Matherson to walk in the walled garden behind the main house. It had been set out by his wife, as near as possible in the traditional Chinese style. Though stark in winter, it was his favourite place. The streams were crossed by graceful wooden bridges. The bare branches of the willow trees rustled in the wind. They used to walk here on a summer's evening. And as he wandered, he felt her there beside him and it gave him comfort.

Balfour brought a stranger. 'May I introduce Mr. Martin?' he began. Martin brushed past Balfour and stepped forward. He was a large, heavily boned man, in his early fifties, with a flat expressionless face and cold, dark eyes. His muscles had long since turned to fat from lack of exercise, but his handshake was firm and his voice, though quiet, was accustomed to authority.

'We have met before, Sir Edward. You may remember. Many years ago in Boston.'

'Ah yes, Mr. Martin, I remember,' Matherson said. 'Wasn't your name a little longer then?'

Martin shrugged. He was immaculately dressed in a conservative English style, but his voice still held a trace of a Boston Italian accent. 'When in England,' he said simply, 'it is important to blend with one's surroundings.'

'However distasteful?' Matherson inquired.

'On the contrary, Sir Edward. I find your country delightful. The pace suits me as I grow older. In fact, I am seriously considering making it my country of adoption.'

'Don't make any rash decision,' Matherson said drily.

The smile left Martin's face as suddenly as it had come. 'I normally reserve Sundays for my family,' he said coldly. 'When I received your invitation, I naturally assumed that it was important.'

'It is, it is,' Matherson said, taking his arm. He stopped. 'You'll stay for lunch?' Martin refused. 'Tell cook that there will only be two for lunch.' Balfour took the hint and left.

'A beautiful garden, don't you think?' Matherson said as they walked. Martin looked at the bleak cold landscape before him and did not reply. 'It gives me great pleasure,' Matherson added softly. He stopped by the bridge for a moment, collecting his thoughts. Martin wondered which mood he would turn on next and mentally damned all Englishmen.

'Mr. Martin,' Matherson said at last. 'I should like you to lift the contract on Janders.'

In spite of himself, Martin was startled. 'No chance,' he replied flatly and walked on. He looked at his watch. 'If that's all, I'm afraid that I shall have to leave you now, Sir Edward. I'm short on time.'

Matherson turned slowly from the bridge. 'You and I have little in common, Mr. Martin,' he said quietly, 'except that we are both extremely ruthless men. Now, understand me, I would like you to lift that contract on Janders.'

Martin looked up. Then he laughed in disbelief. 'You threatening me?' he asked.

'Let us say that I would prefer to reason with you.'

Martin stared into the harsh face, the cold unblinking eyes. The man was serious. 'Look,' he said, 'I'd like to help you, but there's no way. The bodyguard I could forget. He should have known better. But my own brother's son.'

'He was no good.'

43

'His father grieves for him.'

'He was no good. His father's better off without him.'

'You want to tell his father that?' Martin said angrily. 'Besides, he was under my protection.'

'He was cheating you.'

'We could have taken care of that. If we don't look after Janders now, I lose a brother and every cheap hood in London will think he can settle with members of the Family.'

'What about Janders' friends?'

'He has no friends.'

'What about the mercenaries he fought with?'

'What about them?' Martin said scornfully. 'Cheap amateurs only good for roughing up natives.'

'My friend,' Matherson said softly, 'the world is changing. While you are trying to become respectable, a new force is rising. These men work on an international front. They're strong enough to protect wealthy governments and topple weak ones.'

'So?' Martin asked.

'Janders has a friend who can raise, equip and fight a small army within a month. I should hate him to drop everything and concentrate on you.'

'We can look after ourselves.'

'I have no doubt,' Matherson said drily. 'But they have nothing to lose, while you have everything to protect. And it may cost you a lot of blood doing it.'

'Where do you stand in this?'

'Oh, I shall have to hurt you financially as much as I am able. Already, I believe that I can adversely affect some of your Family's major investments. Then, of course, the syndicate which I represent indirectly controls several of the nation's newspapers. I think I can promise you that, from the date of Janders' death, you and your lieutenants will be among the most photographed and written about men in England. A small war between the Mafia and mercenaries could do a lot to improve circulation. Now I ask you,' Matherson said. "Be reasonable. Is a youth of that calibre really worth this much trouble to you?'

'What makes you think that we can't get to you, Sir Edward?' Martin asked quietly.

Matherson stopped. 'I have thought of that,' he admitted. 'And I think that I have made the necessary arrangements. If I or anything that I hold dear to me is hurt, then you and those nearest to you will be broken completely.'

Martin considered the lonely old financier. Then he thought of his wife, children and grandchildren waiting lunch for him and he nodded his understanding. 'The Family won't like it,' he said. 'But if we give you Janders, what can you do for us?'

'What do you want?'

Martin thought for a moment. 'We're going into Real Estate in a major way. Money's tight at the moment. We need medium- and long-term mortgage money.'

'Yes, I think we can help you there. Shall we say three per cent above present bank rate? We can work out the details later.'

'How about bank rate?'

Matherson shook his head.

'One per cent?'

Matherson smiled. There was no warmth in it. 'Shall we agree on one-and-a-half per cent?'

'Agreed,' Martin said uncomfortably.

'You'll lift the contract immediately then.' They were walking across the lawns towards the main house.

Martin shook his head. 'I'll have to call a meeting of the Council. Phone my brother and get his okay.' He looked up. 'That money at one-and-a-half per cent – is it secure?'

Matherson shook his head. 'I'll have to speak to the syndicate.'

'I'll let you know by this evening,' Martin said tightly.

'I should have an answer for you by then,' Matherson answered pleasantly.

Martin entered his car and nodded to the chauffeur.

Matherson leaned forward. 'How much time has Janders got?' he asked.

Martin shrugged. 'Not much. We're getting close. What's this man Janders to you anyway?'

'I have a use for him, so you would be wise to consider my previous remarks in earnest.' A wintry smile crossed Matherson's face. 'I hope that we're able to reach an amicable agreement,' he said.

Martin turned as the car sped down the drive and saw the gaunt old man standing before the steps of his home. He thought back briefly to their conversation in the walled garden. Then he took a clean silk handkerchief from his pocket, raised his hat and wiped a thin film of perspiration from his forehead.

CHAPTER SIX

6 p.m. Sunday

THE telephone was ringing as Balfour entered his house. He lifted the receiver.

'Where have you been?' Faulkner's angry voice challenged him. 'I've been trying to reach you for the last two hours.'

'With Sir Edward,' Balfour replied. 'The contract may be lifted. We're waiting for them to contact us.'

'When do you expect to hear?'

'Some time before midnight.'

'It'll be too damn late by then.'

'There is little more that we can do at the moment, except wait.'

'You said that you had a file on Janders. Where is it?'

'In my offices in the city.'

'I want to see it. I've been going through everything I know about Janders. There's something missing.'

'I did ask you not to interfere.'

'He won't last till midnight,' Faulkner said savagely. 'I've been bumping into the Family's men all day. They're getting so close you can almost hear them baying. Now I need that file.'

'All right, all right,' Balfour said. 'I'll be at the offices in thirty minutes.' He gave Faulkner an address off Chancery Lane.

47

An hour later in the clean but stark first floor offices of Balfour, Whipple and White, Chartered Land Surveyors, Faulkner found what he was looking for. 'I've checked every damn place that he ever lived in. Every pub and club that he drank in. But I never bothered to find out where he worked. He always said that he was going into the gallery business one day.'

'His gallery must have specialized in art forms that no one else appreciated,' Balfour said. 'For as you can see, it slipped steadily into insolvency from the day he took it over.'

'He should have made you his financial adviser.'

'As such, I would have advised him not to enter that particular form of enterprise,' Balfour said drily. 'You will note that the venture finally went insolvent six months ago. The effects were auctioned for a very small sum.'

'Do you know who took over the premises?'

'No. We lost interest when Janders moved on.'

7.45 p.m.

A taxi dropped Faulkner in the Fulham Road, some half a mile before the Fulham Broadway. He walked along the pavement, glancing at the numbers on the doors. When he was satisfied that there was no one watching, he crossed the street to where a gaudily decorated fashion boutique called the Ginger Tom occupied a small corner site by an access road.

The lights of the shop were on. At first no one answered when he knocked. He kept on hammering until at last the door was flung open. A short, chubby man stood before him, dressed in a close-fitting high buttoned suit of dark velvet, his trouser legs tucked into black leather high boots. His face was round and soft, tanned, even in winter, with a flared nose and large, liquid eyes, shadowed by a curly brown mop of hair.

'Well?' he asked, his hands placed theatrically on his hips. 'Can't you see we're closed? Really,' he snorted, 'some people have no consideration.' He looked at Faulkner speculatively. 'Besides, we've got nothing that would suit you here. You're not our sort.'

'I want to talk to you,' Faulkner said. He lifted the little man up by the elbows, set him down on one side and walked into the shop. Inside clothing hung suspended from the ceiling or pinned to the walls in various attitudes of dance. They were made chiefly of three materials: velvet, leather or chain mail. The little man followed him, spluttering with rage.

'Appy,' he shrieked. 'Appy.'

A large, bald headed man loomed on the stairway, dressed in a leather jerkin that exposed two great tattooed arms with metal studded wrist bands. He looked a lot like a public executioner of Henry VIII's time.

'Appy,' ordered the chubby little man. 'Throw this barbarian out.'

Faulkner steeled himself for the charge. It never came. Appy remained on the stairs sewing.

'Appy,' the little man called, 'phone the police.'

Appy checked the hem of the garment he was working on. 'Can't,' he said. 'You know they cut the phone off.'

The little man dropped his hands to his sides in despair. 'Appy is really a very beautiful person,' he said apologetically. 'He hates violence, but if you were to hurt me, Appy would kill you, wouldn't you, Appy?'

'Yes,' Appy said placidly. And Faulkner, with long experience of men, believed him.

'What's your name?'

'Robert.'

'Mine's Faulkner. I need your help.' Robert looked

interested. So Faulkner continued quietly. 'I live in a little village in South Africa. In the Cape. I'm a stranger to your town. And I've come a long way to find a friend. He used to run an art gallery here.' He saw Robert's face harden. 'Look, Robert, his name is Rafer Janders. If you know where he is, you've got to tell me. He's in bad trouble.'

'I've never heard of him,' Robert said. 'You heard of him, Appy?' Appy slowly shook his head.

'Robert, you must know that if I don't get to him before the others do, they'll kill him.'

'I still don't know what you're talking about.'

Faulkner was sure that he knew. For a moment, he thought of beating it out of him, but he knew the Roberts and the Appys of this world. They didn't break easily.

'Robert,' Faulkner said softly. 'Rafer is about the only friend that I've got left. I need him badly. If you know where he is, tell him Allen Faulkner is here.

'Where is the nearest pub?'

'Down the road and on the left.'

'I'll wait there until closing time. After that it will probably be too late.'

Faulkner sat with a bottle of whisky in the corner of a crowded bar, waiting while the time ticked by. There was nothing more he could do. He had just decided to get drunk in the minutes remaining before closing time, when Robert slipped through the door. He sidled up to Faulkner.

'Follow me,' he whispered. He was practically wearing a cloak and dagger. Minutes later Faulkner was hurrying through the narrow side streets towards the King's Road.

'It was your ugly face that did it,' Robert explained, trotting happily beside him. 'I mean, as I said to Appy, anybody with a face like that has simply got to be honest. It was an awful *faux pas* about the phone, wasn't it? I could have died. Things aren't going very well for us at the moment. Appy does the designing and the cutting, while I help with the making and the selling. He's gone quite kinky over chain mail at the moment. We make it out of curtain rings. I think it's very sexy. What do you think?'

'How much further?' Faulkner asked.

'Just up the next street,' Robert replied. He was breathing hard. 'I really am losing my figure,' he said. 'I simply must go back to dancing classes.' He gave a little skip. 'There is this simply delicious man who teaches there. He looks like Nureyev. You know, with flashing eyes and a lean and hungry look. He says that I'd make a very good dancer if I wasn't so lazy.'

Robert stopped in a doorway. A small sign indicated Four Feathers Club with a cupid's arrow pointing the way. There was no lift. They climbed a rickety stairway, badly lit by naked light bulbs suspended above each landing.

On the second floor, they stopped before a door. It was of heavy oak, iron studded and curved at the top. A wrought iron grille was set into the wood at head height. Robert beat on the knocker. A moment's pause. Then the shutter behind the grille opened and a face peered out at them.

'It's only me and a friend,' Robert said. 'Open the door.'

'It's a new club,' Robert explained proudly as the bolts were being slid back. 'Terribly, terribly exclusive. It's not finished yet. The grand opening's next week.'

A tall lean man inspected Faulkner suspiciously as he entered. He had shoulder length hair, dyed white blond. He was wearing an old tee-shirt and a pair of battered Levis. 'Cradle snatcher,' he said to Faulkner in a high sotto voice.

'Oh, do be quiet, darling,' Robert commanded as he pushed past him. 'He'd not one of us. He's straight.'

'He's Maxi,' Robert said to Faulkner, nodding to the blond man. 'He's really a very good interior decorator, but he's terribly, terribly vicious. You see,' Robert indicated through the dim red haze from the concealed lighting, 'he's using some of our chain mail, which also makes him terribly, terribly clever.'

'Someone had to use it, darling,' Maxi said nastily. 'I mean, if you wore it, at the rate you perform, it would all rust up. And then where would we be?'

'Darling, go and do what you're best at,' Robert replied airily. 'I'm busy.'

He led Faulkner through deep pile carpets past a long curved bar and into the back of the club. They climbed two steps through a small dirty kitchen. Beyond that lay another short flight of steps that led to an attic landing. Robert knocked softly on the door.

'Rafer, it's only me. I've brought your friend.'

'Faulkner,' Janders called through the door.

'Yes,' Faulkner replied. He could not think of anything else to say.

'You all right, Robert?' Janders asked.

'Me?' Robert said. 'I'm fine. Why?'

'Good,' Janders said. 'Search him. See if he's got a gun.'

'Who?' Robert asked.

'Faulkner,' Janders replied. 'Who else?'

Robert looked at Faulkner. He turned back to the door. 'No,' he said. 'I can't possibly. We've only just met.'

'Do it,' Janders shouted.

Robert turned back to Faulkner. ' 'Scuse me,' he giggled nervously. He ran his hands lightly through Faulkner's clothes. 'Nothing,' he shouted. 'You ought to be ashamed of yourself, really.'

'The door's open, Allen,' Janders called. 'Just come on in slowly and stand in the light. Keep your hands open and clear of your sides.'

Faulkner stood very still in the doorway. At first he was blind. Then, as his eyes grew accustomed to the dark, he was able to pick out Janders on a narrow cot in the corner of a small, bare, very cold room, directly below the slates and trusses of the roof. Janders was propped up against the wall, swathed in blankets, with a gun resting across his knee pointing in the general direction of Faulkner's stomach.

'You come to collect on the contract, old friend?' Janders asked softly.

Faulkner shook his head. 'I've got other plans for you.'

'Such as?'

Faulkner did not reply.

'Okay,' Janders said tiredly. 'It might as well be you as anybody. There's a light above you.'

Faulkner glanced at a narrow window set into the gable.

'It's blocked,' Janders said.

Faulkner reached up and pulled the cord. A low powered naked bulb glowed to life, swinging from side to side sending the shadows scurrying around the room. Janders was cold, his face drawn, his eyes red from lack of sleep.

Faulkner closed the door, lea·'ng Robert outside, walked over to Janders and sat on the bed beside him. 'You old bastard,' he said affectionately. 'You haven't lost your touch. Who'd think of looking for you in a queer's club?'

'They will,' Janders said. He was trembling slightly. He smelt of stale sweat and fear. 'These boys go heavy on junk. The Mafia withdrew all supplies last night. It's just a matter of time before somebody cracks.' He looked into Faulkner's face. 'Don't knock them,' he said. 'They make good friends when they can.'

'I'd better get you out of here then.'

'I can't go too deep. They'll get my son.'

'All we need is time. We can round up some men. We'll give them a war that will make them cry blood. Come on. If you can't walk, I'll carry you.'

'Forget it. We'll be sitting ducks on the streets. Just stay with me an hour. Let me close my eyes. Then wake me up and you move on. This is my war, not yours.'

'Rafer, what's happened to you? You can't just curl up and die in a hole like this. Come on, get out of here.'

'The fear eats into your soul if it goes on long enough. I've died a little every time I heard a noise outside that door. I'm too old to run. And I've got nowhere to run to.' His eyes closed. 'Just wake me up when you leave. I dearly want to take a couple of them with me when I go.'

Faulkner opened the door. Robert, who was waiting outside, glanced suspiciously in at Janders. 'He's sleeping now,' Faulkner said. Robert seemed satisfied. He had probably been listening at the door. 'There is going to be trouble soon. Get your friends out of here.'

'We'll help,' Robert said.

Faulkner shook his head. 'Not unless you've got a couple of machine guns. Now get out of here. Wait a minute,' Faulkner said as Robert turned to go. He felt in his pocket, drew out a money clip and held out some notes. 'Go to Brighton for a couple of days,' he said. 'Take Appy with you.'

Robert looked at the money. 'No thank you. Besides I simply hate Brighton. So does Appy.'

'All right. Go anywhere you like. But get out of London for a couple of days.'

Faulkner opened the door. Before he went inside he turned back to Robert. 'Thanks,' he said. 'We'll do the same for you one day.'

'You're welcome. Rafer's a friend of ours,' he added by way of explanation. 'He was very good to us over the shop.' He paused. 'I suppose you don't want me to call the police, do you?'

'No,' Faulkner said.

'Well then, do be careful.'

Janders was sleeping heavily. Faulkner took the gun from

his hand and looked around the room. The window was padded with wads of newspaper. There was no furniture, other than the cot.

He waited for a few minutes, then he walked down the stairway, through the kitchen and on into the now empty darkened club. He checked the front door, sliding back the inside latches. Then he retreated through the club, locking each door and piling up furniture behind it. His barricades couldn't stop a determined assault, but they would slow attackers down and every minute was precious. Besides, few men would relish breaking through a door when a man with a gun might be waiting on the other side.

Faulkner tried to weaken the king posts of the attic stairway, but they were too strong. He climbed the stairs and, kneeling on a stair tread towards the middle of the flight, loosened the riser of the next step above with a kitchen knife. When he had finished, a man's weight would cause the unsupported tread to break.

He returned to the room. The musty damp and the cold worked into his bones. Janders was tossing and mumbling in his sleep. Every so often his hand wandered through his nightmare searching for his gun. Faulkner lifted him gently off his cot and set him down by the far wall, wrapping the blankets around him. If things went badly, he would need the cot to block the doorway.

The room and the cold depressed him. He checked the gun. The Tokarev, as hand guns went, was a good, solid, simple weapon, effective between twenty-five and thirty yards with a good stopping power. Faulkner tried the action. It worked smoothly. He looked at his watch. It was a quarter to eleven. He moved over to Janders and searched his pockets for more ammunition. Janders woke up, his hands clawing at Faulkner's throat. 'Easy, easy,' Faulkner said, moving his hands away. 'You all right now?'

Janders raised himself into a sitting position, shaking his head to clear it. 'I'll be okay in a minute.'

'Have you got any benzedrine?' Faulkner asked.

'Some. I've been saving it.'

'Take it, I may need you.'

'Get out of here while you still can.'

'I'm committed now.'

'Friend, you must want me awful bad.'

Faulkner did not reply.

Janders looked old and drawn. 'You going to help me through the night?' he asked.

'The next hour, if we're lucky. We've got someone trying to lift the contract.'

'There's no chance,' Janders said flatly. 'You heard what I did?'

Faulkner nodded. He reached up and turned out the light. They waited in the dark. 'I didn't find any more ammunition.'

'There's none.'

'So much for the best planner in the business.'

'Man, I didn't plan anything. When I found out I was carrying junk, I went berserk.'

They sat in silence for a while. 'What's the time?' Janders asked.

Faulkner glanced at the luminous dial of his watch. 'Just gone eleven.'

'Christ, time goes slowly when you're waiting.' Janders adjusted himself against the wall. 'How's Jenny?' he asked.

'She's dead,' Faulkner replied. 'Two years now.'

'And the kids?'

'They're grown up. I don't see much of them any more.'

'That woman was too good for you.'

'I miss her now.'

'Bit late. Before, each time she turned around, you were gone somewhere else.'

56

'Shut up,' Faulkner said softly from the darkness.

'Just trying to keep awake. So how else did you make out?'

'About the same as you.'

'You mean you're broke?'

'Yes.'

'With me it was paintings. Man, I loved them too much. Bought them too dear and sold them too cheap. But I handled some really good work. Some that'll be good long after I'm dead. What time is it?'

'Nearly quarter past eleven.'

'I wish they'd come. It's better than waiting.'

'You've waited before.'

'I was younger then and stupider.'

'You got married again.'

'How did you know?

'I read a file on you.'

'The people who are trying to lift the contract?'

'Yes.'

'I might have guessed.'

'What happened to her?' Faulkner asked. 'I thought that you'd turned yourself into a living shrine to the first one.'

'For you there will always be lots of women. For me there were just two.'

'So what happened?'

'She left me when the gallery folded,' Janders said without malice. He leaned back against the wall. 'She was French, working as an au pair girl. But what a girl. Man, was she pretty. And, God, did she love life. I felt young just being near her. Maybe I was just too old for her. Or maybe I loved my first wife too much. I don't know. She left me with a son though. That was the best thing she ever did for me. I call him Emile. He looks like his mother. Reminds me of her each time he laughs. Christ, how I love that child.'

'Where is he now?'

'Switzerland. I've got a bit of money aside in trust for him.

He goes to a really good school there. Like a family really. I visit him on holidays. You know, he can ski better than I can. Hey, if you turn on the light, I'll show you a photograph.'

'If I turn the light on,' Faulkner said drily, 'he'll be without a papa.'

'That's what he calls me. Papa.'

Faulkner did not answer. He crossed the room, leapt lightly over the banisters and moved through the kitchen. He heard the high pitched whine of an electric drill. The front door gave. Then came the sound of muttered curses as they struck the furniture.

Janders crawled onto the landing. 'They're in the street below,' he said. 'Christ, if I had a rifle.'

Faulkner waited by the nearside of the kitchen door. He heard them stumble through the bar clawing away the chain mail that hung in the darkness from the ceiling. Someone tried the lights but found that Faulkner had removed the fuse. He estimated two, possibly three men. They tried the kitchen door handle hopefully. It did not move. Someone, rasher than the others, put his shoulder to the door. It would have given, but for the furniture propped against it.

Faulkner moved up to the door. He knew by experience that the best way to winkle out an armed man from a room was with grenades. Without them your only chance was to come through fast. He heard the man beyond the door pacing out his run. Faulkner counted the steps. There was a moment's silence. Then he heard the man begin to run.

Quietly he counted the foot falls as they slammed heavily into the wooden floor. A pace before the man was due to strike the door, Faulkner fired twice. There came a scream like no human sound. Then the crash of a body falling.

Faulkner threw himself flat on the floor, waiting for a fusillade of answering bullets. None came. Instead he heard the sounds of a body being dragged away. He glanced at his watch. It was eleven thirty-five. Still no sound. He moved cautiously back to join Janders on the landing.

'Next time, *I* use the gun,' Janders said. 'I'm going mad just sitting here. Why didn't you bring one with you?'

'You know I don't carry a gun unless I'm in action. If I'd known that on my second night here I was going to be holed up in an attic with half the Mafia after me, I'd have brought a bloody army.'

11.40 p.m.

Matherson was called to the telephone. 'Martin here,' a distant voice said. 'Is the deal still good?'

'One-and-a-half per cent over bank rate,' Matherson confirmed.

'Okay, you can have Janders. The word's out. The contract's lifted.'

'I'm obliged,' Matherson said and replaced the receiver.

11.55 p.m.

'I've been retired a long time,' Janders said out of the darkness. 'I'm no use to you now. You know that – it's been seven years, maybe more since we split up.'

'You're still the best planner in the business,' Faulkner replied, 'and I need you. If you'd been with me in Tel Aviv, I'd never have come unstuck. They're quiet out there. I wonder what they're doing.'

'Whatever it is, they'll have to get it over quickly. They can't risk much more noise.'

'Perhaps the contract's been lifted.'

59

'No chance.'

Suddenly there came a burst of rapid fire from a heavy calibre rifle. Four bullets tore through the attic window, shattering the glass, ripping the newspaper away.

'What did I tell you?' Janders muttered.

'Must be in the house across the street,' Faulkner observed from the safety of the floor. 'Sounds like an F.N. They can't see anything, so it's not going to do them much good.'

'Unless they've got a grenade launcher attachment,' Janders said.

For a moment, neither of them spoke. Then they both rose from the floor as one man, grabbed the mattress from the cot and threw themselves at the window.

Faulkner heard a noise from the kitchen. He left Janders propping up the mattress and ran across the room. Someone was shouting in the street below. As he arrived on the landing, there came a second crash against the kitchen door. He crouched below the banisters, his gun seeking a target. The door still held. Then he saw that it had been holed at the bottom. A hole too small for a man to climb through, but large enough through which to roll an anti-personnel grenade.

Faulkner heard footsteps. He turned. Janders was behind him, leaning against the doorway.

'They've got us,' Faulkner said quietly. 'I should have been watching.'

'Your man came through,' Janders said wearily. 'The contract's off. I heard the man in the street calling off his men.'

A voice from outside the door called to Janders.

Janders lifted his head. 'Yeah.'

'Next time,' the voice promised. Then came the sound of men moving out.

'That's the closest I've been to dying for a long time,' Faulkner said after a while. 'You owe me now.'

Janders slipped down the doorway until he sat on the floor, leaning his back against it. He was shaking. 'Man,' he said. His voice was hoarse. 'I'd got so used to the idea of dying that now I'm scared of living all over again.'

A police siren wailed in the distance. Faulkner turned and walked down the stairs. Janders let him go a few paces, then grudgingly he rose and followed him.

CHAPTER SEVEN

Monday, 30th November

JANDERS awoke to someone shaking him. He found himself alone in a double bed in a darkened room. As his eyes cleared, he saw Faulkner standing above him.

'What's the time?' he asked.

'Ten a.m.,' Faulkner replied.

Janders groaned and rolled back into the pillow.

'You're in a man called Balfour's bed,' Faulkner said, 'and he's not very happy about it. He had to tell his wife to stay in the country. She's giving him hell,' Faulkner chuckled. 'She probably thinks that he's got a woman stashed away here.' He glanced at his watch again. 'Get up. We've got to be at Balfour's office by eleven.'

They were met by a very anxious Balfour. He placed several massive files in a briefcase and handed them to Faulkner. 'My wife's arriving on the noon train,' he explained as he reached for his hat.

'We need a base to work from,' Faulkner said. 'A good sized flat will do. Preferably in a large block so people can come and go without being noticed.'

'I've thought of that,' Balfour replied as he opened the door. 'Got you one in Dolphin Square. My secretary has the keys. You said it would take you forty-eight hours.'

'Yes.'

'I'll see you then. You've got my number if you need anything. Very pleased to see that you're all right Mr. Janders. You caused us all a lot of trouble, you know,' he added reprovingly. He closed the door behind him before Janders could speak. Then he opened it again and put his head round. 'Oh, and if you do need to phone me,' he said anxiously, 'try not to phone me at home. The wife, you know.'

'Now I know why I prefer the company of queers,' Janders said maliciously.

'Don't underestimate him,' Faulkner replied.

The flat in Dolphin Square was situated on the fourth floor of Hood House. 'Not bad,' Janders said as he wandered through the rooms. The refrigerator had been stocked with food, the liquor cabinet filled, mainly with whisky. In the second bedroom he found his clothes neatly laid out with a note attached. Balfour had paid Janders' back rent and removed his possessions from his room in Bayswater. A neat postcript added that the monies would be deducted from the final amount that he was due.

Faulkner found much the same in his room, except that on the dressing-room table was the cheque for expenses which he had carried with him from South Africa. And it had been signed. Janders walked into his room and saw the cheque.

'How come they're so sure that you'll take the contract?' he asked.

'It was part of the deal that I made for you,' Faulkner replied.

'What makes you think I'll come along?'

'You owe me, remember?' Faulkner took the briefcase into the living-room and spread the papers in piles on the floor. He sat back on his haunches. 'Limbani's alive. He's going to be executed in the Albertville barracks on or about 5th January. The contract is to get him out.' He looked up at Janders and saw the disbelief in his eyes. 'He's alive. They know,' he added quietly. 'They're no lightweight organization. They got that contract lifted off you, didn't they?'

In spite of himself, Janders glanced at a scale map of the Albertville army barracks and the area immediately surrounding it. Then he turned away, 'Christ,' he said. 'I might just as well have died in that room.'

'They wouldn't have stopped there,' Faulkner said quietly. 'They would have got your son as well.'

'No, they'd have been happy with me. That's why I didn't go too deep.'

'Well, you're alive now.'

Janders walked over to the window. 'Look at us, Allen,' he pleaded. 'We're a couple of old men. Trouble is we never grew up. Ten years ago we were still too old but at least we could fool ourselves. We can't any longer. There are plenty of younger men in the game. If Limbani really is alive, why don't they do it? Why don't we just retire gracefully while we're still ahead?'

'We tried it once before,' Faulkner said. 'You to an attic room and me to a bottle.'

'I've followed you twice now,' Janders said. 'With men shooting at me with everything from mortars to poison arrows. This time, bugger you.'

'This time I was getting shot at.'

'It was your decision.'

'I did it anyway.'

Janders paced up and down the room. He turned on Faulkner. 'All right,' he said. 'All right, I'll help you plan it. But I'm not going in with you. I'm too bloody old to jump now.'

'You think we'll have to parachute in?' Faulkner asked.

Janders got down on his knees beside him and spread out the map. 'Of course. You're doing a snatch. Not organizing a full scale war. Now the way I see it . . .'

64

Faulkner sat back against the wall. By two o'clock in the morning, Janders was committed.

10.00 a.m. Tuesday, 1st December

Faulkner opened the door of the flat. Balfour entered. With him were two men. He introduced them. 'Major Rushton and Major Simmonds. They're on attachment to the Department. Known affectionately as Tom and Jerry.'

The nickname suited them, for Rushton was a small mousey man in his early thirties, his hair thinning with little furtive eyes. Simmonds was a tall gangling man of about the same age, slowly in movement with long arms and great hands that seemed to touch his knees.

'The Department kindly lent me these gentlemen to establish whether or not your plan is feasible.' Balfour caught the look on Faulkner's face. 'They're completely reliable,' he added quietly. 'Naturally I thought it advisable to ensure that your plan has at least a reasonable chance of success before we outlay any large amounts of capital.'

Faulkner nodded to Janders. 'Tell them,' he said.

Janders walked over to a large map that had been pinned to the wall, covering Central and Southern Africa. 'What experience have you had?' he asked brusquely.

'A little here and there,' Rushton replied. He seemed to have elected himself spokesman for the two. 'Not as much as you, of course, but then you've been out of the business for some time.'

Janders winced and turned to the map. 'You've been briefed about what we're trying to do?'

Rushton nodded, 'We're just interested in how you intend to achieve it.'

'The way we see it, we've got to move in and out fast. We

aim to spend a maximum of three hours on the ground,' Janders stopped to collect his thoughts. 'The best way, I think,' he continued slowly, 'is to take you through the way we planned it. It's still full of holes, but we'll fill them in as we get nearer the day.

'First, we intend to recruit in London. There's still quite a few of the old commando around and we haven't got the time to look elsewhere. We reckon to need fifty men split into five groups of ten, each group led by an officer with an N.C.O. in support. Faulkner's group will carry an R.S.M. who will take charge of discipline and training.' Janders looked at the men before him. 'I know it's top heavy, but we've found that it works better that way.

'We'll group in Mozambique, probably Lourenço Marques, then use a jump-off point in the north. Such as Port Amelio or Lumbo off Mozambique Island. Somewhere in a thousand mile radius of Albertville because we aim to use a Lockheed Hercules C.130. Its range and payload make it the ideal plane for our purposes especially since it'll have to wait around a bit before bringing us back.'

'Can you get the Portuguese to let us use Mozambique?' Faulkner broke in, speaking to Balfour. 'We thought of Angola at first, but we'd be flying over the Congo too long. We also thought that, with the terrorist war going on in Northern Mozambique, we could lose ourselves among their soldiers.'

'This way we can go in over Malawi,' Janders continued, tracing the route on the map. 'Then along the Tanzania–Zambia border. Up Lake Tanganyika following the border between the Congo and Tanzania until we stop off before Albertville. The plane will be on a chartered flight from Beira to Ruanda, carrying urgent medical supplies. It can carry one hundred and thirty-five thousand pounds all-up weight, so there'll be room. After dropping us, the plane will carry on to Ruanda, offload the supplies, pick up fuel and then return for us. As there is a good chance of it being seen at Albertville, we reckon to change the markings to that of a Libyan Air Force transport plane.

'Okay so far? Good. There's a plateau amongst the hills seven miles out of Albertville. We intend to drop in there by parachute, then split into two groups, while the plane moves on to Ruanda. The first group will take the barracks. We aim to use much the same plan as the I.R.A. used on a British barracks during the last troubles when they emptied an armoury, except that we intend to silence the sentries and then use gas on the occupants. The second group will hold the airport which is two-and-a-half miles from the barracks as the crow flies, or four miles by road, if we can borrow their transport.'

Janders pinned up another map. 'I've made up a large scale drawing of the immediate area in which we will be operating. If you move closer, you'll be able to see it.' They gathered around him.

'The dropping zone is in amongst these hills,' he continued. 'It'll be dangerous, but if we drop at eight hundred feet using all three doors of a Lockheed C.130 we should get in. The hills will take care of the noise of the plane and provide us with cover as we fall.'

'Fifty men in the air at once,' Rushton said dubiously. 'It'll be a shambles up there.'

'It's a chance we've got to take,' Janders answered. 'We're dropping in a zone only three hundred yards long by fifty yards wide. We're hoping for a moonless night and we can't risk the men getting scattered in the hills.

'The new barracks are four miles out of Albertville, parallel to the airport. We have allowed an hour for the first group to cover the three miles across country to the barracks and into position. The same for the second group at the

67

airport. They've got a bit further to go, but the country's easier. The second group waits in position until they hear from us.

'According to our information, the airport should be closed for the night. Only a light police guard on duty. With a bit of luck, they'll be drinking in the bar rather than patrolling the perimeter. At least, they always used to.'

'They still do,' Rushton said.

'Okay. On the word, group two takes the tower and establishes radio contact with the returning plane and with group one at the barracks. They also operate the landing lights and talk the plane down. By this time, group one have taken the sentries and are inside the barracks. The barracks normally hold eight hundred men, but according to the information here, if it's accurate . . .'

'It is,' Rushton said quietly. 'We collated it.'

'Well then, we can expect over the Christmas period a strength of between three hundred and three hundred and fifty men. Not more than four hundred.' Janders turned to Rushton. 'Since you collated this information, did you allow for special guards when Limbani arrives?'

'He'll have fifteen of the President's bodyguard as special escort. The General is very anxious to dispatch Limbani quietly. He doesn't want to open up any old sores, especially as Limbani's tribe extends as far as Albertville. The garrison is made up of men from tribes other than those of the district. As is the General's custom, the rest will all be allowed on leave with the exception of the troops from the General's own tribe.'

'Okay. The barrack rooms sleep a hundred men each. We intend to go in with gas masks and cyanide gas. One man each end and two men in the centre with silenced rifles in case anybody wakes up. The gas will come from canisters at either end and in the middle. With luck they'll never know what hit them. We've allowed forty-five minutes to take the barracks and put everyone there to sleep. Thirty-five minutes to get from the barracks to the airport, by which time the plane will be waiting. Ten minutes to load up and off.'

'Limbani will almost certainly be held in the cells under the guard room. It's the only logical place,' Balfour said. 'Do you have to attack the whole garrison? I mean, you're just harming people indiscriminately.'

'If we just hit the guard room and someone alerted the barracks, we might have a rough time trying to board that plane,' Janders explained gently.

'Good Lord. You don't mean to tell me that you intend to kill them all?' Balfour said aghast. No one answered him. 'Couldn't you use some kind of nerve gas to put them to sleep for a while? Then you could damage their transport so that they couldn't follow you when they woke up. Of course, I'm not a military man,' Balfour wilted under their hostile glare.

'Where are we going to get hold of modern nerve gases from?' Janders asked. 'As sure as hell, no government is going to give it to us. Cyanide is cheap and you can get it anywhere. In a large airy barracks, anaesthetic gases would dilute too quickly. If we gave them too much we'd kill them anyway. If we gave them too little, they'd be after us before we got out of there. Things are going to be tough enough as it is. Just remember, if we don't make that plane, we've got no chance. We're over three hundred miles from the nearest friendly border, if you count Malawi, and you can't be sure how friendly Doctor Banda's going to be to a group of mercenaries on the run. I'd hate to have to find out.'

'The United Nations will go mad,' Balfour muttered.

'Not if we can bring Limbani out. Ndofa will have too much explaining to do to want to kick up a fuss. What about

69

the old military barracks in town?' Janders asked Rushton. 'Your information gives that it is now being used as a political prison. Surely they'll hold Limbani there?'

Rushton shrugged his narrow shoulders. 'No, we don't think so. Too many of Limbani's old friends in there. Someone might see him. Besides, they'd have to take him through the town.'

'We'll know for definite before you move in,' Balfour said. 'You'd better study both possibilities just in case.'

'Well,' Janders turned to the army officers. 'What do you think?'

Simmonds leant back in his chair and stretched his long frame.

'I thought you were asleep,' Faulkner said.

The tall man smiled and shook his head. 'My friend here does the talking while I do the thinking. It's a long-standing relationship. How do you propose getting hold of a Lockheed C.130?' he asked suddenly.

'There's quite a few in Africa now,' Janders answered. 'The South African Air Force use them. The Americans used them in the Congo in '65. An Irishman called Mad Malloy runs an air charter firm out of Swaziland. He chartered a couple and ran copper out of Zambia when Rhodesia closed its railways to them a couple of years ago. Now he's running meat and maize and anything else he can, mostly from Beira. He'll carry us for a price.'

'The Chinese have MIGs along the Tan Zam Highway. What makes you so sure that they won't bring you down?'

'One, because we are hoping that, by the time they pull themselves together, we'll be over Malawi on a cleared flight plan and, two, we're counting on China not being ready to use its MIGs in Africa yet. And especially for the Congo.'

'The main radio aerials are in the airport boundaries. You could take care of them while you're at it,' Simmonds said.

'How do you know?'

Simmonds grinned. 'I'm the military attaché at our Embassy there.' He grew more serious. 'Where do you propose to get your arms and how will you transport them at such short notice?'

'There is an Egyptian merchant we know who takes care of these things.'

'Gemel Hassim?' Rushton asked. Janders nodded.

'What else do you want to know?' Faulkner asked.

Rushton looked at Simmonds for confirmation. 'I think that we have enough information at the moment,' he said.

'Perhaps we can answer some questions for you,' Simmonds said.

'What's the calibre of the soldiers in the garrison likely to be?' Janders asked.

'I think that seven years ago, it must have been one of the best all-black armies in Africa,' Simmonds replied thoughtfully. 'However, after Ndofa used it to get to power, he made damn sure by constantly purging the officer ranks and the senior N.C.O.s that no other army officer with political aspirations could follow him. It's probably the weakest, worst-led army in Africa.

'Ndofa formed a new force shortly after he assumed power. He called them the Simbas after the old mob. Made them into a sort of secret police force, loosely modelled on the Ton Ton Macoute. He instilled into them the same witchcraft rigmarole. The whole country's terrified of them.

'Basically, the country has the following forces. You can write off the Air Force as virtually non-operational. That leaves the civil police and the army, which are powerless. The Simbas make up the uniformed paramilitary police which, incidentally, are far better equipped than the army. And the secret police, whose senior men wear a sort of standard civilian uniform of a dark suit and dark glasses. Every

71

second person in the country is an informer to them. The army's lower ranks are riddled with them. You can imagine, discipline has gone to hell. In fact, the whole country has descended into an African version of Papa Doc's Haiti.'

Simmonds rose to his feet. 'I think that's all I can tell you at the moment. Oh yes, the political prisoners in the barracks are guarded by the Simbas. That's probably why they die like flies.'

'You the man who'll be letting Balfour know when Limbani's coming and where he'll be held?' Faulkner asked.

Simmonds smiled. 'Maybe,' he said, 'but Balfour has other sources of information, probably better than mine.'

Rushton turned at the door. 'I think that the plan is about as good as it can be under the circumstances. However, we'll think about it and let Balfour know. Oh, by the way,' he said. 'No doubt you'll be seeing Gemel Hassim soon. When you do, I'd be grateful if you'd tell him from me to keep his mucky fingers out of Northern Ireland. He'll understand.'

Balfour remained behind for a moment. 'I'm sorry,' he said, 'but their Department watches over all movements of mercenary forces and arms. We can't move without their blessing.'

'What are the chances?' Faulkner asked.

'I think they're good,' Balfour replied. 'They want Ndofa toppled nearly as much as we do.'

'What chance have we got of using Mozambique?'

'Again, I think that you have a good chance. Our syndicate is heavily involved in the Cabora Bassa Dam scheme and the Portuguese have no love for the Congo. A lot of the terrorists around Tete have been trained there. I'll be able to let you know for sure in a few days.'

'Well?' Janders asked tiredly after they had gone.

'You were magnificent,' Faulkner answered. 'I could almost smell the cordite burning as you spoke. Come, I shall

72

buy you a truly magnificent lunch. Then we'll run over the plans again.'

Janders reached for his hat. He studied Faulkner with his sad grey eyes. 'You never let up, do you, friend? One day soon you're going to get us both killed.'

'Until then we'll celebrate at the Savoy. Tell me now, honestly. When did you last eat at the Savoy? Eat well, live rich. That's what life's all about. Anybody can die poor.'

'You celebrate. I'll just eat and pray that those two turn the whole scheme down. If they're bright, they'll do just that.'

'Not a chance. Everyone needs Limbani too much. Don't you see, if Matherson gets him, Ndofa's got to be reasonable, or he'll have a civil war on his hands. Besides, it's our lives they're risking.'

Faulkner walked beside Janders. There was a new spring in his step and his eyes were alive. 'Anyway,' he reminded Janders, 'It's the only work we're good at.'

CHAPTER EIGHT

8.00 a.m. Thursday, 3rd December

FAULKNER stood by the window of the flat watching a grey dawn break over London, waiting for the telephone to ring. The clamour of the bell suddenly broke the stillness and he snatched up the receiver. Janders padded into the room, a blanket around his shoulders, warming his hands on a cup of black coffee.

Faulkner replaced the receiver and looked up. 'It's on,' he said, his eyes alight. 'They've agreed. They're sending round files giving the last known addresses of all the old commandos, together with some likely men that we can contact. The 5th of January,' he said, thinking out loud to himself. 'I wish to God they'd contacted us sooner.'

'You know why they left it so late?' Janders said coldly. 'It's because they've tried everyone else – we're the last on the bloody list – the only chance they've got. My God, they must have been desperate. Allen, don't take this contract,' Janders warned. 'Back out now while you've still got the chance. I've got a feeling in me that we're going to die out there. There's too little planning, not enough time.'

'I've already taken it,' Faulkner replied. 'You know that. Rafer,' he said softly, 'I need this contract. I need it more than I've ever needed anything in my life. Don't worry, we'll get back. We may be old, but we're still the best there is.'

'Do you think you can still take Ndofa? He's good.'

'Take him?' Faulkner snorted. 'Of course I can. I *taught* him.'

Janders couldn't shake off the cold feeling inside him yet in spite of himself he smiled. It was the old Faulkner talking – and he still loved him. 'All right,' he said, 'I'm with you.'

Faulkner made a call to Gemel Hassim. They were invited to dine at his house that evening. The rest of the day they spent sorting through the files supplied by Major Rushton, tracing the whereabouts and sending telegrams to the various men who had worked with them before.

At a little after seven, a car owned by Gemel Hassim dropped them before the steps of a pleasant house off Eaton Place. An Arab, dressed in a white burnous, met them at the door and bowed them through a richly carpeted hallway. The living-room was softly lit, decorated and furnished in the Regency style. Only the paintings that hung from the walls were modern. They seemed to blend with and yet accentuate the unspoken wealth of the surroundings.

There came a soft, well-oiled click from behind. Both men swung round. A bookcase set into the far wall revolved and Gemel Hassim stepped into the room.

He was a small man in his early sixties. A small spread of stomach showed through his cummerbund. He had short, black hair and a clean-shaven face with slightly olive skin. His dinner jacket was of baby mohair, his shirt of heavy silk.

Faulkner was conscious of his fading old-fashioned suit. 'Forgive the way we're dressed,' he said after they had made their introductions. 'We travelled light.'

Gemel Hassim smiled. 'My house is yours,' he answered pleasantly. 'You would be welcome in rags.' He clapped his hands. A servant appeared. 'What will you drink?' They both ordered whisky. 'It is my custom to dine early. We can discuss our business after dinner.'

Janders walked slowly around the room inspecting each

75

painting. Gemel Hassim joined him. 'I believe that you were in the gallery business for a while, Mr. Janders,' he said evenly. 'If I had known sooner, I would have dealt through you.

'Shall we go in to dinner?' He moved with an almost feminine grace. He was the kind of man who had his hair trimmed once a week, his nails manicured each day, who would change his shirt for a crease. Though he spoke softly, below the polished surface lay a deep menacing violence.

Gemel Hassim began to trade in arms after his father had lost a major part of the family fortunes. During the years, his enterprises grew until, at one time, he was supplying both the Israelis and the Palestine guerrillas. However, the Israelis became self-sufficient and the Palestine guerrillas tried to assassinate him. Now he confined himself to competing with the French and communist governments providing arms to emergent states and the smaller guerrilla organizations. Competition was increasing, Gemel Hassim told them sadly. When the rest of the world sent food and money for famine relief, France and Czechoslovakia sent arms. It would be a sad world when every guerrilla organization could buy arms directly from legitimate governments.

Brandy was served at the table and he changed the subject.

'I believe that you had a little difficulty with the Mafia,' he addressed Janders. 'I may have to obtain their clearance before I can sell to you.'

'We're clear,' Faulkner said. 'You tied up with them?'

'No, but I find it advisable to live in peace with them. They are gaining strength rapidly here.'

'Some day someone is going to have to do something about them,' Faulkner said. He spoke softly, but his eyes were angry.

'Are you considering it, Colonel Faulkner?'

76

'If they cross me,' Faulkner looked up. 'You'd better believe it.'

'You're from South Africa, I believe.'

'Yes.'

'Things are a little different over here.'

Gemel Hassim leant back in his chair. 'Now gentlemen, you must be impatient to tell me your requirements. At the moment, I can offer you any amount of Second World War material, such as the Thompson and the Schmeissers. Perhaps you would be interested in the French Matt 9 millimetre 1948 ex. Algeria. It depends of course on what you're looking for.'

'We'll be divided into five sections, Janders said. 'Ten men in each section. We need to arm and equip them for up to seven days in the field from a parachute drop. We see each section's fire power divided into two light machine-guns, seven rifles and an assault weapon, self-loading pistols and, of course, grenades.'

'We would require the weapons to be of Russian origin, such as the A.K. 7.62,' Faulkner said. 'Ammunition interchangeable wherever possible.'

'So you intend to operate within the Russian sphere of influence. The Mafia will no doubt be relieved to hear that,' Gemel Hassim said drily. He rose. 'If you'll follow me, gentlemen.' He led them into the living-room, pressed lightly against the panelled wall and the concealed door swung open. He pressed a second switch and a heavy iron grille rose electronically. They followed him down a steep flight of steps into the basement of the building.

Racks of vintage weapons lined the walls of a small antechamber. 'I am, of course, a registered gun collector,' Gemel Hassim commented. A portion of the far wall opened. He led them into a larger chamber, a sound-proofed miniature firing range. His servant was waiting for them.

'Let me see,' Gemel Hassim said. 'The A.K. 7.62 assault rifle and the R.P.D. light machine-gun would be a good combination. The ammunition is, of course, interchangeable. A lot of these weapons are becoming available from Vietnam.' He nodded to his servant who brought him an A.K. He held the banana shaped weapon lovingly in his hands. 'It's obsolete now, of course,' he said, 'but it is still one of the finest weapons of its type.'

Faulkner reached out and took the rifle. He cocked the action, then he suddenly spun round and fired a burst at the target. The noise from the explosions was deafening and the harsh acrid smell of gun oil and burnt cordite filled the confined space of the range.

The servant wheeled in the target. A line of evenly spaced holes ran horizontally across the bulls eye. 'Not bad,' Janders said as Faulkner caught his eye. He noticed that, for all the hard living, Faulkner's hands remained steady as a rock.

Gemel Hassim took the rifle. 'My weapons are in excellent condition,' he said nervously.

An hour later, they returned to the living-room. 'How much ammunition will you require?' Gemel Hassim inquired.

Faulkner consulted a list. 'Each man with an A.K. carries six magazines and a spare two hundred rounds in a bandolier. The R.P.D. machine-guns, four containers of a hundred rounds each and three other men in the section to carry spare belts. The R.P.G. 2 rocket-launcher, one pack of three rockets plus another man in the section to carry a further three. Then each man to carry four grenades.'

'What else will you need?'

'Forty-eight hour ration packs. No tins, just tubes and packets. British army camouflage, German boots and American helmets. Oh yes, and American 5.10 parachutes plus containers. Can you supply?'

'Of course. When and where?'

'We'll need all the equipment landed in Mozambique. We'll confirm that, by the way, not later than the 14th of this month.'

'I'm sorry. I would have liked to have helped you, but that's completely impossible. I was expecting at least two clear months. I'd have to air freight it in within that time.'

'The shipment will be cleared with the Portuguese authorities, so there'll be no problem there. We can arrange with the Royal Air Charter firm of Swaziland to liaise with you.'

'Mad Malloy?' Gemel Hassim asked, amused.

'Why? Do you know him?'

'Of course. We dealt together in Biafra. He charters two Lockheed C.130s from me.'

'We're going to need one of them,' Janders said.

'I thought that you might. I'll pass on your request to Mr. Malloy and arrange for you to visit him, but I am afraid, on the question of arms, it will still be impossible to meet your deadline. I have another shipment to meet first. Perhaps, if you could delay your expedition.'

'That's impossible,' Faulkner said. 'By the way, I have a message for you that might have some bearing on your other shipment. We met a Major Rushton today.'

'I hope that you did not mention my name.'

'He did. He asked me to give you a message when I saw you.'

'Yes?' Gemel Hassim asked coldly.

'Something about him suggesting that you keep your mucky fingers out of Northern Ireland.'

'Did Major Rushton know that you were coming here tonight?'

'Yes.'

Cold anger gathered in Gemel Hassim's eyes. 'Colonel

Faulkner,' he said softly, 'I really feel that you have abused my hospitality in telling him.'

'I didn't. He knew.'

Gemel Hassim crossed the room, deep in thought. 'If I fail to deliver the arms, my principals will be rightfully annoyed. They may take drastic action against me. However, if I do deliver in spite of Major Rushton's warning, the British will certainly ensure that I don't deliver any more. You place me in an impossible situation, Colonel Faulkner. It is widely supposed within the circles in which I move that the British Intelligence Services liquidate more people in a year than the majority of the Western countries put together.'

He thought silently for a moment, then he raised his hands in a gesture of surrender. 'As the British Intelligence Services will almost certainly be operating long after the I.R.A., I think that I can assure you that your arms will be delivered on time.'

'My car and driver are at your disposal,' Gemel Hassim said as he saw them to the door.

The night was clear and cold. The moon was in the first quarter and the stars shone clearly down. Faulkner was elated. 'I think I'll walk a while,' he said. 'How about you?'

'Not me,' Janders answered. The cold feeling was still with him and he disliked the shadows. He caught Faulkner's arm. 'Come in the car,' he said. 'We'll walk some sunny day.'

CHAPTER NINE

Friday, 4th December

JANDERS sat on the floor of the flat in Dolphin Square, surrounded by files. Plans, maps and lists of equipment were pinned to the walls around him. 'We need five officers, five N.C.O.s and forty men,' he said. 'Let's start with the officers. So far there's you and me. We need three more.'

'Where's Jimmy Ashton, now?' Faulkner asked.

Janders picked up a file and tossed it to him. 'You're out of luck,' he answered. 'He's with Peter in the Middle East.'

'Patrick Sillito?'

'He's in the Yemen.'

'My God,' Faulkner said softly, 'the wild geese have scattered.'

'You left them in the lurch last time, remember.'

'Where's Jeremy Chandos then?'

'He's in London, but he's given up the trade. Gone back to his first love, gambling. He's doing well I hear.'

'Is he still disinherited?'

'Yes.'

'Then it's only a matter of time before he's broke again. What do you think of him?'

'Young, wild, doesn't care a damn. Good in a tight spot.'

'We can use a man like that. Who else?'

'I've got someone in mind,' Janders said. 'Someone who can get us across that hundred-yard killing ground which surrounds the barracks.'

'Who?'

'Peter Coetzee. You won't know him. He's from Rhodesia. Worked for the Game Department over Operation Noah when they were filling up Kariba. Then he joined one of their crack police anti-terrorist units. But something went wrong and now he's ended up in London. I bumped into him a couple of times. He's in a pretty bad way. Floundering around the city like a fish out of water.'

'How's he going to help us?'

'Firstly, he knows more about the bush than you and me put together and secondly he worked with the Game Department at the time when they were developing the game darting rifle. If they can put a bloody great elephant to sleep, I don't see why they can't do the same for a sentry.'

'All right. The N.C.O.s and men can wait until we see what the telegrams bring in. You find this Rhodesian. I'll find Jeremy.'

Janders wandered into a dingy pub on the East India Dock Road. The pub's single large bar was called the Fo'c'sle. It was dark and dirty with battered lamps hanging from the rafters and the stump of a sailing mast rising above the bar.

An enormous man with a wide ugly face and long reddish-brown hair stood alone on the far side of the counter. Janders made his way over to him.

'Buy you a beer?' he asked quietly.

The man did not hear him. He was lost in a far off dream. Janders, whose head was barely in line with the man's shoulders, nudged him gently. The big man turned. 'Oh, it's you. Rafer Janders, isn't it?'

Janders nodded, glad that he had remembered him. 'Buy you a beer?' he offered.

'Man,' Peter Coetzee said. He had an Afrikaans accent and, like many really big men, his voice was soft. 'I'd like that.

But you must know that I can't afford to drink with you. What are you doing here anyway?'

'Looking for you. They told me that I'd probably find you here.'

'I'm trying to get on a boat. Mr. Janders,' Peter said seriously, 'I never knew it could be so hard. First I don't want to be a sailor. I hate the sea. All I want is to work my passage to South Africa and then back to Rhodesia, but they say I have to work a round passage. So if I go, I end up back here again. And I think to myself, okay I go there, I come back, then I have enough money to go there again and this time get off the ship. And I say, okay, I'm your man. What do you want me to do? So they say, Nothing, we got more sailors than we know what to do with at the moment. So I tell them straight. I can out-work any sailor that they've got and they say, All right, go to the Union office and then, maybe. So I go there. They take one look at my Federal Rhodesian passport and then they say, Go to hell. We don't want any Rhodesians in this Union.'

Peter raised the pint of bitter that Janders had brought him and finished it five seconds later. Janders nodded to the barmaid.

'Man,' Peter said. 'I'm getting so desperate that I'll swim back just now. You don't realize that this is an island until you want to get off it.'

The barmaid brought the beer. A wide smile spread all over Peter's face. He raised his tankard to thank her. The girl was intrigued. There was something about Peter's great warm ugliness that attracted women. Janders took Peter firmly by the arm and led him away to a seat in the gloom.

'There's a job going,' Janders said when they were seated. 'When it's over, it'll get you a ticket to Rhodesia and a lot of money besides. But it carries one hell of a risk. Are you interested?'

'What do I have to do?' Peter asked.

Janders told him, leaving out most of the details.

'No man,' Peter shook his great head slowly. 'No. I don't think that's for me. Lord knows I don't like Kaffirs, but I don't like killing them for money either.'

'What about when you were hunting terrorists? I heard you were pretty good.'

'That was different. That was my country.'

Peter was a great bear of a man. Two hundred and thirty pounds of solid muscle, gristle and bone, trained by one of the finest anti-guerrilla forces in the world. And Janders had the feeling that Faulkner would need him.

'What exactly did you do out there?' he asked. 'Did you ever lead men?'

'Sometimes, but mostly I was alone. Because I grew up in the bush, they gave me a special job watching the waterholes in the Zambesi Valley. Man, that valley is one of the last great wildernesses in Africa. It's harsh and hot and dry and so filled with tsetse fly that no man can live there. Only the animals. The terrorists had to cross the valley on their way into Rhodesia. And when they went to the waterholes, I'd pick up their spoor and hunt them down one by one.

'I lived in a cave on and off for eighteen months and, Mister, I grew worse than an animal. I never walked in the sunlight, only crept in the shade. And I killed and I killed. Mostly right up close so that I could see them and smell their fear. And at night I'd go back to the cave and stare at the walls.

'That was a bad time for me. I nearly went mad. You know, I started off as a game ranger. I always saw myself protecting things, not destroying them. And I have the feeling that, if I kill any more, I'll get so that I can't do anything else and I'll never wash the blood off my hands. And that, Mister, is why I'm not going with you. That's why I came over here.

84

'But to tell you the truth, Mr. Janders,' Peter said, 'I could never live here either. I'm drowning in this place. I'm homesick for Africa and I've got to get back. But not that way.'

Janders knew better than to press him. He took out a card and scribbled on it. 'I'll be at that address for the next seventy-two hours,' he said, handing it to Peter. 'If you change your mind, let me know.'

Janders stood up. 'Have you heard of Limbani?' he asked.

Peter nodded. 'He died some time ago.'

'He's alive still,' Janders said. 'The contract's to get him out. I know that man. He's worth saving. He's the one African leader who could possibly bridge the gap between black and white and stop the fighting. Limbani could help your country. The contract's worth considering in that light.'

Peter shook his head. 'There's people dying all the time in Africa and nobody gives a damn unless they're killed by white men. And the black leaders get to power by killing all their friends, but they don't last for long. Mister, I'm not fighting for governments any more. I'm just fighting for myself. Thank you for the beer.'

Janders looked at Peter and he felt his sadness. 'I've been down too,' he said softly. 'Could I lend you some money?'

Peter shook his head and smiled and the great warmth within him returned to his face. 'No thanks,' he said. 'I'll manage.'

Later that evening, Jeremy Chandos weaved his way uncertainly around a wrought iron railing and down a flight of steps to the basement of what had once been a gracious house in Bayswater. He hammered loudly against the grimy red door of a gambling club called Johnnie's Place. After a few moments, the door opened. The big doorman recognized him. 'Wait here,' he said gruffly and called the proprietor.

Jeremy was twenty-nine but he looked younger. Tall,

lean, fair-haired, with an open boyish face and not a single scruple. The proprietor came up. 'It's young Chandos, sir,' the doorman said. 'He's drunk again. Shall I throw him out?'

Johnnie the Greek was torn between his natural greed and concern for the reputation of his shabby club. As usual, he succumbed to greed. For Jeremy played at the high table and, win or lose, the club made more from its percentage of that table than from all the other four tables put together. 'Let him in,' he ordered.

The doorman brought Jeremy in from the cold, propped him firmly against the wall and relieved him of his coat. He pointed him across the bare hallway. 'I hope your luck changes tonight, sir,' he said, letting him go.

Jeremy parted the bead curtains that covered the entrance to the gaming room and hung in the doorway, allowing his eyes to grow accustomed to the dim light and his lungs to the smoke that drifted like a mist in the air. Then, summoning his concentration, he weaved his way across to the high table which was situated on a dais at the far end of the room.

The rest of the men at the table were already assembled in their accustomed places. They greeted Jeremy warmly as he fell into his seat. There were several Greeks, a Lebanese who claimed that he was really a member of Al Fatah, a truly dangerous man, and two Persians who rarely spoke. One of the Greeks opened a pack of cards and pushed it across the table for Jeremy to cut. None of the other players alluded to Jeremy's condition by so much as a gesture, but they waited greedily for him to start.

Jeremy had been playing at this club for a month now, three times a week. After an initial win, he had been losing steadily, some five hundred pounds at a time. It was known at the table that Jeremy's family owned a string of racing stables and that was where they thought his money came from.

86

In fact, though the stables could be counted on to produce winners in most of the major races, Jeremy saw none of that money. His father, a stern Irishman and a belligerent Catholic, who far preferred his horses to his children, had laid down a rule that there would be no gambling in the family or among his managers. The rule was rigidly enforced.

Jeremy's older brothers followed in their father's footsteps. But at the age of twelve, Jeremy became an avid punter. He was discovered when he was fifteen and his father had the unfortunate bookmaker barred. By the time he was eighteen, his family reluctantly saw that there was little future for him within the business, for though Jeremy loved horses, his father harboured a grave doubt that his youngest son, in a burst of enthusiasm, would not be above adding a little incentive to a particular animal's bloodstream. He therefore entered Jeremy for Sandhurst.

When Jeremy was urgently asked to leave that establishment for conduct unbecoming an officer and a gentleman, his father disinherited him. But Jeremy had a talent for soldiering and he used it in the Congo. One of his troop, a man called von Brandis, taught him how to open safes. He returned from the Congo a wealthy man.

For a while, things went well for Jeremy. He had gone into partnership with one of his father's trainers but in due course his father found out. The trainer was fired and the winning streak ended. And now Jeremy was in debt to half the bookmakers in the north of England. Consequently Jeremy returned to London to safeguard his health. The money on the table before him was the last he had.

The other players thought that he was cracking. By agreement, they raised the stakes and removed the limit from the game. Then they closed in to make a quick kill. They rode Jeremy, pushing up his call. He seemed too drunk to care and barely turned over his cards. Yet, more often than not, he won. They continued after him relentlessly, convinced that it was just a matter of time.

Somehow he remained conscious. And somehow they kept losing. After three hours they got scared and let him carry a bluff. After five hours the table was dry. Jeremy rose, collected six thousand seven hundred and twenty-seven pounds and thanked them politely. They watched him leave the room stone cold sober. He refused Johnnie's offer to hold the money in his safe, visited the lavatory briefly, then made his way up to the street in search of a taxi.

Two men were waiting for him in an alley. They stepped out behind him as he passed. One of them locked his arm around Jeremy's neck and placed the point of a knife firmly against his throat. The other calmly searched him in full view of the night traffic of London, all the time disregarding Jeremy's strangled protests. They emptied his pockets, then tore off his shoes and socks. The bulk of the money was in the socks. Both men turned and ran into the night, taking with them the shoes and socks, leaving Jeremy barefooted on the pavement, speechless with rage, clutching a bookmaker's card.

Faulkner appeared beside him. 'Did you see them?' Jeremy shouted, recognizing Faulkner. Faulkner nodded. 'You mean you were standing there all the time and you let them rob me. They could have cut my throat.'

Faulkner shook his head. 'You were in good hands,' he said. 'We met outside the club a couple of hours ago while you were making your coup and declared our interests. Apparently they collect for a syndicate of bookmakers. They agreed not to harm you. I agreed not to interfere.' Faulkner began to walk slowly down the street.

Jeremy padded after him. 'You bastard,' he shouted. 'You cold-blooded bastard. You just stood there and let them take me after all I've done for you.'

'I prefer you poor at the moment,' Faulkner said. 'Watch out for cigarette ends,' he warned. It was too late. Jeremy let out an anguished shout and came hopping after him, clutching his foot. Faulkner stopped, allowing him to catch up. 'Would you like to earn a lot of money quickly?' he asked.

Jeremy gingerly allowed his injured foot to touch the pavement. 'Doing what?' he asked suspiciously. 'You still owe me a retainer for the last job you boshed up.'

Faulkner hailed a passing taxi. 'I'll tell you about it on the way.' Faulkner climbed in. Jeremy remained on the pavement. 'Well, come on,' Faulkner said impatiently. 'You can't walk about London with no shoes.'

'Six thousand, seven hundred and twenty-seven pounds,' Jeremy said threateningly. The taxi began to move slowly down the street.

'I dropped in at your flat,' Faulkner called. 'You've been evicted. There's a couple of bloody great West Indians waiting for you for non-payment of rent.'

'Hold it,' Jeremy shouted, hobbling after the departing taxi. 'Hold it. I'm coming.'

Peter Coetzee walked the streets of London half the night. He returned to his bedsitting-room in a basement in Earls Court just as dawn was breaking. Without bothering to turn on the light, he lit the gas fire and huddled over it. The cold of an English winter sapped the strength from his bones. And his whole body ached to feel once again the hot bright sunlight of Africa.

He stared at the walls, trying to think; his face was drawn and his eyes saddened. He had come to this city a lonely man in search of people, trying to make a new life for himself. But he was more lonely now than he had ever been in the bush. His great strength and independence were useless to him here. He was as much out of his element as a wild animal caged in a zoo.

The walls of the cramped room reminded Peter too much of the cave. He got up and made two cups of coffee. In the room next to his lived a thin, shy, young man. They had grown to be friends and they made a strange couple as they went around London together, one weak, cynical, sure of failure and frightened by it, the other huge and gentle with a desperate need of hope.

The young man was down at the moment. Lately he had been withdrawing more and more into himself and Peter brought him the coffee to try and cheer him up. He walked down the dark, damp-smelling corridor. Pinned to the door there was a note written neatly in crayon: *Please be careful of the gas.*

Peter knocked on the door. There was no answer. He knocked again. Someone along the corridor shouted at him to shut up. A horrible thought dawned on him and he tried the handle. The door was locked. He shouted. No one replied. Then Peter went through the door with a splintering crash of wood.

The room was filled with gas. The sudden draught from the open door set a blue bulb swinging, the cold dim light rocking back and forth over a figure sprawled across an unmade bed.

Peter crossed the room, tore open the curtains and smashed the window. He gulped in fresh air then went back and sat by the young man, whose face had been made hideous by the pain of dying. His mouth was wide open and his eyes stared up blindly from hollow sockets. Peter had seen death many times before, but he felt a bitter anger now. This was a life wasted and it sickened him. The young man had left no note. He had just curled up and died alone. Peter's heart cried out in protest at the uselessness of it all.

He picked up the little man in his arms and carried him out into the street. Together they sat on the steps in a cold washed winter's sunlight, the man cradled like a child in Peter's arms. Grey, faceless people hurried past. It's your fault, Peter wanted to shout at them, you did this to him. But nobody knew him, nobody cared. They just hurried on past, oblivious to the suffering.

The landlord came out. He tried to persuade Peter to carry the body back inside, but Peter wouldn't move. It's not right for a man to die alone in a little dark room, he wanted to explain. A man should die free with the sun in his face. But the words would not come.

The police arrived and a crowd began to gather. Peter watched helplessly as his friend's body was taken away. 'He needn't have died alone,' he whispered to himself. 'I'd have stayed with him. Man, I'm scared of cities. I've got to get out of this place. I don't belong here.'

CHAPTER TEN

Saturday, 5th December

JANDERS had worked on the files through the night.

'Where's Jeremy?' Faulkner asked as he entered the room.

'Still sleeping,' Janders answered wearily. 'You picked up that kook. Why didn't you put him in your room?'

'He's not altogether pleased with me,' Faulkner answered. 'Did you find that Rhodesian you were after?'

'Yes.'

'What's he like?'

'He's good,' Janders said. 'We need him.'

'Will he come?'

'I don't know yet. I've just had a call from him. He's coming round to see us this evening.'

Faulkner glanced at his watch. He picked up his briefcase. 'I've got a meeting with Balfour. If he agrees to the bill, I'll sign the contract. By the way, I've given some thought to what you said about us being the last on the list.' Faulkner's eyes went cold. 'And I'll tell you something, old friend. Limbani's going to cost those bastards. My God, but he's going to cost them.'

Jeremy entered the room when he heard Faulkner leave. 'Did you hear what that bastard did to me last night?' he asked indignantly.

'Yes,' Janders said. 'You told me several times.'

'How much is the contract paying then? He wouldn't tell me.'

'You'll know when he gets back. Listen, we need another man. Someone who knows his way around aeroplanes. Have you got any ideas?'

Jeremy thought for a moment. 'I know one man. He'd be ideal, but I don't think he would go for this.'

'Why not?'

'He flew with Mad Malloy into Biafra and he picked up a small fortune out there, so he won't need the money. And if you think he'll come for the love of adventure, forget it,' Jeremy warned. 'He's not that sort. His name's Shaun Fynn. Mad as a hatter, but he can fly anything that's got a pair of wings.'

'I'd like to meet him,' Janders said. 'Where is he?'

'He could be in any bed in London now. A girl called Cynthia's giving a party tonight. We'll find him there. Hey,' Jeremy said, following Janders into the kitchen, 'seeing as I've joined, could you lend me some money? All my belongings are in hock.'

'How much do you want?'

'Three hundred should do it.'

'I'll give you one hundred on account.'

'What about the rest?' Jeremy asked indignantly. 'Do you think I'm going to do a bunk or something?'

'It crossed my mind,' Janders replied drily.

Jeremy changed. 'Hey,' he shouted from the next room. 'Could you lend me a pair of shoes?'

'What size are you?'

'Nine.'

'Try Faulkner's.'

Faulkner returned just before noon, his hat was over his eyes and his face beamed.

'What did you get us?' Janders asked suspiciously.

'A hundred thousand pounds for me, fifty thousand for you, twenty thousand for each officer, fifteen thousand for the R.S.M., ten thousand each N.C.O. and five thousand each man.'

'That's one hell of a wage bill.'

'It's a short sharp contract, no chance of spoils and a bloody good chance of getting killed. Besides,' Faulkner said, 'they can afford it. Have we had any replies to the telegrams yet?'

'Over a hundred so far. The telegraph department are thinking of laying on a special messenger. Thank God we're in with security.'

'I noticed a couple of them outside in a car taking photographs.'

'We'll have to move soon before the Press get on to us.'

'We'll begin recruiting on Monday then.'

'I've made a separate list of the ones we know. Most of them are getting a bit long in the tooth. We had better agree on a maximum age limit. There's even one from Sandy Young.'

'Yes. I wired him personally.'

'Christ, he's sixty,' Janders said startled. 'Wasn't he an N.C.O. in the paras at Arnhem?'

'I want him as R.S.M. If he's in bad shape, he doesn't have to go in with us, but he can train a squad faster than any man I know. For the rest, we'll make a maximum age limit of forty. I'd rather go in with older men who know what it's all about than with some youngster who thinks he's hard and breaks up at the first action.'

Janders groaned. 'A middle-aged army led by old men. I'm telling you, Allen, we're pathetic.'

'I suppose you've worked out that you'll be earning about twenty-five thousand pounds an hour on the ground,' Faulkner answered quietly. 'That's not bad for a couple of old men.'

Faulkner, Janders and Jeremy were waiting in the living-room when Peter arrived that evening.

'All right,' Peter said. 'I'll come with you.' He was unsure of himself, feeling low.

'Good. My name's Faulkner. Sit down, make yourself at home. From what Rafer here tells me, you'll make a good soldier.'

'Man,' said Peter uncomfortably, 'I'm better with cattle.'

'You'll be a lieutenant with an N.C.O. and a squad of eight men under you. Your pay will be twenty thousand pounds on successful completion of the contract, a third of that amount if the mission is unsuccessful. The money will be held for you in Switzerland and paid into any country that you wish. If you die, the monies will be made over to your next of kin or nominee.'

Peter sat back in wonder. 'I can buy a ranch with that,' he said.

'It cheered me up when I heard,' Jeremy admitted.

Faulkner walked over to a large scale map of the barracks. Peter followed him.

'One of the difficulties that we have met so far is how to cross this area,' he indicated the hundred-yard cleared killing ground, 'and get to the sentries. That's where we hope you can help us.'

'We've got an idea that we could use those game dart rifles,' Janders said. 'Can it make the range?'

Peter shook his head. 'The American Police tried to use them, but they didn't work well. In the Game Department we used a .303 adapted to fire a .22 blank with a two-grain cartridge. The dart was an aluminium cylinder like a hypo syringe with a feathered flight at one end.'

'What range does it have?' Faulkner asked.

'About twenty-five yards. If you use any more power, you'll damage it.'

95

'What sort of drug do they use?'

'Depends on what you want. Depressant drugs normally. They're using one called Etorphine now. It's about the best. It depresses the central nervous system and puts everything to sleep.'

'How long does it take to work?'

'About seven minutes.'

'As long as that? I thought they just sort of dropped.'

'Not a chance,' Peter said. 'Unless you're lucky and hit an artery. You won't be able to put down sentries with it. We tried it out in Rhodesia. It takes too long.'

'Isn't there any other sort of drug?'

'There's a killing drug called Succinyl Chlorine. We're using it for game culling, but again you've got to get it in a vein or artery to kill instantly. Otherwise, it takes about five minutes.'

'What would happen if you gave a man the same dose as an elephant?'

'Men are on the whole much less susceptible to the drug than animals. They've found that the same dose needed to kill a man would kill a buffalo weighing eighteen hundred pounds.'

'What are the chances of finding a vein?'

'It's hard enough trying to find one when a man's lying still. It's bloody near impossible at any distance. Besides, at a hundred yards, it's going to be tough enough hitting the target. And I can tell you, that sentry's going to yell loud enough to wake the dead when the needle goes in.'

'Well, that's that,' Janders said dejectedly. 'We'll have to think of something else.'

'Couldn't we just find someone who looks like Limbani, train him up and rescue him from the Algarve or something?' Jeremy asked.

'I've got an idea that might work,' Peter said thoughtfully.

'If we can't get across that killing ground, maybe we could get to the sentries with a cross-bow. Don't laugh,' Peter said seriously to Jeremy. 'I've hunted with them. They've got more stopping power than most rifles.' Peter paused uncertainly.

'Go on,' Faulkner urged.

'You sure there's no sentries in the bush before the barracks?'

'Not according to our information.'

'They use guard dogs?'

'No.'

'So there's just three sentry towers along each side of the wire then?'

'Yes.'

'Well, if you get me that cross-bow,' he said softly, 'I'll take care of them.'

'You're on,' Faulkner said. 'Show us what you want.'

Peter drew a piece of paper towards him and began to sketch. 'The stock is made of aluminium, like a rifle, with a trigger below. The bow is made of steel, five-sixteenths of an inch thick, one-and-a-half inches at its widest point, tapering to five-eighths of an inch at either end.

'The total length of the prod is twenty-four inches. The cord is made up of seventy-two strands of dacron twine interlaced and treated. The breaking strain is about two thousand, five hundred pounds. The bow will kill at five hundred yards. We'll need quarrels which are nine inches long and flighted like an arrow on a five-sixteenths of an inch shaft.

'At one hundred and twenty yards, the quarrel will go straight through a man. What we need is shock, so I reckon we use a hard wood quarrel, split at the end and saturated with a fast acting poison like cyanide. The quarrel will shatter inside the man. If the shock don't kill him, there'll be so much blood around that the cyanide will take effect in a second. End of sentry,' Peter said softly. 'But, man, it's one hell of a way to die.'

'I'll buy you dinner,' Faulkner said delightedly. 'Pick up your kit and move in here. We'll be alone this evening and we'll talk. The other two are going out after a pilot.'

Jeremy looked Janders over. 'You could at least have tried to look a little less American,' he said reprovingly. 'Remove that ridiculous hat, will you?' Janders meekly did as he was told. Jeremy rang the little ship's bell at the head of the gangway of a houseboat. The door was flung open and a girl dressed as an Indian squaw appeared on deck.

'Jeremy darling,' she shrieked, deftly removing the whisky bottle from his hand. 'You're supposed to be in costume. I shouldn't really let you in. You would have made a delicious brave,' she added disappointed.

'I've gone one better,' Jeremy soothed her. 'I've brought a real live American.'

She turned her attention to Janders, who was faltering on the gangway, noticing his grey eyes and battered face. She was interested in the older man. She reached up, tugged at his beard and kissed him. 'You must be new in London,' she said.

'No, ma'am. I've lived around here for a long time,' Janders admitted as he was led down the gangway.

'Is Shaun here yet?' Jeremy asked.

'Yes. The bastard's seducing one of my friends,' Cynthia replied viciously.

'Lead us to him.'

They found Shaun in a corner, a large drink in his hand, the other holding a very pretty girl while he talked intently to her. He was a good-, wild- and reckless-looking man of about thirty-five, tall and strongly made with no spare flesh on him. His eyes were blue and bloodshot, naturally so it seemed.

Jeremy tapped him on the shoulder. Shaun swung round, his face lighting up as he saw Jeremy. He pulled the girl forward, putting his arms possessively around her waist.

'Look what I found. Isn't she gorgeous?' he said. 'Her name's Mandy. I've only just met her and I love her already.'

'This is Rafer Janders,' Jeremy said. 'We want to talk to you.'

'Sure, sure. Go ahead,' Shaun said easily.

'How about outside?' Janders said. 'Too much noise in here.'

Mandy lowered her head possessively against Shaun's chest and her arms encircled his waist. Shaun chuckled. His whole body radiated energy and a sheer love of life. When he laughed, it ran right through him. 'No ways, man. Not right now. I'm living at Priscilla's place. See you there tomorrow.'

The music started, a wild, moody, blues beat came from the speakers suspended from a low ceiling. The noise was deafening.

'It's important,' Janders shouted, but Shaun was already dancing. His body moved as though each limb was independently sprung, powered by some tremendous driving force in his pelvis. Mandy changed from a shy angel-like blonde to a performer who could have topped the bill in Beirut.

'It's no good,' Jeremy said, shrugging his shoulder. He watched the girl wistfully. 'We'll never get any sense out of him. He only concentrates on one thing at a time. We'd better try tomorrow. What are you going to do now?'

'I'm going home,' Janders said.

Jeremy looked around the room. 'I think I'll stay a while.'

Janders pushed his way through the gyrating crowd and

up the steps. It was a clear, cold, starlit night. Below him the tide was rising. The water from the river licking softly against the hull of the converted M.T.B. In the distance, above the sounds from the party, came the noise of the London traffic.

He thought of his dead wife and then of his son. He felt washed out, old and lonely tonight and he wished that they were with him. He crossed the gangway onto the street. A girl was waiting there.

'I can't find a taxi,' she said. 'Could I walk with you until I find one?'

'You from the party?' Janders asked.

She nodded.

'Why don't you phone for one from there?'

She glanced back at the boat. 'I can't go back in there.' In spite of herself, tears formed in her eyes. 'Please. Can't I walk with you? Just until I get a taxi.'

She did not want to be alone. And, Janders, in his loneliness, understood. A wave of warmth swept through him, drowning his own pain. And he was grateful to her. He offered her his arm with old-fashioned courtliness. She took it gratefully.

'Trouble back there?' he asked as they walked from the Embankment towards the King's Road.

She nodded. 'I came with Shaun. He met someone else and he dropped me,' she said simply. They walked on a few paces in silence. 'Oh God,' the girl said softly, and began to cry.

Janders let her rest for a moment against his shoulder. He took out his handkerchief and brushed away the tears that were streaming down her face. 'Hey, hey,' he said softly. 'Stop it. You're spoiling your face. It's not every day that an old guy like me gets to walk with a pretty girl.'

She raised her head. 'If you'll give me your address, I'll

wash the handkerchief and send it back to you.' She took his arm timidly and they began to walk again. 'I'm sorry,' she said after a while. 'You must think I'm very stupid.'

'No. How old are you?'

'Twenty.'

Janders nodded. 'By the time I'd got to that age, I thought I was so hard that I'd forgotten how to cry. It didn't do me any good.'

'It's so stupid really. You see, Shaun's got this line. And I know it's a line, but I still fell for it. When he first meets you, you can almost feel the force coming out of him. There is something animal and yet very exciting about him. He makes you come alive, as though you're the most vital person in his life. Did you meet him?' she asked.

'Yes,' Janders answered briefly.

'Then you know what I mean. Anyway, everybody warns you about him, so you play it cool, but after a few weeks he just wears you down. He's always at your side or phoning you up. It's as though he can't live without you. He tells you that he's terribly lonely – and he is. That he's looking for a wife because he wants to settle down. And when he tells you all this, he says it in such a way that you've got to believe him. And you start trying to be his ideal of a perfect woman. Then he changes. Once, if you cooked him scrambled egg and you burn it, it's the greatest thing that he's ever tasted. Now, if you lay on a four course dinner, he hates every course. Little by little he tells you that you do everything wrong and each day you lose a bit more of your pride. You don't know why things are going wrong and you try harder. He makes you look stupid in front of your friends and you don't care. All you want is for him to love you like he did once.

'Then one day he drops you. And there you are. You've

got nothing left.' The girl began to cry again. Softly this time, but the tears coursed down her cheeks. 'He'll never find her,' she added defiantly, blowing her nose.

'Who?' Janders said.

'The perfect woman. She doesn't exist. He'll just end up a lonely old man. In a way I pity him.'

'What's your name?'

'Jill. Jill Darby. What's yours?'

'Rafer Janders.'

'That's a strange name.'

'I've had several. I chose this one myself.' They were nearing the King's Road. She looked up at him. 'You've got a wise face,' she said.

They reached the King's Road. Janders hailed a passing taxi.

'Would you like to come home with me?' the girl asked. 'There's not much, but . . .'

Janders shook his head. 'If I was twenty years younger,' he said sadly. 'But now I'm no good for you.'

'Couldn't I see you again sometime?'

Janders closed the cab door. 'When I want my handkerchief back, I'll find you,' he said gently. 'Good luck. Keep well, my friend.'

'Thank you,' the girl called after him as the cab moved away. 'I'm glad I met you.'

10 a.m. Sunday, 6th December

Jeremy Chandos and Janders found Shaun in a small house in Drayson Mews. He met them at the top of the stairs, a towel around his waist, and an indignant expression on his face at being disturbed so early in the morning, but within a few minutes he was back to his normal cheerful self.

He collected a bottle of whisky and three glasses and led them into a pleasant living-room.

Mandy crossed the room on her way to the bathroom, dressed only in a blue sheet that rippled as she walked. The men were silent, their eyes following her passing.

'What's she like?' Jeremy asked when the door closed. 'I mean, besides the obvious. Where's she from?'

'I don't know,' Shaun shook his head bemused. 'Each time I get round to trying to talk to her, I get a short circuit between my brains and my balls.' He was sitting cross-legged on the floor. He caught Jeremy's eye and a chuckle rose from deep within him until his whole body shook. It was the kind of warm irrepressible laughter that made everyone else want to laugh too.'

He poured three generous tots. 'Priscilla's in Switzerland,' he answered Jeremy's unspoken question. 'Not due back until next week.'

'Does she know what's between her sheets?'

'Hell, she wouldn't mind. You know Priscilla and me. There's nothing any more. I'm just looking after her house as a friend. Anyway, the whisky's mine, so drink up. It's good to see you again. You owe me fifty quid.'

'Yes, well,' Jeremy said. 'Janders here has got a proposition for you. It could be worth a lot of money.'

'Is it dangerous?'

'Yes.'

'Forget it,' Shaun said.

'The least you can do is listen to him.'

'Show me your hands,' Janders ordered.

Shaun did as he was told. His fingers were coated with nicotine and the tips trembled.

'I heard you were a good pilot once. What happened? Did your nerve go?'

'Just about,' Shaun answered. He looked up. 'You should

have tried flying arms into Biafra for Mad Malloy. I made seventy odd trips, landing at night in jungle airstrips, never sure whether they were still held by our allies or by the enemy. I lost a lot of friends out there. And I flew one of the last planes out of Uli. As I took off, I found I was flying half a ship, the rest was full of holes. And I promised myself then. To hell with the money. I'd never do it again. I've got too much imagination. I kept thinking what they'd do to me if they took me alive.'

'And the money you made?'

'I lost it all. Money doesn't stick to people like me. I changed it all into U.S. dollars. And I thought to myself, man, I'm just going to die of excess. And I went on the biggest bender you've ever seen.' Shaun shrugged his shoulders then he chuckled. 'Trouble was I ran out of money before I died of excess.'

'Malloy recruited you from the South African Air Force. What rank did you hold?'

'Lieutenant.'

'So you handled men?'

'I went through the Academy.'

'You're no use to me in this condition,' Janders said. 'Could you cut out smoking and keep off the bottle for a month?'

'I could if I had to. But then I don't have to. I like the way I am. I live here rent free and there's always a girl who'll keep me in food and booze.'

'This job will require about a month of your time. Of that, you'll only be in danger for a few hours maximum. It'll pay twenty thousand pounds in cash on completion. If things go well, you won't have to fly, just handle a very primitive control tower for about an hour. Could you do it?'

'I could, but I'm not going to. Only running dope could pay that much and I haven't got that low yet.'

'Not dope,' Janders answered. 'It's a mercenary contract.'

'Can you tell me any more?'

Janders shook his head.

'Can I come out now?' A blonde head peered round the bathroom door.

Janders stood up. 'Sure,' he said. 'We're just leaving.' He wrote an address on the back of a card. 'You'll find me here if you change your mind. Maybe we can use you – but on my terms.'

They went down the stairs and into the street. 'We were wasting our time, Janders said. 'He's finished.'

'Behind that foolish talk,' Jeremy answered, 'that man's no fool. If I was in a tight spot that needed a pilot and I broken-nerved, drunk, the lot. He's the best there is. The could choose anyone I wanted, I'd still choose him, half only trouble is,' Jeremy added sombrely, 'he never grew up. He's the oldest teenager in town.'

CHAPTER ELEVEN

8.30 a.m. Monday, 7th December

'RIGHT, gentlemen,' Faulkner said briskly calling the men in the room at Dolphin Square to order. 'Make yourselves comfortable. Smoke if you wish. You all know R.S.M. Young.'

Young stood stiffly to attention. He was a very short man, no more than five foot five inches in height, extremely fit and his body was almost square in build betraying enormous physical strength. His hair was thick, cropped close on a bullet-like skull. His eyes were brown, but with none of the warmth of that colour and they turned a light tan when angered. His lips were a small straight gash, set into a hard, wrinkled, leathery face. They rarely smiled.

Like Faulkner, he had been a professional soldier. One of the few natural-born fighting men whose savage talents are appreciated in time of war but become an embarrassment in time of peace. They were both retired from the army after an incident in Malaya when, in spite of written orders forbidding the crossing of a neighbouring state border, a village known to be harbouring terrorists was wiped out. Since then, Young had followed Faulkner through every campaign. He was a man who had very little love in him and what he had he reserved for Faulkner.

'We're short of an officer at the moment, R.S.M. You'll have to take his place until we can fill the slot. Jeremy, haven't you got a pilot's licence?'

'Yes, sir.'

'You have to know a bit about tower landing and take off procedure, don't you?'

'The minimum, sir.'

'Okay, then you'll take responsibility for the tower. There's nothing complicated about it. Rafer's got the details. Swat it up until you know the layout of the place backwards. You've got to be able to lay your hands on any switch blindfold.'

'Yes, sir.'

'If necessary, we'll have to go in without a pilot. We haven't got time to recruit now and I'm not prepared to risk an unknown quantity.

'Right. We'll be using this place as an interviewing centre. It's not suitable, but we'll have to make do. The living-room here will be the waiting-room. Rafer and I will interview the men in my room. Those we select will be passed on to you. Jeremy, you and Peter will fill in these equipment forms.

'The commandos will be numbered from one to five and, for identification purposes, each commando will have a coloured arm flash. Namely white from number one commando, red, green, gold and blue. Each man will bear a slip from us stating his rank and commando. When he has filled in his form, he is to sign a contract. He will then leave his passport with you. Check that it's in order.

'Here is a list of hotels and boarding houses in which we have reserved rooms for those living out of town. The men will have twenty-four hours to complete their personal affairs. Then they are to report to one of the lodgings that you will select and await further instructions.

'Finally, under no circumstances are the men to be told where they are operating. You will note that the rooms are reserved in the name of the Sun Oil Exploration Company which, by the way, is at present operating in Mozambique

107

waters. The men will be recruited as drillers, riggers, etc., and will travel under that cover. Each man will be given a letter of contract to support this.

'Oh, and try to lodge the men in boarding houses according to their commandos. Give the N.C.O. in charge instructions to keep them out of trouble. It'll give them a chance to get to know each other and weld into a unit. Any questions?'

No one said anything.

'Okay. The first batch are due at 0900 hours. The word's getting out, so we'll have to move fast.'

Janders and the R.S.M. joined Faulkner. The beds had been stacked against the wall. They sat behind two small tables in an already cramped room. There was no chair in front.

'Each of you make your recommendations on a slip of paper and pass them on to me. My decision will be final. My requirements are that each man must have undergone military training or have had a good record with us before. I don't want any wild young men. No man with a criminal record, we know that they normally make bad soldiers. And, above all, no junkies or alcoholics. I'm looking for good, solid, soldier material.'

'What about queers?'

Faulkner thought for a moment. 'We'll take those who have proved themselves with us before. Discard the rest. They'll all come for the money, but we've got to try and choose those with a natural love of fighting.'

The door bell rang.

'Okay, R.S.M. You can start wheeling them in.'

'I've organized them in batches of ten, sir. Twenty minutes each man. Three hours between batches to allow an overlap. Ex-N.C.O.s and possibles are in the first batch.'

'How many men have we got to interview now?' Janders asked.

'One hundred and forty-three so far, sir.'

'March them in R.S.M.,' Faulkner said. 'That way we'll soon get to know if they're bullshitting about previous military experience.'

'Left, right, left, right, left, right. Halt. About turn. State clearly your name, age, previous military experience and rank, if any. At ease.'

'Donaldson, sir. Born 1924. Two years active service in the commandos. Demobbed 1947. Rank of private, sir. Served two tours with you, sir, in 1965 with the rank of sergeant under Tiny Martin, sir.'

'Welcome back, Tosh,' Faulkner said. 'How have the years been treating you?'

'Not too good, sir. I'm with my brother-in-law in a jobbing plumbing business. It's not my line, sir. I just do it to please the wife.'

'Does she know about you coming here?'

'Lord no, sir. She'd do her nut if she knew. If you take me, I'll just leave a note. She'll understand.'

'You must be forty-eight now,' Janders said.

'That's right, sir. But I'm as fit as a fiddle. I'm as good a man as I was at twenty – better.'

'You've got a home, wife, kids. What do you want to come with us for?' Janders asked.

'It's the job I do best, sir,' Tosh said simply. 'I'm growing old at home. If you'll take me, you won't regret it, sir. I promise you.'

'Left, right, left, right, left, right. Halt. About turn.'

'O'Leary, Patrick. Twenty-seven. Six years in the Paras. Left six months ago. Rank – sergeant.'

'Why did you leave?'

'The Irish problem, sir.'

'Are you Southern Irish?'

'Yes, sir, but it wasn't that.'

'Speak then.'

'I'm as good a Catholic as any, sir, but I was a Para first. We could have cleaned them out in nothing flat, but they wouldn't let us at them. After the Bloody Sunday incident, they got to my family in the South. I thought it wiser to leave then.'

'Why do you want to join us?'

'I'm a professional soldier, sir. It's all I've been trained for.'

'Next.'

'Why do you want to join us?'

'That's a bloody silly question. The money, of course.'

'Next.'

'I dunno, really I don't. I thought it was a good idea at the time. You know, make a bit of money, have a few laughs.'

They worked late into the night and then on through the following day. The men heard that Faulkner was back. They forgot their grudges and came streaming in to join him.

'Left, right, left – hold it. Hold it. How old are you then?'

'Eighteen, Sergeant Major.'

'Sir to you. Go on home, sonny. This is no place for you.'

'How are we doing?' Janders asked.

'We're averaging one in three at the moment.'

'We might just make it then, if we scrape the barrel a bit.'

'We'll have to take an extra five with us in case of casualties in training. Pass the word to Jeremy, will you?'

'Next.'

'Left, right, left, right. Halt. About turn.'

'Shaun Fynn. You still got that job for a pilot open? Your conditions.' He was as white as a sheet.

'What happened to your head?' Janders asked.

Shaun put up his hand self-consciously to the bandage which swathed his head. 'You remember Priscilla? The one whose house . . .'

Janders nodded.

'Well, she came home unexpectedly. She was quite friendly at first. I was chatting away while Mandy was getting dressed and thinking to myself, man, this is one good woman, when pow, she hit me on the head with a whisky bottle. No warning. You just never can tell with a woman.'

Faulkner looked across at Janders who nodded. The R.S.M. obviously disapproved.

'How badly are you hurt?' Faulkner asked.

'Not too bad. She caught me a glancing blow as I was putting my trousers on. Just cut the skin. The bottle was empty, thank God. I've got a hell of a headache though.'

'Go in and join Jeremy in the next room,' Faulkner said. 'Oh, and R.S.M., see if you can find some sticking plaster to replace that bandage. We don't want to scare half the men to death before we get there.

'Next . . .'

6 p.m. Wednesday, 9th December

Five exhausted men waited for Faulkner in the living-room of the flat in Dolphin Square. Faulkner entered, throwing off his coat and hat. He never grew tired and his enthusiasm seemed to inject new life into the others.

'Settle down, please. R.S.M., are the men squared away?'

'Yes, sir.'

'Have they all signed their contracts?'

'Yes, sir,' Jeremy said.

'Gemel Hassim got the equipment forms?'

Janders nodded.

'Right, tomorrow we start moving out. So no one leaves the flat tonight, except for the R.S.M. who is lodging with his sister.

'Jeremy, Shaun, Peter. You're going to Lourenço Marques via Lisbon. You'll be met there by a member of P.I.D.E., their secret police. Watch them, they run the country and they're one of the hardest organizations in the business. We're taking over a small police barracks on the outskirts of the city. You'll have less than four days to get it ready to receive the men. Jeremy, you'll be in charge. I'll supply you with a letter of credit drawn on the Bank of Lisbon. You'll require Peter as a second signature. You'll have to account for every penny that you spend, so watch it.

'Rafer, I want you out of the country, so you're going to Johannesburg direct on B.O.A.C. From there you catch a connection to Swaziland. You've got the job of negotiating with Mad Malloy. The R.S.M. and I will hang on here and see the men off. I'll be moving out of the flat tomorrow, so you can contact me through Balfour with anything urgent.

'The men will start moving out on Friday the 11th of December. The R.S.M. will go with the first batch. I'll accompany the last lot, which will be on Sunday the 13th, arriving Monday the 14th early a.m. Training will begin as soon as the R.S.M. arrives. I want the men kept so busy that they haven't got the energy to get into trouble. The officers will train with their men under the directions of the R.S.M. Any questions?'

No one said anything.

'Right, gentlemen,' Faulkner grinned at them. 'A drink. And then I suggest an early night. We're on our way.'

'Speak with you for a moment?' Janders asked, drawing

Faulkner aside. 'I want to stop off in Switzerland, see my son. Okay?'

'See him when you get back.'

'No. I'm going to miss Christmas with him.'

'Can't you send him a bloody great present? We're short on time as it is.'

'Not the same. I've got to see him. I'm all he's got.'

'All right. You can have twenty-four hours. No more.'

'Thanks.' Janders looked embarrassed. 'I want to put my affairs in order – can you give me some of my money on account?'

'You still thinking about not making it back?'

Janders said nothing.

Faulkner's face, softened. 'Rafer, you old bastard,' he said softly. 'You and I, we're the best there is. We're going to make it. Don't worry, old friend, I'll get you back – you'll not leave your son an orphan.'

Zermatt, 5.30 a.m. Friday, 11th December

The first train of the day pulled into the station. It was still dark, the snow had stopped falling and the wind had died, leaving the village silent, almost deathlike in the early morning.

Janders' footsteps echoed as he crossed the deserted platform. A lone horse and sleigh were waiting to meet the train, the driver beating his arms to warm himself in the biting cold air. Cars were banned from the village in winter and sleighs were the only means of transport.

They spoke briefly as the driver tucked the blankets warmly around Janders, then he climbed up into his box, gave a low whistle and cracked the reins. The horse dropped its head and pulled against the harness. The sleigh broke free of the ice and ran smoothly.

Overhead a quarter moon was dropping in the sky, the stars brightening briefly in the darkness before dawn. On either side, snow-capped roofs leaned over the narrow road, glinting ghost-white in the fading moonlight. The soft jangle of the sleigh bell and the muffled thuds of the trotting hooves were all that broke the silence.

Rafer slowed the driver, then leaned back in the blankets. He was anxious not to disturb the household too early. But more than that, he was shy at meeting his son again. Earlier, when they had been together, it had been easy, but now, apart and the boy growing up, they felt awkward in each other's company, each wanting to give the love that the other needed, but not knowing how to offer it and the words came hard and self-consciously.

Outside the village, the sleigh drew up by a small wooden chalet, set apart from the others. Janders paid the driver and knocked on the door. It opened as he knocked. A plump woman in her late fifties stood before him, dressed in a quilted house-coat.

Grey haired, her face was warm and kind. 'Come in,' she said in English. 'You must be freezing.'

The little chalet was warm, the furnishings comfortable and they made you feel welcome. Tidy and yet well lived in. Books lay scattered around the room. Photographs lined the mantelpiece and the walls, mostly of children.

'Emile was so excited when I told him that you were coming,' she said, bustling into the kitchen. 'He kept running to the door last night every time he heard someone passing.'

'Where is he now?'

'He's asleep. I told him that way you'd come faster. Eventually he believed me.'

'Papa, papa,' a little boy burst into the room, barefoot and clad only in pyjamas. 'Papa, it must be Christmas.'

Janders warmed inside and reached out for his son to

swing him into the air. This time he'd make it. He'd cross the gap between them.

The little boy stopped outside his arms. 'You are welcome, papa,' he said gravely in French. 'Did you bring a present?'

'He brought himself. What more do you want?' the woman asked fondly.

'I brought you a present, Emile,' Janders said, hurt at his son's reserve. They stood for a moment watching each other.

'Go and put on your dressing-gown and slippers,' the woman scolded. 'You'll catch cold. Go on this minute.'

The boy looked at his father, then broke away and ran skipping out of the room.

'Maybe I shouldn't have come,' Janders said, sinking into a kitchen chair. 'Maybe I should just get the hell out of his life. That kid's going to have enough troubles without a bum of a father to screw him up.'

'I think that a bum of a father, as you so aptly put it, is better for a child than no father at all. When you're away, he talks about you all the time. When things go wrong for him, he's sure that when you come back you'll fix it.'

'You really believe that?' Janders asked, clutching at straws. 'But I can't get through to him. Sometimes I think he doesn't know me any more.'

'Mr. Janders, you appear very wise about many things, but sometimes you seem blind about your own affairs. A lonely child makes up dream parents. Sometimes he's a trifle startled by his real ones. You pay me well to look after your child and I love him, but I can't be his father and he doesn't want me to. That's something you've got to work out.

'Now, I've packed a picnic lunch. I suggest you spend the day together. Talk to him, Mr. Janders. Stop treating him like a stranger. He'll listen.'

'Ma'am, I've tried. Hell, I've tried. But when the words are important to me, they just don't come.'

'Try harder, Mr. Janders. They'll come. They don't have

to be important. They just have to be there. I've made up a room for you. How long are you staying?'

Janders looked embarrassed. 'I'm leaving tonight. Six p.m. train.'

'You'll be back for Christmas.'

'No. Will you look after him for me? There's something I've got to do then.'

'I'll look after him, Mr. Janders, but I can't take your place.'

'You're one hell of a woman, Mary. Why didn't you marry?'

'The men I loved died in the wars. Now I'm happier alone.'

'Don't you ever get lonely?'

'I've too much to do. Now you haven't got much time. I suggest you get out and enjoy your day.'

'Listen, I stand to make a lot of money on this trip. Enough to retire and settle down. If I do, I'll make a home for you and Emile. Will you come? I'd like you to. I mean, I know I'm not your sort, but I'd be good to you.'

The woman smiled and it warmed her face. 'Thank you. We'll talk again when you come back,' she said.

They were walking down the hill by the canal, warmed by a big breakfast. 'What do you want to do?' Janders asked in French.

'I'm learning German at school.'

'That's great. How are you doing at it?'

'Do I speak French because my mother was French?'

'Yeah, you grew up there for a little while.'

'I remember. Where's my mother now?'

'It's a long story. I'll tell you when you're older. Hell no. I'll tell you now. You want to hold my hand?'

'Why?'

'Because it'll make me feel good.'

'All right.' The little boy reached out for him. And suddenly the words began to come.

'Watch me. Watch me,' Emile called across the frozen ice rink. 'I can skate. I really can. Watch.' He wore a coloured scarf around his neck and a woollen cap with a bobble on it. He looked out on the world with large eyes, sometimes very old for his age, sometimes very young and vulnerable.

He skated out onto the ice and tried to turn. His legs slid from under him and he fell sprawling. Janders watched him anxiously. The little boy rose uncertainly to his feet, clutching a bruised arm. For a moment Janders thought that he was going to cry and moved across the ice to comfort him. The boy watched him but he didn't cry. His face was filled with the hurt of loss of pride in front of his father rather than the hurt of falling.

Janders felt love and warmth and pride for his son well up within him until he was almost bursting. He knelt on the ice beside him. 'I've got an idea,' he said. 'We'll tie a pillow on your backside and you can push a chair in front of you. That way you can skate all day.'

'Did you learn that way?'

'Sure I did.'

'I can ski better than I can skate,' the little boy said gravely. 'I'm only learning this.'

'Boy, I'm proud of you. You're doing well. You just slipped, that's all. Anybody can do that.'

'Papa, why do you always go away? The other boys all have parents, sometimes they tease me.'

'I'm going away just this once more. When I come back I'll stay for good. I promise you that because I love you, Emile.' Janders gathered the boy in his arms and hugged him. 'I really love you,' he said. 'You're all I've got.'

It was the end of a long day. Janders knelt beside his son, helping him off with his boots. 'I've got to go away now, Emile,' he said softly.

'Already, papa?' The little boy's eyes clouded. 'Will you come tomorrow?'

'No, I can't come tomorrow.'

'You will come for Christmas. It's soon now.'

'Emile, I won't be here for Christmas, but I'll come back soon afterwards. Then maybe you and I and Mary can all live together. You'd like that.'

'But you always come for Christmas,' the boy said tearfully. 'You always do. You promised me when I came here.'

'Emile, this is something I've got to do. You've got to understand,' Janders said desperately.

'You promised me,' the little boy said, crying.

The woman gathered him in her arms. 'We'll have Christmas together, you and I,' she promised. 'We'll go to England to my sister. You'll like it there. You've got so many Christmases in front of you, one more won't make any difference, will it? Besides, you're a man now. You've got to stay and look after me.'

The little boy drew himself free of the woman and dried his tears on his sleeve. He studied Janders gravely. 'I don't care if you don't come for Christmas,' he said. 'I don't care if I don't ever see you again. I'm going to look after Mary.'

Janders bowed his head. The words dried inside him and there was nothing more he could say. He turned and walked away. Night was closing. The narrow road dropped sharply and doubled back on itself.

His son watched him silently out of sight. Then he broke free of Mary's hand and ran after him, pounding down the street as though his lungs would burst.

'I didn't mean it,' he shouted. 'Papa, I didn't mean it. Come back. Please come back . . .'

CHAPTER TWELVE

Lourenço Marques, Mozambique, Africa. 5.30 a.m. Tuesday, 15th December

THE great yellow orb of the sun was rising from behind the grass-tufted sandbanks, its pale yellow light washing the early morning mist from the sea and glinting off the high flying cloud, giving promise of the heat that would follow.

The mercenaries were falling in on the sandvelt parade ground, their N.C.O.s quietly chivying them into position according to their commandos. The R.S.M. watched with satisfaction as the unit began to take a well-ordered military aspect. He turned from the billet window and addressed his junior officers.

'The Colonel, gentlemen, has instructed that all officers will train with their men, as is only right and proper for an officer to do. As I shall be in charge of all training, I may have cause to address you, in which case I shall refer to you, in deference to your rank, as Lieutenant Chandos, sir. You will address me as Sir, as well. Do I make myself understood?'

The group muttered their understanding miserably in the still cool half light.

'The only difference is,' the R.S.M. added, 'until you prove yourselves, you'll mean it. Now, gentlemen, let's have you at the head of your men on the parade ground double quick.'

There was something about the quiet, ferocious way in

which the R.S.M. spoke, Shaun admitted to Jeremy later in the day, that never failed to make him move like a startled deer.

Faulkner welcomed the men, telling them briefly what was in store. He had an easy, courteous, confident way that made each man feel as though Faulkner was talking to him personally. And he had the ability of a born leader to make men trust and want to follow him. At the same time, he left them in no doubt that he would deal ruthlessly with any man who stepped out of line.

The R.S.M. took over. He seemed to speak quietly, yet his voice carried clearly across the parade ground. 'For a start, we'll have off your beards, moustaches and most of your hair. Now, some of you on the parade ground think you're hard men. You're looking out and you see a little man standing before you old enough to be some of your fathers.

'Well, some of you know me already and some of you don't. For those that don't, I'd say this to you. A man is as big as his rifle. If you get out of line with me, I'll kill you stone dead. Don't think it would worry me, it wouldn't. I've seen better men than you die. So when I say jump, you just ask how high. Do I make myself clear? Good.

'Right. We'll start off by seeing how fit you are. Walk ten paces, trot twenty paces, run fifty paces, then fall flat on your faces. Then get up and do it again. And keep doing it until I tell you to stop. Space yourselves out in your commandos. Parade walk – trot – run. Run, you bastards. Right – down all of you. All right, get up. Get up you horrible man. Yes, you, up. Get up or I'll kick you up. There's no Queen's regulations out here, you know.'

He kept them moving for ten minutes. As the first men started to drop he kicked them up and they staggered on. One man refused to rise.

'My heart's stopped beating, honest, R.S.M.,' he wheezed.

There came a flat report from a revolver and a bullet buried itself in the sand by his head. The volunteer shot up like a startled rabbit and ran on reserves of adrenalin.

By now most of the mercenaries were reduced to crawling on their hands and knees. Some of the men, including Shaun, were vomiting as they crawled. Only Peter and a very few others continued to run, moving easily as though they could run for ever.

The R.S.M. called a five-minute break. He gathered the men around him. 'If you think that was bad, wait for tomorrow,' he warned. 'By the time I've finished with you, you'll move like machines. And if I decide you're malingering, I promise you I'll come after you like a banshee riding out of hell. But when the going gets tough you'll live a little longer.

'All right, break for breakfast. I want you back on parade in half an hour. That's at six-thirty sharp. Dressed and equipped for foot drill.'

Peter helped Shaun into the officers' mess while Jeremy stumbled behind. 'I'll never make it,' Shaun whispered. 'I sweated so much that I can feel the whisky draining from my blood stream. After all these years, my liver won't stand for it.'

The R.S.M. took a particular pleasure in foot drill. He loved to see well-ordered bodies of men marching in unison, wheeling and turning on the instant of a given word of command. He was from the old school who believed that it only took ten minutes of foot drill to spot a true soldier.

He divided the commandos into the various areas of the parade ground and marched them under the alternate direction of their N.C.O. and officer. Most of the men fell back into the routine quickly. They were tired, but their pace grew appreciably quicker when the R.SM. moved amongst them.

Shaun, now partially recovered, had completely forgotten the words of command, so he placed his N.C.O. in sole charge of the commando and tried to lose himself in the second rank. The R.S.M. marched beside Shaun, who was sweating freely.

'Lieutenant Fynn, sir,' he said politely, but with infinite menace, 'if you don't swing your right arm in unison with your left leg, I shall be forced to cut it off and hit you about the head with the wet end. Do I make myself understood?'

'Sir,' Shaun yelled hoarsely and he marched with a limp.

'Squad, squad, halt,' the R.S.M. barked. 'You're a miserable squad. The worst on the parade ground. Run with your rifles above your head. Hold them high.'

When the men's arms were nearly breaking from the strain, the R.S.M. halted the squad. 'Right, Lieutenant Fynn, sir, shall we try again?'

Alternately he drilled them and ran them with their rifles above their heads until they stumbled rather than ran, their rifles dipping lower and lower as their arms gave under the strain. Their faces became masks of rage, frustration, pain and exhaustion.

He judged their point of collapse. Just before that level, he stopped them. 'Fifteen minutes break, then weapons drill.' The men flung themselves down where they stood on the sand. The stronger ones crawled to shade to escape the now burning glare of the sun.

'Oh, God,' Shaun gasped as Jeremy pulled him into the shade. 'If he keeps this up, it'll be a toss-up whether my commando have me or him first.'

'They won't get him,' Jeremy replied. 'People have tried it before.'

At ten a.m. they staggered into the mess hall which was also to be used as a lecture room. The R.S.M. stood behind a table at one end facing them. In his hands he held a rifle. He waited until they were seated.

'The rifle that you have been issued with is the Kalashnikov assault weapon. You will know it as the A.K. 7.62, commonly called the banana gun, from the shape of its curved magazine.

'Pay attention in the back there,' the R.S.M.'s voice crossed the room like a whip lash. Some of the men, sprawled over their tables, sat up sharply. He walked over to them. 'You're going to know this rifle in the dark – better than you know your own wife,' he spoke softly, his face stamped in a mask of cold rage. 'You're going to listen to every word I say. God help you if you don't, for I'll find a way to hurt you that'll make you cry blood.'

The R.S.M. resumed his position behind the table. 'Now then, this is an assault weapon rather than a rifle. Short range, but very accurate up to two hundred yards with good stopping power. The weapon operates on single shot or automatic fire with a thirty-round magazine. The cyclic rate of fire is approximately six hundred rounds per minute. As the name implies, this weapon is most effective for close attack purposes or in a defensive role in thick bush conditions.

'I have one piece of advice for you. The old soldiers will already know but, for the younger ones, whilst you're in barracks you will carry your weapon with you everywhere you go. To the mess hall, to the ablution block, everywhere. Until it becomes like a third arm and you're lost without it. In your own time, you will strip it, clean it and generally cherish it. Because when you're in action, you can forget your commando and your mates. That weapon is going to be the one thing that stands between you and death.

'Right, now, watch me. The method of stripping and rebuilding this weapon is as follows . . .'

At noon they broke to eat. 'Not you, Lieutenant Fynn, sir,'

the R.S.M. said. 'I suggest we find some shade at the back of my office and brush up your foot drill. We don't want to go through the same embrarrassing performance as we did this morning, do we, sir?'

Shaun groaned. 'I'm a pilot. Blistered feet isn't going to help me fly anything.'

'At the moment, sir,' the R.S.M. said softly, 'You're an infantry officer and you will learn to march like one.

'By the left – quick march. Left, right, left, right, left, right. Halt. About turn. Lieutenant Fynn, with respect, sir, hold your rifle straight. Get your elbows in. Get your head up. Chin in. Your chest out. Hold your ugly stomach in. No one, sir,' the R.S.M. said disbelievingly, 'no one as sloppy as you could fly an aeroplane.'

The range was situated on the sea-shore with the butts against the sand dunes. The men ran all the way.

'You will take your place on the firing line in groups of ten, according to your commandos. Each of you will be issued with a full magazine and you will account for every cartridge. When you're on the firing line, each man will face his front. If I see a man turn with a loaded rifle, I'll count it as an act of aggression and shoot him. Is that clear? And while I'm about it, cover yourselves from the sun. Sunburn will be treated as a self-inflicted injury and will be severely punished as such.'

'What did I tell you?' Volunteer Clark whispered to his mate, Volunteer Scouse Jones, 'the bastard's getting nervous. He can't keep this up without somebody having him.'

'You have a go mate,' Jones advised. 'He frightens the shit out of me.'

They fired from fifty, one hundred, one hundred and fifty and two hundred yards, whilst the two armourers moved among them, truing the sights and checking the weapons.

At five p.m. the R.S.M. called a halt. 'All right, that's enough for today. Clean your weapons. Those with faults report to the armourers. The rest of you can swim if you want to, provided one commando stands guard for sharks.'

Shaun and Jeremy threw themselves down on their beds. 'Oh, thank God,' Shaun muttered weakly. Every muscle ached. 'That's the worst day of my life. My mate, I'll never last another one. Where did we hide the whisky? Come on, come on.'

Peter wandered in. 'The R.S.M. wants all officers and N.C.O.s over in the mess hall now.'

'What for?' Jeremy asked indignantly.

'Wants us to go over the A.K. 7.62 again before supper. Seems we didn't do so well on it this morning.'

'Well, stuff him,' Shaun said. 'I've had it. I'm not moving. You can tell him that from me.'

Peter glanced out of the door. 'Seems like you can tell him yourself. I think he's on his way over.'

Shaun shot out of bed, closely followed by Jeremy. They tumbled onto the parade ground.

'Well, where is he?' Jeremy mumbled.

'Seeing as you're up,' Peter said with a grin, 'you might as well come along quietly.'

'Don't you ever get tired? You bloody gorilla.'

The men queued for their supper in the mess. A huge Scotsman, Volunteer Jock McTaggart, let out a roar of anger when he tasted his food. He threw his plate down and strode up to the counter. He had bright ginger hair, a flaming face, red from anger and the sun and a great hook of a nose with the point of his jaw seeming to jut up to meet it.

He reached out with a large hairy hand, grasped the little

cook by the lapels of his jacket, lifted him onto his toes and shook him. He was a man possessed of enormous strength and, in anger, he shook like a high pressure boiler about to explode with devastating force.

'For three days you've been poisoning me now. What's that we're eating?'

'Stew,' the little man squeaked. 'Irish stew, honest.'

'It's filth,' McTaggart roared. 'Taste it yourself.' He pushed the cook's head into the hot container of stew. 'It's filth.'

The other men in the crowded mess hall cheered McTaggart on. Someone began to beat his knife against his tin plate and stamp his feet. The others took up the chant until the noise became deafening.

'I can't help it,' the little cook wailed. He was trembling violently, his face covered with stew. 'I told 'em my last job was a steward on the P & O line and they made me a cook. I'm doing my best.'

The R.S.M. quietly entered the room. He wore a pistol but it remained in its holster. He was followed by two N.C.O.s who carried rifles. The men were working themselves up into a frenzy. He walked up to the counter then turned to face them. Peter, Jeremy and Shaun entered the mess quietly and took up positions at the far side of the room. They were also armed.

Gradually, in the presence of the R.S.M., the noise died. One brave soul tried to start them up again, but the others failed him. He let his knife drop in the now still room. The R.S.M. helped himself to a plate of stew. He ate it slowly in the silence of the room. The men watched him.

'There's nothing wrong with it,' he stated at last. 'It's perfectly nourishing food.' The men began to mutter against him like a rising tide.

'It's filth, man,' McTaggart roared. He was spoiling for a

fight, anxious to even up the hours spent toiling in the sun.

The R.S.M. filled another plate. He handed it to McTaggart. 'I don't eat filth,' he said softly. His eyes were a menacing tan colour. 'Now you eat it.'

'Get knotted,' McTaggart shouted, his knuckles whitening on the rim of the counter.

'You and me, Jock,' the R.S.M. said softly, 'we're old friends. You still owe me your life from last time.' He held out the plate. 'If you don't eat it, well then, we'll have to sort it out. One of us is going to get crippled.'

The anger cleared in McTaggart's eyes. He reached out grudgingly and took the plate. 'I owed you,' he said. 'Now we're square.'

The R.S.M. shook his head. 'I'm a harder man than you'll ever be, McTaggart.' His hand was in the pocket of his camouflage jacket. He moved it slightly. McTaggart caught the hard outline of a gun pointing at his stomach. 'The only reason that you're still alive is that you're too good a soldier to lose lightly. Now you follow me and the Colonel – anywhere we say.'

'Damn you,' McTaggart whispered. 'Damn you. You're straight from hell.'

The R.S.M. moved amongst the men. 'It's your right to decide whether you want to eat or not, but for those that don't, rather than waste valuable time, we can just fit in an hour's drill before lights out.'

The men began to eat. And the R.S.M. left the mess.

'What's with him?' Shaun asked. 'Is he trying to get himself killed?'

Jeremy chuckled. 'He hasn't got much time and he's shaking the men down fast. In a few days he'll have them where he wants them. Then he'll start welding them into their commandos. Don't worry about him. You're watching one of the last real professionals at work. Between him and

Faulkner they're a great team. The men will love one and fear the other. It's the only way to run a mercenary outfit.'

'A word with you, sir,' the R.S.M. stepped out of the darkness and joined Peter. They walked slowly across the parade ground, still and silver in the light of the rising moon. 'The Colonel is out of barracks at the moment, or else I wouldn't have worried you,' the R.S.M. continued softly. 'I'm expecting a little trouble tonight. I'd appreciate your help.'

'McTaggart?' Peter asked.

'No. McTaggart's not the sort to come in the night. If he was going to try for me, he'd have done it then and there. No, sir, I've got my eye on a couple of the others.'

The camp was woken by the muffled screams of a man in pain. Men came tumbling out of their barracks and ran towards the far end of the parade ground in the direction of the screams. In the waning light of the moon they saw three men lying out-stretched starlike on the sand. They had been crucified with bayonets through their arms and their thighs. They had lain there for some time for their blood had dried on the sand. Each man's face was covered by a sack and, under that, a gag in his mouth. One of them had worked his gag loose.

The mercenaries gathered in a semi-circle around the spread-eagled men. No one moved. Peter pushed his way through the crowd. He removed the bayonets none too gently and cut away the sacks and the gags. Then he ordered that the men be taken to the hospital at the Portuguese Paratroop base nearby.

The R.S.M. marched onto the parade ground. He was dressed, shaved and ready for the day. He glanced casually at the wounded men. One of them had fainted, the others were moaning with pain. All three were covered in fresh blood where their wounds had re-opened with the bayonets being drawn.

'If your commandos are short, choose men from the reserve,' the R.S.M. told the gathering N.C.O.s. 'These men won't be coming back.' He glanced up at the sky. In the east the first rays of the sun were beginning to appear over the sea. 'Seeing as you're all awake,' his voice carried across the cool of the parade ground, 'we might as well start the day early. You've got ten minutes to get back on the parade ground.'

Silently the men turned away. The sentry on that perimeter claimed that he had never heard a movement. He was placed on punishment duty by the R.S.M. No one spoke of the matter again, but then no one ever approached the R.S.M.'s hut at night without shouting a warning first.

'Gentlemen, today we're going to deal with the R.P.D. light machine-gun. Again, this weapon was designed in Russia and, though now obsolete in that country, it is widely used in the Communist block. It is still one of the lightest machine guns in the world, weighing only 19.3 pounds with a loaded belt of a hundred rounds. It fires the same ammuniton as the A.K. at a rate of approximately six hundred and fifty rounds per minute. It is fully automatic and can provide covering fire up to a thousand yards. Again, it is a simply designed weapon. Two men from each commando will carry them.'

Faulkner met Janders at the airport. They drove through shanty town and on past the stark concrete structure of the bull fighting arena.

'Did you manage all right?' Faulkner asked.

'Yes,' Janders answered. He was tired, hunched up in a corner of the car. 'I've got Peter's cross-bow with me. The rest of the equipment, including the parachutes and containers arrive on Monday. How are things going this end?'

'Fine. We're dead on schedule.'

'Did the weapons arrive on time?'

'Yes,' Faulkner said.

'And their condition?'

'Excellent. Gemel Hassim's done us well.'

'I had trouble with Malloy.'

'What happened?'

'Don't worry, we got the plane. It's old and it's been used hard. But it's the only Hercules Malloy's got and he's clucking over it like a mother hen. He told me to tell you that the operation's got to go smoothly. If there's trouble while we're on the ground, he's not risking his plane going in to get us out. He said to be sure and tell you that.'

It was late evening, training was over for the day. The R.S.M. stood at ease in Faulkner's office. Janders was sitting on the the desk, Faulkner behind it. Crickets screamed outside the window and innumerable insects swarmed around the light.

'How are the men shaping up?' Faulkner asked.

'They're coming on, sir,' the R.S.M. replied. 'I'll have them ready for you by the time you need them.'

'And the officers?'

'They'll be all right too, sir. We could have used Peter Coetzee a long time ago though.'

'You had three men transferred out injured,' Janders said glancing at a report. 'And you don't want them back.'

'I don't think it would be a good idea, sir. Besides their replacements are proving themselves adequately.'

Faulkner stretched in his chair. He was pleased with himself. 'We can have Mozambique Island,' he said. 'The Portuguese have turned an old fort there into a rest camp for their men. Between Christmas and New Year, all those due for relief are being brought back to Beira to let them unwind. They've lent us the fort during that time. It hasn't become too much of a tourist attraction yet and the population is isolated. We'll move the men down just before we go in.'

Shaun stretched on his bed just before lights out. Every limb ached but he was feeling fitter. 'Man,' he announced, 'if I don't get my hands on something soft in the next few days, I may announce my engagement to the cook.'

'I had a chat to the P.I.D.E. man when we arrived,' Jeremy replied. 'He gave me the number of a high class escort service. By the amount they charge, it sounds more like a call-girl racket. What do you say?'

Shaun sat up indignantly. 'I've never paid for it in my life before.'

Jeremy shrugged his shoulders. 'If you think you're going to lay your hands on a sweet young Portuguese girl, you can forget it. Their mothers guard them closer than Fort Knox.'

In the middle of the night, Shaun woke Jeremy up. 'Phone them tomorrow. Make a date for the evening. Man, I'm getting desperate.'

CHAPTER THIRTEEN

Saturday, 19th December

THE R.S.M. worked the men until noon, then he let them relax for the rest of the day. Only the officers were allowed to leave camp. The men swam or organized games of football. A limited quantity of beer was made available in the mess.

'Hey, Peter. Do you want to come with us?' Jeremy shouted as he changed.

'Where?'

'We're paying for a date with a couple of hopefully beautiful birds. We could lay another one on for you.'

'No thanks.'

'Come on,' Shaun urged. 'You can't stay here on Saturday night.'

'I've got things to do,' Peter said, 'but thanks anyway.'

Shaun and Jeremy drove a Portuguese Army-issue jeep flat out along a dry weather road into the city. Shaun let the wind play through his hair. It felt good to have a piece of machinery under him instead of his overworked feet.

'How do we decide who gets which girl?'

'Let's see what happens,' Jeremy answered. 'If we both fancy the same one, we can toss for her.'

The jeep tore into the driveway of the Polana Hotel and skidded to a halt before the entrance. The two men walked into the foyer.

'A Miss Mausilowski and a Miss da Silva. They're expecting us,' Jeremy said.

'Indeed, sirs. Indeed,' the Indian receptionist beamed. 'They are at this moment awaiting your arrival in the visitors' lounge. If you will follow me personally, sirs,' he made it obvious that he expected a large tip.

Shaun and Jeremy followed the Indian through the lobby of the beautiful old colonial-style hotel, down a flight of terrazo steps into a large, high ceilinged room with a wall of windows at one end overlooking the gardens.

'If those are them over there, I know which one I want,' Jeremy muttered as they weaved their way between the tables.

'You've got no chance,' Shaun replied hoarsely, looking in the same direction. 'I'm the one who's got to get his hands on something soft, remember?'

The Indian saw the men seated and then, snapping his fingers at a passing waiter, he pocketed his tip and left them with a parting flash of gold teeth.

The hostesses were complete opposites. One was of medium height with a breathtaking figure. She had long, glowing, jet black hair that fell down one side of her face and swept back over her shoulder, a light healthy olive skin and flashing black eyes. Her low-cut dress seemed to be supported only by her magnificent breasts. And both men watched fascinated as she breathed.

The second hostess had a slim, graceful figure, but it lacked the striking dimensions of the other girl. Her hair was a natural brown colour cut short in an urchin style and it framed a young appealing face with a generous mouth and large expressive brown eyes.

'This is Maria and I'm Gabriella. My friends call me Gabby,' she said brightly. She knew that she stood in the shadow of her more glamorous friend and she tried hard to

133

make up for it. For she had learned by now to recognize the disappointment in a man's face when he compared the two of them.

Shaun and Jeremy nodded, hardly noticing her. Jeremy held a ten escudo coin in his hand and he quietly laid it flat on the table, catching Shaun's eye and shielding the face of the coin. 'Heads,' Shaun muttered. Jeremy lifted his hand. It was tails. Shaun was a poor loser. He turned to Gabby.

'You're my date,' he said harshly, ignoring her feelings. 'Come on, let's get out of here.'

'I'm sorry,' Maria cut in firmly, 'but Gabby and I stay together. It's the rules.'

'All right,' Jeremy replied. He was looking forward to the evening and his eyes sparkled mischievously at Maria. 'Where would you like to eat?'

'The Hotel Cardosa,' Maria said. 'It's quite close to here.' She made a face. 'The people in this hotel are too old. In the Cardosa the people are younger and the music better. Is that okay?'

Gabby tried hard to make a conversation as they finished their drinks, but Shaun answered her in monosyllables, his attention distracted elsewhere. Maria didn't bother to talk. She didn't have to. She knew that she had only to move to hold both men's complete attention.

'We'll find a taxi,' Jeremy offered as they reached the lobby, forgetting his natural meanness in an effort to impress Maria.

'What did you come in?' Gabby asked.

'A jeep.'

'Don't worry,' Gabby smiled. 'We'll go in that. You'll find the Cardosa expensive enough.'

'A taxi,' Maria said firmly. 'Gabby has only short hair,' she explained, 'and she forgets about the wind.'

Gabby left them and walked over to where Shaun was standing. 'I know that I will be of great expense to you this evening,' she said gravely. She was conscious of his growing anger and disappointment and it made her feel even more inadequate. 'I'm sorry,' she said softly. 'I shall try to be good company for you.'

Shaun arrogantly misunderstood her meaning. 'You do that,' he said harshly and moved away.

The Commandante Room was situated at the top of the Cardosa Hotel. It was dark, richly decorated and built in a semi-circle mostly of glass, with panoramic views of Lourenço Marques Bay. The girls were well known there and they managed to secure a table by the window. Below them in the moonlight lay a fairy-tale scene of ships riding at anchor awaiting a berth in the harbour. Jeremy and Maria ordered sea foods and wine and then moved on to the dance floor.

Shaun remained at the table. Gabby had not yet grown hard like Maria. There was still warmth and laughter in the girl, innocence and vulnerability. She was hurting now as she struggled to make the evening at least bearable for both of them.

In spite of himself, Shaun found her attractive. Out of the shadow of Maria and in her own light, Gabby was almost beautiful. Deep down inside, Shaun admired her spirit and found himself unbending a little. He started with his old, well-practised lines, but Gabby teased him and the act fell to pieces. Yet she did it so gently that he couldn't feel offended.

Shaun began to suspect that, if he would only go more slowly, he'd find a lot to this girl, more than Maria could ever offer. But he couldn't spare the time. All he wanted was a woman for the night. He stood up, pushing the table away. The girl had eaten, the preliminaries were over.

'Come on,' he said roughly. 'Let's get out of here.'

Gabby followed him, but as they crossed the dance floor she put her arms around his neck and her body swayed to the rhythm of the music. At first Shaun was impatient to be gone, but there was a warmth, a gentleness in the girl's body that soothed him. And he put his arms around her.

Gabby's face lit up as they danced close together and, for the first time in months, she was happy. She felt good with Shaun and if the mood had only lasted, she would have lain in his arms all night. But the band broke into a fast pop number. Shaun moved away and began to gyrate with his accustomed fervour. He danced as he lived, giving it everything he had. Gabby found the sheer male arrogance of the man both attracted and amused her. Shaun looked up. Gabby was standing with her hands by her sides, her shoulders shaking as she tried to suppress her laughter.

'What's the matter?' Shaun asked suspiciously.

'It's you,' Gabby choked. 'When you started to dance like that, I thought you'd dislocated every bone in your body.'

Another time Shaun would have thrown back his head and laughed with her, lifting her up into his arms and holding her. But right now he too was vulnerable. 'And you,' he said coldly, making his way back to the table, 'are as sexless as a dead fish when you dance.'

Gabby stopped laughing and followed him.

'I'm sorry that you don't find me attractive,' she said angrily, 'but then if you think that you've been cheated, go and see the management and get your money back.'

'Woman,' Shaun said cuttingly, 'at least I make my money honestly. I'm not a tart.'

'Neither am I,' Gabby replied hotly. 'I can't get a work permit and I've got to live the best I can.' She relapsed into a miserable silence, her mind filled with all the other evenings that she had spent in this night club. The dull and lecherous men that she had had to entertain. And now this man was no different.

She looked around. The night club had become her cell, its glass windows her bars. Somehow, Gabby told herself, desperately, she had to get out of this place and find a new life. She knew that it was an old promise worn thin with time. But in the morning she would stand in the queue at the Consulate and plead once again for a passport.

Maria danced with Shaun. 'My friend is proud,' she explained. 'But if you report her to the management she'll lose her job, and with no work permit she won't find another one easily. She is a refugee from black Africa, her family are dead. And without a country to go home to or papers to travel she has nothing.'

Shaun felt sorry for Gabby. When he returned to the table, he saw the hurt and loneliness in her face and he reached out and took her hand.

'Come on,' he said, almost kindly, and led her onto the dance floor. But any feelings that Gabby might have had for him were gone now. She was closed and empty inside and Shaun couldn't reach her.

The band was playing the closing number of the evening.

'What do you mean you won't sleep with me?' Shaun shouted impatiently, his voice rising above the noise of the music. He knew that he was making a fool of himself, but he was too drunk and angry to care. 'Hell,' he exploded, 'it was part of the agreement, wasn't it?'

'No,' Gabby shouted back, her eyes growing hot. 'You misunderstood. The agreement is that I have to supply you with company during the course of the evening. It stops there. I told you that I wasn't a tart. You should have believed me and sent me home then.'

'You've had other men, haven't you?'

'Yes, if I found them attractive enough.'

'Well, what the hell's wrong with me?'

All the humiliation of the evening boiled up in Gabby. She threw back her head and let go. 'You're a spoilt, selfish little boy who's never grown up,' she said. 'You're shallow. Oh, I expect that you've had lots of women, but you haven't got enough love in you to hold one woman all her life.'

'Woman,' Shaun said scandalized. 'You don't know me. You know nothing about me.'

'Oh yes I do,' Gabby said triumphantly, glad to be hitting back. 'You've got a face I've seen many times before. You lean on other people's ideas, borrow their lines and laugh at their jokes. Mister, you've got nothing, you're just a shadow in this world.'

'Listen, if I want to be analysed, I'll go to a psychiatrist. No ways, woman, do I need a two-minute lecture from a professional virgin like you.'

'Break it up,' Jeremy parted them angrily. 'The people can't dance and the band's getting bitter.'

'I'm not going to cry,' Gabby said furiously and burst into tears.

Shaun had had enough. 'Let's get out of here,' he shouted. 'This woman's driving me mad.'

They fought their way to the exit.

'Maria,' Jeremy said, taking her aside as they reached the lobby, trying to save a ruined evening. 'I don't want the evening to end yet, you understand. We can get rid of Shaun, put Gabby in a taxi and then go back to your apartment.'

Maria smiled and shook her head.

'You're a warm and fascinating woman,' Jeremy argued desperately, 'and you know I'm going away to sea. Imagine nothing but hundreds of ugly men on an oil rig.'

'Jeremy,' Maria said sweetly, 'when you get back, you'll appreciate me even more, and then, maybe.' She reached up and kissed him. Her tongue ran lightly around his lips and her breasts melted into his chest, making Jeremy fairly glow with frustration.

A taxi drew up. 'One hundred escudos should cover the fare,' she said practically as she climbed in after Gabby.

Shaun flagged down another taxi. Jeremy crossed the street and joined him. He was as white as a sheet and he sank weakly back into the seat. 'You bastard,' he said in a strangled voice. 'We've been robbed, and it's all your fault. Do you know what that evening's cost us?'

The following morning, Shaun dragged himself over to the small Nissen hut that had been set aside as the officers' mess. Jeremy and Peter were having breakfast and he regarded them blearily.

'I don't know what came over me last night,' he said. 'I wasn't myself.'

'Sit down and shut up, will you?' Jeremy said bitterly. 'Just the sight of you is giving me indigestion. Do you know what that bastard did to me last night?' he said Peter.

'It was those bloody great eyes of hers,' Shaun defended himself. 'She had a way of looking at me as if to say, Shaun Fynn, you're lying again. And I was, too.' Shaun was silent for a moment, then he shook his head bemused. 'I keep thinking about her. I can't get her out of my mind. Have you got a number where I can contact her? I've got to see her again.'

'No. Only the agency's and nobody will be there now. Wait until Monday.'

'I've got to see her today. It's important to me.'

'Try the P.I.D.E. man,' Jeremy replied. 'He'll know where to find her.'

Shaun got to his feet. 'Cover for me, will you?'

'You'd better make it back by noon,' Peter warned. 'The R.S.M.'s taking the whole unit on a jungle walk.'

'Oh, God,' Shaun groaned. 'Doesn't he ever let up? That man's going to have me the fittest alcoholic in the Southern hemisphere.'

The unshaven driver of an ancient Mercedes taxi sped across the city, urged on by Shaun, his brakes squealing professionally at every corner, his horn scattering the Sunday drivers. They reached the Cathedral as the service ended and the doors opened. Shaun stood at the bottom of the steps gazing into the faces of the women as they surged past him. He saw Gabby, took her by the arm and led her out of the crowd.

'Thank you for coming,' he said as they walked towards the coast road.

'Don't thank me,' Gabby replied bitterly. 'I came with you because I had to. I have temporary papers and I have to renew them each month with P.I.D.E. If you are something to do with them, you can have them withdrawn.'

'I'm nothing to do with P.I.D.E.,' Shaun said.

'Then what do you want with me? There are many more attractive girls you can sleep with.'

'It's not like that. Not any more.'

'For a man like you, is there anything else?' She watched gravely as Shaun floundered, then suddenly she smiled and the warmth returned to her face. 'If you've come to apologize for last night,' she said, 'I accept. And I know that you must really mean it or a man as vain as you would never have come all this way.'

Shaun relaxed. 'I have a few hours before I have to go back,' he said. 'Could we go for a walk, swim or do something? It's a beautiful day.' He saw the indecision in Gabby's face. 'I won't hurt you again,' he urged gently. 'I'd just like to be with you for a while.'

The R.S.M. took the men out to a jungle swamp land about four miles from the barracks. It was an area of twisted tree ropes and greasy black water teeming with mosquitoes. Dark, eery, silent, but for the constant drip of moisture, the shrieked warning of a bird, the sudden swirl beneath the water as some creature moved for the shore. The men didn't like it.

'This is the sort of country you could be operating in,' the R.S.M. said. 'You think you're fit now, so we'll test your reflexes. Each man will be given five minutes to walk through this section of jungle. Don't step off the path or you'll disappear in the swamp. Hidden amongst the trees are targets operated by wires. The targets will appear before and beside you for a space of between two and five seconds and at varying distances.

'I don't want any wild firing. You will have time to take one, possibly two, shots at each target and you'd better hit it. God help you if you get carried away and loose off a magazine. And remember you'll be using live ammunition and I'll be walking just behind. If you see a target to the back of you, leave it. Any man who swings round more than ninety degrees, I'll have you, so don't try.'

'I'm telling you, boyo,' Taffy Williams said quietly to Tosh Donaldson. 'There's all manner of bleeding creatures in there. Cobras, puff adders, the lot. The R.S.M. knows that you can't look down when you're following a jungle path. He's got it in for you, see, and he's just waiting for someone to catch it.'

The jungle walk was over. The R.S.M. paced before his men. 'What did I tell you?' he raved. 'I knew you were bad, but the safest thing in that jungle was the targets. You,' he yelled, 'yes you, you dirty miserable little man.' Volunteer Roberts, who stood six-feet two in his stockinged feet, waited patiently for the storm to pass. 'You loosed off the whole of your remaining magazine at the third target ten seconds after the bloody thing had gone down. I should have shot you myself and saved the kaffirs the trouble.

'As for you, Sergeant Donaldson, leaping through the bush like a bloody schoolgirl. Half the time you were higher than the targets. Do you know that you cleared a five-minute jungle walk in one minute fifty seconds flat? What were you trying to do, outrun a bullet?

'We'll do it again,' the R.S.M. shouted, 'and again and again and again, until you can hit something. I'll bring you back here at night and I'll bring out floodlights if I have to. Roberts,' the R.S.M. said dangerously. 'You get in there and hit something or I'll take your rifle away and use you as a pack horse.'

Shaun was strangely silent that evening as the others prepared for bed, confused about his feelings for Gabby.

'How did it go with her?' Jeremy asked.

'Not too good,' Shaun replied. 'She won't have that much to do with me. Though God knows, she's got good reason. Listen, she'll be finished work at about two o'clock this morning. I'm going to bunk out and see her then. Cover for me, will you?'

'What about the sentries?'

'Two of them are from my commando. They'll let me through.'

'If the R.S.M. finds out, he'll put a bullet in you.'

'I know, but that's a risk I'm prepared to take.'

They heard Shaun leave in the middle of the night.

'Poor bastard,' Jeremy said softly. 'That girl's really got to him.'

The R.S.M. never let up in the days that followed. Each

commando knit and the men united against him, the strong carrying the weaker members, determined not to let him break them. They ran and crawled and stumbled, but they held together. They cursed him with sweat in their eyes, planned to put a bullet in him when they were in the field.

The R.S.M. seemed to revel in their hatred. He pushed them harder. The men were fast reaching a stage when they would do anything to relieve the long days of training, fight anybody except the R.S.M., who they feared as though the devil walked beside him.

Janders hardly left the office now, working through the night and, when he could keep himself awake no longer, dozing in his chair. In a normal army, it would have taken a whole staff to arm, equip and move a group of fighting men across continents in the time. But Janders had done it alone. He had a brilliant brain, capable of attending to the minutest detail. And until they actually went in, the success or failure of the operation lay largely with him. Faulkner knew this and valued Janders' support.

In the evening, there came a knock at the door.

'Come in, R.S.M.,' Janders said, glancing up from his desk. 'If you'd like to wait, the Colonel will be back in a moment.'

The R.S.M. stood quietly by the wall, a ferocious little man with pale killer eyes. Faulkner entered the room and the R.S.M. stiffened to attention.

'The men are ready for you now, sir,' he reported quietly. 'You can handle them like putty.'

'Good,' Faulkner answered. 'I'll take over tomorrow.'

Janders leant tiredly back from his desk. 'You haven't got much time left,' he warned the two of them. 'I've just had a signal from Balfour. The operation has been put forward from 5th January. Limbani could be coming in any time now so we'll be moving out of here on Christmas Day.'

He turned to the wall map behind him. 'There's an airstrip on the mainland at a place called Lumbo just off Mozambique Island. That will be our jump-off point. It's within a thousand mile radius of the target area and we'll be going in from there.'

CHAPTER FOURTEEN

THE method of training changed. Faulkner handled the men with a lighter rein and they responded to him. Two areas had been set out in the sand dunes, one a facsimile of the airport, the other of the military barracks. The positions of the roads, buildings, fences and other obstacles were marked according to the information coming in from Balfour, together with the expected positions of the sentries.

Shaun and Jeremy's commandos practised attacks on the airport, whilst the others practised attacks on the barracks. In the evening, Faulkner tested Shaun on the layout of the control tower. Peter worked with his cross-bow. When questioned about his performance, he offered to place an apple on Jeremy's head. Jeremy declined.

Shaun had been bunking out of the barracks each night after lights out to see Gabby. Although the others hadn't sensed it yet, his nerve, already half gone, was fast reaching breaking point. As the time for action grew closer, he grew more scared. He desperately needed someone to hold on to and Gabby had become his crutch.

At first, Gabby had had little to do with him, but his persistence had worn her down. He used to meet her after work in the small hours of the morning and they would wander the empty streets. Two lonely people walking, talking, trying to make plans, their relationship deepening quickly with the urgency of his going away.

Shaun's face was drawn with strain and lack of sleep. He

was almost permanently on edge. Jeremy and Peter were tired of covering for him. 'It's got to stop,' Jeremy said that night in their billet. 'Instead of wandering around all night, why in the hell don't you just take her to bed and get it over and done with?'

Shaun sat hunched up in his chair. He was a selfish man, but his need for Gabby was so great that, for the first time in his life, he was giving all of himself to a relationship and, in doing so, he discovered a depth of feeling that he had never known himself capable of. 'I've had hundreds of women,' he tried to explain, 'but they were just bodies passing through my bed and I didn't give a damn about any of them. I really care about this girl. Every man she goes with tries to lay her. It's the only way I can show her that she's different to me – that she's special. Can you undertand that? Don't laugh at me, Jeremy,' Shaun said desperately, knowing his reputation. 'I love this woman. I need her.'

Jeremy was stunned by the change in Shaun. 'Don't worry about it,' he advised lightly. 'You've got the Christmas feeling. It's an occupational hazard with bachelors around this time. You're imagining yourself with your feet up before a warm fire and a good woman fussing around you. I usually go away about this time myself and hang out for the New Year,' he admitted. 'Forget about her. It'll pass.'

But Shaun crawled under the barracks wire again that night and he waited for Gabby on the beach road. She came up eagerly, a waif-like figure in a light summer dress and long brown legs.

'Gabby,' Shaun said. 'I've decided. I'm not going in with the others. I'm staying with you. We'll make a new life together somehow. We'll start clean.'

He picked her up in his arms and held her. 'I can't leave you now,' he said. 'Not now. You're everything I've ever wanted.'

Gabby looked up at him with her enormous dark eyes pleading. 'Shaun, are you serious? Don't tease me. I've got just that much strength left,' she said indicating less than an inch with her fingers, 'and if that breaks, I've got nothing left. Nothing, do you hear? So don't speak to me like that unless you're serious.'

'You were away too long,' Jeremy said to Shaun when he returned. 'I couldn't cover for you that long. Janders wants to see you in his room.'

'Come in,' Janders said, 'Close the door.'

'Does Faulkner know?' Shaun asked.

Janders shook his head. 'I thought I'd let you talk to me about it first.'

Shaun's face was pale with strain, his hands moved nervously. 'I've met a girl,' he said. 'Not just a girl. I love her. I'm not going in with you. I want to pull out now.'

Janders didn't seem surprised. 'I thought maybe that was it,' he said. He rose and moved over to the door. 'You want to walk a while? It's a fine night.'

Shaun recognized the tone of command in Janders' voice and followed him. They walked past the sentries and down to the beach.

'I don't know what's come over me,' Shaun said. 'Look, it might be because we're going in soon and I'm scared of dying. I'm scared of failing again. I'm scared of so many things. But all of a sudden, I care about someone. I really care about her with everything I've got.' He turned to Janders. 'I'm going to marry her,' he blurted.

Janders sat on the beach. He lit a cigarette and handed it to Shaun. For a while he was silent, listening to the surf, then he said, 'You warned me that your nerve was going and I should have listened to you. This love you're talking about, it's nothing special. A lot of men when they're scared of dying want to hold onto someone, want to leave someone behind to grieve for them. What makes you think you're any different? You're as selfish as most.'

'Look, you don't know about her,' Shaun said. 'If I die, I'll leave her with nothing. She's got no papers, no family. They all died in the Congo. And if this country goes black you can imagine what's going to happen to her here. It's more than she's just given me something to live for. I'm responsible for her now, don't you see? And if I leave her, I could lose her.'

'Shaun,' Janders said quietly. 'All your life you've been running away when the going gets tough. And if you back out on us now, some day you'll do the same to her. If she really means that much to you, then put away your fear and come in with us. And if you make it back, well then, maybe you'll have stopped running. And if she's still waiting, you two can start from there. But as you are now, Shaun, you're a frightened man. And you know you're no good to her.'

Janders stood up, brushing the sand from himself. 'You've really got no choice,' he said quietly, 'but I'll leave you to think on it. The sentries have word to let you through when you're ready.'

Faulkner met Janders by the perimeter fence. 'How did you do?' he asked.

'He'll come all right,' Janders said.

Faulkner's eyes glowed coldly in the half light. 'He'd better,' he said softly, 'or he's got an accident coming.'

'Lay off him,' Janders said. 'I'll do it my way.'

Faulkner returned the sentries' salute as they entered the gates. 'No one walks out on a contract with me,' he said. 'Remember that.'

'Well?' Gabby asked, but from the look on his face she already knew the answer. Suddenly she was afraid again – vulnerable and alone. The shutters came down and the warmth went out of her.

'I'm going with them,' Shaun said. 'I've got to, Gabby. There are reasons.'

'I don't know what you're doing, but it's dangerous, isn't it?' Her face had assumed a hard mask of indifference.

Shaun reached out and took her face between his hands. 'Oh Gabby,' he said desperately, trying to reach her. 'I promise you that, as I love you, I'll come back for you.'

She pushed him away. 'It's so easy to make promises when you're leaving.'

'I mean it,' Shaun said desperately. 'All you've got to do is wait for me. Please wait for me.'

'We're being stupid,' Gabby said coldly. 'Like little children. It's over between us now. I'm better with life the way it is. I don't want to wait and I don't want to hope ever again. When I leave you now, I shall forget you. Do you understand? I won't wait for you and I won't care if you live or die. You're just another man who bought an evening.'

'To go through life without feeling,' Shaun said. 'We might as well be dead. You taught me that. It's better to hope, to care, to hurt a bit.'

'You,' Gabby cut in angrily. 'You say that because you don't know what hurt is. You don't know what waiting's like. It dries your soul until you're dead inside. Once I hurt so much that I nearly went mad. I'm never going back there again. Not for you – not for anyone.'

'I'll marry you,' Shaun said. 'This minute. We'll find a preacher. You can have my name, my papers, everything.'

Half angrily and half as though her heart was breaking, Gabby began to cry. 'I don't want that,' she said. 'I want someone to love me. To give me a home and children. To give me warmth.' The anger left her and only the pain remained. 'You wouldn't understand,' she said softly. 'I must go now. I have to work tonight. Goodbye.'

Shaun took her hand. 'It's you that doesn't understand.

You don't have to work any more. I'll give you money. I'll make sure that you never want for anything again.'

'I don't want your money. I'll live my own life.'

'See me tomorrow,' Shaun said desperately. 'It's Christmas Eve. I have to go the next day. Please see me tomorrow.'

'I work on Christmas Eve. There are many lonely men in this town then and they need my company.' She snatched her hand away from Shaun's and ran towards the beach road.

'What about me?' Shaun shouted after her.

She turned and shouted back across the empty sand: 'You have your friends. Go back to them. You belong there.'

Thursday, 24th December

The men were seated in the mess. They rose as Faulkner entered the room.

'At ease, gentlemen. Tomorrow we're moving from this barracks, so I want all your kit except your bedding stowed tonight. As you know, it's Christmas Eve and for everyone other than those on guard duty there will be transport into town at 1800 hours.'

The men began to cheer.

Faulkner grinned at them. 'Right, you've got the night off,' he said. 'You can draw a limited advance on pay from Mr. Janders, but you're to be back in barracks by 0200 hours. And we don't want to have to go looking for you. Is that clear? Any questions?'

One of the N.C.O.s stood up. 'Me and the lads, sir,' he glanced around for support, 'well, we're wondering when you can tell us where we're going.'

'You'll know in good time,' Faulkner replied. 'Very good,

carry on, R.S.M. Oh, and if I don't see you before morning, Happy Christmas.'

'Hold it, hold it,' the R.S.M. bellowed as Faulkner left the room. 'I didn't say move.' He walked amongst the men, distributing forms.

'What's this then?' one of the men asked.

'It's your last will and testament,' the R.S.M. replied. 'Now then,' he ordered, 'fill it in nice and neat. Keep it simple and don't leave any ink blotches on the paper, or the lawyers will make a fortune out of your widow.'

'Do you know where we're going then, R.S.M.?'

'I dunno, lad. I expect I'll find out the same time as you.'

Shortly before midnight, a small group of mercenaries found their way down to the dock area of the city. They came across a narrow street that looked interesting. Tosh Donaldson laboriously read the sign. Rua Majior Araujo. 'That's it,' he announced to his mates gathered around him. 'Sin Street, like the taxi driver told us. The place where all them sinners collect off the ships of an evening.'

'Need another drink,' Taffy Williams announced, propping himself up against a lamp-post. He burst into song. Tosh swung him over his shoulder. 'Keep together lads,' he warned as he staggered across the street. 'They'll cut your throat down here as soon as look at you.'

The pavement and the people were illuminated by the neon lights. Clubs offered their attractions by lurid posters and sleezy doormen who tried to drag the drunks inside as they passed. One poster offered the promise of a rape scene involving a live gorilla and a blonde trapped in a steel cage. Tosh, forgetting his natural caution, was for going in, but the others pulled him back. They wanted a drink first and not at night club prices.

Wide-eyed, they continued down the street until they

came to a bar called the Crazy Horse Saloon. It was lit by neon lights with a juke box in the corner. There were no chairs or tables, just a long line of stools that followed the curve of the counter. And the place smelled of aged stale beer and sweat.

'Beer, Mush,' Tosh said to an African dressed as a cowboy. 'All round and lots of it. Right now, all together lads. It's Christmas, remember. "Good King Wenceslas looked out ..."' Above them hung a sign. In deference to the Christmas spirit, it was decorated with imitation holly. And it read, in three languages: Men come here to drink and forget. Pay before you forget.

The Caves was one of the supposedly better night clubs in Sin Street. Faulkner led the way.

'Where's Shaun got to?' Peter asked.

'He's gone off to try and find Gabby,' Jeremy replied. 'He's got a bloody great Christmas present for her. We're supposed to be meeting him later on and he's going to try and bring her with him.'

They wound down a flight of steps into an enormous cellar. It was packed to capacity, mostly young South African tourists. White and coloured hostesses moved between them. The cellar was dark. From the centre came the glare of spotlights over the tiny dance floor. Noise from the crowd rose and fell like pounding surf and cigarette smoke hung like a mist in the air.

The P.I.D.E. representative had reserved a table for them by the band with a good view of the dance floor. He rose to welcome them. 'Where are the other two?' he shouted above the noise. 'Are they coming?'

'No,' Faulkner shouted back. 'Mr. Young sends his compliments, but he's volunteered for guard commander. Mr. Fynn is absent.'

The P.I.D.E. man courteously offered the vacant seats to some standing tourists.

The floor show was well in progress. A large peroxide stripper about forty years old was struggling through her act. Her face was caked with make-up. Spare flesh hung in rolls from her body. She was trying hard, desperately willing the audience to appreciate her, but her act and her body were grotesque. The audience were far from home and in an ugly mood. A storm of cat-calls and whistles arose and people shouted at her to get off.

'Give us a chance, ducks,' she pleaded. 'It's Christmas.' Her act ground to a halt and she hurried from the stage.

The drums ruffled above the noise of the seething crowd. A spotlight cut through the mist of cigarette smoke and followed an African woman onto the stage. She was tall, and so thin that her bones seemed to show through her skin. She wore her hair naturally without a wig. And she was dressed in an off-the-shoulder gold lamé dress that looked as though it had been discarded by someone larger years before.

She faced the predominantly South African audience nervously. 'Happy Christmas,' she said. About four people answered her. She broke into a loud pop song made famous by Cilla Black. She had a good voice, but the song did not suit her.

The atmosphere in the cellar became cold and breathless, gathering like the lull before a storm. Someone, fearing a riot, sent for the manager. The singer finished her song haltingly. A few of the Portuguese and English in the audience clapped and the noise rang hollow in the otherwise silent room.

The singer was trembling now. She looked ready to collapse or break and run. With a visible effort, she pulled herself together, stared defiantly at the audience and began to sing *Tuli Tuli Baba*, a low haunting song that the Zulu women sang to their children years ago. She faltered through the first few bars, then her voice grew stronger.

The atmosphere in the cellar slowly changed. One by one the South Africans in the audience began to join in, swaying on their benches to the slow theme of the song. The sound of their singing swelled in the darkened cellar. Peter sang and tears began to run down his face. He was an African and he felt a long way from his home.

The manager came running onto the stage and made as if to pull the singer off. An angry roar rose from the audience. Peter leapt up and ran across the tables towards the manager. The South Africans moved forward and formed a circle around the stage, protecting her. The manager and his staff fled.

She sang on and they wouldn't let her leave. They refused to let any other acts onto the stage and they threatened the band. The haunting songs that she sung were the carols of Africa, more real to her audience than the European carols of snow and holly. At this moment in time, both black and white, they were Africans. It was Christmas, they were all a long way from home and they loved her. She was crying now as she sang, her thin bony shoulders shaking over the microphone. And the audience shared her emotion.

Jeremy crept up to where Peter was sitting. He moved quietly for he felt that if he made the slightest noise he would be lynched on the spot. He stared in wonder at Peter's great frame and tear-stained face. 'You're all bloody mad,' he said softly.

Peter shifted uncomfortably, suddenly ashamed of his emotion. 'I think with my heart,' he said simply. 'Man, you don't understand us. You never will unless you're born here.'

They carried the singer around the room on their shoulders while the audience cheered and shouted and stamped their feet, then reluctantly they allowed her to leave, having first made the terrified manager promise to look after her.

Peter resumed his seat.

'Tomorrow,' Jeremy said cynically, 'they'll all be back to bloody kaffirs and apartheid.'

'Maybe,' Peter answered, 'but some of them will remember tonight, like me. We make a lot of mistakes and sometimes we're just plain stupid. But we're the only people who are going to sort our problems out. And maybe my generation's starting to do it. But you people leave us alone,' he warned, 'because when you interfere, we stand with our fathers.'

'Christ, there you go, you bloody Dutchman. Straight back into laager.'

'Better we don't talk about it any more,' Peter said, 'because, man, I'm getting angry.'

'Okay, okay, leave it,' Jeremy said. He could always out-argue Peter, but on a previous occasion, in the heat of the moment, Peter had run out of words. His face went blank wondering how best to express himself, then his fist swung with the speed of light, not with malice, merely as though to punctuate a lost sentence. And Jeremy had ended up ten feet across the room.

Faulkner couldn't sleep and he walked alone along the beach below the barracks. It seemed to stretch for miles below him, deserted but for stuttered clumps of palm trees swaying gently with the wind.

From the base of a palm tree, a cigarette end glowed briefly. 'You want to rest awhile?' Janders' voice asked softly out of the dark.

'I've been looking for you,' Faulkner said sitting down beside him. 'What's been eating you all evening?'

'My boy,' Janders said. 'I'm wondering what sort of

Christmas he's having. I got him a good present, but I should have been there to give it to him.'

'He'll be all right.'

'Maybe. I feel very close to him tonight.'

'Somehow I can't see you sneaking around with a stocking.'

'I do,' Janders said seriously. 'He's too young to care who I am or what I am. He just loves me – and that feels good.'

'You'll be back soon. You can make it up to him then.'

'I've been thinking about that. If I get back I'm going to try and be a good father to him, give him a proper home. So that when he's older, he'll respect me. It's easy when they're young, but when they're older you've got to work at it.'

'I'll come over and visit the two of you.'

'You do that. Come for Christmas.'

Faulkner chuckled. 'I can just see us. Two old men and a young boy gathered round a Christmas tree and both of us trying to stay sober.'

'You'll enjoy it,' Janders said. 'Try it some time.'

Faulkner knew what Janders was thinking and he weakened. 'If you'd rather not go in,' he said, letting him off the hook, 'I'll understand. You've done the planning. Just get me as far as the jump off point. I'll take over from there. And I'll see that you get all of your money. You'll have earned it.'

There was a warmth in Faulkner, an understanding of the men he led, that made the rest of his character worth while. And it was that which made Janders committed. 'I've come this far,' he said gruffly, 'I'll go in with you. But I know how Shaun's feeling tonight. When you're scared and you're lonely, you grab at anything that's real to save yourself from drowning. With me it's my son. With him it's the girl. What are you going to do about bringing him in?'

'That's being attended to,' Faulkner said quietly. He was glad that Janders hadn't backed out on him. He needed him badly. They sat quietly on the beach together, the warmth of an old friendship between them.

In the early hours of Christmas morning, Peter and Jeremy called in at the Polana Hotel looking for Shaun.

'Have you seen a fairly big bloke with sort of bloodshot eyes?' Peter asked naïvely, for the hotel was full of drunken men with bloodshot eyes.

The night porter recognized Jeremy. 'Would it be the man you came with before, sir?' he inquired.

'Yes,' Jeremy replied.

'He was here earlier, sir, inquiring after a young lady. He had a few drinks and then he left. I don't know where.'

'Where else did you go that night?' Peter asked once they were outside.

'To the Cardosa Hotel. Listen,' Jeremy grumbled, tired of having to look after Shaun. 'Let's go home. He's a big boy now. He can take care of himself. Besides, the place is running out of taxis.'

'All right then. We walk.'

'Where to?'

'The Cardosa.'

'You must be mad. It's miles.'

'Walk,' Peter ordered.

They walked up the Avenue do Simas and into a small square with a statue in the centre. On the left was the Cardosa Hotel. Waiting under a street lamp was the dim figure of a man.

Shaun turned away as they approached. 'Bugger off,' he said.

'Where is she?' Peter asked, always a man of few words.

'In there,' Shaun answered. 'Eating with some fat oily bastard old enough to be her father.'

Peter noticed the crumpled parcel at Shaun's feet. 'Have you been here all night?' he asked suspiciously.

Shaun nodded. 'I just wanted to see her,' he muttered.

'You're out of your bloody mind,' Jeremy said aghast. 'Look, she's just not worth it. She's only a glorified tart.'

Shaun swung round, his fists clenched. Peter stepped quickly between them. Shaun slumped back against the lamp post. He was a man at the end of his tether. And Jeremy stared at him in shock.

'I know what you're thinking,' Shaun said weakly. 'I've called myself every name under the sun, but I'm going mad waiting here. I don't care about my pride any more. I just feel dead inside. I never knew I could hurt so much.'

'What are you going to do about it?' Peter asked.

'I don't know. I can't think straight any more. I thought of going in there and smashing the place apart, but it wouldn't do any good. I've been trying to give her this present but she's with another man. And I don't want her to know that I'm hanging around like a spare part.' He looked at both of them in turn, with a face as forlorn as a rejected teenager.

'You poor bastard,' Jeremy said. 'Well, we'd better go in there and get her out. I'll tell you what we do. We phone the night club and tell her that she's wanted urgently in reception. Then when she comes down, we grab her.'

'You keep out of this,' Shaun warned.

'We can't leave you standing under a lamp post all night. His mind's unhinged,' Jeremy said to Peter. 'Had to happen one day.'

'Go on, bugger off,' Shaun said. 'I don't need you here. Either of you.'

Peter reached out and patted Shaun reassuringly on the shoulder. 'Man,' he said gently. 'We stay with you. Don't worry, we'll think of something. Jeremy,' he ordered. 'Think of something better than that.'

They waited silently under a lamp post. After a while Jeremy returned. 'I got hold of the singer,' he said. 'They're coming down in a minute. Maria and another bloke are with them.'

Maria and her escort, a tall, lean, middle-aged American, left the lift first. Jeremy was waiting in the foyer. Maria's face registered a moment of surprise before Jeremy caught her up in his arms and kissed her. He then insisted on being introduced to her embarrassed escort. 'Happy Christmas,' he said cheerfully, wringing the American's hand. 'Does your wife know about this?'

The American thought that he was being framed and he made for the door with Jeremy following him.

'How much has she cost you so far?' Jeremy asked.

'I don't think that concerns you,' the American said. He was almost running now.

'You're not going to sleep with her, you know,' Jeremy said maliciously, ignoring Maria's vicious kick at his ankles. 'I know. I've tried.'

The American reached his car. He opened the door for Maria, then fairly leapt into the driver's seat. But Jeremy was at his window. 'Hang on,' he said. 'You're going to have a passenger.' And he reached in and took the keys.

As Gabby left the lift, she found an enormous man towering above her. He picked her up with a roar of delight and hugged her warmly. Then he set her down and turned to her escort, who waited nervously nearby. He looked like a cartoon caricature of a Middle Eastern banker with black greasy hair and a thin moustache. Peter picked the little man up and hugged him in a manner that made him feel as though his ribs had flattened on his back bone.

'My sister,' Peter said. 'You treated her well.' He still had a great grin all over his ugly face, but his words were menacing. The little man was terrified of him and he nodded breathlessly. 'Good,' Peter said. 'It's Christmas now. I take her back to her family. Thank you very much.'

'I was just trying to warn you,' Jeremy was saying outside by the car. 'I mean, do you know how much she cost me?' Jeremy always knew to a penny what a girl cost him.

'I've never seen him before,' Maria said desperately.

'Gimme my keys or I'll call the police,' the embarrassed American shouted.

Peter appeared with the little man running in front of him. Jeremy opened the back door invitingly and the little man fell into the car. Jeremy tossed the keys to the driver. Peter put his head through the window and the little man pressed back against his seat. 'Happy Christmas,' he beamed and the car roared off.

Peter appeared in the lamp light, pulling Gabby along behind him. He reached out and took Shaun's hand. Then he placed Gabby's hand within it and closed them one over another. His face broke into a happy grin. 'Happy Christmas, both of you,' he said. 'God bless you.' Then he disappeared into the darkness.

'Get that bloody grin off your face,' Jeremy said indignantly when he reappeared. 'Do you know how far we've got to walk back?'

'Stop complaining,' Peter said happily. 'I feel good now. It's really Christmas. I'll tell you what I'll do,' he said enthusiastically. 'I'll teach you some songs like that singer sung. It's about time you reinecks learnt some decent songs.' He looked up. 'The night is full of stars,' he said. 'I wonder which one guided the wise men. Maybe that one.' He pointed to an especially bright star. 'Just think, Christ was probably born now. And already he has all the troubles of the world on his shoulders.'

'You never cease to amaze me,' Jeremy said. 'Do you honestly believe all that?'

'Course I do,' Peter said firmly. 'Now this song – you've got to sing it low – with lots of feeling, because it's about a baby being born.'

'You great drip.'

'Stop complaining and sing. You've got twelve miles to walk.'

'Well,' Gabby asked angrily, 'what in the hell do you think you're doing?'

Shaun dropped her hand. Then shyly he picked up the battered parcel and handed it to her.

She took the parcel but she was looking into his face. 'How long have you been waiting here?' she demanded.

Shaun said nothing.

'So you really care,' she said, her eyes filling with tears. 'Oh, you fool,' she said softly. 'You great fool. You know it can't work.'

'It can,' Shaun said doggedly. 'It can. You love me too. I can see it in your face.' Suddenly he reached out and, picking her up, swung her round and round. He was laughing now, the tension leaving him. She began to laugh with him.

'Put me down,' she protested. 'This is ridiculous.'

'I love you,' Shaun said. 'I've said that to lots of people in lots of different ways. But now I only want to say it just to you. I love you. I love you. I love you. Over and over again.'

They walked by the sea, carrying their shoes, barefoot through the surf, her arm through his and her head on his shoulder. Two desperately lonely people, drawing together, needing each other, aware that the hours were ticking away.

They spoke very little – words were useless – there was nothing in the past that either of them wanted to remember and Gabby refused to discuss the future. Yet above them the stars shone like crystals in a velvet African sky – a night so clear and so beautiful that it brought an almost physical ache to their hearts. The sea was gentle and warm on their feet and the dark waves broke in a soft incessant roar that filled their ears and their senses.

They lived greedily each moment that they had together, trying to cram a lifetime of emotion into one night. They stripped off their clothes and swam out to sea, chasing the moonbeams, plunging and laughing. When they returned to the shore, Gabby stood before Shaun, deeply happy, lifting her head so that it showed in her eyes, offering her body to him. And that slim frail girl was beautiful to Shaun, more beautiful than any woman he had ever seen.

They tasted the salt on each other's lips the sensuous feel of each other's bodies. They made love on the beach, slowly, gently, both of them praying that the night would never end. And such was the urgency, the need, the love they bore one another that, at that moment, it was as though their minds and their bodies fused and they became one. For the first time in his life, Shaun reached out and touched the flame of another person's soul. It was more than just physical, it was a mental exaltation that so filled him with power and emotion that he knew that he would never experience a depth of feeling as great as this again.

Afterwards, they lay together, arms around one another, holding each other, and Gabby brought Shaun peace. She drew the sadness out of him, took his fear upon her shoulders and made him strong once more.

They awoke with the dawn, stiff from lying on the sand. The air was cool and the sea grey in the morning light. Everything seemed harsh and real after the magic of the night.

'I have to go,' Shaun said softly, 'but before I do I want to explain why.'

The sleep left Gabby's face and the loneliness and pain awoke in her again. 'Don't tell me,' she said. 'I don't want to know. Just come back.'

'You'll wait for me?'

She shrugged her shoulders, hard again. 'I've got no other place to go.'

'I'll come back.'

'I'll give you two months. If you're not back by then, somehow I'll get out of this place and find another country.'

She made him leave her on the beach. By the time she reached the road the taxis would be running and she would take one from there. She refused to take any money and she refused to give up her job. Her hair was tousled, her face drawn and her dress was full of sand, clinging round her. She reached up and kissed him hard on the mouth. Then, without saying goodbye, she turned and walked down the beach.

The African fishermen in dugout canoes were paddling in from a night at sea. Seagulls were beginning to wheel and cry in the grey morning air, waiting for the fish to spill from the nets, and a limping mongrel was beachcombing in the tide.

Shaun watched her figure receding into the distance, growing smaller and smaller. In a moment she would be lost among the fishermen. A sudden panic seized him and he cupped his hands.

'I'll be back,' he shouted. 'Wait for me. I'll be back.' His voice echoed in the still air of the beach, but she didn't seem to hear him, for she didn't turn. She just kept walking away.

CHAPTER FIFTEEN

Christmas Day, Friday, 25th December

The R.S.M. reported to Faulkner.

'Well?' Faulkner asked. 'Have we got all the men back yet?'

'There's still a few in outlying police stations, sir, but they're all accounted for.'

'What happened to Number Three Commando? You can't see Donaldson for sticking plaster.'

'He'll be all right, sir. Apparently a fight broke out and he went through a plate glass window. The manager of the Crazy Horse Saloon claims that he's never seen anything like it. There was a lot of damage.'

'Deduct that and all other damage claims from the men's pay,' Faulkner ordered. He leaned back against his chair, relaxing. 'Anyway, it's done them good to let off steam. They must have gone through town like a whirlwind.'

'Yes, sir,' the R.S.M. agreed. 'They're about ready for anything now. Do you have any more information about when we're likely to go in?'

'There should be a signal waiting for us in Mozambique Island. I want the men paraded at 2000 hours ready to move out. Oh, and R.S.M., every one is to be confined to barracks until then. That includes the officers.'

A convoy of closed Portuguese army trucks roared

164

through the city. Due to the terrorist war being waged in the north, no one paid any attention to troops on the move on Christmas night. The men inside were mostly silent, swaying in the darkness of the trucks, knowing that the time for action was drawing near.

They passed through a high wire perimeter fence and onto a landing strip. At the far end, two Dakotas waited with their engines ticking over. The men debussed quickly. Kit and equipment were loaded. Then the men filed on board and sat facing each other on canvas stretcher seats that ran along either side of the fuselage.

The engines revved. The noise in the dimly lit unpressurized cabin became deafening. The first Dakota began to roll, gathering speed. Now it was bumping across the grass, the fuselage groaning and rattling as though it were straining apart. The aeroplane lumbered into the air, made a wide circuit gathering height as it crossed the city. The other plane followed immediately behind.

The men talked, told jokes or dozed through the night. It was too uncomfortable to sleep. Shaun made his way up to the flight deck. The pilots could speak English and he talked flying with them for a while.

The Dakotas landed to refuel at Beira, the second largest city in Mozambique. They taxied to a military enclosure away from the terminal. And the men were allowed to disembark and stretch their legs. Then they took off again, climbing over Macuti beach, swinging north following the coast. In the dawn, they crossed the huge mouth of the Zambezi, where the river stained the sea with mud from Rhodesia. And later, when the sun was well clear of the horizon, the planes banked sharply and came in low over Mozambique Island.

The island was beautiful from the air, less than three thousand metres long and six hundred metres wide, surrounded by a clear jade-like sea and coral reefs. It was too small to accommodate an airstrip, so the Dakotas landed at Lumbo, a sand strip on the sea-shore off the mainland. As the doors opened, the first waves of heat struck the men. Sweat started on their faces and under their clothes. In a few minutes, the surface of the aeroplanes was too hot to touch and a hot sand-laden wind blew across the strip.

The mercenaries formed into their commandos, telling off for an equipment check. Boxes of ammunition and kit lay beside them. A man in his early forties dressed in a white shirt and shorts detached himself from the shade of some palm trees and strolled across the sand towards Faulkner.

'Welcome,' he said in good English. 'My name is José Pereira. I am to help you while you are here.'

'You from P.I.D.E.?' Faulkner asked.

Pereira shrugged his shoulders. 'I am connected with them,' he admitted, 'but here on the island, you will find things very different. Once we were the capital of the whole country, now we are forgotten. And we like it that way.'

He led them past a tiny control tower to where some army lorries were waiting. The men embussed, sweating and swearing in a heat that grew appreciably as the sun rose. Pereira climbed into the leading truck beside Faulkner and nodded to the driver.

'Have you received a signal for me yet?' Faulkner asked.

'Yes. Limbani is on the move. Our information is that they will be bringing him across the lake from Tanzania tomorrow. General Ndofa is due to arrive the following morning to see him executed. Until then, Limbani will be held in the military barracks. Balfour is very worried. The strike now has to be launched ten days ahead of schedule. Will you be ready?'

'We're ready now,' Faulkner said quietly. He and Janders had planned for a contingency such as this.

'In that case, you're to wait here for the Go signal. Malloy is sending his plane to Lourenço Marques and will be holding it there in readiness. Balfour is expecting information in the next few hours which will confirm Limbani's time of arrival in Albertville.'

The convoy crossed a two-kilometre long causeway built on concrete stilts over the sea and rumbled onto the island. They thundered down a narrow cobbled road, horns shrieking at hairpin corners and tyres mounting the pavements. On either side, below the road, grew a maze of conical-roofed, thatched huts. The road dropped and the huts gave way to walls of ancient double storey, white-washed houses with large wooden shutters and heavy doors.

Pereira watched Faulkner looking curiously about him. At the northern end, the trucks drew up below a massive fort. Pereira gazed up at it affectionately. He was proud of his island. 'We must walk from here,' he said. 'This was built in 1545 and they had no motor vehicles then.'

Two sentries on either side of the open doors stiffened to attention as they passed into an enormous sun-baked courtyard. The fort was shaped like a butterfly with its wings oustretched, guarded on three sides by the sea. Barracks rooms were set deep into the stone walls and rusted cannons watched from the ramparts above.

The men were fed and their equipment stowed. A radio was set up and Faulkner and Janders began to send and decode messages from Lourenço Marques. The day wore on. The sun burned overhead. Not a breath of wind stirred and the air shimmered in a heat so intense that each breath seemed to sear into your lungs until it felt as though your blood would boil. And the men, confined to their barrack rooms, dozed on sweat-stained mattresses supported by iron bunks, too uncomfortable to lie still and too tired and listless to move. Every so often, they staggered over to the ablution block and hung under tepid salt water showers. And their tempers grew short.

In the late afternoon, Faulkner called the R.S.M. into his office. 'I think it's on for tomorrow night,' he said. 'Are the men ready?'

The R.S.M. stood stiffly to attention, immaculate, his pale, death-like eyes fixed on Faulkner's face. His very perfection, his ruthlessness in preparing the men for action was just a small measure of the love he bore his colonel.

'I'd have liked a few more days with them, sir, just to polish off the rough edges on their training, but they'll do. They'll not let you down, sir. I'll see to that.

'It's growing cooler now, sir,' the R.S.M. added. 'I'd like to work the men for a while before dark. The waiting's getting them down and it's better to keep them occupied.'

'Very good, R.S.M.,' Faulkner said. 'Carry on.'

He climbed a stairway set into the walls that led up to the ramparts. Below him the R.S.M. paraded the men in the courtyard.

'Now most of you,' the R.S.M. said, and his voice cracked across them like a whiplash, 'will remember your parachute drill – and those of you that don't, well you've got the next two hours in which to learn. Remember, if you break your legs when you come down in enemy territory, there'll be no ambulances, no hospitals, no sympathy. Just me.' His pale eyes glowed. 'And I'll put a bullet in you because you'll be no damn use to me with a broken leg. So pay attention.

'You'll be coming out of the aeroplane in three sticks, like the prongs of a fork. You'll only be in the air for a matter of seconds, but for Christ's sake keep apart. If you tangle with each other you've both had it. And remember, let your container drop before you hit the ground – but not from more than forty feet up or you'll drop it through somebody else's parachute.

'You,' the R.S.M. picked on a man. 'Yes, you. What size is your reserve chute?'

'Twenty-two feet, sir.'

'Where's the quick release ring?'

'Here, sir.'

'Good. Now we'll go over all the things that can go wrong and you tell me how to right them.'

Faulkner found Janders leaning over the ramparts staring out to sea and he leant beside him. The sun was setting, leaving a glow across the whole horizon.

'There's something sad about the sun going down,' Janders said softly. 'You find yourself trying to catch it, trying to hold the colours and the mood in your mind but you never can.'

'It's the same with me,' Faulkner said, understanding him. 'When I'm ready to go into action, I notice everything. I care about everything: the sound of the sea, the smell of the air. The world suddenly seems very beautiful and I promise myself that, if I ever get out of this alive, I'll never neglect life again. But I always do. When I'm not in action, I'm dead inside.

'I've been thinking,' Faulkner said after a while. 'When this is over, maybe we should retire like you said. Pereira tells me that, now the port's been moved up the coast, this island's dying. Perhaps we could come back here. We could do a lot for this place. The island's got everything. Sun, the clearest sea you've ever seen, spear fishing in the coral and deep sea fishing beyond the reef. We could turn this old fort into one hell of an hotel, maybe we could even get a casino started. Tourists would make this island come alive.'

Janders knew Faulkner's schemes of old, but he needed something to hold onto and he was tempted. 'My boy could grow up well here,' he admitted. 'I hate the thought of tourists though.'

'Only the best clientèle,' Faulkner assured him. 'And we could buy a boat and sail up the coast when the mood took us, or out to the Forgotten Islands. This is a good place to grow old in. What do you say? The R.S.M. would be keen to come in with us.'

'Sounds good,' Janders said gruffly. 'We'll talk about it some more when we get back.'

The mercenary manning the radio room brought Faulkner a message. He read it in the fading light. 'The operation's on,' Faulkner said. 'Take off is 2100 hours tomorrow night.'

Sunday, 27th December

At 1800 hours Faulkner held his final briefing. The men were assembled in the largest of the barrack rooms. There was a hum of tension in the air and the R.S.M. barked for silence as Faulkner entered.

'We're going in tonight,' Faulkner said. 'An aircraft's picking us up at Lumbo. Take off at 2100 hours.' He turned and took the covers from the maps pinned against the walls. 'Now this is what we're going to do . . .'

'Crikey,' a man whispered to his mate. 'I thought we were going to attack Rhodesia.'

'Just be bloody glad you're not,' Peter Coetzee said softly from behind.

Janders took over the briefing to explain the details. He positioned himself before a large scale map of Albertville. 'As you know,' he said, 'the timing's been moved forward. Limbani is being delivered to the military barracks this evening and Ndofa is believed to be flying down at first light tomorrow – at which time Limbani will be executed. We have just received a signal that a group of Simbas have moved into the area. Their numbers are estimated to be in the region of two to three hundred men – and they have been billeted in the centre of town. Here,' he indicated the site on the map. 'In the old prison. Their presence is not altogether unusual, as we know that when General Ndofa moves into an area, he likes to keep a balance of power between the army and his paramilitary police, to avoid the possibility of a coup.

This large body of men presents a danger to us. But we have studied the problem and altered our plans accordingly.' He turned to the map and indicated with a ruler. 'The positions of the airport. The military barracks and the prison resemble a triangle with the airport at the apex and the barracks and the prison forming the base line. They are all connected by a link road, so that we now intend to blow the armoury and the munitions dump as we leave the barracks. The detonations, we believe, will cause the Simbas to panic and come hotfoot to the aid of the garrison – this will draw them off us and leave us a clear run to the airport without fear of an attack on our flank.

'The success of this operation depends on speed and surprise. The timing is all important. You must keep to your schedules. You must move in and out of your positions to the minute. If things go well, we'll be on the ground for less than three hours. But if they go wrong, we will have very little chance of getting out of there alive.'

The briefing was over and Faulkner stood before his men, hardly able to keep the excitement from his face. The days of preparing had created a bond between them, as though they had been together a long time – and he had grown to care for them. 'It's a good plan,' he told them. 'Nothing will go wrong. Good luck,' he said quietly. 'The trucks are waiting outside.'

The convoy rumbled through the narrow streets. The island seemed deserted, as though its people had been warned to stay indoors. They crossed the causeway, drove onto the strip and backed against the huge Lockheed Hercules that loomed out of the night, seeming to dominate the tiny airstrip. The plane had brought extra fuel with it and the ground crew were pumping it into the tanks. There was a roll call and yet another equipment check by the tireless R.S.M. as the men waited to board.

Pereira led Faulkner to one side. 'I have a message to pass on to you which I very much regret,' he said and his face was creased with worry. 'If all goes well, you are expected to recross our borders by not later than eight o'clock tomorrow morning. If you have not crossed by that time, then I'm afraid that our borders will be closed to you and your men. I'm very sorry to have to tell you this, but you understand, I have to pass on the message.'

'What exactly do you mean when you say that you are closing your borders?' Faulkner asked coldly.

'It means that if you try to cross by air after that time, you will be shot down. If you try to cross on foot, our border patrols will be alerted to stop you. You understand that, if you fail, in the eyes of the world we must be blameless.'

The refuelling was finished and the men were filing on board.

'We'll be back before eight,' Faulkner said. Abruptly he turned away and joined his men.

'Good luck,' Pereira called after him. 'I will pray for your safe return.'

Faulkner joined Janders in the starboard doorway. A few wistful clouds were drawn up across the sky like waves. And between them rode a huge yellow moon like a ship on a gentle sea.

'That's a bad moon rising for us,' Janders said softly. 'It'll light us coming down.'

'Pray for cloud over the Congo tonight,' Faulkner answered.

The doors closed and one by one the four huge Allison engines kicked into life. The cabin was brightly lit. There were no windows and the shell was thickly padded. The men were ready, dressed in dark jungle-green camouflage with blackened faces. The aeroplane taxied to the very end of the strip.

'We've had it,' Taffy Williams whispered. 'This dirty great monster will never get out of here.'

'Shut up, will you?' Tosh Donaldson whispered nervously. 'It landed, didn't it?'

'That's before we got on, boyo.'

The engines reached a screaming pitch. The Hercules lurched forward on its brakes as the propellers bit into the air. Then suddenly it was running, accelerating hard across the sand. The men confined in the cabin waited nervously, concentrating on the noise of the wheels pounding against the ridges of the strip. The aeroplane jolted as though it had struck a large bump. Then they felt it heave itself into the air and begin to climb.

A young pilot in a heavy fur-lined flying jacket and a cap pulled rakishly over his head made his way through the fuselage. 'Faulkner?' he asked. The R.S.M. pointed further down the cabin.

'Colonel Faulkner?' the pilot asked. Faulkner nodded. 'You're acting as your own jump masters,' the pilot confirmed.

'Yes,' Faulkner answered briefly. He had other things on his mind.

'We've rigged up jump lights over the doors. There's a telephone connection to the flight deck by the starboard door. The light will come on when the skipper wants to talk to you. He'll let you know when we're half an hour out of the dropping zone. Okay. Is there anything else?'

'Yes. Are we on time?'

'There's a strong head wind, but we're doing all right. Are your men comfortable? I'm afraid that we haven't got anything for them.'

'They're all right. I'd like to talk to the captain.'

'I'll get the skipper to give you a buzz when he's free. You just follow your nose up to the flight deck.' The young pilot moved back down the aisle.

He stopped. 'Hey, Shaun,' he said delightedly. 'What are you doing here? Last I heard, you were a gigolo in London.'

Shaun looked up. 'Jerry,' he said miserably. 'I wish I knew. What are you still doing in this outfit anyway?'

'I tried an airline, but it was like flying a bus route. Besides, I'm making a packet flying for Malloy. You must be our man in the control tower – have you studied the layout of the airport?'

Shaun nodded.

'Then you'll know it's a bastard of a place to land in. I'll be coming in very low over the lake. There'll probably be cloud, so watch for my lights. I'm relying on you to talk me down safely. For God's sake, don't fly me into one of those mountains.'

'I'll get you down,' Shaun said.

'I know you will,' Jerry answered reassuringly. 'I'm the only chance you've got of getting out of there. I'll just get your Colonel through first, then come up to the flight deck, we've got some coffee up there. You ever flown one of these jobs before?'

'Never. Are they as good as they say?'

'Better. For all their size, they handle like a mini and with J.A.T.O. rockets attached, they'll take off in under two hundred yards. I'll get the skipper's okay.'

'Do I know him?'

'No. He was with Lufthansa. Good pilot though. He won't mind. There's plenty of room up there.' Jerry looked at Shaun reflectively for a moment. 'For a man who swore when he left the outfit that he'd never risk his neck again, you do the strangest things,' he said. Then he made his way up to the flight deck.

Half an hour before reaching the dropping zone, the cabin lights were dimmed to allow the men's eyes to become accustomed to the dark. The doors were swung inwards and fastened into position. The cabin filled with the noise of the engines and the slip stream. Those nearest the opening shrank back from the empty darkness outside.

The men were all awake now and tension began to build. Some were silent – insular – their fear contained within them. Others told jokes and laughed too loudly. Jeremy wondered who'd miss him. He tried to count and was shocked at an honest answer. Some men prayed, Janders amongst them.

'Oh God,' he whispered into his beard. 'Before you sits a hypocrite, because you know that you only hear from me when I'm in trouble. Well tonight, Lord, I'm scareder than I've ever been. Maybe I'm getting old, Lord, but I need you badly now, so stay with me a while.'

Shaun was feeling sick. He had never jumped before. It was bad enough in daylight when you could at least see the sky and the earth, but to launch yourself into the rushing darkness seemed unnatural to man. His mind wandered back to the beach, saw Gabby walking away. She could at least have turned back, waved or something. She had never actually told him that she loved him.

Peter was staring into space, his face immobile, a great lonely sadness covering him. He thought of the ranch in Rhodesia he would buy with the money. He saw it after the rains with the tall grass moving in the wind and the cattle roaming through the stunted Mopani trees, their coats mottled in the sunlight. He saw himself returning to the farm house at the end of the day – but it, too, was empty. He was a man with a lot of love in him and he needed someone to give it to.

Beside him sat Jock McTaggart with his red hair and hook nose. He had become number two in Peter's commando. The big raw-boned man was a professional of the old school – an ex-N.C.O. of the Black Watch. During training, the two of them had worked well together and without the need for words a bond of friendship had grown between them. He caught Peter's eye and he grinned, his hot blood rising at the prospect of action.

Peter smiled in answer and then withdrew inside himself again. There had been a girl once – it seemed like long ago. Peter had wanted to marry her, but she turned him down. He took her out from the darkness of his mind and walked with her a while.

Fifteen minutes from the dropping zone. The men were darkening their faces. Faulkner rose and stood in the aisle.

'Prepare for action,' he shouted.

The aeroplane was losing height. The men attached their containers to the lower D string of their parachute harness, tightened the restraining straps around their knees.

Ten minutes from the dropping zone. Faulkner shouted, 'Stick up, hook up.'

Each man took his strop and attached the hook to one of the three cables that ran down the ceiling of the fuselage.

Faulkner gave the command, 'Check equipment.' Each man checked that the man in front of him's hook was secure, that his container was properly fastened and that his parachute harness was secure. The R.S.M. moved quickly between the lines, checking that the men had fastened their

176

strops to the right cables. He tugged at the hooks of the last two men in the sticks, ran quickly over their equipment, then tapped one of them on the back.

They began to tell off by number. 'Fifty, okay.' 'Forty-nine, okay.' 'Forty-eight, okay.' 'Forty-seven, okay.' Everything inside the fuselage seemed to rattle. They were dropping through cloud and, for a moment, the openings were white. It was bitterly cold. Even so, beneath their camouflage, the men were sweating, their back and legs aching from their harnesses and the weight of their equipment.

'One, okay,' Janders shouted. The men gave a shuffle step forward towards the opening, the junior officers first, followed by the N.C.O.s; the R.S.M., Janders and Faulkner took up their positions by the opening, watching the lights. No one spoke. The noise was deafening. The dropping aeroplane left their stomachs behind.

The aeroplane levelled out. There came the noise of the engines being throttled back. Clouds of sparks passed in the slip stream.

'Oh, my God,' Shaun thought wildly, 'my parachute will catch fire.'

The red light came on. The dispatchers shouted, 'Stand in the door.' Shaun looked pleadingly at the R.S.M. who did not notice him. He was watching the lights.

Jeremy hung in the doorway, his hands clutching the sides, his head and shoulders in the rushing night, a shield protecting him from the immediate slip stream. The aeroplane seemed to hang in the air.

The green light blinked on. The dispatchers gave their men a clout on the shoulders and shouted, 'Go.' The men launched themselves into space. Shaun faltered. 'No ways,' he thought, trying to see into the night, 'am I going out there.' A fist clouted him again. He jumped wildly into the dark, trying to avoid the sparks.

Other men filled the doorways, then jumped into the night. They moved fast, jumping at intervals of about one-and-a-half seconds between each man, the dispatchers screaming, 'Go. Go. Go,' the pilot throttling back as the aeroplane lightened.

The slip stream hit Peter with a physical thump. He felt himself hurled through the air as his static line paid out. A second later it took. There came a tremendous slowing jerk across his torso. He looked up with relief to see the dark canopy of the parachute opening above him. He pulled the quick release ring and the container dropped on a line and swung fifteen feet below him.

Shaun made a bad exit. He was dropping like a stone, head first, when the slip stream hit him. He began to spin. The static line paid out. The parachute opened, the jerk taking him across his shoulders. He righted suddenly, feeling his legs fall below him. He looked up. He was falling too fast. Above him he could see that his rigging lines had crossed the canopy, causing it to look like a woman's brassière, the air spilling out, he began to fall faster.

From somewhere near, he heard a man's voice screaming at him hoarsely. He did not dare look round. He opened his mouth, but all that came out was a moan of terror. He was dropping faster, leaving the voice behind. He caught the words, 'Pull chute'. His brain seemed paralysed. He could not think what they meant. Somewhere below, the ground was rushing up out of the dark to meet him.

Suddenly he knew. His fingers tore at his reserve parachute release. 'Oh, God,' he prayed as it billowed out in front of him. 'Don't let it tangle with the other one or I'll drop like a stone.'

There came another jerk, slowing his descent as the reserve took. He looked up praying. The canopy swelled clear of the main chute. Instinct told him that he was still dropping too fast. He released his container and let it drop, hoping that there was no one below. His rate of descent slowed.

The last three men jumped. The cabin looked strangely empty. The young pilot was standing by the telephone. Faulkner hooked up his strop, tested it, grinned at Janders and the R.S.M., who were doing the same, and then jumped.

A few seconds later, Faulkner was floating easily down. He heard the noise of the aeroplane engines deepen as it began to climb away. The navigation lights came on and the pilot dipped his wings in salute before disappearing into the darkness.

Faulkner felt good. Better than he had felt in a long while. He felt free, drifting in space between the sky and the earth, as though apart from the strictures of society that tied him down and trapped his will in the monotony of everyday living. He heard the wind hum in the rigging. Above him the moon glowed through a cloud, lighting its edges into luminous figures and the stars were bright and clear. It was with regret that he touched the ground.

CHAPTER SIXTEEN

0100 hours. Monday, 28th December

PETER gathered his commando, then he sought out Shaun who was seated on the ground, his head in his hands.

'This yours?' he demanded, throwing the container at him. Shaun nodded without looking up. 'You bastard,' Peter whispered furiously. 'You bloody nearly brained me with it.'

Shaun looked up. He was still trembling. 'Nothing,' he said firmly, 'will ever get me to do that again.'

'I thought all you bloody pilots knew how to jump.'

'We know better. You don't catch us up there without a pair of wings with bloody great engines attached.'

Jeremy came up to Peter. 'Leave him alone,' he said. 'He nearly bought it up there.'

Dark shapes were coming in from all around the landing area. It was quiet, there were no lights in the surrounding hills. The men quickly unpacked their containers, checked their equipment and formed into their commandos.

A three-quarter moon scudded between regiments of dark cloud drawn up against the sky, filling the patches and flooding the bush in bursts of pale yellow light. Faulkner moved up.

'Number one commando all present and correct, sir,' the R.S.M. reported quietly.

'Number two commando all present and correct,' Janders said. It was a habit with him. He called no man sir.

'Number three commando all present and correct, sir,' Jeremy said.

The moon passed behind a barrier of cloud and the darkness rushed in. The men heaved a sigh of relief.

'Number four commando all present and correct, sir,' Peter said.

'Number five commando all present and correct, sir,' Shaun reported.

'I hear you had a rough drop,' Faulkner said. 'You all right now?'

'Yes, sir.' The ground had never felt so good beneath Shaun's feet.

'All right, officers to me. The rest of you break. Bury your chutes and containers. I want the job done well. Carry on, R.S.M.'

The officers gathered around Faulkner.

'Right, we're twelve minutes behind schedule. Set your watches by mine. Are you ready? In ten seconds, the time will be 0100 hours and twelve minutes. Six, five, four . . .

'Everybody got it? Good. We'll let you know when we've got Limbani. Good luck, gentlemen. I'd like to think that God was with us. Anyway, I'm sure that he can't disapprove too much.'

Shaun's and Jeremy's commandos filed out first. Five minutes later the remaining commandos followed. Two men in each of these commandos humped two seventeen-pound plastic cylinders of cyanide gas on their backs. The other men helped out with their kit. Peter slung his rifle over his back. He carried an evil-looking cross-bow in his arms. The quarrels hung in a leather quiver by his side.

They were on the north side of Albertville, coming in through the hills towards the lake, moving fast in single file, following the tracks where they could. As they drew nearer to the town, they began to skirt stunted mealie lands, Kaffir dogs from dark kraals in the valleys below barked thinly in the night.

They did not slacken their pace. It was a country in which few people ventured out after dark for fear of drunken Simbas. The track dropped sharply. They followed it down to a narrow dirt road. Faulkner stopped to check his map. The men silently took up covering positions on either side. Faulkner glanced at his watch. They were making up time. The narrow dirt road formed one side of a triangle and led to the military barracks. The track on the other side of the triangle led to the airport. It was as though the mercenaries had dropped into the centre of the triangle and the base line led between the barracks and the airport.

Before independence these had been fairly good roads but, in the confusion that reigned afterwards, they were neglected. In an area that experiences a hundred and fifteen inches of rain a year, a neglected road soon becomes a pot-holed track.

The mercenaries fanned out on either side of the road, the men on point well forward of the rest. Now the moon was almost continually behind cloud and, with the stars obscured, the night became dark. Lush vegetation grew over the track and brushed against the men as they passed.

For the men on the eastern apex, it had begun to rain. Softly at first, then harder and harder until great drops beat against their clothes. Shaun looked up anxiously, trying to judge the visibility. Albertville Airport was going to be hard enough to land in anyway, especially if they looked after their runways as they did their roads. If the weather closed in . . .

A message was whispered down the line from the point. Before it reached Faulkner, he caught the distant sound of a lorry engine grinding through the potholes. The rain was just reaching them, beating lightly on their helmets, making the road slippery underfoot. A wind followed sighing in the dark through the trees like a river rushing towards them.

The lights from the lorry glowed briefly against the low scudding cloud. The men vanished into the darkness on either side of the road. Faulkner watched the lorry draw near, its lights dipping and rising as it fought its way through the potholes.

The wind struck and the rain beat down. The lorry had drawn almost level, sliding sideways as the wheels churned up the mud. In the reflected light, Faulkner saw the camouflage paint of an army lorry. 'Don't let it get stuck here,' he pleaded silently. The driver changed down a gear and tried to accelerate out of a skid. He lost control. The truck struck the bank, tried to climb it, then lurched back into the ditch, settling into the mud.

The mercenaries waited while the driver gunned the engine, but the wheels buried themselves. The R.S.M. found his hands clutching an imaginary steering wheel, willing the vehicle out of the ditch.

The A.N.C. driver got out, walked around the truck, stumbling and cursing in the rain and the dark. Angrily he kicked one of the tyres. Faulkner glanced at his watch for the third time. The storm was passing and the rain easing. A dim glow of the moon penetrated the thinning cloud. They could try to detour the truck through the bush, but they would make a hell of a noise and, in the dark, men could get lost.

The driver shouted something to a person in the cab. A brief argument followed. The driver re-entered the cab wound up the window amd switched off the lights.

The R.S.M. squirmed forward on his belly towards Faulkner. He made a cutting motion across his throat. Faulkner shook his head and indicated that he was to check the back of the lorry.

Peter was lying on the other side of Faulkner. He reached

across and touched the R.S.M.'s shoulder, telling him to wait. Then, followed by McTaggart, the two big men moved silently onto the road. They waited, listening for movement, by the canvas-covered tail of the truck. Then McTaggart covered Peter as he raised a corner of the canvas flap. Peter appeared a moment later and indicated that the back was clear. The windows of the cab were steamed up. It looked as though the men inside had settled down for the night. The two mercenaries took up positions by either cab door. An untoward movement by the men inside would have brought them a sudden death. The mercenaries filed silently past. Peter and McTaggart broke away from the truck and followed behind.

The rain left as suddenly as it had come. Thunder rumbled in the distance. Lightning scarred the sky and flashed into the nearby hills. Janders had walked this road before in much the same weather, but many years ago – when Limbani had been fighting for his country's life during the wars that followed the Congo's Independence. Ndofa was then Limbani's trusted commander-in-chief and Janders and Faulkner had organized their army. Ghosts of long-dead companions of that time walked with Janders. The prospect of action no longer excited him for now he was wet and his bones ached. But without the clouding emotion of excitement, his brain worked like a computer.

Faulkner glanced at his watch again, conning the luminous dial with his hand. They were well behind schedule. The men were pushing on as hard as they could, sweating under the weight of their equipment. With the warm moist air buffeting against the men's faces, their feet slipping and sliding on the wet, mud-packed road, muttered curses came from a man who stumbled knee-deep in slime into a pothole. Soft laughter lifted in the air from the others. The N.C.O.s moved through the men silencing them and urging them on.

Faulkner sent word down the line for Peter. He came up, sure on his feet like a great cat silently materializing out of the night.

'Any idea what that truck was doing?' Faulkner asked.

'I don't know. The back was filled with monkey nuts. You want some?' He had filled his pockets.

'They were probably working some kind of fiddle, sir,' the R.S.M. said, 'using army transport.'

Faulkner checked his watch again. By now the Hercules should be landing at Burundi. The points rounded a sharp corner. Steep hills rose on either side of them. The road had been hacked through a cutting, the untended banks crumbling on either side. Faulkner made a note of another ambush site. He was a man who could remember terrain and map it in his mind. A few thousand feet above them a wind was breaking up the clouds. The light from the moon stuttered between them, silhouetting the men in flashes of light.

A message came down from the point. They were nearing the barracks. Faulkner slowed the men. On the left a narrow track led steeply up to a small plateau on which, in the cooler air and commanding a view of the lake, Faulkner could dimly make out the small, white, darkened houses of the senior officers who lived apart from the main barracks.

On the left, a narrow, rocky footpath wound down to a maze of huts and tin shanties where the soldiers' wives and camp followers lived. Starving dogs barked at their passing. There was a commotion in the front and there came the sound of drumming hooves. The word came down the line – a herd of goats grazing at the side of the road. The dogs barked louder. The points tried to pass the goats, but they ran in front, stopping every few yards to look back curiously, as though enjoying the game.

'If we don't wake up everybody this side of Sunday, they

deserve what's coming to them,' Janders muttered help-lessly.

Faulkner halted the column and checked his map. They should now be within a few hundred yards of the barracks. The way they were going, the goats would announce them at the main gate. The men lay against the banks, on either side of the road.

'We've found the telephone lines, sir,' an N.C.O.'s voice came out of the dark.

'Cut them,' Faulkner ordered. He sent a message on to the two points men to scout forward.

A man's voice rose up from the shanties below. He drew the words out so that they would carry and his voice rose thinly.

'What's he saying?' Faulkner demanded.

Peter listened for a moment. 'There's a goat guard up here somewhere,' he answered. 'Probably asleep.'

'Only a Congolese could sleep through this,' Faulkner muttered. 'Find him.'

The voice was persistent. Peter's commando fanned out searching for the goat guard. Eventually, from far ahead, a sleepy voice answered. Faulkner called Peter in.

'Leave it,' he ordered. 'The points will get him. What's he saying?'

'Everything's okay,' Peter translated.

The man below cursed the dogs. For a moment, Faulkner was tempted to send a commando up to the officers' quarters. It would have made a nice, clean sweep. He decided against it. A few officers would constitute little threat to their flank and he made it a rule never to deviate from the main plan once it was in operation.

The points reported back. The target was four hundred yards ahead, surrounded by a hundred-yard killing ground on which the goats now grazed. The barracks were situated within a small depression on fairly flat ground. The killing area extended evenly up the shallow sides of the depression, fading out into thick bush. They had used the area constantly for grazing. The grass was too short for a man to crawl through. The points had found goat tracks leading through the thick bush from the road and on to the killing ground. The goat guard was dead.

Faulkner glanced at his watch. They were now seventeen minutes behind schedule. Soon the aeroplane would be leaving Burundi. The points led the column through the tracks. The bush was high and so dense that without the tracks to follow the men would have had to cut their way through. The tracks, worn into channels by the rain, led over a hill and into the depression. The cover was good. The points gave a signal. The men silently fanned out, sank on their haunches and waited.

Peter and Faulkner moved forward to the edge of the killing ground. The area was littered with boulders, twisted trees and elephant grass growing between. Janders made radio contact with the rear guard, who had been left to cover the road. It was clear and quiet.

CHAPTER SEVENTEEN

0200 hours. Monday, 28th December

FAULKNER scanned the area below, then handed Peter his night glasses. The barracks consisted of a small area of long, dark, wooden Nissen huts with corrugated iron roofs. They covered, at right angles, three sides of a square, part of which was a concrete parade ground. The armoury, a low concrete building with its own wire guard, was situated in the far corner. The guard house was a brick building situated to one side of the main gates. On the other side was a single, smaller Nissen hut that served as the camp office.

The whole area was surrounded by a ten-foot heavy mesh perimeter fence, capped with two feet of slanted barbed wire. From within the barracks, banks of raised, fixed lights were supposed to illuminate the perimeter wire and the immediately surrounding area, but several of the lights had fused, leaving patches of shadow.

Situated at three intervals along the north and south side of the wire were small turret-like guard posts. They rose on narrow stilts some thirty feet above the ground, supporting an open platform protected by two thick rails with a small thatched roof above. The only access was from within the wire and by a linked chain of ten-foot ladders.

The mercenaries were on the north side of the barracks. The south side faced towards the town several miles distant. Peter studied the guard turrets carefully. He ascertained that only three of the turrets were manned, two on the east and west ends of the north side and one overlooking the east perimeter on the south side. There would also be sentries on the main gates by the guard room. The two sentries guarding the eastern perimeter appeared to be asleep. The sentry guarding the north and western perimeter was awake, leaning against one of the roof posts smoking a cigarette. He would have to be the first one.

Peter lowered the binoculars. He nodded to Faulkner then gave a low whistle. McTaggart came up carrying the cross-bow. Faulkner picked up the binoculars and scanned the barracks again. There was no movement within the wire.

'Which are you going to hit first?' Faulkner asked.

'North-west,' Peter answered.

'Okay. After that hit north-east. We'll go in through the shadow under the centre guard tower.' Faulkner looked at his watch. 'We're way behind time. I can give you twelve minutes. After that we'll just have to blast our way in.'

Peter nodded in answer. He handed his rifle to McTaggart to carry and took the cross-bow. They moved back and then along the perimeter wire into position. When they were level with the sentry, Peter sank onto his haunches in the bush. The cross-bow was shaped like a sawn-off double barrelled shot-gun, with a steel-sprung bow across the barrel. He fitted in the loader shaped like a pickaxe handle and began to crank the cord back. The pressure required to load the bow was between two hundred and forty and two hundred and fifty pounds. The loader gave a six to one advantage. The whole operation took about four seconds.

From the quiver at his waist, Peter selected a short quarrel. He checked the flights and the true of the shaft. Then carefully he began to unwind a khaki bandage covering the tip. The quarrel was made of polished hard wood. The tip was blunted and slightly split into four quarters, hollowed out to contain a small glass phial of concentrated cyanide.

Without seeming to hurry, he fitted the quarrel carefully into the prod, checked the calibrations of the sights then, lifting the cross-bow, he waited for the moon. He was slightly below the level of the platform and some hundred and five yards away.

McTaggart looked up. The moon glowed from behind a cloud, racing for a gap. He began to count, four, three, two one. Peter pulled the stock tightly into his shoulders. He would have about ten seconds of light. He stood up, placing his feet to balance himself against the recoil. The light flooded through, almost as bright as daylight. The sentry saw Peter as he released the quarrel. There came a dull thump and the dark shaft crossed the air.

The sentry had time only to open his mouth in a soundless scream before the quarrel took him in the chest, smashing through his ribs and bursting inside his body. He was picked up and thrown against the far guard rail. But he was dead before he hit it.

Peter did not wait. As the quarrel struck, he was moving fast towards the other end of the perimeter fence. The mercenaries were forming up as he passed.

Janders called up the other commandos at the airport on the radio.

'How's it?' Shaun's voice came over the air. He sounded relaxed. The radio squawked when he was told that they were only just beginning to move in.

'What's it like your end?' Janders asked.

'Dead quiet,' came the answer. 'We're in position and ready to go. Jeremy's found a couple of sentries by the wire halfway down the field, but they can be dead any time. The rest are hanging out in the airport building. Hey, is the sky clearing your end?'

'Yes,' Janders said. 'Can the plane get in okay?'

'If you get a move on. It's going to cloud again soon.'

'We're moving in now. Wait till you hear from me before you go in.'

'Okay.'

Janders called up the rear guard. It was clear and quiet.

Peter unwrapped the tip of the second quarrel and fitted it into the prod. The sentry appeared to be curled up on the floor of the platform. He could not see him clearly enough to get a shot at him. He would have to move in closer. He fitted an infra-red telescopic sight to the cross-bow. It was blurred to useless at a range of over eighty yards.

Faulkner led the first five men across the killing ground. They moved low and fast, hurling themselves down beside the wire. Faulkner waited until his breath came easily, then he tested the wire for current. There was none. A trip wire alarm system had long since rotted with neglect. He signalled two of the men forward. They moved against the fence with long handled wire clippers.

The sentry on the south-eastern perimeter turret stirred. Janders must have been watching through the night glasses and signalled, for work on the wire stopped.

Peter ran on until he was in line with the tower. Then he moved out at right angles across the open killing ground. McTaggart covered the north-eastern tower. The sentry had propped his rifle against the top guard rail and was sleepily relieving himself over the side.

When he was within sixty yards, Peter stopped and braced himself. There was no moon and he blended with the dark bush behind. Through the infra-red sight, everything took on a ghostly faded greenish effect. The figure of the kneeling sentry became silhouetted like a frame from a film negative. The quarrel left the cross-bow with a dull thud, streaked through the air, glanced off the lower guard rail and disintegrated in the sentry's stomach. The sentry was thrown onto his back, his rifle falling across him. No other sound came.

The men began work on the wire again. Peter moved back to the north-eastern turret. He had heard that many of the A.N.C. were on dagga. This sentry must have been one of the worst offenders. He still had not moved. The wire was open and the first men through. The remaining mercenaries were crossing the killing ground in batches of five.

The dark shape of a man began to climb the ladders leading to the platform. Peter glanced round. McTaggart was behind him. He estimated the distance between his new position and the tower, then carefully focused the sights. He had been lucky the last time. If this sentry was able to give the alarm, a lot of the mercenaries would die.

The climbing man was nearing the top, the light frame of the tower swaying under his weight. Suddenly there came the noise of a rifle scraping aginst the wooden floor of the turret. The climbing figure froze against the top ladder. Peter raised the cross-bow. Men were still moving under the wire, pulling through the containers of gas, oblivious to what was happening to one side of them. The silhouette of the sentry rose above the guard rail. Any second now he'd turn and see the men below. Peter tried to zero him into the crossed hairs of the sight. Sweat stung in his eyes, clouding his vision. The cross-bow seemed heavy in his hands. The man below, thinking that the sentry had just stirred in his sleep, began to climb again.

The sentry leaned down. Peter wiped his eyes. He rose again, throwing open the trap door. Peter sighted the cross-bow. He loosed the quarrel and prayed while it was in flight. The sentry saw the man below, heard the thud from the cross-bow. Then he died.

By now most of the men were through the wire, moving

behind the lights into the shadow of the parade ground towards the Nissen huts. Peter, followed by McTaggart, ran along the killing ground towards the western boundary and the main gates. It was raining again and, together with sweat, it matted their hair and ran down their faces.

The men within the barracks broke into sections and took up positions at either end of each of the three long Nissen huts. The men who were to enter donned gas masks attached by an expansile tube to respirators on their chests. They wore gloves and light, semi-transparent polythene protective clothing. In the pale light they looked grotesque. The only distinguishing human factor was the menace of their rifles. The R.S.M., followed by two men, headed for the armoury.

By the main gates, two sentries dozed in their boxes. The lights from the nearby guard room were blazing. From inside came the sounds of men drinking. Peter laid down his crossbow, drew his knife, nodded to McTaggart to take the other one and moved in.

The Nissen huts were divided into sections by thin plywood partitions. Each major section slept a hundred men in three rows of cots, twenty-four inches apart. The N.C.O.s slept near the doors in the main section. Their officers slept beyond the partition in small cubicles. A passage led through these into the next major section.

The windows were closed and the air inside was foul. Mercenary guards took up positions two at each end and two in the middle. They carried low velocity weapons with silencers fitted. Attached to their helmets and lowered over their eyes were infra-red sights. By moving their heads, they could throw the light up and down the rows of cots checking for movement. Many of the cots were empty. Greenish shadows with cylinders on their backs began to move slowly through the hut. There came a low hiss of escaping gas.

The sentries died silently in their boxes. The main gates

were locked, but there was a small side gate for the guard. It was open. Peter and McTaggart slipped through. Then they waited by the guard room door.

The gas passed from the cylinders through a tube with a nozzle at the end, directed into the faces of the sleeping men. Cyanide gas has a bitter almond smell and no colour, bringing death almost instantly at a hundred parts to a million in air. The gas attacks the respiratory system. The lips go blue and, after a brief unconscious spasm, death is painless. Few of the men woke up. Those that did died before their eyes grew accustomed to the dark.

The mercenaries moved steadily through the hut as they had been trained, on through the partition and into the officers' cubicles, then on again into the next major section. A few of the men threw themselves off their cots when the gas tore at their lungs. Others choked out a brief cry.

The R.S.M. waited impatiently while his men cut through the armoury wire, then he wriggled through whispering to them to wait while he looked for the guard. He moved silently around the building. There were two guards at the back awake and seemingly alert. One of them was grinding the handle of a field telephone attached to the wall. They were talking excitedly to each other in low voices.

The R.S.M. fitted a silencer to the barrel of his pistol, checked it, then raised the Tokarev and, using his left arm as a rest, he pulled the trigger.

Peter heard the jangle of a telephone bell in the guard room. It rang several times. There came a muttered curse, then the scrape of a chair as someone got up to answer it. As he did so, the telephone stopped ringing. The man inside cursed it again and resumed his seat.

The two other men crawled through the wire and joined the R.S.M. They searched the dead guards for the armoury keys on the unlikely chance that they might be carrying them. There were no keys. They laid charges against the steel doors and then they waited.

'It's going well,' Janders reported. 'Better than I thought. They're going through the last section now.'

'Not bad for a bunch of old men and youngsters,' Faulkner replied.

'Who was it who said of the A.N.C. that they were many things but never soldiers?' Janders snorted. He moved over to the radio. 'I'll call the rear guard in.'

Faulkner whistled up the men of Peter's commando and set off for the guard house. Peter met him.

'We've got troubles,' he said. 'There are Simbas in there. Hard-looking bunch.'

'How many?' Faulkner asked.

'Eight Simbas in the guard room. They're being entertained by the orderly officer and his guard commander. There's a couple of army N.C.O.s in there as well. The grille leading down to the cells is locked.'

'Are they drunk?'

Peter shook his head. 'Drinking, but not drunk. There must be some more down in the cells with Limbani. I saw them pass some beer through the grille. If we go in there blasting, they'll get Limbani before we do.'

'We're in emergency time already. If we get the lights, can you get the keys?'

'No chance. I reckon one of the Simbas is hanging on to them and I don't know which one. How about a shot of gas?'

'Too dangerous. Limbani's got a weak heart. If he gets a whiff of it, he's gone. No, we'll just have to walk in and introduce ourselves. It's worked before. Take it very easy so that we don't scare them into doing something rash.'

The men gathered in the guard room looked up casually as the door opened. The Simbas were seated comfortably in a semi-circle on chairs. Their hosts, including the officers, squatted on the floor. The room was large and bare. A few desks and discarded bottles of beer littered the room. On the north wall hung an enormous portrait of Ndofa in general's uniform looking sternly down. Other bright posters depicting Ndofa leading the nation covered the white-washed walls. Inset into the far wall was a large steel grille which blocked off a stairway down to the cells.

Peter loomed through the doorway closely followed by McTaggart. He was talking softly in Swahili, telling them to be still. Other mercenaries were filing into the room. The Congolese sat as though frozen. Those with their backs exposed to the mercenaries taking their cue from the ones facing. The room was slowly filling with armed white men in dirty camouflage and blackened faces. Peter's rifle trained continuously across them, his voice monotonous and soothing. McTaggart stood beside him grinning hugely. The grin alone did more to terrify the Simbas than all the rifles pointed at them.

In a matter of seconds, there were twelve mercenaries within the guard room. The look of bewilderment on the faces of the Congolese changed to one of horror. One large Simba who had been swinging back in his chair when Peter entered toppled over to fall sprawling on the floor.

The spell was broken. Two of the Simbas reached for their weapons. McTaggart let out a low animal growl and they stopped. The tension eased. Peter began to talk again, asking for the keys.

No one moved. A man from the cells called up asking about the silence. The man called again and began to mount the stairs. One of the mercenaries moved over to the grille. He raised his rifle but Faulkner shook his head and looked desperately to Peter.

'Be silent,' Peter called softly, 'the President is on the telephone.'

The man on the stairs stopped dead, then quietly began to descend. Such was the power of Ndofa.

A mercenary held his pistol to the head of the most likely looking Simba while Faulkner searched him. On the third try he found the keys. The Simba, knowing that he would die anyway if he lost Limbani and that the president's method of execution was far more painful, made a grab for the keys. Faulkner snatched them out of his reach and tossed them across the room to Peter. The Simba attacked Faulkner. The mercenary beside him pulled the trigger.

Pandemonium broke out in the guard room as the Simbas broke for their weapons. Peter threw open the grille door and ran down the stairs three at a time. The stairs spiralled sharply towards the bottom. He cannoned off the wall and leapt for the ground. He caught a glimpse of a guard at the bottom step with his rifle raised. The report of the shot in the confined space smashed into his ear drums, then he landed feet first on the guard. They went down in a tangled heap Peter's momentum carrying him on. He rolled forward and rose to his feet. His right leg buckled under his weight and he went down again. The guard was trying to rise. He was badly winded, whistling for breath and his arm hung loosely from his shoulder socket.

McTaggart, who was following closely, tried to shoot the guard from the hip in mid-air and missed, the bullet ricocheting along the passage, narrowly missing Peter. Two more guards ran out from an open cell where they had been resting. McTaggart shot them both, then collided with the unfortunate guard. Their bodies met with a mighty thump. The guard spun off against the wall. McTaggart staggered and then regained his balance. He was screaming with rage and excitement.

Peter was running along the passage dragging his right leg. The injured guard slipped slowly down the wall. The third mercenary to pass shot him twice.

Ten large, steel-grilled cells opened on to one side of the passage with dividing walls between them. The other side was a curved, white-washed, tunnel wall. The cells they passed were empty. The dank air reeked of stale urine and sweat. Peter was nearing the end of the passage. From the last cell he saw a rifle barrel protruding through the grille, trying to reach him. He threw himself down and rolled. The gun began to fire. Bullets hummed in the air above him, ricocheting off the curved walls and on down the passages. The following mercenaries threw themselves down as the bullets screamed madly over their heads.

The man with the rifle was shouting, 'Kill him. Kill him,' to someone else in the cell. McTaggart, crouched against the wall in full view of the guard, was pumping bullets into the cell shoulder high. Peter, using the cover, rolled into the passage, bringing his rifle up as he did so. A shot took the guard, the force of the bullet sending him flying backwards.

An African was lying curled up facing the wall, with his head in his hands, on a cot suspended from the wall by two iron chains. A second guard was trying to point a rifle at his head, but he was shaking so much that he had already missed once and the bullet scarred the wall. Peter fired, the bullets hitting the guard high up in his back. He pitched forward across the African, his rifle flying out of his hands.

McTaggart tried the cell door. It was locked. Peter knelt down and, clasping the ankle of the guard on the floor, began to pull him towards the grille. There came the sound of running footsteps as the other mercenaries came up. One of them was carrying the bunch of keys that Peter had dropped. He tried them in the lock. One fitted and the door swung open.

Peter sank weakly back against the grille, his leg bleeding above the knee. He smiled at McTaggart. 'You silly bugger,' he said fondly. 'Don't you want to live?'

McTaggart shrugged his shoulders. 'Sometimes I forget,' he said. Then he grinned.

Peter became silent. He felt the pain coming.

Faulkner knelt beside Peter. 'You all right?'

Peter nodded, moving his leg. 'Nothing bad.'

'The medical orderly's coming up. He'll have a look at it for you.' Faulkner stood up. 'You earned your pay tonight. Both of you.'

The R.S.M. blew the armoury door at the sound of the first shot. Within the building, there were three more doors. The first opened into a small office, the second to the workshops where the armourers' benches lay neglected and littered with partly assembled weapons. The third door opened into a large chamber, lined with gun racks. At the far end was a heavy steel door leading into a cool room where ammunition and explosives were stored. The men began to place small charges of explosives against the door.

'Easy, easy,' the R.S.M. said nervously. 'Too much and we'll all go up. Here,' he said, pulling one of the men away, 'let me at it. I've forgotten more than you'll ever know.'

The medical orderly knelt beside Peter and loosened a haversack from off his back. The nearest that he had been to the medical profession was assistant to a ship's doctor. Beneath his helmet he wore a ginger toupé. What he lacked in medical knowledge, he made up with compassion and enthusiasm.

'Hello, love,' he said. 'Let's have a look at that poor old leg. If you drop your trousers, I won't have to cut the cloth, will I? Now lie still and I'll just clean it up. There, it's just a flesh wound. No real damage. But keep your weight off it. Limp all you like, ducks. I won't tell a soul.'

'Whity,' Peter said, surveying the neat bandage around his thigh, 'you're as good as a proper doctor.'

Whity flushed with pleasure and gathered up his haversack.

Limbani was semi-conscious, grey with fear and pain. He was wearing a grey canvas shirt and trousers that clung to him as though they had not been off him for months. His wrists and ankles had been manacled and he had been lightly but professionally beaten up.

'Limbani,' Faulkner said. 'Limbani. Do you remember me? It's good to see you again. We're going to get you out.'

Whity bustled forward. 'You poor, poor man,' he said loosening Limbani's shirt. 'What have they done to you? Well, we'll just have to patch you up, won't we? Then we'll get you into a nice warm hospital with crisp, crinkly sheets.'

Limbani muttered something. Whity leaned forward. 'Your pills,' he echoed. 'Don't worry about them, love. I've got some nice ones from London. They gave them to me specially to give to you. Now, you take one of these and it'll do your poor old heart the world of good. My, my,' he clucked sympathetically, 'they have been beastly to poor old you, haven't they? It's a wonder you've survived.'

'Peter, you're responsible for him.' Faulkner said. 'You'd better keep Whity with you. From now on don't let him out of your sight. And for Christ's sake, keep him alive, or we'll have come all this way for nothing. All right, let's move.'

Peter limped into Limbani's cell. 'Right, kaffir,' he said, 'we're going.'

'You be careful with him,' Whity said indignantly. 'He's a very sick man. Here, you'd better carry a packet of these pills as well, just in case. He's got to have one every two hours – on the dot, mind.'

They blew the door of the explosives room and set their charges. The R.S.M. looked around. 'This lot's going to make one hell of a bang,' he said happily. Then he left.

The vehicle park was in the open end of the parade ground. An N.C.O. chose the ones he wanted. The trucks were American and fairly new. They dropped pencil time bombs into the petrol tanks of the others.

'Start up,' the N.C.O. shouted to the drivers. Their lights flashed on. The N.C.O. jumped onto the running board of the first truck. 'All right,' he shouted. 'Move out.'

Janders called up the airport on the radio. Jeremy answered.

'We thought you'd decided to stay for breakfast,' he grumbled.

'We're moving out now,' Janders said. 'We've got Limbani. Take the airport.'

CHAPTER EIGHTEEN

0310 hours. Monday, 28th December

JEREMY crawled over to Shaun. 'They're on their way.'

Shaun was watching the sky. 'They'd better hurry,' he said worriedly.

'They'll be here in thirty minutes. You set?'

'Okay.'

Three men were sent off to dispatch the guard on the bottom perimeter. Shaun and two men made for the small control tower. The rest followed Jeremy.

The wooden door at the base of the control tower was locked and the building deserted. Shaun waited by the door, the two men covering him on either side.

A boom blocked the road with a sentry box to one side. An N.C.O. with a second mercenary appeared from the bush behind the sentry box and the boom opened. Jeremy ran through followed by his men. The N.C.O. threw a chain around the concrete weight at the end of the boom to hold it open. The guard in the sentry box was already dead. They faded back into the bush to wait.

The ground floor of the terminal was empty. A bare, unswept, concrete floor, ticket counters and weigh bays on the far side. A stairway led to the bar and concourse. Their boots beat against the floor. Two men detached themselves from the unit to guard the bottom of the stairs. Jeremy was nearing the top, bounding up three steps at a time. The other mercenaries followed him.

As he reached the top step, Jeremy pulled the pin of a grenade. He swung onto the landing. Someone shouted. The swing doors leading to the bar were wire glazed. He kicked open one side, tossed in his grenade, then threw himself down. There came another startled shout followed by a wild burst of sub-machine-gun fire. The grenade exploded.

A second mercenary ran past, kicked open the door and lobbed in his grenade. Dust and screams were rising from within the bar. The mercenary threw himself down beside Jeremy. The second grenade exploded. The blast was closer, fracturing the glass in the doors until it hung starred to the wire mesh. A third grenade exploded. They went in with their guns flashing through the dust.

Shaun blasted the lock in the control tower and raced up the steps. One of the mercenaries guarded the door. The other followed him. Shaun reached in the dark for where the light switch should be and found it. Dim lights blinked on. The sound of gunfire died in the terminal.

'Fan out and check the building,' Jeremy shouted.

The bar was a shambles of dead and dying men. Suddenly there came a burst of automatic fire from the ground floor, a pause and then the sharp crack of a grenade going off. Jeremy ran down the stairs. Tosh Donaldson was standing over a body.

'Taff bought it,' he said sadly. 'There was a bugger in the lavatory.'

'Have you got him?'

'I lobbed a grenade in after him. The bastard's splattered all over the wall. But Taff ought to have known better, going in like that.'

In the distance came a rolling noise like muffled thunder.

'That must be the barracks going up. Take four men and a bazooka. Get down to the cross roads where you can see them pass on their way to relieve the barracks. Move, man. Move.'

'Are we going to take Taff out with us and put him down proper?'

'You can pick him up on your way back.' Jeremy turned. 'Where's the other N.C.O.?'

'Here, sir.'

'Post your men, then take a strong patrol to the bottom perimeter.'

It was raining again. Faulkner's convoy was moving too slowly, each truck playing follow my leader with the next through the potholes. The sky behind lit up briefly in a weird white glow, then came a torrent of sound as the armoury blew. Faulkner looked at his watch.

'Try and raise the airport,' he ordered.

Jeremy ran up the steps of the control tower. 'How are you doing?' he asked of Shaun. 'Have you made contact with the areoplane?'

'I've only just got the bloody radio working. It's one of those Russian jobs. All the knobs work the wrong way.'

The radio hummed and then spluttered into life. 'Iron Man calling Wild Geese.' It was Jerry's voice. 'Iron Man calling Wild Geese. Come in Wild Geese.'

Shaun picked up the microphone. 'Wild Geese to Iron man. Come in Iron Man. Receiving you strength four. Over.'

'Iron Man to Wild Geese. My God, where have you been? We've been growing old up here. We've got total cloud cover at six thousand feet. What's it like your side?'

'Wild Geese to Iron Man. Visibility here seven hundred yards and closing. You'd better get down fast.'

'Iron Man to Wild Geese. We're beginning our descent over the lake. Over and out.'

A mercenary pounded up the stairs. 'You're wanted on the radio, sir,' he said to Jeremy.

'All right, bring it up here. Hey,' he said to Shaun. 'I think I can hear the plane.'

Shaun shook his head. 'It's a long way out yet.'

The radio came up 'Wild Geese leader to Wild Geese three. Come in please.'

'Wild Geese three to Wild Geese leader, receiving you strength five. Over.' There came a crackle as the microphone was handed to Faulkner.

'Everything go all right?' Faulkner asked. The sounds of the lurching truck came through with his voice.

'One dead, but the airport's secure. We've made contact with the aeroplane. It's coming in now.'

'You'll have to hold it on the ground,' Faulkner said, bracing himself. 'We're having to go slow. We'll be coming in late.'

'How late?'

'Fifteen minutes if the road stays as it is. Hold that plane. Over and out.'

Tosh Donaldson and his commando lay in the bush near the cross roads. He heard the rumble of vehicles rising from the direction of the town. 'Can you hear that bloody plane yet?' he demanded.

''Ere, Tosh,' a mercenary shouted. 'Them bloody trucks. They're turning in here.'

'You,' Tosh shouted. 'Get on the blower and tell them. The rest of you come with me.'

Shaun was on the radio. 'For Christ's sake, Iron man. Hurry up,' he pleaded. 'The cloud's coming down.'

'We're doing our best,' Jerry came back. 'We're in cloud now. It's thicker than pea soup. How many yards have we got now?'

'About five-fifty and closing.'

'Bloody liar. I bet it's more like three hundred and closing. We're liable to run slap into a hill.'

Tosh strapped down the ear muffs from his helmet, picked

up the bazooka and balanced it on his shoulder. 'Load,' he ordered.

The radio by Jeremy crackled into life. They're coming in here,' a voice shouted. 'Masses of the bleeders.'

Jeremy heard clearly the whoosh of a rocket exploding against the leading truck. 'Where are you?' he asked quietly, his heart sinking.

'In a bleeding ditch under a ruddy great tree.'

'No, you fool ... Your position. Which commando are you?'

'I'm with Tosh at the cross roads. There goes another one. Christ those rockets make a mess.'

'Get me the N.C.O.'

'I can't. Tosh is on the bazooka. He's doing all right, too. He's fairly loosing the bloody thing off like a machine gun.'

'Listen, you,' Jeremy's voice was savage. 'If you don't calm down, I'll shoot you myself. I'm sending you reinforcements. Now you get a grip of yourself and then come back and tell me exactly what's happening down there.'

'Wild Geese three to Wild Geese leader. Come in please.'

'I've got you strength five,' Faulkner said, his voice quiet and controlled. 'I heard your last transmission. Hold on. We're moving in as fast as we can. Just hold on.'

'We should be about three miles out now,' Jerry was saying. 'Still can't see the lake.'

'Put all your lights on,' Shaun replied. 'Maybe I can pick up your landing lights.' He searched the eastern sky. 'Nothing yet. Nothing yet.'

Tosh came on the radio. 'They came in soft skinned vehicles. No sign of armour yet,' he reported. 'We've blocked the road. It'll take a tank to get past.'

'Hold them,' Jeremy ordered. 'Reinforcements should be reaching you any second now.'

Shaun picked up the lights. 'Got you,' he shouted. 'Got

you, Iron Man. You're about five hundred feet too high.'

'So would you be if you were up here,' Jerry came back. 'We're coming down now. How does it look?'

'Good; down a bit, down a bit. Level up. You're doing fine.'

'There's a bloody great fire burning down there.'

'Yeah, it's nothing much. Use it as a beacon. Keep it on your starboard wing. Can you see the landing lights? They're weak, generator powered.'

'Not yet, but they'd better be there. The skipper's crapping himself in German.'

Faulkner came on the radio. 'Wild Geese leader to Wild Geese three. We're no more than a couple of minutes out now.'

The trucks were flying from pothole to pothole. Janders silently blessed all American truck builders and prayed that this truck would continue to hold together. Whity cradled Limbani in his arms to soften the shocks.

Tosh came over the radio. 'We're falling back,' he said. 'They are spilling out around us into the bush. About two hundred of them half naked and screaming like buggery. There's some clever bastard directing them.'

'Try and pick him off,' Jeremy shouted. 'Keep them away from the runway. Just hold them for ten minutes, will you? I'm sending you every man I've got.'

The commando unit on the far perimeter came on the radio. 'There's a whole pile of bandits coming through the bush towards us, sir.'

'Hold them,' Jeremy said desperately. 'You'll see Tosh's men coming down towards you. The aeroplane will be over you in a minute. Keep their heads down while it passes.'

'You're doing fine,' Shaun said. 'You must be able to see the lights now.'

'Yes, we've got them, we've got them. We're coming in now. How are you at praying?

'Roll right up to the terminal, will you? Don't wait around on the strip.'

'Hey,' the radio squawked. 'There's someone firing at us.'

'Don't worry. We're taking care of it. Just get in will you?'

Tosh's voice came over the radio. 'We're too thin on the ground. They've broken through. They're on the runway.'

The big plane landed hard and bounced once and then disappeared into a cloud of steam and mud. It emerged a second later and slowed in five hundred yards. 'She's down, she's down,' Shaun yelled excitedly.

'We're coming into the airport now,' Faulkner's voice came over the radio.

The aeroplane swung off the runway and taxied fast towards the tower. 'That was bloody hairy,' Jerry reported. 'Your men ready? The skipper doesn't like it down here.'

A long burst of machine-gun fire came from the end of the runway, winking orange in the dark.

Jeremy seized the microphone. 'Tosh, pick that machine-gun off,' he shouted.

Suddenly the big plane was moving back onto the runway. It's engines revved to a screaming pitch. A burst of flame spouted from the J.A.T.O. rockets under the wings. The aeroplane leaped forward, ran for a hundred and fifty yards, accelerating at an amazing speed, then it was up and airborne.

'You bastards,' Shaun shouted into the microphone. 'You bastards, come back.'

The aeroplane rose steeply and disappeared from view. All that was left above the gunfire was the drone of its engines receding into the night.

Jerry's voice came briefly over the radio. 'Sorry,' he said. 'Orders. Good luck to you, Shaun. Over and out.'

Faulkner arrived in the control tower. Shaun was pleading with a dead microphone.

Jeremy was almost hysterical. 'We're stuffed now,' he yelled.

Faulkner ignored him. His features were cold and emotionless. He took the situation in. Then he gave his orders quietly. Some of the men were sent to the terminal. Others were positioned on either side and covering the road. 'Call your men in,' he ordered Jeremy. 'Cover them. This place is too exposed to hold for long.'

Faulkner motioned Janders to follow him. They walked into a small operations room. Faulkner closed the door and leant against it. He was trembling. 'Oh, Christ,' he whispered. 'I thought that we had it in the bag.'

Janders drew up a chair and sat astride it. His eyes red-rimmed and tired. 'Ndofa's out there,' he answered. 'No one else could have got the Simbas out that quick or deployed them over the runway. If it wasn't for him, it would have been a fair gamble.'

Both men were silent. A dim overhead light swung gently over a matchwood table. Outside the mercenaries were knocking the glass out of the control tower window, using it as a fire base. The night was filled with the sound of gunfire . . .

CHAPTER NINETEEN

0340 hours. Monday, 28th December

THERE came a knock on the operations room door. Faulkner pulled himself together.

The R.S.M. reported. 'The men are nearly in now, sir. I don't know the losses yet. The Simbas are on the airfield, but we can hold them all right from here unless they bring up something heavy.'

'Didn't we pass some petrol pumps by the terminal car park as we came in?' Faulkner queried. The R.S.M. nodded. 'Fill up the trucks and load on all the spare fuel you can. Let me know when you're ready.'

'Very good, sir,' the R.S.M. saluted.

'Oh, and send Chandos in.'

Jeremy entered. Faulkner spread a map over the table. He de-briefed Jeremy. 'All right, leave us,' he said. He turned back and studied the map.

'North,' Janders said, 'like we planned. It's got to be north. Maybe Matherson can buy us out of Burundi.' He leaned forward. 'Maybe if we got our hands on the Albertville Ferry.'

Faulkner shook his head. 'We keep off the lake,' he said decisively. 'Without air cover, Ndofa's Cubans will pick us off like sitting ducks. The north has nothing for us but the off-chance that Burundi or Ruanda will let us in.' He was thinking aloud. 'Maybe we've got a better chance if we head south.'

'The Albertville road's blocked,' Janders said. 'By the time we've blasted it clear, they'll have mined the bridge.' He drew a line across the map. 'If we head west for Angola, we'll be crossing by Kaina, the largest military base in the Congo and it's an awful long way back to the white south.' He pointed to the Zambia/Tanzania border. 'There's twenty thousand Chinese somewhere down there.'

'As long as we've got Limbani, Ndofa knows he's in trouble,' Faulkner argued. 'He'll think we're heading north and he'll come after us like a banshee out of hell. If we double back and cross the river here, he pointed to the map, 'there's an old all-weather bridge thirteen miles out of Albertville and then south into Limbani country. We can hole up in the high ground by the lake. Maybe Kilimbi. Yes, Kilimbi. He'll have a hell of a job to winkle us out of those hills.'

'And then what?' Janders asked.

'Two things,' Faulkner replied. 'One, we need time to consolidate and then maybe bargain a bit. Maybe we could sell Limbani for our freedom if we had to.

'The other, Ndofa will have to go easy once he's in Limbani country, or he'll have a civil war on his hands. In fact,' Faulkner was thinking fast, 'maybe we could do just that. The people are about ready for a civil war. If we can hole up, maybe we can just turn this whole thing around.'

Janders shook his head wearily. 'You never give up, do you? We're in bad trouble; with fifty men and less some and you're going to take over the country.'

Faulkner was grinning now, his old optimism returning. 'That would really be something,' he said softly. 'We could sell Matherson a shareholding in our mines. He'd go mad. What do you think?'

'Maybe,' Janders agreed wearily. 'It's about our best chance. But forget the civil war bit. That takes money we haven't got.'

'If we can start one that looks like it can topple Ndofa, we'll find backers. If not, it'll take the heat off us long enough to get out.'

'We're ready to go, sir,' the R.S.M. reported. He saw Faulkner grinning and watched him curiously. 'We picked up three jeeps from the airport guard and their ammunition.'

'How many men have we lost?'

'Five so far, sir. Three walking wounded.'

Faulkner knew that seriously wounded men were counted as dead. 'All right, position a rear guard and start loading the men. Send the officers to me.'

Ten minutes later the convoy started up. The rear guard came running out of the airport buildings and jumped into the last trucks. Lights dimmed, the trucks headed north, back the way they had come. Peter had commandeered a jeep and travelled in the centre of the convoy, McTaggart driving, Limbani and Whity in the back. Limbani was conscious, his eyes wide open and watching. Whity clucked over him like a mother hen.

The road sunk between two fifteen foot shoulders. At the top, where the ground levelled, a jeep turned into the bush and switched off its lights. Four men jumped out and ran back on either side of the embankment. Two of them carried bamboo bazookas. When they found a clear view of the road well below they waited.

The convoy roared through the night, dipping and swaying back over the potholed road. The men were silent, clutching at the roof frames for support. Faulkner had moved among them before leaving the airport. The men could not understand why but his sense of purpose and his optimism cheered them. Those who had lost friends had no time to grieve for them. Each man was glad that he was still alive and worried for the future.

The leading jeep roared past the deserted barracks, its

windscreen laid flat, a machine-gun poking over the bonnet. Three miles past the barracks, they disabled a truck across the road, then the convoy turned and back tracked for a mile. As they crested a hill, the sky lit then came the sound of a rocket exploding carried on the wind. The convoy swung onto the southerly track.

The men at the ambush point heard the Simba trucks approaching, saw their headlights flashing in turn as they cornered into the embankment. The mercenaries had marked a killing area, a twenty yard stretch of road. They waited for the first vehicle to enter that area. The Simba trucks were bunched closely together, loaded to capacity with chanting men flushed with victory.

A rocket took the first vehicle squarely in the bonnet. A second rocket took it in the side. The truck lit up like a Christmas light, slewing across the road. Then it exploded, men and debris rising high into the air.

The second truck, in trying to stop ran into the blaze. In a moment, the fire reached the petrol tank and the truck erupted into a sheet of flame. The chanting turned to screams. Blazing figures ran out of the inferno. A light machine-gun stammered down from the embankment.

A third truck rammed the bank. A rocket took it as it struck. In a minute the road was closed. Flames lit the night. The dying screamed and the living ran aimlessly about searching for cover. The first hesitant stutter of a machine-gun began to return fire from below the embankment, the noise almost drowned in the crackle of flames. The mercenaries drew back and ran for their jeep.

The main convoy entered a seemingly deserted village. Faulkner's hackles rose in warning, but he maintained his pace. As if in understanding, the other vehicles began to space themselves out. The leading vehicles were almost through the village when an ambush opened up from the bush at the side of the road. The rhythmic hammer of a heavy machine-gun beat into the night. A bazooka shell, fired wild and low, passed between the wheels of a truck, glanced off the ground and exploded against the walls of an African store.

The truck in front of Peter took the next shell on its near side front wheel, the blast demolishing the bonnet and the cab. It swung across the road, forcing Peter's jeep into the ditch. Machine-gun bullets began to lace the canvas covering the rear. The truck caught fire. Drums of petrol began to explode sending great ghosts of flame up into the dark, blinding the ambushers.

McTaggart was trying to get the jeep back onto the road but the trucks behind them roared past filling the gap. Bullets screamed from each passing truck over their heads and into the trees above the ambush point. Peter was lobbing grenades into the bush. The machine-gun turned, trying to find him. Then the grenades exploded in quick succession and the ambush point fell silent. There were no survivors from the burnt-out truck. The jeep pulled out and joined the rear of the convoy.

The rear guard mercenaries were working feverishly, burrowing above and into the sides of a high embankment. It was slow work, for the walls were mostly of rock. Each man kept looking over his shoulder back down the road. At last the charges were fixed and fused. In the distance they heard the approaching rumble of the Simba trucks, moving cautiously this time.

The earthen wall of the embankment seemed to rise slowly into the air. There came an ear-splitting crack and a burst of flame, then rock and earth blocked the road. The jeep swung round and roared off, leaping over the potholes, passed the barracks and slowed, searching for the southerly track, then, finding it, the jeep accelerated once more.

A small tree was down across the track. The driver slowed, measuring it in his headlights, then, fearing an ambush, he accelerated and tried to jump the tree at the thinnest point. He saw too late the dark shape of a larger log behind. Engine screaming, the jeep rose into the air, fell on its side and turned over. Three of the men were thrown clear and lay stunned or injured on the track. The fourth was trapped, screaming, under the jeep. Dark shapes emerged from the bush. One of them began to toss lighted matches onto the oil-soaked chassis.

The track was too narrow for Peter to pass. Limbani seemed to have fallen asleep, cradled in Whity's arms. Faulkner's jeep skidded to a halt in front of the bridge. The driver ran back to warn the oncoming trucks. Banks rose on either side of the track, overgrown and the vegetation dripped wetly in the lights. Men jumped from the trucks and ran up the banks. The bridge was built of wood and rarely used now, other than by oxen carts. The advance guard ran across, their feet pounding hollow on the planks. The river was some fifty feet wide, grey, rushing, swollen with the rain. At either end, the king posts were supported by rusted steel hawsers embedded into the bank with concrete. The wood of the bridge was rotted.

The advance guard signalled that it was clear on the other side and took up covering positions. Faulkner's jeep crossed cautiously. When it reached the other side, the first truck started to cross. The bridge groaned and swayed, but it held. Other vehicles were arriving and being signalled to cross. The heavy wooden railway sleepers that comprised the platform churned under their wheels. Men were already setting demolition charges against the steel hawsers at the far end.

Peter's jeep was still out of sight and catching up with the main convoy. The last truck was heavily laden with fuel and it took the bridge too fast, bucketing over the torn sleepers towards the centre. Two of the sleepers gave and the rear wheels slipped between them, locking the truck. The whole bridge lurched forward under the momentum of the arrested vehicle. The guards jumped down from the banks and shouted instructions. The terrified driver revved the engine. The rear wheels tore into the remaining sleepers like a buzz saw. One of the hawsers parted. The steel cable lashed forward, killing the men at the bridge head, sweeping their bodies into the river. One side of the bridge began to fall and the truck tipped sideways. For a moment longer, the second hawser held the total weight of the bridge. Then the strands of steel parted and it gave too.

Almost as if in slow motion, the lorry was tossed clear of the collapsing bridge. It seemed to hang suspended in the air. Then, tail first, wheels spinning, it struck the river. The current took it like a fallen log. The truck slowly turned over, its lights still glowing under the water. It seemed to turn over again, then the lights went out.

Peter's jeep rounded the corner and then on down a steep embankment towards the bridge. They braked sharply. The lights shone out over the naked edge. They saw the bridge rising out of the river on the other side.

'I think it's Peter,' Janders said quietly from beside him.

'It can't be. He was in the centre.'

The R.S.M. was taking a roll call. Faulkner called him over.

'Thirteen missing or dead. Three walking wounded. Two trucks gone,' he reported. 'That doesn't account for the four rear guard who are in a right mess now.'

'Is Coetzee accounted for?'

'No, sir. That must be him over there. Lieutenant Fynn says that he got left behind after the ambush in the village. Mr. Limbani's with him, together with Volunteer White and McTaggart.'

'Oh, God,' Faulkner said softly.

The jeep lights dimmed and a voice called to him from across the river. Faulkner walked up to the bank.

'You okay?' he shouted.

'Yes,' Peter answered. 'Can you get us a line across?'

The R.S.M. checked in the trucks, 'We've got nothing, sir,' he reported back. 'Just some lengths of towing chain. We'd never get that across.'

Faulkner shouted the information across to Peter. McTaggart came up from the river.

'We'd never swim that,' he said. 'Too much current.'

Peter sat on the bonnet of the jeep ignoring the shouts from across the river. He had a good brain, but he had little faith in it. He thought slowly and he needed time. It was growing light and somewhere behind were the Simbas. When he was ready, he stood up and walked down to the bank.

'You go on,' he shouted to Faulkner. 'I'm going downstream through the bush until I find a boat or a bridge. I'll meet you in Kilimbi in forty-eight hours.'

Faulkner waved to show that he understood. He shouted something about meeting up with the rear guard who had a radio. Then he turned and walked back to his jeep. He had wanted to tell Peter how important it was to get Limbani through, how everything depended upon it. But the words were of no use, so he saved them.

'What happened to the luck we used to have?' he asked Janders bitterly as he passed.

'She's looking the other way,' Janders answered and climbed into his truck.

They both knew what would happen if Peter failed to get Limbani through. And it was too late to run north now.

CHAPTER TWENTY

0450 hours. Monday, 28th December

PETER watched the trucks leave. He glanced at the sky again. The first, faint, cold tinges of pink were showing. Guti clouds, resting on the hill tops, would soon begin to rise and disperse. It was going to be a hot day. Limbani was standing by the jeep supported by Whity.

'Kaffir, can you speak English?' Peter asked. In the still of the early morning, his voice was hushed.

The African nodded.

'We're going to walk on from here, so get what you need from the jeep.'

Whity squawked in protest for both of them.

'We walk,' Peter said firmly. 'It's safer. Me and McTaggart, we're good in the bush, so don't worry. Just do what we tell you. We'll walk for an hour then we'll find a place to lay up. Tonight, we'll cross the river.'

McTaggart started up the jeep, rammed it into gear then ran beside, steering until it plunged into the river.

'What about the rear guard? Whity asked.

'We're better on our own. I'll take the point. You help the kaffir in the middle. McTaggart, you watch the rear.'

'Mr. Limbani is no kaffir,' Whity protested hotly. 'He is an ex-Prime Minister.' The African watched silently.

Peter shrugged his shoulders. 'To me he is a kaffir,' he said simply. 'Where there is a river there is always a path. We've got to find it. As we go you watch me in the bush and you learn my ways fast. After this there is no talking, no smoking and no noise. You move quietly. You watch and listen all the time. You learn to think and move like an animal. You don't ever relax your senses. That way you stay alive. Now move on, both of you.'

The day broke gentle and beautiful, like a new world starting. The aeroplane touched down at Lumbo to take on fuel. Pereira waited on the runway. Beard stubble showed on his chin, his face was lined with fatigue and worry. He waited for the doors to be thrown open and the mercenaries to disembark. Only the captain swung down off the steps. Pereira led him to the small airport office. Neither spoke as they walked.

The news flashed to Lourenço Marques and from there to England.

'Make sure that we are covered,' Matherson said to Balfour when he was told. 'When the storm breaks, we'll know that Ndofa has got Limbani. Until then we've still got a chance. In the meantime, find me something else to bargain with.'

The aeroplane touched down in Lourenço Marques, loaded a legitimate cargo and returned normally to Swaziland.

The Congo quietly declared an internal state of emergency. The borders, radio and telephone links were closed to all countries. The airports shut down other than for military traffic and a dusk to dawn curfew was imposed. A statement was issued to the foreign press claiming that the Congo feared imminent acts of aggression from the Portuguese in retaliation for harbouring freedom fighters. All soldiers from Limbani's province were confined to barracks and disarmed. General Ndofa was said to be conducting military manoeuvres in the bush. The world paid little attention to the state of emergency. But in the Congo bush, the village drums carried rumour where the telegraph wires failed.

Faulkner drew his convoy off the track and camouflaged the vehicles in the trees. There the men rested, waiting for dark before pushing on over some of the worst roads in Africa.

Peter returned to the small camp hidden in the bush by the river. He was tired and limping, bothered by the flies which were attracted to the blood forming through the bandages on his thigh. 'There's a village where the river broadens three miles downstream,' he said. 'They've got some dugouts that'll get us across, but it's hard going.'

Whity replaced the bandages. 'It's going to get infected,' he accused.

'Just so long as it gets me there,' Peter replied. 'Bury the bandages deep and put some heavy stones on top. Then guard the point. I need some rest.'

'There's some congealed soup we saved for you,' Whity offered. He stirred it distastefully. 'Made from river water. There's more mud in it than soup. Lord only knows what it'll do to our stomachs. What with not being able to boil the water.' He moved off and subsided angrily into the bush.

'You all right, kaffir?'

The African raised his wrist where the manacles had worn. 'I bleed red like you, white man. Don't call me kaffir.'

'I didn't mean to offend you. Where I come from, a black man has always been called kaffir. Long before it became a swear word.'

'From now on you may refer to me as Limbani. Mr. Limbani.'

'Oh, go to hell,' Peter said exasperated, lying back in the bush. 'I've got more things to worry about than your feelings right now.'

'Would you prefer me to address you as Baas?' Limbani asked. 'Yes, Baas. No, Baas. Would you feel more comfortable with a black man then?'

Peter turned, opening his eyes. 'I don't want to talk politics with you now,' he said miserably. 'I just want to sleep. Leave me alone, will you?'

'Where do you come from?' Limbani asked. 'South Africa?'

'Rhodesia,' Peter answered, in spite of himself, stung to reply at that question like all Rhodesians.

'Rhodesia,' Limbani mused. 'I knew Welensky a long time ago. He was a good man.'

'Well, I didn't,' Peter whispered fiercely. 'I don't get to meet Prime Ministers. Even ex-prime Ministers. Now shut up, will you?' He rolled away from the African and pretended that he was asleep.

'White man,' the African asked of his back, 'why should you think that I would thank you for saving my life? It was because of the white man that I lost my country. It was because of the white man that I spent so many years in a cell. Do you know what it's like to lose all hope for life a little bit each day until there is nothing left; to watch the white governments jostle with each other for power in your backward country? And you, as the pawn, to be tossed aside and forgotten.

'You at least I can understand for the animal that you are, the governments for their simple greed. It is the white liberal that I despise. The men who made me trust them with those wonderful words about human rights and freedoms. The men who left me to rot in a cell and forgot me when I was no longer a figure-head to build a cause on. Those men built monuments to their goodness and Christianity over the dead bodies of Africa, the millions of my brothers who have starved and died and slaughtered each other across this continent. All those good ideals, when in Africa freedom is only a word for a change of oppressor.'

'Man,' Peter said, rising on his elbows. 'Have you finished? Good.' He shook his head. 'I don't know what you're talking about. I don't even understand the politics of my own country. It's way beyond me. Now, if you don't shut up, I'll shut you up, sick man or not. Oh and another thing, don't call me white man. My name's Coetzee. Mr. Coetzee.'

'Why? Does it sound like a swear word? Do you dislike being addressed by the colour of your skin?'

Peter growled. Limbani fell silent, watching while Peter slept.

It was cool and damp beneath the trees, dark for the sunlight barely filtered through. The R.S.M. moved about quietly checking sentries, noting the men who appeared to be cracking under the strain, barking at or encouraging them according to their characters. The remainder of the men were kept fully occupied. One group checked the vehicles. Another endeavoured to heat a weak stew on pocket gas primus stoves. The N.C.O. in charge muttered that it was like trying to feed the five thousand on a single fish. A select group of men sat well away from the others constructing home-made land mines.

In the late afternoon, a spotter plane flying high wove uncertainly over them. The men waited with their faces down until the noise passed, searching south. The convoy started up after sunset and continued with all possible speed towards Kilimbi.

Limbani lay with his back against a tree. The warm light from the afternoon sun filtered through the bush, latticing his face and his body with shadow. The hot, moist air carried the smell of the bush and the noise from the river comforted him. This was how he had remembered his country from his cell. With African fatalism, he had accepted death. Now he was beginning to savour life. He thought of his wife and children and of the future, then firmly he locked it all away in the darkness of his mind. He needed the bitterness to keep him moving. The rain had held off, but in the east it was building up for a wild storm.

Peter awoke and stretched himself like a cat, testing each limb. His leg was stiff and painful, but it would carry him.

'I had a bodyguard like you once,' Limbani said. 'He died.'

'You still talking?' Peter asked indignantly. 'My God, no wonder you're a politician.'

'I meant to ask you. Which government am I now obliged to?'

'I don't know,' Peter answered honestly. 'I think we're getting paid out of your money though. That's one thing about you African politicians. You certainly learn to stash it away. You must rob your people blind.'

'In Africa there are very few elder statesmen. You are either alive and in power or you're dead. Money is of more use than an army.'

'Hey,' Whity called. Peter moved over to him. 'Listen, love, I'm getting eaten alive,' he complained plaintively. 'Those dirty great mosquitoes are going to pick me up and carry me away. When am I going to be relieved?'

'Just now,' Peter said. 'I'll see McTaggart then I'll come back. You can look after Limbani. That kaffir's driving me mad. No wonder Ndofa wants to kill him.'

'He's had a rough time. I think he's trying to hang onto his sanity. You'd be bitter if you were him. And why don't you stop calling him a kaffir? You know it upsets him.'

'Whity, don't you go taking his side. That bastard's been telling me my fortune all afternoon.'

'Don't you worry, love,' Whity said patting his knee. 'You know I'm with you. Want me to take another look at your leg?'

Peter grinned at him. Whity, you really as queer as you make out?'

'Queer as a coot, I'm afraid, love. Does it shock you?'

'Doesn't seem to matter out here. What's it feel like?'

'Buy me dinner when we get back and I'll show you,' Whity flashed back.

'You know I'm not like that,' Peter said embarrassed.

Whity smiled. 'I know, love. I was just teasing you. I can't imagine you in London or in any city come to that.'

'I wasn't much good there.'

'I'm not much good here. But I'm glad I'm with you. You'll get us through, won't you? I hate this place.'

'You're doing fine, Whity. You're as good as any man I know. Oh, and about before, I'm sorry, I just wondered. You know.'

'About what it felt like to be a queer?'

'Yes, but forget it. It's none of my business.'

'It's the loneliest feeling in the world, love. Some day I'll tell you.'

McTaggart grinned at Peter. He seemed to blend with the shadows like a gnarled, old tree stump.

'You okay?' Peter asked.

McTaggart nodded.

'All right,' Peter said, 'we'll move out an hour after sundown. It'll take us about two hours to get to the village. You ever paddled a dugout before? Good. You take Whity. I'd better look after the kaffir.'

The storm struck and passed, leaving them wet and miserable. An hour after sunset they moved off. The path fell sharply with the river. Sheer earth walls on the one side and the river swirling below on the other. Limbani collapsed within the first twenty minutes and had to be carried. It took them three hours to reach the village. There the river was wide and dark with a centre stream of current tossing the water. The dugout canoes lay bottom up on a narrow strip of sand. On the other side, they could just make out a corresponding strip of sand glinting whitely in the starlight below the sheer walls of the bank.

The village lay in darkness some two hundred yards up from the sand. The rising moon sheltered behind the hills. Peter and McTaggart snaked out from the covering bush on their bellies through the sand. They righted two small dugouts, and one at a time they carried them down to the water's edge.

At a signal, Whity emerged from the bush supporting Limbani, stumbling under his weight as he ran. They had joined the dugouts with a length of rope. Limbani was lowered into Peter's dugout. Whity jumped into the second dugout as McTaggart pushed it into the water. They both began to paddle. Peter pushed his dugout into the water as the rope took up the slack. The dugouts moved quietly upstream in slack water then they crossed current, paddling furiously.

Native dugouts are heavy, cumbersome craft, difficult to handle. The current seized them, sweeping them down river. The sound of their frenzied paddling was lost in the rushing noise. They broke from the current and paddled upstream to the opposite strip of sand. Whity half carried Limbani into the bush while Peter and McTaggart loosed the ropes and pushed the dugouts back into the current.

They rested for ten minutes, then, finding a track leading south, they staggered on through the night, each taking it in turn to carry Limbani. Dawn found them with Limbani stretched out on the back of an ox cart. Whity rode with a nervous African driver. Peter and McTaggart walked point and guard.

CHAPTER TWENTY-ONE

Tuesday, 29th December

THE main convoy of mercenaries arrived at the outskirts of Kilimbi with the first light of dawn. It had taken the whole night to cover thirty miles. They had lost two more trucks to the road. The men rested, waiting for the sun to rise. Then they moved cautiously into the village.

The village boasted one main dirt street, wide with trees planted through the centre. White, peeling, narrow-fronted, single storey buildings lined either side, reminiscent of what a frontier town in California must have looked like in the days of the old west. Shop windows were guarded and padlocked with heavy steel mesh. Beyond lay a shanty town and a few faded residential buildings left over from the Belgian era.

The village was completely deserted, silent, eerie in the grey, early morning light. The men were nervous, waiting for the storm to break, their guns swinging to train on shadows. Moving forward, covering, checking, moving forward again. The noise of a door banging, the rattle of a can carried on the silence. The sun rose. They had covered every inch of the village. There was no one there. The occupants had left everything as it was and moved out.

Faulkner, Janders and the R.S.M. made a detailed tour of the area. They checked on the water supply, gathered up all available food and placed guards on it. Janders destroyed all the liquor that he could find. The village occupied a good defensive position in the hills. They placed their men accordingly and the R.S.M. set them to work.

Faulkner established his office in the police station. There were no prisoners, though the cells had recently been occupied. The absence of the people, the silence and the waiting in the gathering heat, made the fear become almost tangible. The men spoke softly with one another, automatically seeking cover if they moved. They waited for the first shout, the first shot to shatter the silence.

A forward patrol found some Africans making hesitantly for the village. They brought them blindfold through the defences. Three elderly, dignified and very frightened men stood before Faulkner's desk. In the background, a radio operator was endeavouring to make contact with the missing rear guard. Faulkner questioned them haltingly in Swahili. They were frightened of his eyes, of the wild violence that lay close beneath the surface.

They told him that the villagers were hiding in the nearby hills. The old men had been selected as their spokesmen because of their standing in the community and, at their age, they were considered expendable. The small garrison had fled in the direction of Boudeville. There were no other troops in the area yet, but they were worried by a rumour that the Simbas were coming. These people kill everybody. Therefore the elders politely requested that the mercenaries move on to some other village and leave theirs in peace.

After about thirty minutes of questioning, one of the elders summoned up the courage to ask if it was true that the spirit of Limbani had returned.

Faulkner assured them that Limbani was expected within the next twenty-four hours. The old men talked animatedly amongst themselves.

'Will your people help us when Limbani comes?' Faulkner asked.

'When we see him,' one of the old men said firmly, 'he will tell us what to do, for he is our mother and our father.'

One of the Africans left to report back to the villagers. The other two left behind as hostages squatted patiently against the wall. An hour later a drum in the hills began to beat, hesitantly at first as though the drummer was making contact, then it broke out into a full throbbing beat.

'They have sent for the white God man,' the elders translated. Faulkner passed word around the defences to expect a white priest and to let him through.

At noon the rain came again and, with it, came the priest, plodding slowly down the main street on a donkey. Behind him at a respectful distance followed the elders and several of the villagers. The priest was tall, sitting straight backed, his head jutting through a hole cut in a great tarpaulin that covered him and most of the tiny donkey. His legs trailed on the ground. He was in his late sixties with a lean, lined, hard face which seemed to have been carelessly chiselled from granite, bushy grey eyebrows that rose towards his temples and wild blue-grey eyes, a mane of long grey hair swept back over his head and ears, matted in the rain. The mercenaries rose from their cover to watch him pass. The priest stared straight ahead.

The donkey came to a halt of its own accord in the middle of the road, stood with its legs spread as though it would walk no more. The priest swore, swung his leg off the donkey and walked behind it. The donkey brayed, then lashed out with both hooves. For an old man, the priest jumped surprisingly quickly. Even so, one of the hooves struck the trailing tarpaulin with a noise like a pistol shot.

The priest launched a kick at the donkey. 'You heathen beast,' he roared in a broad Irish accent. The donkey brayed loudly as the kick connected and lashed out in all directions, scattering the villagers. The priest seemed satisfied and strode towards Faulkner. He pulled off the tarpaulin as he mounted the steps. Underneath he wore heavy boots tied with leather thongs, faded khaki trousers and a short-sleeved, open necked khaki shirt. His exposed walnut-stained arms appeared to be all bone with wide wrists and strong hands.

'So you're the murdering heathen I've come to see,' he greeted Faulkner. He stretched out his hand. Faulkner took it. The priest noticed Faulkner's expression. 'I haven't worn a collar in twenty years,' he said. 'I wear my cassock on Sundays. Does that suit you? What day is it today?' he continued before Faulkner could speak. 'Tuesday,' he answered for Faulkner. 'And what were you doing on Sunday, the Lord's day? By all accounts you were running wild, murdering your fellow men left, right and centre. Am I right?' the priest thundered. 'I'm right,' he confirmed before Faulkner could speak.

When the priest spoke, he held his right fist upraised and clenched by his cheek like a boxer. When he made a point, he lowered his head between his shoulders, fixed his wild eyes on yours, then he snorted. At any moment you felt that his fist might come smashing into your face. His manner commanded complete attention.

'And when you were running wild, murdering your fellow men on Sunday,' the priest roared to the gathering crowd of curious mercenaries, 'did any of you pay your respects to your Maker? You didn't. No, you didn't, you murdering heathens. So now you pray. Before we talk further, you pray that the good Lord will lighten the load of your black sins from off your shoulders. Down there.' He pointed to the muddy road. 'On your kneees, all of you.'

'I heard of him last time we were through here,' Janders muttered. 'Thought he died years ago. He's got bush madness. Better do what he says. Keep him happy.'

The villagers and the mercenaries knelt in the mud and

the rain, following Faulkner's example. One mercenary remained standing.

'I'm a Jew,' he shouted, wincing under the flashing eyes of the priest.

'Down you heathen thing,' the priest roared, rocking on his heels. 'Pray even harder for your lost soul.'

The Jew knelt, in spite of himself.

'Lord,' the priest began. He was a man who seemed to pulsate with power, certain that God was at his elbow. 'Before you, like swine in the mud, are the very dregs of humanity. Mercenaries, murdering heathens, every mother's son. Lord, they are a blasphemy on your good earth.'

Faulkner rose. 'That's enough,' he said.

'Kneel,' the priest roared. 'That's what I said and that's what you are. Anyway, I'm coming to the good bit.

'As I was saying, Sweet Lord, they're sinners every one and, by all accounts, they excelled themselves last Sunday. But then, you'll know about that better than me. However, Lord, I would remind you that, during the last troubles, these sinners did a good bit to save your servants from being chopped up, though why the murdering savages always aim to chop up your servants first I'll never know. Unless it is you're short of martyrs. Now, there's a thought.'

The men shuffled uncomfortably, the rain beating off their ponchos.

'Anyway, Lord, if you can see your way clear to letting these sinners depart with a whole skin, bearing in mind what I've said before, I'd be grateful.'

The mercenaries began to rise. The priest signalled them back on their knees.

'However, Lord,' he thundered, 'if there be amongst them the Godless swine who stole the jewels from the crucifix in your church at Boudeville back in '65, you wouldn't hear me objecting if you made an exception of him, though why you didn't strike him down there and then I'll never know.'

A peal of thunder accentuated his words. The priest's gaze travelled across the kneeling men. No one had fallen.

'However, hallowed be thy ways,' he muttered, disappointed. He gave the blessing, made the sign of the cross and allowed them to rise.

'Amen,' the mercenaries chorused fervently and hurried for shelter. Faulkner led the priest to a map.

'Can you tell us what's happening outside?' he asked.

The priest glanced at the map. 'Not being a military man,' he said and snorted, 'all I can tell you is that you're in real trouble, bad trouble. Ndofa's got you boxed in. He's got the terrorists in training on the Zambian–Tanzanian border coming up from the south, the army's coming in from Kamina in the east and, if that's not all, he's got his very own Simbas coming in from the north behind you. There now,' he stood back from the map. 'What do you think of that? You ask me how he's doing it when nothing can travel over these roads and I'll tell you. He's got Cuban pilots, good Catholics gone Communist, every one of them, flying them in.'

'How long have we got?' Faulkner asked.

'The first of them should be here some time tonight. Before midnight anyway. That's how long you've got. Now, if you're listening, I'll make you a bargain. By all accounts, you've got Limbani himself stashed away somewhere. The country's ready to rise, especially his own people. But if you raise your standard here, civil war will break out. The people will get murdered in the long run because they haven't got the arms.

'Now, my bargain is this. There's a mine about six miles from here. And it's got a little airstrip with an old Dakota standing on it this very minute. The Dakota will fly all right. I've flown in it myself. What do you say to that?'

Faulkner paced up and down the room, head bent, deep in thought. 'Limbani is somewhere between here and the River Lukuga,' he said at last. 'He should be coming in. I intend to wait for him as long as possible.'

'So it's true, is it?' the priest said softly. 'Lord and there was I just humouring the rumour. And then you go?' he demanded.

'And then I'll decide,' Faulkner answered. 'Do you speak the language?'

'Of course, haven't I been here close on forty years?'

'Well, there's the telephone and the line's still open. Try and raise Ndofa. We'll see if we can bargain for some time.'

Faulkner walked Janders outside while the priest wrestled with the telephone. 'I don't trust him,' Faulkner said. 'That man would bow to the devil to save these people from a civil war. Check with the other Africans. For all we know, the Simbas may be waiting for us at that mine.'

'Maybe,' Janders agreed. 'That was a pretty good summary of our position for a priest. Mind you, I told you I've heard of this guy before. That's when we were looking for him – trying to get him out. He was virtually leading his own army then. I still can't figure out how he gets to know where everybody is.'

'You can find that out,' Faulkner said. 'I'll watch him in here. You watch him outside. Make sure he doesn't talk to anybody.'

The R.S.M. reported. 'There's more of them wanting to wait for Limbani and more of them coming in.'

'Choose a leader from each group. Bring him in and guard him. Keep the rest well outside the defences,' Faulkner ordered and went indoors.

All through the afternoon, men appeared at the town perimeter, either singly or in groups. The head men, elders, chiefs and politicians of the surrounding area. The head men and chiefs representing the old and the politicians representing the young. Some of them must have started to walk on the morning they took Limbani, following the drums, each dressed according to his standing in the community. They squatted quietly in the shade under an armed guard and waited for the coming of Limbani.

Peter decided to move on through the day accepting the added risk in an effort to make up time. They abandoned the ox cart, using the driver as a guide, branched into the innumerable narrow footpaths that led through the bush. Peter was carrying Limbani, whose mind was clear but his body weak. They were both in pain.

Limbani began to chuckle.

'What's it now?' Peter demanded angrily. He had insisted on carrying Limbani until it became a form of masochism, his mind filled with a dull red ache from the exhaustion of his body as he plodded mechanically on.

'White man, if your friends in the south could see you now,' Limbani began to chuckle again.

Peter sank to his knees, rolled over and tossed the African off his back. He signalled to McTaggart and Whity to rest. 'Kaffir,' he said bitterly, 'if you think you're going to ride me round the bush like a bloody mule and then laugh at me, you can bloody well walk. We whites have carried you blacks for years now.'

'You mean it the other way round, don't you?'

'You don't see people carving each other up in Rhodesia like they do here.'

'Your turn is still to come. But you can leave me here. I don't need you.'

'Man you need me to save your miserable black life.'

'On the contrary, you need me to save your miserable white life and those of your men. In fact, we both need each other. That's the way it should be. If only the white and black of Africa realized it.'

'Now, listen, I don't want any more of your politics. I've had enough.'

'Are you afraid of new ideas? Unwilling to bend even a little bit?'

'Mister, it's not that. Maybe I don't see the world so clear as some because I haven't been around that much, but what I do know is that you don't destroy the old ways until you've got something better to put in their place. So I'll stick with the old ways until someone comes up with something better – but not just words.'

'They'd better do it fast,' Limbani warned, 'Africa is like an hour-glass and the sand is running out. Apart from white and black, we've got China, Russia, America, England and France all struggling for control, isolating groups of people and setting them against each other. We're like a ripe plum ready to fall off the tree. And when it happens there will be an almighty blood-bath across the continent. First between black and white and then between black and black. But I don't suppose that would worry you. You whites can all go back to your countries of origin.'

'That's where you're wrong,' Peter replied between his clenched teeth. 'We whites are African and we're staying. Listen, it's like there's a thin white line drawn across the southern end of this continent. You blacks have got two-thirds of Africa and you do what the hell you like with it. But leave us alone. Don't try to cross that line or you'll get hurt. And mister, you must know that behind that line we whites have done more for your people than all you blacks put together. We started by building your countries and now, while you black politicians are living on foreign aid, carving each other up and robbing your people blind, we're giving our blacks a better education, better hospitals, better everything. Do you wonder that as soon as your people are old enough to walk, they make a bee-line for the white south? I'll tell you why. They're sick and tired of you lot. That's why. You're the ripe plum, not us. When you sort yourselves out and you've got something to offer, come and talk to us. Until then, we don't want to know.'

'If what you say is true, white man, then why is the tide of terrorism growing? Why the restriction camps? Terrorists and agitators cannot operate without the support of the people regardless of what the countries beyond your borders wish. The old order's changing. When your famous unarmed police force arms, then you'll know that you're losing your people and with them eventually your country.

'Your governments claim to be the last bastion of democracy in Africa. You're supposed to be fighting to preserve your way of life, but hasn't it occurred to you yet, white man, that when your governments say to you, "we're taking away all the rights and liberties that you've had since the Magna Carta, so that we may defend democracy; we're building restriction camps, internment without trial, so that we may defend democracy; a man may fall to his death from the top floor of a police station, so that we may defend democracy", then you no longer live in a democracy, white man? So what are you fighting for? It can't be your traditional way of life because it's changed. It hasn't affected you yet – just the Africans.'

Peter stood up. 'You're like all the rest. You're good at tearing things apart, but you don't put anything sensible back. You're the man who told me that in Africa freedom was just a word for a change in oppressor. And in your countries that's dead right. Me, I can only speak for Rhodesia. I'm not happy about everything there, but I'm telling you the people are happier than here. Okay, a few die and some are restricted, but at least the rest can expect to grow old in peace. And those that die are less than one per cent of the people who have died here, let alone in the rest of Africa. Democracy wasn't built to stand against communist infiltration and an illiterate people. Like civilized law wasn't built to stand against organized crime. I'll bet more people have died from drugs alone in America than have died in political violence in Rhodesia. You can either live with the criminals until they own you or you can lose a bit of your freedom and wipe them out.

'Anyway,' Peter said impatiently. 'As long as the people are hard enough and strong enough, you hold your country. When the people get fat and weak, you lose it. It's always been that way. Nothing's going to change it, especially in Africa, because the Africans follow whoever is the strongest. And I'm telling you, I'm as hard as hell.'

Peter signalled to McTaggart and Whity that they were moving out. He turned his back to Limbani. 'Get up,' he said and grunted under Limbani's weight. He began to plod forward.

'There are other ways of holding a country,' Limbani began.

'Shut up,' Peter said. 'I haven't got the breath to argue.'

Faulkner joined Janders on the stoep. 'We got through to Albertville,' he said. 'Ndofa's somewhere in the bush. They're trying to find him. It'll take another couple of hours.' He looked up. 'Seen any planes about?' He asked.

Janders shook his head.

'Strange,' Faulkner said softly.

'Maybe he wants to snuff us out quietly.'

'He's going to have a hell of a job without air strikes. How much food have we got?'

'About two weeks if we go careful. Plenty of water.'

'Ammunition?'

'Close on a thousand rounds per man. We picked up some more from the army garrison here. But we're short on rockets.'

Faulkner glanced at his watch and then again at the sky. 'Four o'clock,' he said. 'All we need is time. There's nothing in the news, so he hasn't got Limbani yet.'

'I checked with the Africans. According to them, that priest stands right next to God and they're scared silly of him. There is a small mine with a few Europeans about six or seven miles from here across the hills, but it's rough going. They don't know if the plane is there, so I sent a couple of them with a small patrol and a radio to find out. I also sent out a patrol to see if they can meet up with Peter. There's a few men fanned out in the bush all around waiting to make contact with the enemy. So we'll know in plenty of time.'

'Good,' Faulkner said. 'I'm not worried about the army such as it is, or the terrorists. They'll have no stomach for a fight, but we'd better strengthen the north against the Simbas.'

'You still thinking of holding out?' Janders asked.

Faulkner grinned. 'All I need is time,' he replied. 'Maybe Ndofa will pay us double what Matherson offered, just to get us out before we're finished.'

The priest stamped angrily onto the stoep. 'Telephones,' he declared, 'Are designed purely to drive men mad. And those operators must have been trained by the devil himself.'

Faulkner rose.

'You going?' the priest demanded.

'Just to look round the men,' Faulkner replied.

The priest groaned mightily as he sat down beside Janders. 'Now there's a fine, cool, fighting man for you,' he said, nodding to Faulkner's retreating back. 'I wish he'd take himself away from here. I wonder now,' the priest continued thoughtfully, 'if he hasn't Irish blood in him. Faulkner. Faulkner.' He tried to place the name. 'Must have,' he said and gave up. We could have used a man like him in the troubles, but then you'd be too young to remember them.'

He turned to Janders. 'Where are you from? You sound American, bless the people. They've been good to Ireland.'

'Sort of,' Janders replied briefly.

'You know I'll stop you if you try a civil war here,' the priest said. 'I'll use anything I've got, just so long as you understand that.'

'Yes, I know,' Janders said quietly. 'But you'll find Faulkner takes a bit of stopping. Anyway, what's an Irishman doing here?'

The priest grinned. An infectious smile lit up in his craggy face. 'Well, then, I'll tell you. I had to leave Ireland in a little bit of a hurry. Ah, but that was a long time ago.' Janders offered him a cigarette. The priest refused, fumbling in his pocket. 'It'll spoil me for this,' he said, holding up a battered, short-stemmed pipe. 'I grow my own tobacco. It tastes terrible.

'Now, where was I? Ah yes. I was a wild young lad then with an English price on my head. We had a priest in the village. Now there was a man. Deaf as a post and a voice like a fog horn. At least, I'm not so sure he was as deaf as all that. He had a way with him you see. I remember there was always a long queue at confession. God help the man who didn't go. There would be the priest, deaf as a post and a man would creep into the box to confess his sins. And he'd whisper, "I slept with O'Flagherty's wife," and the priest would say, "What, what? Speak up, my son." And the poor man would say, "I slept with O'Flagherty's wife." "Speak up speak up," the priest would shout. "I can't hear you." And the poor man, terrified of the priest, would yell, "I slept with O'Flagherty's wife." The priest would give him penance but sure now O'Flagherty himself would be waiting outside. And that was the punishment.'

The priest pulled on his pipe and smiled to himself as he remembered. 'Sinning in our village was a terrible dangerous thing,' he said softly. 'I remember when I was in bad trouble for killing an English soldier so I went to see the priest. When I told him the next thing I knew he was round the confessional box beating the living daylights out of me. That's the sort of man he was. A fine priest but with a bit of a temper on him. Anyway, he got me out of Ireland to Belgium. I took my orders there. That's where I heard of the Congo. I thought, that's a heathen country with a fine ring to its name. And here I am.'

'Didn't you have a vocation for the priesthood?' Janders asked, astonished that a man could lose himself in the bush without some form of burning faith to hold him.

'Well now, I was a good Catholic, but I don't think I had a vocation. I never really thought on it. In Ireland when I was a lad, you were either a carpenter, a plumber or a priest. It was as simple as that. Vocation, now there's a thought. It's got a fine ring to the word. Vocation. Rolls off your tongue.'

'What keeps you in the bush?'

The priest's eyes smiled. 'I've heard that people say I've got bush madness but then God and I, we know better. Besides, haven't I got a job to do? It's an easy enough thing to convert these heathens, but it's terrible hard to keep them converted after that. Once they grow up, the slightest temptation and the devil's in them. And I've got to drive him out again.

'I know. I know you're thinking that my Catholic doctrine is a bit weak and, to tell the truth, maybe you're right. But it would be useful if the seminaries taught us a little less doctrine and a lot more on how to change a wheel. You see my

39

people like their religion straight. A little fire and a little brimstone. A burning hell below and Saint Peter above with the heavenly keys. Sure, you know what I mean. They like a God who knows his own mind.'

'Don't you have any doubts about your God?' Janders asked.

'Well, now I've never really thought about that. There's a thought now. Have I any doubts about God?' The priest puzzled for a moment. 'How could I?' he demanded belligerently, his eyes growing wild. 'God's God. He's there all right, as sure as we're here. I talk to him and he talks to me. If I get out of hand, he punishes me there and then. Snake bite, fever. No,' he shook his head, 'God's there all right. And it's not for us to question him. Just to keep away from the devil and do what he tells us.'

Suddenly the priest grinned. 'You're sounding like that miserable man of a Bishop,' he accused. 'They think I've been in the bush too long. Twice they've sent for me now. I just disappear and the Bishop himself is shit-scared of coming to look for me.'

He rose. 'I think I'll try that telephone again.'

1750 hours

Jeremy crawled through the bush to Shaun. 'How's it going?' he asked.

'Nothing,' Shaun replied. 'It's so quiet that I'm scared sick just waiting for something to happen.'

'Well, the sun's going down. You'd better alert your men. They like to come with the dusk when all shadows look alike.'

'Don't you worry. We're alert all right. If someone even coughs out there, he'll be full of holes. Hey,' Shaun asked, needing company, 'do you find if you look into the bush long enough you start to imagine things?'

'Yes, it happens to everybody.'

'Good,' Shaun said glumly. 'I thought it was just me cracking up. I keep seeing these bandits crawling towards me. I tell you this place is getting me down. If I'm not panicking for my life, I'm hurting about Gabby. Did I tell you?'

'Many times,' Jeremy cut in firmly. 'You know you're some kind of special hypochondriac. When they're in trouble, some people lean on religion. With you it's a woman. If you get out of here, you'll probably never see her again.'

'No ways,' Shaun said firmly. 'That's what I'm doing here. I'd be with Gabby now if it wasn't for Janders talking me into this. I'm telling you if I die I hope something horrible happens to him.'

'Peter should be coming in soon,' Jeremy said, watching the darkening sky.

'If he's not dead already,' Shaun said morosely. 'They can't raise the rear guard, you know.'

'He'll be all right,' Jeremy said. 'He's got McTaggart with him and they had a head start. Those two will take a hell of a lot of killing. They're better in the bush than the animals.'

CHAPTER TWENTY-TWO

1750 hours. Tuesday, 29th December

PETER was on point. He walked briefly with the guide then he signalled a halt. McTaggart laid Limbani on the ground. He stretched himself, his body bathed in sweat, then he walked over to Peter.

'This black man,' he asked, rubbing the small of his back, 'is he so important to you?'

'Yes,' Peter answered. 'The sun is going soon. We'll rest until just before dark, then we'll make the last run in. You take the point.'

Whity removed the dirty fly-stained bandages. 'Infection's spreading all over your leg,' he said accusingly. 'We've got no more bandages.'

'Use leaves,' Peter said. 'We're on the last run now. As soon as we reach Kilimbi we're home. Man, but those leaves feel good and cool against my leg. You still all right, Whity? When I first saw you, I didn't think you'd walk a mile.'

Whity flushed with pleasure. 'Just because I'm queer doesn't mean I can't walk. You know, I've been thinking,' he said binding the leaves. 'I might go to Rhodesia when this is over. Find myself a nice, hairy, jungle man. You never know, do you?'

'Bugger you.'

'That's what I mean, love,' Whity grinned and patted the bandage.

'Day after tomorrow is New Year's Eve,' Peter said. 'Where were you last New Year's Eve?'

'I had a boyfriend,' Whity said. 'I brought him all the way over from Germany for Christmas. Showed him all round London. I did everything for him.' Whity shook his head sadly. 'I really hoped that it might work out for us. You know, long term. But it never does. The little bastard went off and left me for someone else. I got so low that I spent New Year in Amsterdam, just sleeping around.'

'What about you, McTaggart?' Peter called softly.

McTaggart was sitting further up the track in the bush with his rifle across his knees. 'Me. I danced, got drunk, ended up in a fight. I half killed a man and they put me in gaol.' He shrugged his shoulders. 'It wasn't my fault. A group of them were riding me – I have this temper – they should have known . . .'

'What about you?' Whity asked of Peter.

'I was proposing to a woman who turned me down flat for a commercial artist on the bum. God, I didn't know anything could hurt so much. All right,' Peter said to Whity. 'Take the rear guard for a while. We'll rest for another fifteen minutes, then we'll move out.'

Peter flopped down beside Limbani. He said, 'I've been thinking. 'I've got just one more thing I want to tell you and then I don't want to talk about it any more.

'When I was first in the police in Rhodesia, special branch brought a terrorist to our station. They wanted him kept out of the way and guarded. There weren't very many of us and I drew the night shift. We sat there trying to ignore each other, then somehow we got to talking. It turned out that he had a couple of "A" levels, which is more than I ever got. Man, we talked about everything all through the night. Black versus white, apartheid, justice. And for all the things I've got wrong, I've got a love of justice born in me. We found that we agreed on a hell of a lot of things. We talked so much I forgot he was black, but towards the morning he said to me, "You're white and if the blacks were marching on Salisbury and the whites were definitely in the wrong, which side would you take?" I thought about it. Then, for all my love of justice, I knew that I'd fight for the whites. No doubt about it. When everything is said and done, you fight for your own. That's the way man is and I told him.

'So I asked him, if the whites marched on Harari and the blacks were wrong, where would you stand? And he said, "With the blacks." So there we were. We had talked all night about justice. I liked him and I think he liked me. But if we met in the bush it would be on different sides and we'd kill each other. It might not have been nice, but it was the truth and both of us knew. Since then, I've never wanted to talk politics again. Because it's all just so many words.'

'That night,' Limbani said, sitting up, 'you both reached out and tried to understand each other. You wouldn't have bothered if you hadn't been locked in a cell together. And when you failed, you both just gave up and went back to your nice safe positions. But the point is you found that you actually liked an African.'

'Hell, I like lots of kaffirs.'

'But you respected him.'

'Yes, but he was different, like you.'

'How do you know? How many of the educated Africans in your country have you bothered to talk to? And I don't mean as Master and Servant. I mean like you did with him.'

'I don't get to meet them. We lead different lives.'

'Well, if white and black Africans could be made to meet, if somebody could lock them up away from the rest of the world and they really had to talk to each other and talk and talk and talk, they'd still be different, but perhaps they'd begin to understand each other. Perhaps they would get to like each other enough to form a platform of understanding on which their children could build.

'I can explain it better this way. Once your great-great-grandfather sweated on his lands beside his Africans. They were a simple backward people, happy and well cared for in a feudal society. Your great-great-grandfather was probably also a simple man. He spoke their language and you can't sweat in a field all day beside a man without getting to know him a little bit, understanding him. And they needed each other. If the year was bad they both went hungry.

'Then came the cities and the industry. They both left the land and drifted in. There they were separated. The white depended on and lived with his own kind. The black went to his ghetto. The white man forgot how to talk to them. He didn't know what they were thinking any more or how they felt. He educated them, but he didn't see the product of his education growing up, trying to break out of the feudal system. The white man's son grew up in the town and didn't care any more.

'Do you know that the black man has always admired the white man? As soon as he rose above the others, if he couldn't change the colour of his skin, above all else he wanted to be liked and respected by the white man. His education taught him to despise his fellow African. It was the same with me. But no matter what you are, lawyer, doctor, politician, the whites never let you forget that you're black. They never let you in.

'Have you any idea what it is like to be an educated black African, to stand between two cultures, despising one and not being accepted by the other? Do you know what it is like to be an educated African in your country with a good job? And you go to a store and you stand patiently in a queue while the whites push in front of you. They're not being consciously rude, they just don't notice you. When you

246

eventually reach the counter, the woman shop assistant says, "get to the back, kaffir", and serves the whites.

'Do you know what it is like to travel between two cities and to carry a tent, because the white hotels won't have you, even though you have a better job and you're better educated than most of the white men in it – and you don't want to sleep in a hovel? To provide the best education you can for your son and know that he will tramp the streets fruitlessly in search of employment?

'It's the longing to be accepted, to talk with the white man on equal terms, other than a liberal who invites you to his house and watches to see how you hold your knife and fork. And then the day-by-day humiliations of your skin, until you give up and sink back to the level of the masses. And your emotions are in the colour of your skin. God is black and black is beautiful. You hate the white man and you'd do anything to hurt him, because you once admired him. Every year you're turning these men out of your schools and your universities. You give them education but you deny them opportunity. They can see no future. You're sowing your whirlwind. You're looking outside but it will come from within.'

'So what do you reckon?' Peter asked uncomfortably.

'You learn from history. You learn to bend with the storm of progress rather than break. You take your educated Africans and you let them in little by little, so that the others have hope. You can make them start at the bottom and work up. But you accept them when they prove themselves. You bring them gradually into your civil service. You have patience with them when they fail. And you breed a middle-class that is more Rhodesian than you are.

'As the middle-class forms you will have to sacrifice direct power for influence, but your middle-class will now have a stake in the country. They need stability to prosper. And you control the purse strings through the banks, industries and major firms until the African middle-classes become more conservative than you. They will protect you from the lower-classes because if you fall, they fall. As more and more Africans prosper, so you become more secure.

'But learn to bend quickly, white man, before it is too late. You'll have to face change and change is always uncomfortable. But you will survive and that's what matters in the final analysis.'

'Why should you care what happens to us?'

Limbani shrugged his shoulders tiredly. 'Because we need the white man. Not just the casual white who wanders in and out of the continent. But people like you who really care, who have no other home. The African is growing up too fast in a world alien to his culture. He needs a stable white heritage to live up to. The ideal of an incorruptible civil service, justly enforced laws, an honest police force and some form of strong but democratic government. We need all this and a lot more from the whites. Don't just scoff at our faults. If you want to live in this continent according to your heritage, teach us your ways.'

'Mister,' Peter said suspiciously. 'I'm beginning to believe you. I've got a head like a lump of iron. It takes me a long time to see things, but when I do I take a hell of a lot of stopping. If I ever believe in you wholly, I'll follow you. Somehow I'll make the peoples listen to you. But if you're lying to me, if you're just proving that you're cleverer than me, I'll destroy you. I promise you that.'

'If I get out of here,' Limbani said tiredly, 'I'll say what I've told you over and over again. Until someone listens.'

'All right,' Peter said rising. 'Let's move on. Now you hang on tight, bloke. I've got to get you back. Maybe you're what we need. Maybe you're the man we're looking for.'

A violent, blood-red sun dipped behind the hills, its rays

beating scarlet against the fragile cloud. The bush was quiet, empty, eerie. A light wind stirred the tall grass, then the crickets began to sing. Whity was desperately tired, his body ached and his vision when he tried to concentrate swam before his eyes. He thought he saw movement in the bush some thirty feet down the path. Tiredly, he raised his head, tried to focus his eyes unaccustomed to the half light of dusk.

He heard Peter whisper to him, telling him to pull out. But there was something moving out there. A shadow moving relentlessly towards him. He shook his head trying to clear his vision. It was an African crawling towards him, a darkened knife in his outstretched hand. The African was in the jungle green of Ndofa's Simba police. Fear crawled in Whity's spine, knotted his belly. Commands rushed into his brain, but he could not move, watching the man crawl towards him, hypnotized with fear, like a rabbit before a snake. He wanted to break and run, but his body would not respond. Perhaps, if he sat very still, the man would pass him by. Then he could steal away into the bush and hide.

Peter called softly again, worried now. In a moment, Peter would move down the track to Whity. Peter would protect him. No man could stand against Peter. Whity felt a surge of affection for the strong, kind, slow-thinking man. He couldn't risk him dying. Not Peter.

Whity's rifle seemed to come alive in his hands, swinging down into the direction of the shadow. There seemed noises in the bush all round him now. His voice broke into a warning shout, rising to a broken scream of fear. His rifle began to crack, bullets whining madly through the bush. If he could just hold them off long enough for Peter to get out. Get out, Peter. Get out. A noise came from the bush close by. He swung round to meet it. A grenade. If he could just loose off a grenade. The man with the knife was nearly on him. He couldn't train his rifle. Oh God, Peter, help me. Help me. Help me ...

When Whity failed to answer Peter's first low call, his hackles began to rise in warning. He crouched low in the bush, like a great cat waiting, signalled to McTaggart to cover him. Listening, he thought he heard Whity move and called softly again. He was running forward when he heard the first strained rasping shout of warning.

Like a buffalo that rarely turns once it has begun its charge, Peter continued to move forward, Then he remembered Limbani. He swung back, running low along the track, his boots pounding in the dirt. From behind a wavering scream of terror cut through and a rifle began to fire. Limbani was on his feet waiting for him, his mouth open, shouting something. Peter's arm circled his back, half lifting him off his feet. They began to run.

McTaggart moved quietly in behind them. He squatted on the path, his rifle cradled in his left hand. Unhurriedly he unhooked two grenades from his belt, laid one on the ground before him, the other he held ready in his hand. He heard the pounding of many feet on the path coming towards him. Over that he heard the high wavering scream of Whity in pain.

He tossed both grenades in quick succession. Then, in an easy fluid motion, he raised his rifle, spacing his shots through the bush. As the grenades exploded, he rose and followed Peter.

Limbani's legs collapsed beneath him. Peter caught him as he fell, dragging him along. Then, without slowing, Peter swung Limbani onto his back. Limbani, half conscious, clung on, locking his arms round Peter's neck. They were running along the floor of a shallow valley. Hills towered out of the gathering darkness on either side. They crashed out of the bush, slid down a bank and waded knee deep through a fast-running stream. The other bank was almost vertical.

Peter clawed his way up, loose stones and earth slipping beneath his hands and feet, blood pounding in his head. Huge gulps of air rasped through his throat and on into his lungs. Lining the top of the bank were boulders. The path led round them and on, climbing upwards through the valley.

'Leave me, you'll go faster,' Limbani shouted.

'Christ no, kaffir. I've only just found you. Hang on, will you? You're doing fine.'

McTaggart caught them up. They stopped for a moment while Peter loaded Limbani onto McTaggart's back. Peter sank down behind the rocks and McTaggart began to run.

They had gained five minutes before Peter heard the Simbas coming. They were shouting excitedly to each other, crashing through the bush, each encouraging the other on. In the distance, a light from a Very pistol drifted slowly down, calling in the other Simba patrols and lighting the bush in a weird red glow.

Peter laid two grenades on the rock in front of him. He waited until he heard them crossing the stream. Then he lobbed the grenades over the rock. He rose with his rifle, picking off shadows that were forming on the opposite bank. A submachine-gun opened up, filling the dusk with its harsh metallic stammer, the bullets screaming, searching in the rocks with steel fingers for his body. The grenades exploded one after the other. The stream ran red. Peter turned and followed McTaggart.

The noise of the fight drifted softly towards Kilimbi, carried on the wind. The R.S.M., leading the search patrol, heard it. He halted the patrol, checked the direction of the noise, spaced the men out, then he began to jog towards it. Each man held his rifle a little tighter, watching the R.S.M., ready to drop or move on at his signal.

Peter caught up with McTaggart. The uphill run was beginning to tell on them. The Simbas, gathering strength as fresh men joined them, were closing in, baying like frenzied hounds at the kill.

McTaggart slipped Limbani onto Peter's back. He took the remainder of Peter's grenades. The Simbas had split up and were crashing through the bush, closing in like three points of an arrow head.

'Hold them off long enough to give me a start,' Peter panted, 'then you follow. Okay?'

'We fought well together you and I,' McTaggart panted. 'Go well, my friend.'

Peter was running with Limbani now, his boots pounding wearily on the ground. Limbani was moaning with pain.

McTaggart stood up and looked around him carefully. A pale moon was rising too faint yet to light the earth. His eyes tried to pierce the dusk. He listened for the noise of the advancing Simbas, trying to gauge their distance from him. Then he sank quietly back into the bush and waited.

McTaggart let the first two scouts pass him, cutting off his retreat. As the main body drew level, he lobbed a grenade, then loosed off a magazine into their midst at point blank range. The scouts had turned and were firing wildly through the bush at him. A lucky bullet caught his side as he turned, slicing through his webbing belt and out the other side. He grunted with pain, dropped to his knees and began to crawl through the thick bush away from the track, up the side of the valley towards a huge dark kopje.

The Simbas regrouped on the track, shouting among themselves. Then they began to follow cautiously after him. A lot of their men were dead or dying along the track. The screams from the wounded filled the night. McTaggart inserted a fresh magazine. The rifle felt good in his hands. He began to climb the side of the kopje.

Peter breasted a small hillock. The path sloped steeply down between rock walls and disappeared at the bottom around a corner. Running towards him, halfway up the path and confined into a compact group by the rock walls, were a patrol of five Simbas. They saw each other at the same time. Peter raised his rifle to his hip, his left hand crossed his body to steady it. He came thundering down the hill towards them, unable to turn or stop, the muzzle of his rifle flashing in the dark.

The first Simba bullet smashed into his left arm and on into his stomach. The second took him in the upper thigh. His rifle was wrenched out of his hands and clattered against the path. The impact of the bullets half spun him round and stopped his forward rush. He cannoned against a smooth rock wall, then, righting himself, his feet began to move again, gathering momentum from his own weight and the added weight of Limbani. He picked up speed. Adrenalin surged through his body. He was roaring and cursing with blind rage.

Two of the Simbas were down. A third was slowly sinking onto his knees, holding his belly. In a brief second, Peter burst through them, swinging the load on his back, like a battering ram. He reached the bottom at a full run, failed to take the corner and went crashing into the bush.

Within a few yards of the path, he tripped and fell sprawling. Limbani, who was thrown clear of his back, rolled and lay still. In a moment Peter was on his feet again. His head thrown back, his eyes wild, air screaming into his lungs.

'Get up,' he yelled. 'Get up.'

Limbani lay still, his eyes closed. Peter grabbed one of his legs in his massive hands and began to pull him through the bush.

The R.S.M. halted the patrol again. The noise of the fight had left the path and was moving across the valley. He was just about to cut through the bush towards it, when the noise of a second gun battle erupted some two hundred yards in front of him. His scouts raced towards it.

Peter felt no pain, just a gathering numbness spreading

through his body. He was growing weaker as the blood drained from him, angry at the massive body that was failing him when he needed it most, his eyes blinded by a red film which he could not blink away, but he inched forward, pulling Limbani, pace by faltering pace.

'Don't die, kaffir. Don't die, Limbani. Don't die now.' He thought he was pleading silently in his mind, but he was shouting out loud.

Limbani was conscious again, struggling weakly against the iron grip that held his leg, trying to shout to Peter. But Peter could not hear. His legs buckled under him and he began to crawl, hurt now that his limbs were deserting him, that his strength was leaving him. One thought kept thudding into his brain in time with his receding pulse. 'Don't die. Don't die. Don't die.' He whispered it on his knees, pulling ineffectually at Limbani's leg as his life drained out of him, his blood staining the sand. Then he pitched forward onto his face.

Shadowy figures of the mercenary scouts passed them. Limbani crawled up to Peter. The R.S.M. heard a noise in the bush. His men fanned out to cover him as he went in. He found Limbani with his hands around Peter's wrist, weakly trying to drag him onto the path.

The R.S.M. knelt by Peter's head. 'You can leave him now, sir,' he said respectfully. 'He's dead.'

Limbani kept tugging at Peter's arm.

'He's dead, sir,' the R.S.M. looked curiously up at Limbani. Then he rose and prised his fingers loose. 'I'm very sorry, sir,' the R.S.M. said again gently. 'I'm afraid we'll have to leave him, sir.'

To his surprise, the African was crying, great silent tears streaming down his face.

CHAPTER TWENTY-THREE

1845 hours. Tuesday, 29th December

THE sound of gunfire in the north whispered and died. In the police station, Faulkner waited, hiding his nervousness. Tilly lamps hissed from the rafters. Beside him on a table rested the telephone and the radio. At the back of the room Janders and the priest waited. No one spoke. Words would only betray their anxiety.

The operator at Albertville had made contact over an hour ago, assuring Faulkner that the president would contact him within the next twenty minutes. No call had come through as yet. It seemed to Faulkner as though Ndofa too was stalling for time, while his men encircled the village. The mercenaries on perimeter were constantly sending back reports of movements in the bush below.

The radio crackled into life. Faulkner almost snatched the microphone from the radio operator's hand.

'One commando to base,' the R.S.M.'s voice came through calm and unhurried.

'Base leader to one commando. Reading you strength five. Come in. Over.'

'We've got Limbani, sir. The others are dead or missing.'

'Is he all right?'

'He's alive, sir. We're coming in now. Will you alert the perimeter guards?'

Faulkner nodded to Janders. 'You're clear to come in. Do you need reinforcements?'

'We'll make it all right, sir. Someone has drawn the Simbas off us. Over and out.'

Faulkner leant back in his chair. Above all else now he needed a drink. He bitterly regretted having allowed Janders to destroy the liquor.

'You're not through yet,' the priest warned. 'Not by a long way.'

Faulkner did not answer. He knew that soon the telephone would ring and Ndofa would be on the other end ready to bargain. He turned coldly to the priest. 'You said they wouldn't be here much before midnight.'

'Sure now, but that was just my estimate. I think you'll find that this is the first wave of Simbas. The main body are still to come. Go on man, where's your sense? You can still break out easy,' the priest urged. 'You'll be long gone before they come.'

The radio called. 'Two commando to base. Come in please.' Faulkner acknowledged. 'We're at the village now, sir. It's all quiet. We can see the aeroplane. It's there right enough. Do you want us to move in?'

'Base leader to two commando. Negative. Repeat, negative. Wait in the bush and keep out of sight. Watch out for Simbas. They may be between you and base. Let me know if there is any movement. Over and out.'

'So, you didn't trust me,' the priest said. He did not seem unduly hurt.

'I check all information where I can,' Faulkner replied.

The priest stared at him. 'My son,' he said softly after a moment. 'You may never go to heaven, but you'll do for now as a soldier. And seeing as we're coming to bare facts, I'll tell you this.' His voice rose in anger, his wild eyes fixed on Faulkner's, holding them. 'If you're trying to start a civil war here, then you'll have me and God against you and we're no mean opponents. I'm telling you that. I'll use every bit of influence I have against you. I'll curse you from every hilltop in the country. You'll die without a God, my son.'

As suddenly as the priest's anger rose, it left him. He relaxed against his chair. 'There now,' he said. 'My cards are on the table. Take your heathen self away from here.'

McTaggart reached the top of the kopje. He turned, for the running fight was over. He had hurt them until they all followed him, knowing that he was cornered, their officers unable to stop them, howling like jackals, blood mad for revenge.

The pain in his side was like a ridge of fire. Below him the Simbas had encircled the kopje and moved upwards. A hail of covering fire continually swept over him, the bullets screaming and whining through the rocks.

He fired a quick burst from his rifle, then it went dead. He laid his weapon reverently aside. There was no more ammunition. He sank to the ground and watched the Simbas closing in, brave now that there was no returning fire.

McTaggart knew that shortly he would die. He felt no fear, for the madness of battle was still in him, warming his blood and glowing in his eyes. He unclipped the last two grenades, grinned when he saw that they were going to try to take him alive so that he might die more slowly in their hands. Briefly he commended his soul to his Maker and rose to his feet.

'I'm McTaggart,' he shouted, 'late of the Black Watch.' His voice echoed in the sudden silence. In his mind he heard the massed pipes of his old regiment bidding him to battle. 'Come,' he jeered at the closing ring of chanting men. 'Come closer. Come see how a brave man dies.' He pulled the pins.

With a grenade in either hand, he ran down to meet the astonished Simbas.

Limbani was brought to the police station on a stretcher. He was very weak, but conscious. Someone found an old horsehair mattress and they laid him upon it. Janders lit a paraffin lamp and held it over his head. His people began to file into the room. Helmeted mercenaries stood in the doorway, their rifles held slantwise across their chests.

The priest knelt beside Limbani and helped him to sit up. His people gathered round him in a half circle, their faces shining with sweat in the heat of the night. One by one they stepped into the small circle of light and examined him. Then their spokesman stepped forward, a wizened old chief in a battered sun-helmet.

'You are Limbani,' he announced in a shaky voice, tears filling his eyes. 'We thought to see the spirit, not the man.'

'I am both the man and the spirit,' Limbani replied.

'May I speak for the people?' the chief asked humbly.

'You may speak.'

'The people have said that their hearts cry out to you for help, you are their mother and their father. You are . . .'

Limbani interrupted the beginning of a long traditional address. 'Please be brief,' he said. 'I ask this not through disrespect, but because my body is weak. I must rest soon.'

The wizened chief shuffled his feet uncomfortably. 'Your people cry out against Ndofa,' he said. 'They are weak and he is cruel. The taxes are so great that a man must watch his children starve. Those that speak their minds are killed by the Simbas. Everywhere within your country there is pain.' The chief ended simply. 'What must we do?'

A younger man stepped forward, heavily built, dressed in a shabby blue suit. He had a deep voice. 'If you lead us, the people everywhere will rise against Ndofa. They will follow you.'

'There are Simbas everywhere,' an elder interjected. 'They have guns. We do not. We will all die. If we fight, you must give us guns.'

'Your people will fight anyway,' the young man said. 'I speak for the young people. They are brave with hunger, strong with anger. We can fight from the jungle with spears if you ask us.'

'It is better that the people suffer and still live than fight without guns and surely die,' the elder argued.

'It is better to go to the jungle and die fighting but with hope,' the young man pleaded, 'than to die slowly of hunger with no hope. If you will lead us, the other tribes will follow you. The Simbas have grown fat on the land. They will not follow us into the jungle.'

'My men could form the nucleus of a strong fighting force,' Faulkner urged. 'We could train your men, get your country back for you, if you can raise the people.'

'Don't listen to him,' the priest ordered, fixing Limbani with his wild grey eyes. 'He's purely a fighting man looking for blood and profit. I know your people here better than you do. If they rise now they're surely dead. If you must go against Ndofa, the heathen swine that he is, though I baptized him myself, then do it in your own sweet time, on your own ground. And do the job properly. Now that's good sense for you.'

'Why wait?' Faulkner asked. 'You raise the people, we'll look after Ndofa. Of course we work for money, but if we get your country back for you, it'll be cheap at the price.'

'He's lying I tell you,' the priest thundered. 'Listen to your elders, man. Think on it. Your starving people armed with spears against machine-guns. And what are you going to feed them on in the jungle? Tell me that. It'll cost you more in human lives than you've dreamed of. Your country will wallow knee-deep in blood and you'll be responsible. If there's any goodness sheltering under your black hide, you'll never let that happen.'

'Once we get it off the ground, we'll find backers,' Faulkner argued. 'We got your country back for you before, remember.'

'There's an aeroplane near here,' Janders cut in quietly. 'We can get you out. The priest will look after your people until you come back.'

'It is for you to decide,' the chief said. 'Lead us and we will follow. Tell us to wait and we will wait.'

The room waited in silence while Limbani gathered enough strength to speak. His eyes were tired, infinitely sad, as thought they had seen more pain than a man could bear. His face was grey and beaded with sweat.

'It was in my mind,' he said with great effort, 'that if I lived I would never return to my country. I would shake the pain from my heart, the tears from my eyes and play with my children at peace in the sun, but I have heard your cries and my heart has cried with you.

'I will leave you now and I will say this to you. Your people will not rise. Your people will not cry out against Ndofa. They will bear their pain in silence, but in every town, in every village, in every kraal the people will organize and you will tell them that Limbani is alive, that Limbani will return and they must be ready for that day. All this I promise.' Limbani leant weakly back against the mattress.

'Ndofa will know of this meeting,' the wizened chief said. 'Many here will die before your coming. But the people will know. They will wait for you. Go in peace Limbani.'

The telephone began to ring, its harsh clamour shattering the stillness of the room.

'Clear the place,' Faulkner ordered harshly. 'Get everyone

260

out. You too,' he said to the priest, 'and take him with you.'
He indicated Limbani.

The mercenary guards herded the tribesmen from the
room.

'Remember whose side you're on,' Faulkner said softly to
Janders as he passed. When the room was clear Faulkner
walked over to the telephone and lifted the receiver. 'My
French is not good,' he said, 'so speak slowly.'

The receiver at the other end was handed to another man.
'It is Ndofa here,' a deep voice said.

'Faulkner here.'

'I thought it might be you,' Ndofa sounded calm but there
was steel in his voice. 'Are you well after all these years?'

'I'm well,' Faulkner said. 'I've been following your progress enviously. But you really must do something about
your army. Their security's terrible.'

'I find my army these days more trouble than it's worth. I
think I might send them against you first. They're expendable and they will serve to deplete your supplies of ammunition.'

'When I knew you last, you were a fanatic about your
army.'

'That was before I discovered that each soldier thought he
could be a president. You have Limbani I believe.'

'Yes.'

'May I speak with him?'

'No.'

'Then how can I be sure that he is still alive?'

'When the country rises, you're riding the tiger, not me.'

'You'll never get him out of there.'

Faulkner chuckled. 'Don't try and bullshit me, Ndofa. We
worked together, remember. I can break out of here any
time within the next twenty-four hours and you'll never get
enough men up to stop me.'

'What would you suggest then?'

'That's better. I thought you hadn't changed that much. I'll accept one million U.S. dollars, the whole amount to be paid in cash against handing over Limbani.'

'I'm afraid that our treasury cannot stretch to one million at such short notice. I can offer you a quarter of a million and your skin.'

'One million. You can find it, or you'll have a civil war on your hands. And don't try those old counterfeit notes on me, will you? By the way, are you sure that you can trust your army with Limbani around?'

'Where would such an exchange take place?'

'Albertville Airport. You lay on a plane for us fuelled up and ready to go.'

There was a pause. 'Very good,' Ndofa said. 'But I have two conditions. One, I would prefer Limbani dead on arrival. I find him very difficult to kill. Sight of his body will be sufficient to complete the contract. Two, I don't want any of his people to see him. I'll supply a couple of unarmed observers to ensure this.'

'You've got the second one,' Faulkner said cheerfully. 'But you'll get him alive. He's no passport for me dead.

'Now I've got a clause. The aeroplane is to be capable of reaching the white south non-stop. It is to belong to a major airline, flown by their crew and it is to have at least three ranking United Nations observers on board. And you pull your men off. Pull them right back. Agreed?'

'Agreed,' Ndofa said tiredly.

'Don't cross me now,' Faulkner warned. 'You know I'll be watching for you. I'll move out at day break. Have your men out of the area before then. One wrong move and the whole world will know about Limbani. See you in Albertville.'

Faulkner lowered the receiver. 'One million,' he said softly to himself. 'The bastard's squirming now.' He chuckled. Then he felt a presence behind him and turned sharply. Janders was standing in the doorway, a gun in his hand, pointing at Faulkner's stomach.

'I've come a long way with you,' Janders said quietly, 'but here I stop.'

'What in the hell's the matter with you?' Faulkner demanded, watching the gun.

'We were always bad bastards, but we honoured our contracts. That's what we're going to do now.'

'When that plane took off and left us, they broke the contract, not us. Think on it, man. One million dollars in cash and a passport out of here.'

'The old contract stands good. The plane was our affair. There's an awful lot of bush between here and Albertville. Ndofa can pick us off any time he likes. You thought of that? All he needs is to get us out of here. Besides, I've kind of got to like the thought of having Limbani alive. That's what Peter died for.'

'Who's to know?'

'I will. I've sent for the officers and the R.S.M. We'll take a vote on it, okay?'

'Put that gun away will you?'

'After the vote.'

Jeremy, Shaun and the R.S.M. filed into the room. Janders stood by the door. It was only after they had entered did they realize he was holding a gun. Janders explained the proposition.

'Is that fair?' he asked of Faulkner. 'All right, now we vote.'

'I'm in command,' Faulkner reminded them. 'You all took an oath to follow me.'

'That was under the old contract,' Janders said. 'You want a new one now, so we vote.' He raised his gun. 'I'm the chairman. R.S.M., what's your vote?'

'I'll follow the Colonel, sir.'

'Shaun?'

'Against. We stick to the old contract and get the hell out of here.'

'Jeremy?'

'Against. The men will never go for it. They didn't sign up for a full scale war.'

'Three to two. You lose,' Janders said.

'All right,' Faulkner ordered. 'Get the men together. We'll make a break for the airstrip while Ndofa's on the hop. Janders, you stay behind. I want a word with you.' The others left.

'You owed me, remember,' Faulkner said angrily. 'And now you turn on me.'

'I'm about the only friend you've got,' Janders said softly. 'I'm just seeing you through a period of temporary insanity. Allen, I don't know what's in your mind at the moment, but if you're thinking of knocking me off, just remember it'll split the others and you won't survive Ndofa that way.'

'Oh, for Christ's sake, put that gun away. You must think I'm losing my mind if you think I'm going to kill you.'

Janders lowered the gun. 'You're just getting greedy. I've seen it happen to all kinds.'

'All right,' Faulkner said. 'We've had our say and it's over. It was a good idea, that's all. Now, let's get down to work. And don't worry about turning your back. You'll see your son again.'

'I'd like to be sure of that,' Janders said and he smiled.

Faulkner grinned back. 'You know,' he said, 'maybe getting Limbani out is not such a bad idea after all. There'll be a big juicy contract waiting to be picked up for when he comes back.'

CHAPTER TWENTY-FOUR

2000 hours. Tuesday 29th December

A blood-red moon was rising, lifting through cloud and lighting the earth. The air was still, hot and moist. Mosquitoes swarmed and the night was filled with the shriek of insects.

Apart from the perimeter guards, the main body of mercenaries were drawn up in the street. The R.S.M. marched to the front, turned and faced them as though he were on an Aldershot parade ground. The weary men stiffened automatically as his harsh gaze swept over them.

'In a moment, the Colonel will be addressing you. Before he does, there is something I want to say.

'I've fought with a lot of men in my time.' The R.S.M. cleared his throat, uncertain as to how to continue. 'Well, what I want to say is that, if pride is a sin, well then I'm a sinful man. Because I'm proud of you. You've done all right. Good as any men I know. That's all,' he barked. For a brief moment the men loved him.

Faulkner walked into the street. 'Parade. Parade, 'shun,' the R.S.M. wheeled. 'Parade all present and correct, sir.'

'Thank you, R.S.M.,' Faulkner acknowledged his salute. 'At ease. We're going to break out of here,' he told the men. 'There's an air-strip about six miles away with an aeroplane waiting on it. The going may be rough, but well make it all right.' He spoke easily, an infectious optimism in his voice; a leader certain that no matter whether his men loved or hated him they would follow where he led. 'We'll be falling back, leap-frogging in three waves, a quarter of mile between each. Our intelligence is that there is only a light force of Simbas surrounding us at the moment. The main body is still a long way off. So we'll be out of here before they know what hit them. And of course, we've got Limbani, so the local people will support us where they can. Your officers will brief you fully before we move out.

'I overheard the R.S.M.'s comments. I echo them fully. I'm proud to have commanded you.' Faulkner grinned. 'In fact, I'll buy you all a drink when we get back. All right, carry on, R.S.M. First group moves out in fifteen minutes.'

'Base leader to two commando. Base leader to two commando. Are you receiving me? Over.'

'Two commando to base leader. Receiving you strength five. Come in. Over.'

'Base leader to two commando. Everything still clear your end?'

'Yes, sir. All quiet. A few of the locals still moving about. That's all. No sign of the Simbas.'

'Base leader to two commando. We're moving out now. Maintain radio listening watch. Keep out of sight until the first group hits the village. Then I want that plane fuelled up and ready to go, but watch that plane. Don't let anyone near it, understand?'

'Do you want us to grab the pilot?'

'Negative. Just mark where he is, but don't show yourselves until we hold the village.'

'Two commando to base leader. Understood. Over and out.'

'I can't see why they're not using the strip themselves,' Janders asked anxiously.

'You don't know the New Congo,' the priest scoffed. 'The

mine only levelled it less than a year ago. Them Simbas never leave their offices if they can help it. And they've only got the old Belgian maps to follow. Sure now, it's well known they get lost a mile outside the cities and they won't find any of the locals to guide them.'

'Well, we're committed now,' Faulkner said. 'You're coming with us,' he added to the priest. 'If you're leading us into an ambush, I'm personally going to put a bullet in you.'

'Well now, there's a thing,' the priest chuckled. 'Threatening will do you no good at all. I'm old now don't you see, looking to die soon. A martyr to the faith would suit me fine. Sure of a place in heaven. But you now,' he said coldly, 'it's the raging fires for you, my son, and don't you forget that.'

Faulkner ignored him. 'Tell Limbani that he can choose the nucleus of a small fighting force to take out with him. Young ones that can be trained. Tell him no more than fifteen men. We'll see how many we can fit on board when we get there.'

'You still planning for the future?' Janders asked.

'Naturally,' Faulkner replied cheerfully.

Jeremy, Shaun and the R.S.M. filed into the room.

'Everything ready to go?' Faulkner asked.

'Yes sir,' Jeremy replied. 'It's dead quiet out there.'

'Too quiet,' Shaun said. 'They're waiting for us.'

'No, Faulkner said. 'Ndofa will be pulling his men back. He thinks he's going to get Limbani the easy way. Anyway, it's going to be all a matter of how fast we can break out. Tosh Donaldson, three men and a radio go first. Janders, you follow him with your men. Jeremy, Shaun, you go next and take Limbani with you. If any of his people know how to use a gun, arm them. Right. Now you pass through Janders' men and find a good covering position behind them. Leave Limbani with Janders. I want him kept in the centre at all times – understand? I'll be the last out of here. I'll take up Janders'

267

positions and he'll fall back on you. Then you move on again. Keep Tosh in front looking for trouble.

'If it comes, I think I'll catch it at the back first, so R.S.M. take over what's left of Peter's men and keep with me. If you hear shooting, close up, but keep leap-frogging and keep pushing on as hard as you can. I can't impress on you enough that speed is what counts in this kind of action. If I start getting hurt, Rafer, I'll fall back through your men taking Limbani with me and you cover us. When I've found fresh positions, you fall back on me and I'll cover you. Got the idea? We never stop moving.

'Jeremy, Shaun, you'll be the first in the village. Position your men to cover our retreat and protect that aeroplane. Shaun, you have my permission to keep yourself out of trouble. We may need you to fly us out of here. Work out a flight plan for Rhodesia.'

'Christ, why Rhodesia? Why not Angola or Mozambique? Man, that's near enough eight hundred miles. That's pushing a Dak.'

'Because the Portuguese won't let us in and there's nowhere else. Can you do it?'

'Depends on the load factor and the condition of the aircraft,' Shaun said dubiously. 'I suppose we could do it.'

'We'll have to overfly Zambia,' Faulkner said.

'That's no problem if we keep low and wide of Lusaka. They've got bugger-all radar. The problem's going to be staying up that long. I'll have to work it out, but I expect our maximum range is going to be about eight-fifty miles. Man,' Shaun said softly, 'that's close.'

'That's your problem,' Faulkner said. 'You get us there. That's what you're paid for. All right, gentlemen. Any other questions?' No one spoke. 'All right, Rafer. Move out. Good luck, my friend.'

CHAPTER TWENTY-FIVE

2100 hours. Tuesday, 29th December

'Oh God. Oh my God. They're coming again. Look over there, hundreds of them. Oh my God, we're dead.'

The R.S.M. walked over to where the gibbering man lay crouching behind a low cover of rocks and kicked him hard in the ribs. 'Samuels,' his voice cut like a whip lash, 'you're not dead until I tell you – understand?'

Samuels looked up. Blood seeped from under a grimy dressing on his thigh. His young eyes flickered uncertainly over the R.S.M.'s face. They were the eyes of a man who had nearly reached his limit. 'We're dead,' he said softly. 'We can't run any further. Oh my God, we're dead.' He started to cry as he turned back to his rifle. Tears streaked the sweat and dirt on his face. 'Our Father,' he prayed as he pulled the trigger and the rifle kicked against his shoulder, 'who art in Heaven . . .'

The R.S.M. touched an N.C.O. on the shoulder 'Move over there and keep an eye on Samuels. If he cracks up completely, shoot him before the others get to know.'

Across the vlei a machine-gun began to stutter. Others joined in until the rocks were alive with the scream of ricocheting bullets. Faulkner was on the radio.

'Tosh?'

'It's all clear here, sir.'

'Shaun?'

'All clear here, sir.'

'Rafer, you receiving me?'

'Yeah, I got you.'

'You in position?'

'Yes.'

'Okay, I'm falling back on you now. Cover me. The rest of you push on as hard as you can. Over and out.'

Faulkner spun round. 'R.S.M.,' he shouted.

'Sir,' the R.S.M. came up.

'What's it like?'

'Not too bad, sir,' he said evenly. 'Simbas are firing wild as usual.'

'How many do you reckon?'

' 'Bout eighty, sir. We can hold them all right, depending on their reserves. They're full of dagga though, just like the old days. If they can get in amongst these rocks with their knives, we might have a rough time.'

'We're pulling back on Janders. Get the men moving out quietly. You pull out last. Before you go, shoot all the men who are too badly wounded to make it. That's an order, understand? Don't leave them to die in the hands of the Simbas.'

The R.S.M. nodded and moved off.

'One commando, this is advance guard. Come in please.'

'Advance guard, this is one commando leader, receiving you strength five. Go ahead. Over.'

'We're on a hill, sir. There's a party of bandits outflanking you – heading for the village. They're carrying torches and moving fast.'

'Can you cut them off? Keep the way open?'

'I think so, sir.'

'All right, move. Let me know when you make contact.'

'Moving now, sir. Over and out.'

'Three commando. This is one commando leader. Come in. Over.'

'Leader, receiving you.'

'Jeremy, send out scouts to take over Tosh's position.'

'Very good, sir. Over and out.'

Faulkner looked down. To his disgust, his hands were shaking. The shadowy figures of the departing squads were forming up silently in the dark. In the distance a lone drummer started a slow rhythmic throb on his tomtom. Soon other drummers would join him, whipping the Simbas into a frenzy. When the drummers reached their crescendo the Simbas would rush the rocks. From his perch high up in a rock, the R.S.M. felt his skin start to crawl and he cursed.

The flanking Simbas were running in a massed bunch, following a path, flaming torches lighting their way, shouting and crashing through the bush, oblivious of noise.

Tosh Donaldson chose a fairly open stretch of ground for his ambush position, one which would afford the Simbas little cover. He positioned one man forty feet down the track, another forty feet above. In the centre he sited his machine-gun. He marked a killing ground fifteen feet on either side of the gun with stones. When the Simbas were between these points, he would open fire. His men sank into the bush and waited.

Faulkner threw himself down beside Janders. There came a whoosh of a rocket passing over their heads. They both ducked instinctively, then the brilliant flash of the explosion lit the night. The mercenaries were firing steadily, conserving their ammunition, their snipers with infra-red sights picking off targets as they moved into the eighty-yard range.

'Looks like friend Ndofa was waiting for us,' Janders muttered.

Faulkner grunted. 'Okay, you were right, but he was wait-ing in the north. He didn't expect us to break out here. It'll take him time to get his men over.'

'There's more of them coming up every minute,' Janders said sombrely.

'We'll make it,' Faulkner said firmly. 'I'll have that bas-tard yet. Jeremy reckons it's clear up front. All right, you pull back now. Leave me some of your men to fill my losses. I'll cover you.'

'Fire,' Tosh shouted. The machine-gun chattered, wink-ing orange in the dark. The points opened up. Bullets swept over the killing ground scything the Simbas down. Trip-wired grenades exploded amongst their writhing bodies. The few Simbas at the rear turned and fled.

'All right, pull back,' Tosh shouted.

'Advance guard to one commando leader. Come in.'

'Leader to advance guard. Go ahead.'

'We got them, sir. No casualties our end.'

'Pull back on the village. Cover Jeremy coming in.'

'Very good, sir. Over and out.'

Running – running hard. Their boots drumming on the soil, slipping on the loose stone, sweat blinding their eyes, their breath coming in great panting gasps, the moon climb-ing higher, yellow now, floating between the clouds, Lim-bani swaying on a make-shift stretcher, the old priest stag-gering beside him. A shout from the point. The men dived for cover.

'It's Tosh, sir.' The word came down the line. Jeremy moved up to meet him.

'The village is just up front, sir,' Tosh reported. 'Ham-mond says it's all quiet. Want me to stay back and cover the Colonel while you move in?'

'Right. Keep six men. Spread them out. Limbani and his men can stay with you until I sent for him. Shaun, you and three men come with me. You too,' Jeremy said to the priest 'I may need you.'

The sounds of gunfire whispered across the bush behind them.

Jeremy paused, his eyes searching slowly up the deserted street of the mining village for signs of an ambush. One by one, his men stole through the shadows to take up positions in doorways or in any other places that offered cover. Each time they moved a little further up the street.

Sporadic bursts of firing rippled in the distance, growing closer. Faulkner would be falling back bit by bit, giving way to superior numbers. There was no time left for caution. Jeremy started to run up the cobbled street, his men following him, their boots crashing against the cobbles.

The figures of the running men silhouetted in the moonlight against the white-washed walls of the small mine houses, sweat streaming down Jeremy's chest, soaking into his camouflage jacket, his eyes searching the eerie, empty, darkened windows of the houses, every moment expecting to hear the crack of a rifle, feel a bullet tear into his flesh.

Then they were through the village, running onto the short grass of the landing strip that reached out like an accusing finger in the bush. Jeremy branched sharply right. Above him towered the head gear of the mine shaft. He ran along the verge. At the end of the strip stood a small corrugated iron shed. A little to one side stood a transport Dakota with the moon glinting silver on its wings. Hammond and his men were waiting for him.

'Where's the pilot?' Jeremy panted.

'Over there, sir,' Hammond pointed to a figure in mechanics overalls sprawled on the grass by the shed.

'Christ, what have you done to him?'

'Nothing, sir. He was stoned out of his mind before we could grab him. Colonel's orders, sir. We couldn't move in before.'

'Where are the people?'.

'They did a bunk for it. The whole lot of them, both black and white, into the bush as soon as they heard the gunfire getting closer.'

'You reckon you can still fly one of these, Shaun?'

'Well, it looks like you're going to find out,' Shaun answered. 'Hammond, is that plane fuelled up?'

'Yes, sir.'

'Both mains and auxiliaries?'

'It'll not hold another drop, sir. We grabbed one of the black mechanics. He showed us how. We let him go after. He was bawling like a baby. You want us to keep trying to sober up the pilot?'

'Forget it. He's no good to us now. Give me a lift up will you. Hey, Jeremy, how about trying to find us something to drink?'

'Nothing doing. Hammond, take your men down to the bottom of the village and give Tosh a hand. Janders should be coming in soon. Let me know as soon as he does.'

For the twentieth time in five minutes, Faulkner searched the sky for the Very light. What in the hell was Jeremy doing? A semi-circle of scarlet flashes kept closing in around him.

The R.S.M. crawled up. 'There's fourteen men dead, sir. Two more just bought it.'

Faulkner nodded. 'Did everything go all right back there in the rocks?'

'I did it quiet like, sir, with my knife. They never knew a thing.'

'I'm sorry it had to be you, R.S.M.'

'Never mind, sir. It was for the best. I think we'd better

fall back again, sir. They're getting a bit close and there's more of them arriving.'

'All right, R.S.M. Pass the word.'

The R.S.M. started to crawl away, then he turned. 'Shall I do the same with the other wounded, sir?'

'No. Bring every man who's still alive back with us. I've lost enough of my men,' Faulkner said quietly. 'I'm not going to lose any more.'

Janders passed through Tosh Donaldson's perimeter guards, taking Limbani and his men with him, running through the deserted village and onto the landing strip.

Shaun had thrown himself into the left-hand seat on the flight deck. He studied the cockpit layout, familiarizing himself with the panels, then he reached up above the window, flicking on the starboard engine booster pump. His fingers found the energizer switch and the engage switch, holding them down. He switched the magneto on. The engine fired. Immediately he released the switches and pushed the mixture control up to auto-rich. The engine backfired, belching a sudden flash of flame. Smoke billowed from the exhaust. He wrenched the throttle back and reaching up he pulled the switches again. The engine turned, started, then coughed and died. He adjusted the throttle. Praying, he pulled the switches again. They were loading Limbani on board. The sound of gunfire had reached the villager perimeter. The propeller spun, the engine caught.

'Oh God. Oh, thank God,' Shaun breathed. He waited for the revs to rise, then he pulled the port switches.

'Easy there. Easy there,' the R.S.M. warned, walking calmly behind his men. 'Don't let 'em rattle you. Take your time, draw your bead, pick your target. That's it. That's the way.'

Faulkner followed a trail of sparks as they crossed the

path of the moon. Then a scarlet flare drifted slowly earthwards.

'Has Hammond got the injured back yet?'

'Yes, sir,' the R.S.M. replied. 'It's just us now.'

'All right, get back,' Faulkner shouted above the noise of gunfire. 'Everybody break for the plane.'

Faulkner was one of the last to leave. He walked slowly backwards firing all the time into the dark expanse of bush at the end of the village street. As he drew near to the last of the houses, he turned and started to run. A ricocheting bullet took him in the back, knocking him over. In a moment, he was on his feet again, still running, but slower and slower as his legs began to buckle under him. A second bullet took his shoulder, spinning him round, pitching him onto his back. This time he knew that he couldn't get up.

In the distance, he heard the chant of the Simbas as they started up the street towards him. 'Oh God,' he thought. 'I nearly made it. I so nearly made it.'

Suddenly he felt a hand on his shoulder.

'Who is it?' he shouted. 'My Christ. My eyes. I can't see. Who is it?'

'It's only me, sir,' the R.S.M. said softly.

'Well, get out of here. Can't you hear them coming?'

'Hear them, sir,' the R.S.M. snorted. 'I can bleeding smell them, they're that close.'

'Then get out, man.'

'I can't, sir,' he lied. 'My legs are smashed.'

'So we're both stuck here.'

'Yes, sir.'

'I'm sorry,' Faulkner said softly. 'About your legs I mean.' Suddenly he clutched at the R.S.M.'s arm. 'What's that noise? I can hear a noise.'

'It's the aeroplane, sir. The engines. They've bloody made it. Christ, if only I had wings, we'd race it home.'

'You feel much pain?' Faulkner asked.

'Not much, sir.' The R.S.M. was uninjured and he cradled Faulkner's head in his arms.

'Same with me. Just a sort of gathering numbness. Must have got my spine. I can't move my legs.' Faulkner reached up to touch the R.S.M. 'I'm glad you're here,' he whispered. 'I was frightened of dying alone. You know what I mean. Not being able to see when it comes. You did well with the men. You turned them into a pretty good unit.'

'We were a good team, sir,' the R.S.M. replied softly. 'They won't see the like of us again. If I say it myself.'

'You got the guts to put a bullet in me?' Faulkner asked.

'No, sir,' the R.S.M. replied sadly. He had already thought of that.

For a moment, the two men lay side by side in the deserted street. Suddenly the R.S.M. whispered. 'They're not far off now, sir. Taking it cautious like. How about us playing dead until they get real close. I'll tell you where to point your rifle and we'll make a bit of a fight of it before we die.

'They're coming now, sir. Goodbye, sir. Up a bit. Up a bit more ... little to the left ... that's it. Now hold it there. Christ,' the R.S.M. chuckled, 'they're going to get a nasty surprise before they chop us up ...'

CHAPTER TWENTY-SIX

2150 hours. Tuesday, 29th December

JEREMY stood beside the Dakota anxiously watching the exhausted men from the rear guard stagger onto the airfield, dragging their wounded between them. Above, the Very light drifted slowly down, lighting the village and the bush all around in its harsh blood-red glare.

Suddenly from the far perimeter of the airfield came the sound of gunfire, carrying softly on the wind. He spun round, his hand shielding his eyes.

'Rafer,' he shouted. 'For Christ's sake, look over there. The bastards are trying to cut us off.'

Through the dense bush at the end of the landing strip came the advancing ripple of scarlet flashes that glowed against the dark. Janders followed Jeremy's oustretched arm. He paused, counting the flashes.

'Fifteen ... maybe twenty. No more,' he said calmly, his voice only just rising above the howl of the revving engines. 'The rest are still on the other side. You take over here. I'll hold them off until you get the plane moving. The Colonel should be back any minute now. Hammond,' Janders shouted, 'pick four men and follow me.'

Hammond, the number two in Janders' commando, a short man of about forty with a barrel chest and a bald shining skull shouted, 'Rubens, Ferguson, McFarlane, Williams, bring the R.P.D. and a bazooka.' He started down the landing strip at a steady jog trot, the others falling into line behind him.

'For Christ's sake, hold them until we've got the plane moving,' Jeremy shouted after Janders. 'Then make a run for it.'

Janders did not bother to turn. He just raised his hand to show that he had heard.

Jeremy ran up and down the line. 'Hurry, blast you, hurry,' he screamed. 'Can't you see they're boxing us in?' The exhausted men shuffled faster. 'Oh God,' Jeremy whispered to himself. 'Where's Faulkner got to? I can't take much more of this.'

Two men came staggering towards him, gasping for breath, bent almost double under the weight of a wounded man they were dragging between them. The wounded man kept trying to walk, but his legs buckled as they took his weight and he cursed softly to himself in his pain. Jeremy's eyes narrowed. The Very light had gone, but in the half-light of the moon he recognized the wounded man.

'Tosh,' he shouted as he ran towards them. 'Thank Christ. I heard you were dead.'

The men stopped. Tosh slowly raised his head. His face was streaked with blood and sweat. 'Not yet, sir,' he answered softly, managing to smile. 'Not yet.'

'Have you seen the Colonel?'

Tosh shook his head. 'Not since I caught it, sir.' He saw Jermey staring at his stomach. It was swathed an inch thick in bandages and between them seeped an ever increasing stain of blood. 'I'll make it all right,' Tosh said firmly, then he fainted.

Jeremy glanced up at the men. 'Have either of you seen the Colonel?'

One of the men nodded. 'He bought it back there in the village. The R.S.M. stayed with him.'

'Are you sure?' Jeremy felt the panic rise within him.

The mercenary nodded again. 'Caught it in the back. The bullets fairly ripped him up. He didn't have a chance.'

One of the rear guards stationed nearest the village fired a burst into the air to attract attention. Jeremy ran towards him. 'What is it?' he panted.

The engines were warming evenly. Shaun increased the throttle setting. The plane began to vibrate. He estimated that the landing strip was some five thousand feet above sea level. Overladen, he would require fourteen hundred yards to lift off. As it was night and the air a few degrees cooler, he could possibly cut that distance by two hundred yards. The landing strip, including the emergency area, was about two thousand yards long. He had room to run and should be gaining height as he crossed the Simbas.

The guard pointed with his rifle to where a group of villagers waited at the bottom of an incline. 'They want to come too,' he said. 'They reckon that if they stay, the Simbas will have them.'

'Tell them no,' Jeremy said and turned to walk away.

The villagers started after him.

'Stop them,' Jeremy ordered. 'Fire a burst.'

The gun stammered in the mercenary's hands. The villagers ducked as the bullets whined over their heads, the echoes crashing against the nearby walls. They pushed their terrified spokesman forward. He was an old man with a white mane of hair and a small goatee beard. He clutched his hat nervously in his hands.

'Please, sir,' he addressed Jeremy in broken English. 'Please, sir, take us with you. When the Simbas come they will kill us. They will say we helped you.'

'And did you?' Jeremy asked viciously.

'No, sir,' the old man replied honestly. 'But they will kill us just the same. Please, sir,' the old man repeated. 'Take us with you.'

'No,' Jeremy said fiercely. 'We don't even know if the plane will take off with us in it, let alone any extra weight. Go and hide in the bush while you've still got time.'

The old man shook his head. 'They'll find us, sir. They'll kill us. I have a daughter and two grandchildren. They haven't done anything wrong. Please take them with you. It doesn't matter about me. Please, sir, I beg of you.'

'No,' Jeremy shouted. He was beginning to lose his nerve. 'None of you have done anything wrong. I can't take you, that's all. There isn't any room.'

The old man hung his head. A groan came up from the crowd behind him when they realized that he had failed. Women held up their children, begging Jeremy to take them.

'How can you refuse the children?' the old man pleaded.

'There are too many of them. What do you think I am, God or something? I can't choose who's going to live and who's to die. Go on,' Jeremy shouted desperately. 'Go and hide while there's still time.' The villagers did not move. 'Oh God. Go and get the priest,' he shouted to the guard.

'I'm here. I'm here,' the priest muttered at his elbow.

'Tell them, will you?' Jeremy said. 'Explain to them. Then get back on that aeroplane.'

'I'll be staying with them,' the priest said softly. 'They're my people.'

'Well, if you want to die, that's your problem.'

'So it is,' the priest agreed. He looked at Jeremy. 'It's because of people like you innocent people die. Let that hang upon your soul – all the days of your life.' The priest strode towards the villagers, his arms upraised, commanding their silence.

'It's not me that's going to kill them,' Jeremy shouted after him.

A woman broke free from the crowd and started walking up the incline towards him. In her late thirties, hard faced with high cheek bones, the moonlight shining in her dark hair. Once she might have been beautiful. She stopped five feet in front of Jeremy, her hands on her hips. 'I'm coming with you,' she said softly.

'Why you?'

'Because I'm a trained nurse. Because you have many wounded. You need me much as I need you.'

'How about your friends down there?' Jeremy asked contemptuously.

The woman shrugged her shoulders. 'They are nothing to me. All I care about is myself. I don't want to die at the hands of the Simbas. Now,' she asked impatiently, 'what's it to be? If you leave me I will die, but so will most of your men without proper care.'

'All right,' Jeremy said uncertainly.

'Then we'd better hurry,' she said looking over his shoulder. 'Already you've wasted too much time talking.'

Jeremy spun round. The R.P.D. in the centre of the landing strip was firing almost continuously now. 'Come on,' he shouted as he broke into a run.

'Do you believe in God Almighty?' the priest demanded of the villagers. 'You do. Yes, you do,' he answered himself. 'Then pray, you heathens,' he shouted.

'Sweet Lord, before you kneel a bunch of hypocrites. Normally at this time they wouldn't be giving you a thought. But now, if you're listening, Lord, they're about to do some serious praying. And, Lord, though you know I'd be pleased to die a martyr in your service, these people haven't the same inclination. And to tell the truth Lord, I have a little more living left in me – if you're feeling so inclined. Therefore, oh Lord, protect us this day . . .'

As they neared the aircraft, Jeremy glanced behind. The villagers were kneeling on the open ground, the priest before them leading their prayers, God on his shoulder and in his voice. He hoisted the woman into the open doorway. Willing hands reached out to help her. 'Christ,' someone exclaimed, 'where in the hell did you find her?'

'Shut up,' Jeremy shouted angrily as he scrambled in. 'Just take her down and show her the wounded. And you,' he turned to the woman, 'you'd just better be worth it.' He raced up to the flight deck. 'Get going,' he shouted to Shaun.

'The Colonel on board?' Shaun asked, pushing up the throttles. The engines screamed, the plane shuddering against its brakes as the propellors bit into the air.

'He's dead,' Jeremy shouted. 'The R.S.M. Oh, God, everybody's dead.'

Shaun let go the brakes and the plane began to roll. 'Who's that?' he shouted, pointing out of the window to where Janders and his section were running towards the plane.

'It's Rafer. Oh God, I'd forgotten.'

Shaun gauged the distance. 'I'll taxi towards them. It'll cut down take-off distance by a quarter, so I'll keep picking up speed. They can jump in. Get down the back and help them. They've got one chance.'

Rubens and Williams were dead, Hammond dying, his hands still clutching the R.P.D. Only McFarlane and Janders were left now, racing across the open stretch of landing strip towards the plane.

Jeremy wedged himself in the door, his arms outstretched to catch them. The plane was picking up speed. Janders and McFarlane were closing in at right angles to avoid the propellors.

'Come on.' Jeremy shouted desperately. 'Come on.' More hands reached out through the opening to grab them. They were opposite the doorway, it was now or never. A bullet caught McFarlane in the chest. He crumpled back into

Janders' arms, his legs buckling beneath him. Janders scooped him up and threw him at the doorway. Someone caught his jacket. Someone caught his hair, another caught his arm and McFarlane was dragged into the plane.

But Janders' chance was gone. The doorway was past him now and the plane was still picking up speed. 'My son. My son,' Janders' brain beat. He tried to run faster, his short legs became a blur under him, his mouth wide open screaming with exertion.

Jeremy climbed out of the doorway. Somebody grasped his belt. He reached out towards Janders. 'Rafer,' he pleaded. 'Come on. Come on, Rafer, run.'

For a moment their fingers touched, trying vainly for a grip. Then, inch by inch, they separated as Janders fell back.

'My son. Look after my son,' Jeremy heard Janders scream above the noise of the engines. 'Oh God, don't leave me alive.'

Jeremy climbed back into the plane. He rested a rifle against his shoulder, steadying himself against the vibrations of the plane. He looked carefully along the sights, then gently he squeezed the trigger. 'Don't miss,' he breathed softly to himself as the rifle recoiled aginst his shoulder. Janders was still running as he died gratefully with a bullet through his brain. For a moment Jeremy stared after the tiny doll-like figure sprawled on the runway. Then he handed the rifle back.

The Dakota was caught in a cross fire. Bullets whipping through the fuselage, screaming off the metal struts. Suddenly the plane began to yaw violently, losing speed. It ground looped, throwing the men about the cabin, then it began to run back the way it had come. They passed Janders.

Jeremy trampled through the screaming wounded, making for the flight deck. 'You bastard,' he was screaming, out of

284

control. 'I killed Janders.' The woman and Benson were on the flight deck when he reached it. 'I killed Rafer,' Jeremy said more softly, his eyes searching their faces, willing them to understand.

'Mr. Fynn's hit, sir,' Benson said straightening. He was the last of the N.C.O.s. 'I said Mr. Flynn's hit, sir,' Benson said again. 'We don't know how bad yet.'

'Oh no,' Jeremy whispered as the words sunk in. 'Oh dear God, no.' He began to crumple, his nerve going.

Benson reached out and pulled him roughly up.

'Begging your pardon, sir,' he said. 'Pull yourself together. You're the last officer we've got left. The men are relying on you, sir. That's what you're for.'

'I've given him one-third of a grain of Omnopon. It has an equivalent effect to morphine, but it's more stable,' the woman said. 'The bullet was almost spent. It entered through his side and I think it's lodged somewhere near his lower spine. He's still conscious.'

'My legs,' Shaun muttered. 'I can't feel my legs.' He was white, shaking, in a cold sweat, his face twisted with pain. 'How bad is it?'

'It depends on whether the bullet severed the nerve. If not, it could just be massive spinal shock, in which case, under proper treatment, the paralysis will ease within a few days. The Omnopon will help with the pain. It will begin to take effect in ten minutes, fully effective in thirty minutes.'

'Will he stay conscious?' Jeremy asked.

'It depends on him – if he's got the guts to fight off the drowsiness, he can stay conscious. He's not bleeding too much.'

'Can you give him something?' Benson indicated Jeremy.

The woman stared at Jeremy. 'I've got wounded who need me.' She answered and stalked into the cabin.

Shaun's eyes were closed.

'Shaun,' Jeremy asked, 'can you hear me?'

'Yeh, I hear you,' Shaun muttered.

'What are we going to do?'

'We're going to get this plane out of here. Get in that seat.'

'You're mad. I can't fly this.'

'You'll die before I do,' Shaun promised. 'Benson put him in that seat.'

Jeremy moved in of his own accord.

'You ever flown twin engines before?'

'Yes, but I'm not rated.'

'Taking off is not much harder than in a small plane. Now, you listen to me and I'll tell you where the controls are. It's coming down again that's the cow.'

Shaun was surprisingly calm, his fingers whitening on the arm rests as he tried to control the surges of pain that swept over him. He had no feeling below his belly, only a deep heaviness.

'All right now, Jeremy, relax. Put your feet on the rudder bars and bring her round. Use the outboard engine to help you turn. That's good. That's good. Right, now brake on. It's over there. That's good.'

'He's passing out,' Jeremy yelled.

Shaun opened his eyes and shook his head to clear it. 'No, I'm not. Benson, get back and make sure everyone's up forward.

'All right, Jeremy, now open the throttles right up. Let me know when you get 48′ manifold pressure. R.P.M. twenty-seven hundred. Mixture control on auto-rich.'

The engines howled. 'Got it,' Jeremy shouted.

'Right now. Brakes off and let her roll. Flaps down to a quarter. That's it there. That's enough. Now, as your airspeed reaches fifty knots, push down like hell on the stick to get the tail up. The tail should unstick at about fifty-five to fifty-eight knots. And watch for the swing as the tail comes up.'

Benson returned. 'They're all up forward, sir.'

'Good, I've got a job for you. As soon as this plane unsticks and I mean when we're three foot off the ground, you pull the undercarriage up. Brakes on, undercarriage up. Got it. Brakes on, undercarriage up. In that order. The first is the latch lock lever on the floor at the right of my seat. You see it?'

'Yes, sir.'

'Right, the other lever is on the hydraulic panel immediately behind Jeremy's seat. It's coloured red. Just pull it out and knock it up. See it?'

'Yes, sir.'

'All right, wait for my word.'

The aeroplane was tearing across the grass towards the gunfire, dark figures turning in panic and running out of their path.

'When you're making fifty-eight knots start easing the stick back,' Shaun ordered. 'Normal lift-off is about sixty, but with an overload we could get up to eighty. You've just got to feel it on the stick.'

Jeremy was urging every ounce of power from his engines and praying out loud to himself. 'Oh God,' he repeated. 'Don't let them hit the tyres. Don't let them hit the fuel tanks. Don't let them hit the engines. And God, especially, don't let them hit me.'

A dark expanse of bush and trees loomed before the windscreen.

'The tail's up,' Jeremy shouted.

'Let her run,' Shaun ordered.

'Seventy knots,' Jeremy shouted.

'Now,' Shaun shouted. 'It's got to be now, lift off.'

Jeremy pulled back the stick, willing the plane into the air. The Dakota lurched, then leapt free of the ground.

'The undercarriage,' Shaun shouted. The aeroplane was

rising sluggishly, engines going mad, the retracting wheels tearing through the tops of the trees.

'Eighty knots,' Jeremy shouted.

'We're just above a clean stall. Start milking the flaps up.'

Slowly, very slowly the airspeed increased to eighty-five knots. The aeroplane in a gradual climb hanging on its propellers.

'We've got to go off max. power within five minutes or the engines will start blowing. How's she doing?'

'Eighty-seven knots. Still climbing. Still climbing.'

'Level off at seven thousand feet.'

'We're at six-two. Look at the cylinder head temperatures.'

'Time's up. The engines are going to blow. Bring her down to 2550 revs $42\frac{1}{2}'$ boost.'

'Ninety-one knots. Stay with me, Shaun.'

Benson rose awkwardly from where he had been hiding behind the seat. 'Well done,' he said gruffly.

'We're not there yet. Get them throwing everything out of the back. Weapons, everything, understand.'

'Seven thousand,' Jeremy announced.

'Right, level her off. As the airspeed climbs, bring the throttles back slowly. R.P.H. 1750, cruising speed 105 knots. Mixture to auto-lean. Got it? I'll give you a course in a minute.'

CHAPTER TWENTY-SEVEN

2350 hours

IT was bitterly cold in the cabin, the noise deafening, everything vibrating as though the plane would tear itself apart. A man screamed hoarsely in his pain. Others groaned and cursed, lying in their blood and vomit. The lights were dimmed. The woman moved amongst the men, her hands bloodied, her hair tied back out of her eyes with a strip of cloth. Benson followed her carrying the first-aid box. The smell and the noise sickened him.

The woman knelt beside the screaming man, her hands cooling his face. She opened his jacket and cut through his shirt with a pair of scissors, exposing the wound.

'Give me something,' the man pleaded. 'Give me something for the pain. Oh God, my pain, my pain.'

She did not bother to dress the wound, just pulled the jacket back to cover it. Her fingers left bloody marks where they stroked his face. Her words soothed him. She reached into the box, took out a bottle and gave him five pills. She helped him to swallow from a canteen.

'Thank you,' he whispered as he lay back. 'Thank you.'

'I'll come back in a few minutes,' she promised, her fingers stroking the hair off his forehead. 'Lie still until then. You're going to be all right. We'll have you in a hospital soon.' She handed the bottle to Benson and moved on down the aisle.

Benson glanced at the label. 'They were codeine. Why

didn't you give him something proper?' he demanded as he followed her.

'Because he's dying,' she answered. 'I've got to save what little there is for the ones who still have a chance.'

Limbani was surrounded by his followers. Of the fifteen men who had joined him, only eight had managed to board the aeroplane. Out of those, two were wounded. Limbani lay in their midst, his legs drawn up in his belly and his head in his arms.

'Can you give him something?' one of the Africans asked, his face was grey and his teeth chattered, either from the cold or from fear of flying.

The woman touched Limbani on the shoulder. He rolled over.

'Are you wounded?' she asked.

Limbani silently shook his head, his face grey, strained, streaked with tears.

'He is sad unto death,' his follower tried to explain.

'He's got something wrong with his heart,' Benson volunteered.

'I should give him some kind of tranquillizer,' the woman said worriedly. She sorted through the box, reading the labels, then she knelt forward empty handed. 'Mr. Limbani, I'm sorry,' she said softly. 'I'm not really a nurse. It was a long time ago and I never finished the training. I can give Omnopon because it's in a kit and I can follow the instructions easily, but it's not what you need. If I were to give you something else, I could kill you. Can you hold on, Mr. Limbani? We're nearly there. Just hold on and lie still.

'Keep him warm,' she ordered. She tended his other wounded. 'I'll come back,' she promised before moving on.

'You bitch,' Benson said viciously. 'So that's how you got on the plane.'

The woman paused. She looked Benson full in the face. 'If

you were going to die, what would you have done?' she asked. Then she pushed past him and carried on down the aisle, her arms full of bandages.

A hand reached up and tugged at Benson's arm. 'Leave her alone,' Tosh ordered weakly. 'She's the best thing that ever happened to us.'

Benson knelt beside him, searching through his pockets for a cigarette. 'You want one?' he asked.

Tosh nodded. Benson lit it for him and placed it between his lips.

'How are we doing then?'

'Well, we've got a wounded pilot, nineteen other wounded and seven hundred odd miles to go. We're nearing Zambia at the moment. But don't worry, Tosh,' Benson said with forced cheerfulness, 'we've got this far, we'll get you home all right.'

'You'll do it,' Tosh said softly, 'but I won't. I'm going just now. I can feel it. What do you reckon on that woman then?' Tosh asked after a moment.

'She's a tart,' Benson said. 'I've seen 'em before. When they're going down, they end up on the mines. She probably came in on a truck. She'd have left on one if it hadn't been for us.'

'She's done all right,' Tosh said again. 'You keep an eye on her after this, will you? You know, see she's all right. The lads would want you to and you'll see the money gets to my old woman, will you?' Tosh's eyes widened as a thought crossed his mind. 'My old woman,' he whispered, 'she's going to do her nut when she finds out I've gone off and died on her.'

Smoke caught in this throat. He began to cough, the effort racking his body. Blood formed on his lips and dribbled down his chin. Benson held him still, trying to ease the pain.

Shaun's eyes were closing. 'Stay with me,' Jeremy pleaded. 'I can't fly this thing without you. You've got to help me. You've got to fight it off. Talk about anything. Talk about Gabby. Talk, man, talk.

'What's your height?' Shaun's voice came from far away.

'We're holding seven thousand.'

'Can you call that woman?' Shaun asked.

'Benson,' Jeremy shouted. 'Can you get that woman up here?'

'Watch your speed,' Shaun warned. 'As we burn fuel, she'll pick up. You've got to hold her on a hundred and five knots if we're going to stay up that long. You're feeding off the auxiliary tanks now. Port auxiliary to port engine. Starboard auxiliary to starboard engine. Check?'

'Check. The gauges are nearly on empty.'

The woman came forward. 'How are you feeling?' she asked of Shaun.

'It's like I've got waves of pain, waves of sickness and waves of sleep all washing over me. And one wave of pain is worse than all the pain I've ever felt in my life all added up and it's getting worse. Can you give me another shot?'

The woman glanced at Jeremy. 'Yes,' she said dubiously.

'What will happen to him?' Jeremy asked.

'It will cut down his pain, but I don't think he'll be able to fight off the drowsiness.'

'How long will he sleep for?'

'Maybe four, six hours. I don't know.'

'Can we wake him if we need him?'

The woman shrugged her shoulders. 'I don't know.'

'What do you mean you don't know?' Jeremy shouted angrily.

The woman shrugged her shoulders. 'I just don't know. Look, I'm not really . . .'

'She's doing all right, sir,' Benson cut in defensively. 'She's doing wonders back there with the men.'

'Can you give him half of it? Shaun, is that okay? I can't risk you right under if there's an emergency.'

Shaun nodded. The woman tore open a kit and injected the jelly-like substance into his arm muscle.

'I'll come back and check on your dressing when you're out,' she promised. 'There'll be less pain then.'

'When the gauges are on empty, you'll still have ten to fifteen minutes endurance left. Watch your fuel pressure. When it drops the engines will start running rough and missing. Then switch over to the main tanks. One engine will go before the other, so you'll still have a few minutes left in one tank in reserve.

'Keep checking on your course. When you're within a couple of hundred miles of Rhodesia, start calling up Salisbury Control. Trim her down and watch your speed. You've got to save every pint of fuel you can.' Shaun's head was drooping, his eyes closing, drifting into unconsciousness as the drug took effect, moaning softly in his pain.

The hours dragged by. There was no cloud and the moon shone cold from a starlit sky, gleaming off the wings, turning the propellers into arcs of pale silver light. As the men died, they threw them out to lighten the load.

Apart from the noise, it was still on the flight deck. Shaun slumped in his seat. Jeremy had never felt so alone, imagining helplessly all the things that could go wrong, constantly checking on his course, trimming the aircraft, agonizedly watching the fuel flow meters.

In the rear of the cabin, Samuels was crying softly to himself. His whole body felt numb and he could not lift his head. The bouts of coughing were growing worse and he could taste blood in his mouth. Suddenly he looked up. There was a woman standing over him. 'I'm hurt,' he whispered through his tears and his coughing. 'I'm hurt bad, aren't I?'

The woman knelt beside him, cradling his head in her arms. 'You're going to be all right. You'll be all right. You'll be in a hospital soon.'

He felt comforted by the warm softness of her breasts, by her soothing of his fear.

'You're so young,' she whispered as she wiped his face. 'You could almost be my son.'

'Do you have a son?'

She nodded.

'Where is he?'

'I don't know.' She laid his head gently back against a folded coat.

'Where are you going?' he asked, panic stricken. 'Don't leave me.'

'I must go now. The others need me too.'

'What's your name?'

'Simone.'

'You're beautiful, Simone.'

The Omnopon released the clamps from Shaun's self-control. He was calling hoarsely, cursing in a meaningless jumble of words, red wreaths of pain swirled like a mist within his brain. He heard deep distant echoing sounds of people calling him and he tried to answer, to tell them of his pain, but he couldn't form the words.

The woman straightened, checking Shaun's pulse.

'How is he?' Jeremy asked worriedly.

'He's weakening,' the woman said. 'I think the bullet's in his spine.'

'Will he last?'

'I don't know.'

'Can you help him?'

'No. He needs a surgeon. Keep him warm. That's all you can do.'

'Will he wake?'

'I think so, but let him rest as long as you can. If he is to die, it would be better for him to die gently.'

'Christ, don't talk like that. He's got to get us down. I can't do it.'

Jeremy switched the radio on to H.F. The pitched whine of the static beat into his ears. He glanced down to a plaque in the cockpit that bore the aircraft registration number.

'Salisbury Control. This is Nine Quebec November X-ray Alpha on 6603 kilocycles. Do you read? Over.

'Salisbury Control. This is ...' he kept calling. Eventually he heard them answering him.

'Nine Quebec November X-ray Alpha, this is Salisbury Control reading you strength two. Go ahead. Over.'

Jeremy adjusted the tuning bands. Control's words were weak, drifting hollow through the static.

'Salisbury Control, this is Nine Quebec November X-ray Alpha, crossing Zambia, height seven thousand feet. Speed one hundred and five knots. Position approximately forty miles south-west Lusaka. Low on fuel. Urgently request permission to land Kariba. Over.'

'X-ray Alpha, say again all after Lusaka.'

'Salisbury Control. This is X-ray Alpha. I repeat, low on fuel. Request flare path Kariba.'

'X-ray Alpha, this is Salisbury Control. Identify yourself and purpose of flight. What is your airfield of departure?'

'Salisbury Control. This is X-ray Alpha. We are a mercenary unit departing Congo. Fourteen wounded men on board. Low on fuel. Urgently request permission to land on humanitarian grounds.'

Benson came forward.

'Correction, Salisbury Control. Thirteen wounded men on board. One more just died.'

'X-ray Alpha. This is Salisbury Control. Stand by.'

Jeremy could imagine a sleepy airtraffic controller phoning madly for instructions. He reached across.

'Shaun, wake up. Come on, Shaun, wake up.'

The woman came forward. She seemed almost too tired to stand. 'How much longer?' she asked.

'About another hour and a half. How are they doing back there?'

'They're dying,' the woman said and returned to the cabin.

'Benson, see if you can wake Shaun up, will you?'

'X-ray Alpha, this is Salisbury Control. Permission to land denied. Do not enter Salisbury flight region. I repeat, under no circumstances cross our borders. Over and out.'

'Have you got him awake yet?'

'No, sir.'

'Try slapping his face.'

'If I hit him much harder, sir, I'll knock him out.'

'Well, get that woman up here. Maybe she can give him something.'

'He'll come through just now, sir. I'll keep trying.'

'X-ray Alpha, this is Salisbury Control. We have you on our radar screen. Turn back. Repeat, turn back. You will not be allowed to land in Rhodesia.'

'Salisbury Control. This is X-ray Alpha. I have wounded on board. You've got to let me land. We can sort it out afterwards.'

'X-ray Alpha, this is Salisbury Control. I regret I have my instructions. If you continue on your present course, we will alert our Air Force.'

'Salisbury Control, this is X-ray Alpha. I have Julius Limbani on board this aircraft. I repeat, I have Julius Limbani on board and he's alive. Now you get hold of anybody you can, the Prime Minister if possible, and tell him that.'

'X-ray Alpha. Stand by.'

'He's coming round, sir,' Benson reported.

'Thank Christ for that. Shaun, can you hear me? Shaun!'

Shaun cried out as the waves of pain took him. Then he regained control of himself, his body washed in a cold sweat. 'What's the position?' he asked.

'We're about a hundred miles out of Kariba. Salisbury Control won't let us land. I've told them we've got Limbani on board. Let's hope they believe us. I'm waiting to hear.'

'How's the fuel?'

'Low.'

'X-ray Alpha, this is Salisbury Control. Confirm Julius Limbani. Over.'

'Salisbury Control, this is X-ray Alpha. I confirm Julius Limbani and he's alive.'

'X-ray Alpha, stand by.'

'How bad am I?' Shaun asked.

'The woman had a look at you. She says you'll be okay.'

'You're a bloody liar. It's bad and I know it. I'm as weak as hell.'

'You'll be in hospital in a couple of hours. All you've got to do is hang on and get us down.'

'That's if they let us in.'

'I'm coming in anyway. There's no place else to go.'

'Too many hills around Kariba. You'll need lights.'

'X-ray Alpha, this is Salisbury Control. Can you provide any proof Julius Limbani?'

'Salisbury Control, stand by. Can we provide any proof of Julius Limbani'?

'I don't know,' Shaun said. 'Ask him.'

'Benson, is Limbani conscious?'

'Just, sir.'

297

'See if he can remember anything that will click with Salisbury. It better be good. And hurry. Oh God, look at the fuel. We're not going to make it.'

'What time is it?'

'0340 hours. We'll be coming in with the dark.'

'Listen,' Shaun said. 'About Gabby. She gave me two months to get back. If I don't make it ...'

'Of course you'll make it.'

'In case I don't. Look, I want you to see her. She's got to know I tried. Oh God, how I tried. She's got to get my money, understand. She's got to know I tried.'

'Forget it, Shaun. If we get down, you'll be in hospital and I'll be in gaol. There's no way I can get to see her.'

'You can get a message to her. Something. You've got to do it,' Shaun said fiercely. 'You just can't leave her waiting, understand.'

'Okay, okay. I'll see her.'

Benson came forward. 'Mr. Limbani says there was a secret meeting on the now Zambia–Congo border, April, 1960, concerning Federal intervention in the Congo crisis. The following were present at the meeting. The minutes will be recorded in the Rhodesian Special Branch files.'

Jeremy called up Salisbury Control.

'Benson,' Shaun tugged at his arm. 'Look, if you get out of this, I want you to do something for me.'

'Yes, sir.'

'I want you to find a girl called Gabby. She's in Lourenço Marques. You'll find her address in my flap pocket. And you tell her that I tried to get back. You tell her that, understand. You've got two months. Don't leave her waiting. You tell her. Tell the other men. Someone's got to make it.'

'Shut up, will you?' Jeremy said. 'You're going to be all right. It's just his mind wandering,' Jeremy said to Benson.

'You tell her.' Shaun pleaded, his voice straining just above a whisper.

'X-ray Alpha, this is Salisbury Control. You're clear to land Kariba. We have alerted the police post in the village. They will see that Kariba tower is manned. They are also asking all the people to turn on their lights. The village is in the hills. You'll pick up the lights as you come in over the lake. Kariba tower will contact you as soon as it is operational. They'll take over from there.'

Samuels sat up, his eyes wide with terror. 'Simone,' he screamed. 'Simone. Simone.'

She moved over to him. 'I'm here,' she said softly.

'Simone,' he was reaching out to her. 'I'm dying. Hold me. I'm dying.'

'X-ray Alpha, this is Salisbury Control. Handing you over to Kariba tower now. Good luck to you.'

'X-ray Alpha, this is Kariba tower,' a breathless voice came over the air. 'Flare path lit. You're clear to land. Ambulances standing by for your wounded.'

'Look at those bloody gauges,' Jeremy shouted. 'They're on empty.'

'We're over the lake,' Benson shouted.

Jeremy looked down. He saw the dark shadow of the Dakota crossing the moonlit waters. Shaun was fighting to remain conscious, waves of pain and sleep were swamping his mind. He longed to drop his head and let the sleep take him.

'Ahead,' Benson shouted. 'The lights. They've lit the whole bloody place up for us.'

'Stay with me, Shaun,' Jeremy shouted. 'For Christ's sake, don't go now. Where's the strip? For God's sake, where's the strip?'

Benson crawled back into the cabin. 'We've made it, lads,' he shouted. 'We've bloody made it.' Everyone was cheering.

Simone closed Samuels' eyes.

The fuel pressure dropped and the port engine began to run rough.

'It's going,' Jeremy screamed.

'Bring the starboard engine up to 2550 revs. Punch the port feather button. Watch it, she'll yaw towards the dead engine as it goes. We'll have to get down fast. Speed?'

'Ninety-seven knots.'

'Throw out three-quarter flap. Hold her. Hold her.'

They crossed over the village on one engine. In the cabin the men heard the engine go, felt the aeroplane bucket as the flaps came down. No one spoke. Each man sat alone with his own private prayer. The plane was dropping steeply as they crossed the bush, dark and menacing beneath them.

'Oh Lord,' Jeremy prayed. 'You got us this far. Don't leave us now.' Suddenly the lights of the airport were in front of them.

'Benson, you ready with the undercarriage?'

'Yes, sir.'

'I'll tell you when. Jeremy, you got any fuel left in the starboard auxiliary?'

'A little. The port went first last time.'

'Get ready to open the fuel lines.'

The ground came rushing up to meet them. The runway lights still seemed a long way off.

'X-ray Alpha,' the tower came through. The voice urgent. 'You're too low. You're coming into the power lines. Get up.'

'Bring the flap to a quarter. Gun the engine.'

The thick, high-voltage strands of the main Kariba power lines loomed before them. Jeremy pulled on the stick. The Dakota lumbered higher, the air speed dropping. They cleared the power lines, the plane just above a stall. Instinctively Jeremy put the nose down, picked up speed, then levelled out.

'Undercarriage down.'

There came a bump as the wheels dropped. The increased drag brought the nose down. They were dangerously close to the ground. The starboard engine died. Jeremy was struggling to keep the nose up.

Airspeed dropped to seventy knots. He punched the feather button. All was silent now, but for the rushing wind. It was obvious to Benson that they were going to crash into the bush before the runway and he braced himself for the shock.

Shaun was holding himself upright in his seat, the effort straining the last reserves of his will power. Just before impact he shouted, 'Get the nose up.' Jeremy hauled back on the stick. The aeroplane flattened out gaining those desperately needed yards. Then it started to stall. 'Let her drop,' Shaun shouted. The aeroplane struck a hundred yards before the runway in the short grass emergency area, the impact throwing Shaun down into his seat. He screamed with pain. The Dakota rose thirty feet into the air and bounced again. Jeremy pushed the stick hard forward, trying to hold it on the ground.

Ambulances broke from the tower and came racing out to meet the plane.

'X-ray Alpha, this is Kariba tower. The police require that all your men remain on board until Limbani is off. Is that understood?'

Shaun felt consciousness leaving him, as though his soul was wandering free of his body. He saw Gabby waiting on that beach in the dusk, heard the sound of the surf, the wind in her hair, the pain in her eyes. 'Waiting is like dying a little more each day.' 'Tell her I tried,' his mind struggled to form

301

the words, but they seemed to drift off ino the gathering darkness. 'Oh God, how I tried.'

The aeroplane was slowing, its wheels drumming on the tarmac, a police jeep running beside, the ambulances following.

Jeremy lay back in his seat, his whole body trembling as the tension left him. His mind wandered back and he saw Peter, a strong, gentle, slow-spoken man who cared so deeply about everything he did; that warm smile that lit his ugly face; his dream of a ranch way out in the Rhodesian bush and of a woman to love and need him.

The old priest riding in through the rain. His feet trailing from a donkey. His craggy, hawk-like face and those wide grey eyes. He was a man who knew a simple God and loved him. What was it he had said? 'Let that hang upon your soul.'

And Janders. Oh God, Janders with his lonely eyes and son.

The R.S.M., marching onto the parade ground. That hard little ramrod of a man who had so little love in him that all he had he reserved for Faulkner.

And Faulkner, with his wild grin and cold eyes. A man who lived every second of his life. It seemed impossible for him to die.

Shaun slumped in the seat beside him. Searching somewhere deep within himself for the strength to live. His love of life and that laugh that seemed to rise from his belly. The man who promised to die of excesses. Who waited that night outside the Cardosa Hotel, a crumpled package in his hands.

The Dakota stopped. There came a sudden silence.

THE END

A COFFIN FULL OF DREAMS by FRISCO HITT

Les Affreux – the name of one of the most savage groups of mercenaries ever. They killed, they raped, they destroyed – nothing was beyond the reach of their cruelty.
A COFFIN FULL OF DREAMS
is the nerve-jangling story of a man who abandoned his respectable life as a schoolteacher to become a mercenary in a violent and war-torn land. In a world where the defeated choked on their own dismembered limbs, where sex meant rape, and where love was a weakness that led only to death, he had his baptism of horror . . .

0 552 10246 6   85p

THE DOGS OF WAR by FREDERICK FORSYTH

Sir James Manson – smooth, ruthless City tycoon – discovered the existence of a ten-billion-dollar mountain of platinum in the remote African republic of Zangaro. With a hired army of trained mercenaries, Manson planned to topple the government of Zangaro and replace its dictator with a puppet president. But news of the platinum had leaked to Russia – and suddenly Manson found he no longer made the rules in a power-game where the stakes had become terrifyingly high . . .

0 552 10050 1   £1.00

A SELECTED LIST OF
WAR BOOKS PUBLISHED
BY CORGI

☐	10889 8	HOLOCAUST	Gerald Green £1.25
☐	10400 0	THE BLOODY ROAD TO DEATH	Sven Hassel 95p
☐	09761 6	BLITZFREEZE	Sven Hassel 95p
☐	09178 2	REIGN OF HELL	Sven Hassel 95p
☐	08874 9	SS GENERAL	Sven Hassel 95p
☐	08779 3	ASSIGNMENT GESTAPO	Sven Hassel 95p
☐	08603 7	LIQUIDATE PARIS	Sven Hassel 95p
☐	08528 6	MARCH BATTALION	Sven Hassel 85p
☐	08168 X	MONTE CASINO	Sven Hassel 95p
☐	07871 9	COMRADES OF WAR	Sven Hassel 95p
☐	07242 7	WHEELS OF TERROR	Sven Hassel 95p
☐	07241 9	LEGION OF THE DAMNED	Sven Hassel 85p
☐	10343 8	CROSS OF IRON	Willi Heinrich 75p
☐	09485 4	THE SAVAGE MOUNTAIN	Willi Heinrich 65p
☐	10393 4	THE BLUE MAX	Jack D. Hunter 75p
☐	08371 2	THE DIRTY DOZEN	E. M. Nathanson £1.25
☐	10300 4	THE SCOURGE OF THE SWASTIKA	Lard Russell of Liverpool 85p
☐	10300 4	THE KNIGHTS OF BUSHIDO	Lord Russell of Liverpool 85p
☐	10741 7	633 SQUADRON: OPERATION CRUCIBLE	Frederick E. Smith 85p
☐	10155 9	633 SQUADRON: OPERATION RHINE MAIDEN	Frederick E. Smith 85p
☐	08169 8	633 SQUADRON	Frederick E. Smith 75p

ORDER FORM

All these books are available at your bookshop or newsagent, or can be ordered direct from the publisher. Just tick the titles you want and fill in the form below.

CORGI BOOKS, Cash Sales Department, P.O. Box 11, Falmouth, Cornwall.

Please send cheque or postal order, no currency.

U.K. send 22p for first book plus 10p per copy for each additional book ordered to a maximum charge of 82p to cover the cost of postage and packing.

B.F.P.O. and Eire allow 22p for first book plus 10p per copy for the next six books, and thereafter 4p per book.

Overseas Customers. Please allow 30p for the first book and 10p per copy for each additional book.

NAME (block letters) ....

ADDRESS ....

(JAN 79) ....

While every effort is made to keep prices low, it is sometimes necessary to increase prices at short notice. Corgi Books reserve the right to show new retail prices on covers which may differ from those previously advertised in the text or elsewhere.